Haunted

Is someone here? Polly asked.

She wasn't sure if she had phrased the question in her mind or said it out loud. She called out again, loud enough this time to hear the muffled flutter of her own voice in the darkness.

Where are you? Polly asked the darkness.

After another lengthening moment, a response finally came to her, so faint it wafted over her like unseen smoke in the night.

—*I don't know where I am . . . I'm . . . just . . . here*—

She couldn't believe that she had actually heard a reply. The words—if they had been spoken at all—were gone as if they had never been, but she had the clear impression that they weren't just thoughts inside her head. Someone was in the dark room with her.

the white room

A. J. MATTHEWS

BERKLEY BOOKS, NEW YORK

THE WHITE ROOM

A Berkley Book / published by arrangement with
the author

PRINTING HISTORY
Berkley edition / July 2001

ISBN: 0-425-18072-7

BERKLEY®
Berkley Books are published by The Berkley Publishing Group,
a division of Penguin Putnam Inc.,
375 Hudson Street, New York, New York 10014.
BERKLEY and the "B" design
are trademarks belonging to Penguin Putnam Inc.

PRINTED IN THE UNITED STATES OF AMERICA

10 9 8 7 6 5 4 3 2 1

To the memory of

VENNIE MARIE PISTENMAA

Her garden was her church.
Her church was her family.
And her family was her garden.

Alas, how many hours and years have passed,
Since human forms have round this table sat,
Or lamp, or taper, on its surface gleam'd!
Methinks, I hear the sound of time long pass'd
Still murmuring o'er us, in the lofty void
Of these dark arches, like ling'ring voices
Of those who long within their graves have slept.

—*Orra*, a Tragedy

. . . there are frail forms fainting at the door.
Though their voices are silenced,
Their pleading looks will say,
Oh, hard times come again no more.

—Stephen Foster

one

It was the smell that got her.

It always did.

As soon as the automatic front doors of the emergency room swung open, the sharp, antiseptic smell hit her like she'd run into a solid wall.

Cold . . . clean . . . and sterile.

But beneath that nauseating, sanitized aroma was something else—something that she would never be able to blot out of her memory—the stench and the deep ache of loss and misery.

For what had to have been at least the hundredth time this morning, Polly Harris tried to talk herself out of doing what she was about to do. She glanced back over her shoulder, up at the clear, blue June sky.

There wasn't a cloud in sight. The fringe of trees at the far end of the hospital parking lot was bursting with green. Their long, ink-wash thin shadows stretched out, reaching toward her like two-dimensional hands sliding across the slope of grass and parking lot. A flock of brown sparrows chirped noisily in the shrubbery as they darted about from branch to branch. A cool, fresh breeze was blowing inland from the Atlantic Ocean, carrying with it the sharp tang of salty air.

There's freedom out there . . . new life . . . new hope . . . new possibilities. . . . You've got to remember that, Polly told herself as the almost unbearable urge to turn and flee swept through her.

No one was forcing her to do this, after all, but no matter how much she reminded herself of that, she found herself being drawn irresistibly inside the air-conditioned coolness of the emergency room.

As far as she was concerned—or anyone else, for that matter—she didn't have to go through with this. She hadn't even told her husband, Tim, what she planned to do today. She might have mentioned something about it to him once or twice a couple of weeks ago, and Tim—as always—had been supportive and understanding. In fact, although he was supportive, he had voiced the concern that perhaps volunteering to work as an aid at Stonepoint General Hospital might not be such a great idea, considering everything that had happened. But Polly had insisted that she was over it, all the while thinking to herself that, even if she wasn't over it, it at least was time to put the past behind and try to move ahead. She had to get outside of herself and back into life sometime.

The past was dead, dead and gone, just as her daughter—her unborn baby girl, Crystal—was dead and gone . . . four years now.

How could it be that long? Polly wondered, feeling the pain as fresh and sharp as if it had been only yesterday.

The backs of her legs felt unhinged and ready to fold up on her as she passed through the second set of automatic doors. They swung shut behind her, cutting off the chirping song of the birds and the distant rush of traffic. The antiseptic smell was even stronger now, almost enough to gag her. That old, familiar warm sting of gathering tears came to her eyes, and a tight, sour taste filled the back of her throat.

I'm not gonna make it, she thought. *There's no way in hell I'm gonna make it.*

But in spite of herself, her legs kept moving. Hesitating

in the hallway, she couldn't help but wonder how she must look to an outsider.

Did she look bold and confident, the way she hoped to present herself?

Or could anyone who even glanced at her see the damaged woman she really was inside—fragile and oh so close to shattering?

She tried not to breathe the hospital air too deeply as she turned to the left and walked the short distance to the glassed-in enclosure of the emergency room admissions desk. A large-breasted woman with thinning gray hair was leaning over the desk, supporting herself on two clenched fists as she scanned the file that was spread open in front of her.

Polly recognized her from around town, but all she experienced was a slight measure of relief that at least it wasn't Rachel Parsons. Rachel had been the triage nurse on duty that night four years ago. The emergency room had been renovated since then, but it was still familiar enough to jack Polly's tension up another notch or two.

"May I help you?" the nurse asked, looking up. After a second or two, she registered who Polly was, and a smile spread across her wide, pale face. "Why, Mrs. Harris. Hello."

Feeling so numbed it was like she was flying on automatic, Polly stepped into the small office. She was trying hard to place the woman's face but coming up empty as she held out her hand for the woman to shake. The woman's grip was soft but firm.

"I'm Anna Kincaid," she said. "I was the school nurse at Wescott Elementary. Your son, Brian, was in first grade with my daughter, Shaunalee."

"Oh, yes. Yes, of course," Polly said, cringing at the curious flatness she heard in her own voice. "Nice to see you again."

Mrs. Kincaid regarded Polly in silence for a moment, then frowned slightly.

"Is there something I could help you with?" Nurse Kincaid asked.

Polly had the disorienting sensation that there was a thick

sheet of plate glass separating her from Anna. She had to ponder the question for a moment as if to let it sink in.

"Are you all right?" Mrs. Kincaid asked.

"Yes . . . yes, I'm fine," Polly said, nodding as she struggled to snap out of her daze and focus on why she was here. "I was just . . . I've been out of work for . . . for a while, now, and I was just . . . I wanted to talk to someone about possibly volunteering to work here . . . in the hospital."

"Oh," Mrs. Kincaid said, arching her eyebrows and nodding. Polly thought she could sense the woman's relief that, thankfully, this wasn't an emergency. "You have to go up to the personnel office. It's on the second floor. Room two sixteen."

"Of course," Polly said softly.

She suddenly realized how foolish she must appear. Of course she should have gone to the front entrance and asked at the information desk in the main lobby. What was she thinking? Why in heaven's name had she come to the emergency room first? Was it force of habit . . . or something else?

"So tell me, how's Brian doing?" Nurse Kincaid asked before Polly had a chance to turn and leave. "I remember that he seemed to have a lot of trouble with allergies. He was in my office at least a couple of times a week. Especially in the spring. I got to know him quite well that year." She laughed softly at the memory.

"Oh, he outgrew that years ago," Polly said. "He's doing fine now, just fine."

"Glad to hear it," Mrs. Kincaid said. Leaning forward and lowering her voice as though sharing a professional secret, she whispered, "You know, to tell you the truth, I always thought it was just nerves more than anything else."

Polly shrugged tightly, feeling suddenly defensive about her son.

"How's Shaunalee doing?" she asked. "I haven't heard Brian mention her in . . . quite a while."

"Oh, she's doing terrific. She's a student at Bishop Connolly High, in Beverley."

Polly made a slight sound in the back of her throat as

she nodded. She was at a total loss as to how to disengage from this conversation without appearing awkward. She had already been one-upped by Anna Kincaid twice: first when she mentioned Brian's allergies and "nerves," and a second time when she threw out so casually that her daughter was attending an exclusive Catholic private school that was known to be quite expensive.

"Well," Polly said, nervously rubbing her hands together as she started backing out of the office, "I won't take any more of your time, Mrs. Kincaid. You've been most kind."

Mrs. Kincaid smiled warmly at her and said, "Say hello to Brian for me, okay?"

Polly nodded that she would.

She kept telling herself that there was nothing else behind what Mrs. Kincaid had said. She was simply being as helpful and friendly as she could.

But all the encounter left Polly with was an almost overwhelming conviction that, as nervous as this was making her, she was doing the right thing. It had been four years since she and Tim had lost their baby daughter during delivery, and it was time—well past time—to get back into the feel and flow of life, and get a real job even if it was—for now—only volunteering at the hospital.

She was vaguely aware of the open door behind her as she took another backward step before turning to leave. Her neck and face were flushed, and she could feel a low tremor deep in her stomach.

I don't have to do this, she told herself. *It's not too late to walk out to the car, get in, and leave. Even if Mrs. Kincaid notices me driving off, she might think I'm just driving around to the front.*

So intent was she on escaping—yes, *escaping* was the word—that she only distantly registered the sudden noise and flurry of activity when the interior set of automatic doors slid open.

With a swiftness that belied her size, Mrs. Kincaid wheeled around the side of her desk and rushed past Polly into the hall. As Polly exited the office, she saw a three-person medical emergency crew coming toward her, wheeling a gurney. Her first impression was that the gurney was empty, but then she saw the small shape strapped onto it. One of the EMTs—a thin, young man with black hair and glasses—was leaning over the figure, holding an oxygen mask in place with one hand.

"What are her vitals?" Mrs. Kincaid asked sharply.

Her brow was furrowed, and Polly was impressed by how quickly she snapped into professional mode.

Another of the emergency crew—an older-looking man with a blond crew cut—answered her.

"BP's eighty over forty and dropping. Pulse is high. A bit over one forty."

"Left pupil is blown," the man with dark hair and glasses said.

Polly could hear the tremor in his voice, and although she didn't know exactly what a "blown pupil" was, she knew it couldn't be good.

"Take her to trauma room one," Mrs. Kincaid said.

As the medical crew rushed past her, Polly couldn't help but look down at the small figure lying on the gurney. Her vision suddenly telescoped to a tiny circle with the accident victim's face in its center. All of the sounds of the hospital around her seemed to close down with an audible *whoosh*.

That looks like . . . No! It can't be!

It was a little girl, no older than ten or eleven years old. The oxygen mask covered the bottom half of her face, and the top part of her head was horribly distorted. The crew cut EMT was holding a thick wad of blood-soaked gauze to the left side of the girl's head, and Polly suddenly realized what a "blown pupil" was. The center of the little girl's left eye was so fully dilated that only a thin rim of blue showed around the wet, black circle. The whites of her eyes were so bloodshot they looked solid red.

And the little girl was looking up at her . . . staring straight at Polly with a distant, glazed look.

A terrifying sense of recognition hit Polly, but she was

too stunned to let it sink in. She could hear a faint, almost insectlike buzzing sound and realized that the little girl was trying to say something only when the EMT holding the oxygen mask in place leaned forward and whispered to her, "There, there . . . just relax . . . We're going to take good care of you."

Before they moved past Polly, she stepped up to the gurney. Holding the railing lightly with one hand, she started pacing along beside it.

Her voice felt thick in the back of her throat when she tore her gaze away from the little girl's dilated pupil and asked the EMT across the gurney from her, "Where did this happen? Where did you find her?"

"Hit and run over on Martindale Street," the EMT replied solemnly without looking at Polly.

As soon as he said those words, an icy rush filled Polly's stomach.

Oh my God! she thought.

Tears stung her eyes, blurring her vision. The light in the corridor seemed to suddenly dim to a murky yellow. Polly had to tighten her grip on the gurney railing to keep from falling down.

"I live on Martindale," Polly said, not even sure if she was speaking out loud. "I think I . . . know her."

At that, the EMT glanced at Polly. She could read the deep concern in his eyes.

This isn't good, Polly thought, and the coldness tightened unbearably inside her. *She isn't going to make it.*

"Her name is Heather . . . Heather Olsen."

The EMT nodded, but before he could say anything, they burst through a set of double doors and went the short distance down the corridor to the first trauma room on the left.

Polly was feeling so weak in the knees she was afraid she was going to collapse into a heap on the floor as she stepped back and watched the sudden flurry of activity around the gurney. Two more of the medical staff joined Mrs. Kincaid as they set to work examining Heather. Their shouted commands and reading of stats became a meaningless cacophony. All Polly could think was how small and frail Heather's body looked, lying there as if it were nowhere near large enough or strong enough to keep the life inside her from leaking away.

My God, she's dying, and there's nothing I or anyone else can do about it!

The doctor who was obviously in charge—a heavyset, balding man wearing green hospital scrubs—said in a steady, commanding voice, "Okay, let's get her into the OR, stat."

His voice sounded curiously flat, and Polly was nearly overwhelmed by a feeling of helplessness. Everything looked like she was moving in a dream as she stepped up to the gurney and took hold of Heather's hand.

It felt cold and lifeless, totally limp.

Fresh tears filled Polly's eyes as she squeezed the little girl's hand, wishing she could send her courage and strength. She could feel the tears, running down the sides of her face.

It may have just been from the motion of the gurney as the emergency team swung it around to leave the room, but Heather's head rolled to one side, and Polly realized that the girl was staring up at her. Her gaze was distant and hazed, but—thankfully—Polly didn't see any pain in her clouded eyes.

She's in shock, Polly thought even though she knew that it was more than that. Heather was dying, right there in front of her. Polly tried to keep the memory away, but she couldn't help but remember another day almost four years ago when she had watched helplessly as another little girl—a newborn, baby girl they were going to name Crystal—had died here in the same hospital.

Polly was barely aware of everything going on around her. Her entire attention was focused on Heather's eyes and the dimming light she saw there.

"I'm here, baby," Polly whispered, still not sure if she was even speaking out loud or not. She squeezed Heather's hand gently but firmly, hanging on to it, feeling its limp lifelessness. She knew—she could tell—that she and

Heather were connected, if only by this fragile touch and their steady eye contact.

"I won't leave you. I promise. I won't let you go."

Polly looked around when the medical team burst through a set of doors into the operating room. She felt a gentle tug on her shoulder and saw Mrs. Kincaid standing behind her. The woman's mouth was moving, but Polly couldn't hear a word she was saying over the faint, indistinct buzz that filled the room.

Polly turned back to Heather. The girl's face looked like it had slipped away from her and was disappearing into a blurry lens of failing light.

"No . . . please . . . don't leave me. . . ." Polly whispered to her in a voice that had a dull, dragging quality to it.

But she knew it was already too late.

The faint glow in Heather's eyes was fading.

". . . Mrs. Harris . . ."

Polly was distantly aware of the sounds in the room around her. She thought she could hear someone calling her name, but it was far away and echoing. Once again— or still—she felt the gentle tugging on her shoulder, but she gripped Heather's hand all the tighter, determined not to let her go . . . not until . . .

Not until she passes through.

Polly locked her gaze on Heather's eyes and wouldn't turn away. Deep inside, she knew that would break the contact, that it would be deserting Heather at the last moment.

"I'm here with you, baby," Polly whispered, feeling a ragged dryness clutch her throat. "I won't let you go. . . . You're safe here with me, baby. . . ."

But Polly knew that Heather was no longer in the room with her. She was fading away slowly, like a dying ember drifting on a faint breeze. They stared at each other with an intensity that was frightening, and Polly could feel herself being pulled under along with Heather. Swelling blackness surrounded her, closing in from all sides like seething storm clouds. The only thing that was real was the intensity of their eye contact, their touch, and the unspoken words and thoughts—the love and the fears—that they shared.

"... Mrs. Harris ... please ..."

The voice sounded muffled and so far away Polly thought it might be coming from the next room or from outside the building, but it cut into her awareness with a torchlike brilliance and began to draw her back.

"... You'll have to leave now, Mrs. Harris. ..."

Is that Mrs. Kincaid's voice? Is she talking to me?

"... There's nothing more you can do here, Mrs. Harris. ..."

Before Polly could respond, she noticed a sudden change in Heather's eyes. A dull white film cast across her gaze like a skimming of frost, and a dim lifelessness transformed the darker depths of the little girl's eyes so her eyes mirrored the bright lights of the operating room with a frightening intensity.

In that instant, Polly felt a subtle electrical current shoot up her fingertips and through her hand. In a flash, it passed up her arm to her shoulder, tingling and growing stronger with an amazing simultaneous warmth and cold as it spread across her shoulders and up the back of her neck. Then, still gathering strength, it seemed to penetrate deep inside her body, gripping her lungs and stomach with a burning cold touch.

Polly was only dimly aware of the faint whimpering sound she made as she released Heather's lifeless hand and stepped away from the gurney. A terrible sense of vertigo swept through her as that odd tingling sensation went deeper, touching her heart and mind with a curious, warm prickling sensation.

"... She's gone. ..."

Polly clearly heard the words—*Yes, it was Mrs. Kincaid's voice*—echo her own thought as the terrifying truth gradually sank into her mind. Too stunned to move, she just stood there rigidly. She had experienced death this intensely only once before, that day four years ago when her baby died, struggling to be born, but she had *never* felt anything like this before. It was as if with just that touch, something . . . she had no idea what, but a small fragment of Heather had entered her.

Her what?

Her *body?*

Her *mind?*

Her *soul?*

Polly just stood there, blinking her eyes stupidly as she turned slowly and looked over her shoulder at Mrs. Kincaid.

"We'll have to leave now," Mrs. Kincaid said in a soft, soothing voice that did nothing to quell the deep sense of loss and loneliness that gripped Polly.

She knew this feeling all too well.

It was how you felt when you were lying on a hospital operating table yourself, and you knew that no matter what you or the doctors and nurses tried to do, no one was going to be able to save the life you so desperately wanted to cling to.

"I tried . . ." Polly said in a shattered voice. "I tried to . . . keep her here and I . . . couldn't."

She licked her lips, acutely aware of their dry roughness as she closed her eyes and tried to concentrate. She wanted to hold on to the feeling of soothing warmth that seemed to have settled around her heart as though holding it, cradling it, like warm, loving hands.

With her eyes still closed, Polly smiled weakly and inhaled gently. A sudden cold fear clenched inside her when her nostrils were assaulted by a terrible stench unlike anything she had ever experienced before.

It was more than a smell.

It was a sickening taste that invaded her nasal passages and clung to the back of her throat like the nauseating stench of burned hair and rotting flesh and sour milk and . . . *and something else* . . . something she couldn't identify even as it made her stomach roil and churn.

"My God! What is that smell?" she asked, frowning with concern as she glanced around the operating room.

There was no longer a sense of urgency in the room. Polly could see that the monitors connected to Heather were all displaying flat, green lines on their black screens. There was a high-pitched buzzing sound that, thankfully, someone quickly shut off. When she glanced over at the gurney, she saw that someone had pulled the white sheet up over Heather's face. Polly stared numbly at the bulging outline of the gauze pad and the faint red stain that was blossoming on the sheet as blood seeped into it.

"You'll have to leave now," Mrs. Kincaid repeated softly. "There's nothing more you can do."

A choking flood of emotion welled up inside Polly. She reached out, grateful for the support Mrs. Kincaid offered her as she turned and started from the room. At the door, Polly hesitated and glanced back at the tiny sheet-draped form on the table, unable to process or accept the fact that there really was a little girl under there who, no more than an hour or two ago, had been happily living her life. Now she was gone . . . forever.

The emotions that welled up inside Polly were almost too much to bear but somehow she found the strength to leave the room. As the Emergency OR doors whooshed shut behind her, Polly's only thought was, *That's the smell of death in there. . . . And now it's inside me!*

"What kind of tea is this?"

It was half an hour later, and Polly was seated in the nursing staff room. She held a Styrofoam cup of hot tea tightly in both hands and sniffed as thin tendrils of steam rose from the cup and curled around her face. Her hands were still trembling deep inside, but she felt at least a little better.

"'S just regular old tea," Mrs. Kincaid said, indicating the box of Red Rose Tea that was on the table beside the staff coffeemaker.

"Ummm . . . It smells . . . different, though," Polly said, nodding as she brought the cup up closer to her face and inhaled more deeply.

A frown creased her brow as she tried to match this aroma with her memory of what "just regular old tea" was supposed to smell like. No matter how hard she tried, she couldn't make the two fit. This tea smelled . . . odd. It had a thick, almost cloying damp earth smell that made her stomach do a little flip-flop.

"You can use the phone on the wall beside you if you'd like to call your husband," Mrs. Kincaid said. "Just dial nine to get an outside line."

"No. I have my cell phone, but there's no sense getting him worried. I'm feeling considerably better now."

Polly was aware of the slight drag in her voice and how it might make Mrs. Kincaid think she wasn't feeling much better, but she couldn't stop thinking about how odd the tea smelled, like it was something she had never smelled before in her life. Her frown deepened as she looked over at Mrs. Kincaid.

"So what happens next?" she asked. "About Heather, I mean."

"We've contacted her mother at work," Mrs. Kincaid said. "She's on her way over."

"So there's nothing else . . ."

Polly left the question unfinished and swallowed with difficulty as another heated rush ran through her. The sensation seemed to be centered in her chest, close to her heart, and she wondered again about that curious feeling she'd had the instant Heather died.

No, not died, Polly thought. *She passed over.*

"There was nothing more you or anyone else could have done," Mrs. Kincaid said. Polly knew that the sympathy she heard in the woman's voice was genuine, and she chided herself for suspecting earlier that Mrs. Kincaid had been trying to one-up her.

"We did everything we could, but sometimes . . . you know?" Mrs. Kincaid took a slight breath, and Polly could hear her shudder as she exhaled and shook her head. "Sometimes there's nothing we can do. It's especially hard when it's a child." She blinked away the tears forming in her eyes. "It was a good thing that you did, being there and holding her hand. It was very courageous."

"What else could I do?"

Polly looked down at the cup of tea she was still holding tightly with both hands. The surface of the tea reflected the fluorescent lights overhead, and for a frightening instant, she recalled how, at the instant Heather died, her eyes had suddenly glazed over and reflected the lights in the operating room like polished mirrors.

"I guess we can only hope that there's someone there to do the same for us when we—" She almost said *died,* but finished—"when we pass on."

All this time, though, Polly couldn't stop thinking about what had happened, what she had felt in that terrible instant when the spark of life left Heather Olsen. She didn't doubt that she had experienced . . . something.

She just wasn't sure what.

As she mulled it over, she became convinced that the instant Heather died, some essential part of Heather had somehow been transferred to her. Even more frightening, Polly was beginning to think also at that same instant, some part of her had been lost or replaced by whatever it was of Heather that had entered her. Leaning forward with her eyes closed, she tried to make that thought go away, but now that it had been planted, it wouldn't let go.

Is something like that even possible? she wondered as a tightening nervous fear gripped her.

Polly wasn't a strictly religious person. She didn't attend church or say prayers regularly, but she was to some degree what she would consider religious. She believed that there was a spiritual—if not supernatural—aspect to life, so if there really was a soul, and if it resided somewhere within all of us while we're alive, why wouldn't something like that be possible?

Thinking these thoughts with her eyes closed, she felt the warmth curling around her heart intensify. For a panicky instant, Polly wondered if, under the stress of what had just happened, she might have ruptured a blood vessel that was leaking blood internally and would eventually kill her.

The rising panic took hold as she opened her eyes and looked at Mrs. Kincaid, hoping to find something to anchor her sight on, but her vision suddenly clouded over, and a sprinkling of white dots zigzagged in front of her.

Polly wanted desperately to get up and leave, right now. She felt compelled to run out of there, but she was afraid that, the instant she stood up, she would pass out. Her vision, especially around the edges, was jittering with a blurry red and black darkness that seeped across her eyes like a slowly spreading ink stain.

Oh Jesus! What's happening to me?

She looked around the staff room, wanting desperately to find something to focus on. Determined not to lose control—not here . . . not now . . . not in front of Mrs. Kincaid—she clung desperately to consciousness.

When she took a deep breath of air through her mouth, her chest felt like it was filling with warm water, not air. The warm, liquid sensation spread out slowly, radiating into her shoulders and deep down into her abdomen. As her panic spiked, a feathery *whoosh*ing sound filled her ears, keeping time with the almost painful throb of her pulse.

Moving with slow deliberation, Polly turned to her left and tried to place the cup of tea on the table beside her before she spilled it, but her hands were trembling so badly that some of the tea sloshed onto her thumb, scalding her with its sharp burn.

"I don't—"

That was all she managed to say before the darkness at the edges of her vision closed down around her with a dull, muffled roar. She was already unconscious by the time she pitched forward out of the chair and landed face first on the threadbare, carpeted floor.

two

"Jesus, Polly, you should have called me sooner," Tim Harris said the instant he entered the kitchen and saw the expression on his wife's face. He let the screen door swing shut behind him and rushed over to her.

It was late in the afternoon, and it had been several hours since Polly had gotten home following her ordeal at the hospital. For the past half hour, she'd been sitting at the kitchen table, waiting for Tim to get home. The cell phone was on the table by her elbow where she had left it ever since she had called him at his office at the university and told him what had happened. She stood up shakily, her face pale and moist with tears. Whimpering softly and unable to say anything, she practically fell into her husband's arms and clung desperately to him.

Tim frowned, unable to disguise the worry he felt as he embraced his wife for a moment. Then he pushed her away and looked at her. She smiled at him, but it looked thin and forced. There was a distant glaze in her eyes that made him think of a thin skimming of ice over a pond that was just starting to freeze. Although she was looking directly into his eyes, she seemed to be focusing on something else . . . something in the distance behind him.

"What the hell were you thinking?" he asked, not doing a good job of hiding his anger.

"I thought I . . . that it would be all right," Polly replied in a high, tremulous voice.

"Well, I just don't get it," Tim said, shaking his head and taking a step away from her. "I mean . . . Christ! What on earth possessed you to go there in the first place?"

Polly shrugged. Tim could see that she was feeling really bad about what had happened, and that his anger wasn't what she needed right now.

"I just thought it was time to start looking for something to do," she said weakly. "We'd been saying how I had to get out of the house more, get involved with something."

"Yeah, but that was *months* ago," Tim said, still fighting his anger. "I didn't think you were actually going to *do* it. Certainly not today, anyway. You never even mentioned it to me."

"I didn't think I needed your permission," Polly said with a sudden flush of anger. "It was a beautiful morning, and I was feeling pretty good, so I figured today was as good a day as any."

"Not if you're going to call me fifteen minutes before I'm supposed to administer a final exam and inform me that you passed out in the hospital staff room. And what's this?"

Tim took hold of Polly's left hand and raised it so he could get a better look at the thick wadding of bandage on her thumb.

"Oh that . . . I burned my hand a little when I spilled some tea. Nothing serious."

"You burned your hand," Tim echoed.

"If it had been real serious, what better place to be than in a hospital, right?"

Polly chuckled softy, but no matter how hard he tried, Tim couldn't find even the slightest trace of humor in the situation.

"But you . . . I mean . . . What the hell were you think-ing, putting yourself into a situation like that? You're not trained to . . . That's not what . . ." Unable to find the right words, he let his voice trail away. Pressing his hands against his forehead, he shook his head with exasperation.

"I didn't really have a choice," Polly said softly, regarding him with a dark, steady stare that he couldn't begin to read. "Once I was there, things just . . . happened. And anyway, forget about me. Fuck me! Think about the Olsens and what they have to deal with now. Think about their child . . ."

Polly's voice hitched as she looked at him, her eyes brimming with tears.

"Their daughter is *dead*, Tim! She's really *dead*!"

"I know . . . I know," Tim replied, but Polly was looking at him like she thought it was painfully obvious that he *didn't* know, that there was no way in hell he could ever know or understand. Her tears were running down both sides of her face, and she sniffed loudly as she wiped her nose with the back of her hand.

"I was there, Tim . . . I was holding her . . . her hand, and I—"

She sniffed again and almost choked, but forced herself to continue.

"And there was nothing I could do, Tim. *Nothing!* I had to just stand there and watch as she . . . as she . . . she slowly faded away and then . . . then she was . . . gone. Just like when our—"

Before she could finish the sentence, Tim drew her to him again and hugged her closely, pressing her face against his chest and running his hands up and down her back. She was trembling terribly as deep sobs ripped through her. She felt so small and fragile in his embrace that he almost started crying, too; but this was one of those times, he told himself, when he couldn't let himself feel the emotion and hurt. He had to put his own concerns and irritation aside and just be strong for her.

"I was holding her hand," Polly said, her voice muffled against his shoulder. "Her tiny, little hand . . . And I was the last one . . . I was the last person she ever saw before she . . . before she—"

Polly's voice broke off. Her body collapsed against him as she cried all the harder and pressed her face into his shoulder as if somehow he could protect her from what she had experienced and what she was feeling right now.

"There, there," Tim whispered, cupping the back of her head with one hand and crushing her against him.

They stood that way for a long time, saying nothing, just feeling each other.

"You weren't there. . . . You have no idea what it was like. . . ."

"I know."

After a minute or two, once she seemed to gain a measure of control and her tears had begun to subside, Polly pulled away from him. It was only with difficulty that she was able to make eye contact with him. When she tried to speak, nothing came out. Biting her lower lip, she simply shook her head and, closing her eyes, pressed her face against him once again.

"It must have been horrible," Tim whispered. "Absolutely horrible."

But even as he soothed her, rubbing her back and holding her tightly, he sensed just by the way she stiffened in his embrace that Polly was thinking there was no way he could even begin to understand what she was feeling. He realized that he had reacted the same way when their daughter had died. The awakened pain of that terrible day four years ago was like a knife jab to his heart, but he told himself that he couldn't let it show.

He had to be strong . . . for Polly.

Later that day, once she had calmed down, they sat side by side on the couch in the living room, not saying much but trying to find comfort in each other's presence.

Polly still felt utterly alone in her grief. Her husband didn't seem to understand. Lois McIssac, her best friend and confidante, was traveling in Europe with her new husband. Her other friends, she was sure, wouldn't understand what she was feeling. So that left her stranded, all alone . . . alone except for the subtle sensation of warmth that shimmered in her chest like two tiny, fragile hands, holding and caressing her heart.

A mild shiver of fear raced through her when she thought about what she had felt the instant Heather had died. She knew that she didn't have the words to communicate what she was feeling to her husband.

There's something new inside me.

A bone-deep shudder ran through her.

And, at the same time, I've lost something. . . . There's something missing.

"It's like . . . like a little piece of me died with her," she finally whispered with tears in her eyes as she shifted closer to Tim and placed her hand lightly on his elbow. "It's just like when . . . when Crystal died . . . I feel like I . . . I've lost something . . . a piece of myself."

Tim said nothing as he stared at the glass of beer in his hand. Polly was grateful for that because she knew there was nothing he could say.

He didn't understand.

He couldn't understand.

No one could!

She wasn't entirely sure that she knew what she had been through, but watching Heather die had opened up old wounds, wounds she had never thought were healed but were now bleeding fresh and strong.

After taking a deep breath, Polly let it out in a sigh and leaned closer, her head resting on his shoulder. It was then that she became aware of something else, of a faint, musky scent that filled her nose.

"What's that smell? Is that on your jacket?" she asked as she pulled quickly away from him.

"Huh? What smell?"

"Your jacket," Polly said, frowning. "It smells . . . funny."

Tim raised his arm to his nose and noisily sniffed the sleeve, then looked at her with a deepening frown. Polly was tempted to lean forward and sniff him again, but even through the congestion of having just finished crying, the pungent smell was strong in her nostrils.

Her memory of Tim, especially when he wore this particular herringbone jacket, was that he always smelled tweedy, the way a college professor should. But now there was a different smell about him.

Polly tried to get a fix on what it was, but the scent was elusive—a mixture of damp wool and soap and something else—a faint flowery aroma and something like citrus, orange peels, maybe, from an orange that had gone bad and dried out.

"Did you let some fruit rot in your coat pocket or something?" she asked.

Tim shifted forward and patted both pockets, all the while shaking his head.

"No. Are you sure you're feeling all right?" he asked.

Polly winced as if he had slapped her.

"*No!*" she said sharply. "I'm *not* feeling all right at *all,* but there's . . ."

She closed her eyes for a moment and rubbed the bridge of her nose, all the while telling herself just to drop it.

It's nothing.

She told herself she was focusing too much on little things, letting them become more important than they really were. His jacket probably just needed a cleaning, that's all.

Still, there was *something* about it that seemed . . . different, and it bothered her that her sense of smell seemed to have changed so dramatically.

Maybe it's somebody's perfume, Polly thought, surprising herself with this sudden suspicion. *Maybe he's having an affair with a colleague or with a coed from one of his English literature classes.*

Polly's eyes widened as she stared at her husband, trying to divine the truth from his expression; but as far as she could tell, he was just as perplexed as she was. If he was hiding anything like an affair, he was masking it extremely well.

But maybe he's had a lot of practice, she thought.

What she said was, "We should probably send that old thing out to the cleaners."

"It's my favorite sports coat," Tim said.

"Yeah, well, the semester's pretty much over, so you won't be needing it until the fall, anyway."

Tim raised his sleeve up to his nose again and sniffed loudly. Before he could reply, they heard the front door open and then slam shut.

"Anybody home?" a voice called out.

Footsteps approached from the entryway, and both Polly and Tim turned as Brian, their thirteen-year-old son, entered the living room. He swung his backpack off his shoulder and slid it like a bowling ball across the floor until it hit the foot of the stairs with a loud *thump*.

"Am I interrupting anything?" Brian asked.

"We . . . your mother's had a pretty rough day," Tim said. "She was at the hospital—in the emergency room— when Heather Olsen was brought in."

"Oh, yeah," Brian said, nodding. "I heard something about that at school today. Someone said she'd been hit by a car or something on her way to school this morning."

"She was," Polly said. Her voice almost broke, but she tried to keep it steady. "She . . . didn't make it."

"What? You mean she died?" Brian asked, his eyes widening with surprise. "Oh, man. That really sucks."

Polly tried to say something more, but now her voice failed her.

"That's what you have to say?" Tim said sternly, glowering at Brian. "It *sucks*?"

"Yeah," Brian said, raising his hands and looking around, genuinely confused. "Well, it does."

"Oh, never mind," Polly said softly.

Another flood of tears was building up inside her as she allowed herself the fleeting thought of how she would feel if it had been Brian who'd been struck and killed by a car and "That really sucks" was the extent of his friends' reaction.

An awkward silence filled the kitchen. For an instant, Polly thought—just to create the illusion of normalcy—that maybe she should say something to Brian—again—about not sliding his backpack across the floor like that; but she wasn't in any mood right now to start harping at him about anything, so she let it drop.

"You know," Tim said, suddenly clapping his hands together and rubbing them, "now that we're all together, I figure it's as good a time as any to tell you something."

Polly tensed, suddenly—irrationally—expecting the worst.

Is he going to drop the bombshell now? What's he going to do, admit to having an affair right here in front of both of us and tell us he's leaving?

Tim cleared his throat as he looked back and forth between his wife and son. Then, adopting the same slouched stance she had seen him assume whenever he lectured a class, he said, "What do you say we all go on a family trip this summer?"

"What?" Brian said, unable to contain his surprise.

Polly did a little bit better than that and checked any overt expression of surprise, but this was so different—and benign—compared to what she had been expecting that it caught her completely off guard. She had to struggle not to burst out laughing. After a moment, though, she composed herself and gave her husband an inquisitive look.

"A vacation?" she said, enunciating the word and hearing just a trace of skepticism in her tone of voice.

"Yeah . . . a vacation," Tim repeated, his eyes lighting up as he fired to the idea. "I've been thinking about this for a while, now, and I think this is gonna be our best chance—probably our last chance—to take off for the whole summer and get away."

"Get away?" Polly said skeptically.

"The whole summer?" Brian said at the same instant.

His expression said it all: He wasn't the least bit interested in taking off for even part of the summer much less the whole of it, especially with his mother and father.

"Yeah, but we haven't taken a family vacation since . . . gosh, since we went to Quebec when Brian was five or six," Polly said hesitantly. She was trying to keep her re-action in check because she didn't want to say anything too committal either way before she had some time to think about it.

"Exactly," Tim said emphatically. "We work and go to school and never take any time off except for weekends and holidays, and then we end up either just hanging around here or doing housework. We've never taken time for the three of us to be together."

Polly raised one eyebrow and shook her head but said nothing.

"My classes are over in a week," Tim continued, "and Brian's done with school the middle of June. If we start planning now, we can make reservations at the places we want to go."

"Uh-huh. Like where?" Polly asked, seeing her own hesitation reflected in Brian's perplexed expression.

"I don't know. Like Glacier National Park and Yellow-stone and the Grand Tetons," Tim said enthusiastically. "We could drive out, taking a northern route across the Great Plains and Rockies, then come back by a southern route, through New Mexico and Texas and Alabama."

Brian sniffed with laughter as he shook his head. "Oh, yeah. Alabama. That's my idea of an ideal vacation spot, especially in the middle of the summer."

"That's not what I'm talking about," Tim said, sounding a shade exasperated as he registered his family's resistance to his proposal. "I'm talking about all the national parks and monuments. Haven't you ever wanted to see the Alamo?"

"Not particularly," Brian said with a sly smirk. "And as for this summer, I was thinking more along the lines of get-ting a job doing lawns or something."

Tim sniffed and shook his head. "Hold on a second," he said. "Are you telling me that you'd rather stay here in this little town and work instead of travel cross country and back?"

Brian started to reply, then checked himself.

Sensing that this could easily turn into a heated argument between Brian and his father, Polly spoke up.

"We don't have to commit to anything either way . . . at least not right now. I think it's a good idea."

She looked directly at Tim and smiled, even though her smile felt forced, and all she could think right now was that this wasn't such a good idea, and Tim wasn't thinking at all to mention it now, after the kind of day she'd had.

"Let's think it over," she finished. "We have to take into account what all of us are looking for this summer."

Tim's expression hardened. "I'm just saying, if we don't do it this summer, we might never get to do it as a family."

"Fine by me," Brian muttered, shaking his head, but Tim kept talking right over him.

"We've been saying for years that it's something we should do, and I think we'd better grab this summer to do it. Otherwise, Brian's going to be too old to want to do it."

"Maybe I'm too old to want to do it now."

Brian spoke in a whisper that Polly heard, but she wasn't sure if Tim heard it or not until his face flushed with anger, and he wheeled around on his son.

"If we decide that we're driving cross country, you're coming with us, and that's the end of it," Tim said. His face turned bright red as he jabbed a pointed finger at his son.

"Why don't just you and Mom go. I could stay here," Brian offered. He cowered from his father but didn't back down.

"Alone? For the whole summer? I don't think so," Tim snapped as he shook his head in disgust.

"Why not?" Brian said, rising to the fight. "It'd be a lot better than being stuck in a car all summer."

"A trip cross country might be fun," Polly said, stepping

between them. "But like I said, let's think it over and talk about it later. Right now, I—"

Before she could finish, a sudden rush of chills filled her chest like a flood of water. For a second or two, her lungs felt constricted, and she found it almost impossible to take a deep enough breath. Her eyes went out of focus, and little white dots shot like tiny comets across her vision.

"Right now . . . all I . . . want to do is . . . sit down and . . . relax."

Her voice dragged and sounded strangely distant to herself as the chilly prickling sensation rippled up her back. She wanted desperately to close her eyes and just put her head back, but even as simple an act as that seemed impossible to do. She was paralyzed, too frightened even to move. The couch seemed to be pitching gently from side to side, like the heaving motion of a boat at sea. When she looked over at her husband, his face looked subtly distorted, as though she were looking at him through an oddly curved lens.

". . . Polly . . . ?"

She saw his mouth move, and she knew that Tim had spoken, but his words didn't seem to match the motion of his lips. His voice echoed thinly in her ears, sounding impossibly far away.

Polly struggled against the dark rush of vertigo that was sweeping over her, but all she could think was, *This is exactly how I felt at the hospital, just before I passed out.*

She grabbed the arm of the couch like it was a lifeline. Her heart was racing high and fast, making the pulse in her neck almost painful. She looked down at her hands, surprised how far away they looked.

Is that really my hand? she wondered with just a trace of amusement cutting through her rising panic.

The hand—her hand—looked so thin and pale and . . . foreign. For a shattering instant, Polly had the distinct impression that her body was nothing more than a puppet for someone else who was controlling her every move.

Somehow, she managed to cling onto consciousness as

she leaned back, her head bouncing heavily against the cushion. A tingling electrical shock raced up her shoulders, but it felt so distant that it was only mildly painful. Polly laughed softly to herself as she cupped her hands over her eyes.

"Polly! Are you all right?"

"Mom?"

She could hear the frantic edge in both Tim's and Brian's voices, but she was drifting too far away, too numbed to be worried, and she couldn't help but wonder why they would be upset. Her eyes remained open behind her cupped hands as she stared into the darkness that swelled there. The white dots had multiplied and were now part of a vast, vibrating field of white energy that jiggled and swelled within the darkness, keeping time with the hard, steady pulses of her heart.

I don't like it here. . . . I'm afraid.

Polly heard as much as thought the words. She was positive that this was her own thought, but she was feeling so detached from her body that the words seemed to be coming from somewhere other than inside her mind.

"Do you need to see a doctor?"

It was Tim's voice again, and this time he sounded much closer. Polly took her hands away from her eyes and looked at him. He was kneeling in front of the couch, holding her knees. She could see the earnest concern in his large brown eyes and wanted to say something, but the voice was still echoing inside her head.

I'm all alone. . . . I'm afraid.

Beyond Tim, Polly could see Brian standing in the doorway. He was staring at her with a mixed expression of concern and fear.

Yes, fear! Polly thought. *He's afraid there's something wrong with me . . . that I might be dying!*

"I . . . I'm all right," she whispered, even though it pained her to speak.

Somehow, she managed to smile as she looked at her husband. His eyes looked glassy and moist, as though he'd been so frightened that he'd been about to cry.

"Seriously," Polly said, bracing herself and speaking with more strength that she really felt. "I'm all right. I'm still just a little freaked out about what happened today, and I . . . I just can't take it when you two start arguing like that."

Tim and Brian exchanged guilty glances, and then Tim mumbled, "Sorry."

"We'll talk about your idea after supper," Polly said, feeling stronger now. "But for now, don't even mention it." She took a deep breath, grateful to feel the clean flow of air into her lungs. "I don't really feel like cooking anything tonight, so what do you say we eat out. How does pizza at Artie's sound?"

Tim and Brian both nodded, but Polly thought that they were agreeing just to make her happy. The muscles in the backs of her legs felt loose and shaky as she stood up. She had to lean on the couch arm with both hands for a few seconds to make sure she wasn't going to collapse.

"And please," she said after taking another deep breath and letting it out slowly. "No more arguing tonight. All right?"

Father and son glanced at each other, and both of them nodded.

"I just can't take it," Polly finished, "because when you think about what we have and what . . ." She choked up and almost couldn't speak. "And what the Olsens have lost."

She took another deep breath and, reaching out, grasped each of their hands in hers.

"Let's just appreciate what we've got while we've got it, okay?"

Both of them mumbled, "Okay."

•   •   •

Considering the day's events, the family had a fine evening out. First they had pizza at Artie's. Then, for dessert, they swung by Friendly's for ice cream sundaes, even though Polly complained that she didn't really need the extra calories. Throughout the meal and even after dessert, though, there hadn't been any more discussion of Tim's road trip. Polly didn't even think about it, and Tim didn't mention it because he realized just how deeply the day's events had shaken Polly. He was making an effort not to be insensitive or distant. Brian didn't mention it because he wasn't at all keen on the idea in the first place, and he was hoping it would just go away if he didn't bring it up.

It was now nearly nine o'clock. Since seven o'clock, Polly had been hunched up on the couch, channel surfing, but mostly staring blankly at whatever happened to be on the Cooking Channel. Tim was upstairs in his office grading final exams, and Brian was off with his friends until his curfew, which on school nights was nine o'clock. He should be home any minute.

Try as she might, Polly couldn't stop wondering what—if anything—she could do for Craig and Marlene Olsen. Although they lived on the same street as Polly and Tim, they weren't close friends. The Olsens' sons, Alan and Scott, were a bit younger than Brian, so they never played together. And Brian hadn't paid any attention at all to Heather, who was so much younger than he.

Polly knew that the Olsens had to deal with their grief and anguish on their own terms, but because she had been there with Heather, she felt an intense, personal bond with the family. Polly recognized that the Olsens' situation was much different and had to be much worse than hers. She and Tim had lost a baby in childbirth. Their daughter, Crystal, had never even had a chance at life. Polly and Tim didn't have ten years of memories and hopes and dreams so suddenly shattered.

Still, the loss of a child, no matter what the circumstances, was the worst pain imaginable. The terrible thing was, Polly had no idea what she could do to help the Olsens.

Should she call them tonight to express her sympathies, or would sending a sympathy card suffice?

Or should she go over to their house and visit so she could express to them just how sorry she was about what had happened?

Would the Olsens even want to hear from her?

Maybe they had no interest in hearing about their daughter's final moments of life, her struggle for life. The agony that would put them through might be intolerable.

Certainly the family was grieving, but that was probably something they would want to do alone or with relatives and close friends and their priest or minister. Still, Polly felt an unusually strong compulsion to visit them as much for her own peace of mind as theirs.

At least for now, though, she did nothing.

She didn't want to intrude on their sorrow. Of course, she and Tim would attend Heather's funeral if it wasn't a private affair for just the family. Polly thought that might provide an opportunity for her to speak with them.

Then again, she couldn't imagine what she could possibly say to them. Although they no doubt would not want to hear the gruesome details of the accident, she yearned to try to communicate to them the intensity of the connection she had felt with Heather just before she . . . *passed on.*

Polly still couldn't fully grasp the fact that Heather, like Crystal, was dead.

Dead sounded too final, too hopeless, and what Polly was sure she felt with Heather had not felt final. Something unusual had happened, so as much as Polly might want to talk about it to Heather's family, she didn't want to see them until she had a better grasp on exactly what had happened.

"But what did happen?" she whispered to herself as she stared blankly at the flickering TV screen.

"What's that, honey?" Tim called out from the kitchen.

Polly was surprised to realize that he was downstairs and had overheard her. She hadn't even noticed when he walked by.

"Huh? Oh, nothing. Just talking to myself. How're the papers going?"

"Just about done," Tim said. "The trouble is, I've had so much coffee, I'll probably be up till dawn anyway."

"I know what you mean," Polly whispered to herself, knowing that it wasn't coffee, it was thoughts of Heather Olsen that were going to be keeping her awake tonight.

As far as Polly was concerned, any telephone calls after eleven o'clock at night meant only one thing: trouble.

Brian had come home only a minute or two past his curfew. Not late enough to make an issue about it. He claimed that his homework was all done for tomorrow and had gone to bed by ten-thirty without much complaining. Tim had been wrong about the coffee he'd consumed and was snoring peacefully by eleven.

All of this left Polly alone, lying in the darkness and staring up at the ceiling until her vision began to blur with tears. She couldn't stop thinking about Heather Olsen and what her family must be going through right now. No doubt both parents and probably both brothers were still awake, crying and grieving and trying to figure out how and why something like this could have happened to them, and what—if anything—they could have done to prevent it.

But I was there, and there was nothing anyone could have done to prevent it.

Grief sliced through her heart like the cut of a cold razor blade. She became terribly conscious of her breathing. There was a weight on her chest, even though she was wearing only a light nightgown and was lying outside the covers. The air in the bedroom felt dense and oppressive, as though it wanted to squeeze the life out of her with a slow, steadily building pressure.

That's when the telephone rang.

The sudden, sharp, electronic *beep-beep* shattered the silence, making Polly jump as if she'd received an electric shock. The clutching sensation around her throat tightened so much she couldn't make a sound.

The telephone shattered the silence a second time, and this time, Tim stirred in his sleep. Groaning softly as he rolled over, he smacked his lips and muttered something unintelligible.

Polly shifted her eyes to the alarm clock and saw, just as the phone rang a third time, that it was 11:48, almost midnight.

The cold tightness around her throat spread like grasping fingers down into her chest.

Something's wrong. . . . Someone's been hurt.

Her first thought was that Brian might not be in bed after all, that he might have waited until he thought she and Tim were asleep and sneaked out to meet up with his friends.

Maybe this was the police calling to inform them that there had been some trouble . . . an accident.

Halfway through the fourth ring, Tim reached out blindly in the darkness and grabbed the receiver.

"Hello?" he said, his voice thick with sleep.

Polly tensed as she waited in the darkness to hear what he said next. Her mind was rifling through a series of worst-case scenarios even though she realized that the worst couldn't have happened. Her family was all safe and sound at home.

So who is it? What's happened?

Tim's folks were both dead, and her parents had moved to Bradenton, Florida, a few years ago. Had something happened to one of them? Maybe Dad's heart had finally given out.

"Yeah," Tim said, still sounding groggy and a bit irritated at being awakened at such a late hour. "Yeah, it's been a while."

Every fiber of Polly's being tingled with anticipation as she waited for some indication from Tim as to who was on the phone and what the hell had happened.

After a moment, Tim whispered, "Oh, Jesus," and now Polly knew that—whatever it was—it wasn't good.

Tim let out a long, shuddering breath, then said, "Oh, Jesus," again.

Polly heard a rustle of sheets as Tim rolled over, then a dull click as he snapped on the light on the bed stand. The sudden brightness brought tears to Polly's eyes, and she had to squint to shut out the burst of pain.

"Who is it?" she whispered, surprised to find that she had the strength to speak at all. Tim waved her off with an impatient flick of his hand as he swung his feet to the floor and sat up on the edge of the bed.

"I see," he said softly into the phone. "Uh-huh. . . . Yes, yes . . . of course. No. No problem."

Polly could barely stand the tension that was winding up inside her. She was instantly angry at Tim for not telling her right away what was going on and had to restrain herself from slapping him to get his attention, but he turned away, avoiding eye contact with her as he cupped the phone close to his ear.

"Yes . . . yes," he said, nodding. Then, with a low sigh, he held the phone at arm's length and flicked off the power button.

"Who was that?" Polly asked in a dry, croaking voice. "What happened?"

"That was Doc Greenberg, in Hilton," Tim said softly. He was looking straight at Polly now, his eyes looking unfocused.

"Doc Greenberg," Polly said with a slight shake of her head. "I don't remember—"

"He was our family doctor when I was a kid."

Tim's eyes twitched back and forth as though he were

trying to track something that Polly couldn't see over her shoulder.

"My brother, Rob, had an accident at work today," Tim said with an unmistakable catch in his voice. "He's in the hospital."

An hour later, Tim and Polly were facing each other across the kitchen table. Following the phone call from Dr. Greenberg, they had come downstairs to talk so they wouldn't disturb Brian. The dark night pressed against the windows like an animal, wanting to be let in. The soft yellow glow of the single light they had on did little to dispel the gloom that had settled around them.

"It just seems so . . . unreal," Tim said with a slow shake of the head. "I mean . . . he's my big brother, and I just can't think of him as . . . as . . ." His voice drifted off as he shook his head, trying to absorb what had happened.

"Vulnerable?" Polly offered.

Tim glanced at her and nodded, then looked past her and out the windows, his eyes unfocused.

"Hey, these things happen," she said softly, and even as she said it, she thought for the hundredth time since the phone call that Rob's accident must have happened right around the time she was in the hospital with Heather. There was no way the two events could be connected, but still, Polly had the unnerving feeling that somehow they were.

"Why do you think Dr. Greenberg waited so long to call you?" Polly asked.

Again, Tim shrugged.

"My guess is that Rob's being the tough guy, you know? He probably told Doc not to call me, insisting that he could deal with it himself. I figure Doc held off for a while but later, once his conscience got the better of him or whatever, he phoned."

"Why'd he have to call so late?" Polly said. "I was having enough trouble getting to sleep as it was."

"Umm," Tim said, nodding, but he seemed distracted, his mind elsewhere.

"Do you think it's as bad as the doctor said?" Polly asked. "Would he exaggerate it?"

Tim shrugged again and, leaning back in the chair, took a deep breath.

"If anything, he'd probably understate things. . . . At least that's how I remember him. But Doc's a lot older, now. Got to be in his midsixties, at least, so . . ." He shrugged again. "I just don't know."

"Well, even though it sounds pretty serious—multiple fractures of his lower leg and foot and all—I don't see how anything like that could be life threatening."

"Not unless there's something he's not telling me until I get there."

Polly's eyes widened, and a slight chill jabbed her when she looked at her husband.

"What do you mean, until you get there?"

Tim's frown deepened. His eyes were veiled and dark when he turned to her.

"We—or I, anyway—have to go up and see how he's doing," Tim said. "We can't very well send a get-well card and forget about it."

Polly could hear the effort it took Tim to control his voice.

"I'm not gonna leave my brother alone in the hospital!"

Polly took a moment to consider her words carefully before responding.

"Well," she said, "it obviously can't be *too* serious or else the doctor would have called right away, don't you think?" She took a breath, knowing that she had to say what was on her mind. "If you ask me, it sounds like another one of your brother's attempts to manipulate—"

"Hold it right there," Tim said, shooting an angry look at Polly and shaking a warning finger at her. After a second or two, he relaxed his posture and leaned his head back so he was staring at the ceiling. When he spoke, it was with more exasperation than anything else. "I know you're not my brother's biggest fan, okay? But there's no reason for you to disparage him."

"No reason?" Polly snapped, unable to choke back the words before they were out of her mouth. "Come on, Tim . . ."

Tim started to speak again but then apparently thought better of it and said nothing as he folded his hands behind his head and continued to stare up at the ceiling.

"He's a master manipulator, Tim," Polly said, keeping her voice as flat and emotionless as possible. She knew she should just shut up. This wasn't going to help, but she had already said too much and couldn't stop herself. "It's not like this is anything new. I swear, from the first day I met him, I could tell that Rob was a . . . a complete—"

Finally, she cut herself off, but it was already too late. The word *loser* hung in the air between them like a heavy charge of electricity, just waiting to ground out through someone. They'd had this discussion so many times over the years that it was all too predictable. The lines were clearly drawn. Polly didn't like Rob. End of story. And at least as far as she was concerned, Tim was one hundred percent blind to his brother's character flaws. He would defend him, no matter what.

"He's not perfect. I know that," Tim said in a low voice that sounded absolutely defeated, "but he's my brother, Pol. He's all the family I have left."

"I know that, but that doesn't excuse some of the bullshit he's pulled over the years," Polly said, trying to cool down.

"No, it doesn't," Tim replied evenly, "but it also doesn't mean that I can ignore him when he needs help."

"And what makes you think he needs help now?" Anger bubbled up out of her so fast she could almost taste it. "*He* didn't call you. Dr. Greenberg did. As far as he's concerned, you don't even know what's happened."

"Oh, I'll bet he knew that Doc Greenberg would call me," Tim said.

"Exactly," Polly practically shouted. "And you don't see that as him trying to manipulate the situation?"

Tim rolled his head to the side and looked over at her. His eyes gleamed in the dim light; his face looked pale and drawn.

"If *he* had called and told you what had happened, that'd be different," Polly said, struggling to calm down. "Then you wouldn't be feeling this way. You'd figure he was doing all right and not be worried. But don't you see? This way he gets you to worry . . . and to react."

"Yeah? And how do you think he wants me to react?"

"Exactly the way you are! He's got you worried about him now, and you're actually thinking about going up there to help him out."

Tim turned away from her and let out an exasperated sigh as he shook his head and looked at the wall of night outside the window.

"So what you are saying is, I'm not supposed to be concerned?" Tim snickered softly. "You're saying I should ignore him when he needs help? I'll bet if this was *your* brother, you'd offer to help in a flash. Wouldn't you?"

"That's not really the point, is it?" Polly said evenly. "Look, I don't dislike your brother. I just don't *trust* him. He's always got an angle, and something like this is right up his alley. It's just the kind of thing he'll use to take advantage of you. He'll hit you up for money, at the very least."

"I want to help him if I can. There's nothing wrong with that. And since we were thinking about taking a family vacation this summer, anyway, I was just thinking that maybe we'd spend some time up in Hilton first."

"Until he's out of the hospital and able to get around on his own, huh?" She tried, but Polly was unable to hide the disgust in her voice. Tim snickered again, louder, but said nothing.

"If we do something like that, we could end up staying there the whole summer."

Tim sniffed. "I can think of worse places to spend the summer."

"Yeah, well I can think of *better* places. If you want to go up there and see how he's doing, then fine. But I don't think it's fair for you to be dragging me and Brian along with you. I'm not going to spend my summer baby-sitting your brother."

"Jesus, I'm not asking you to *baby-sit* him," Tim said. He sounded tired, and Polly could see that he was getting exasperated with her. "I'm just saying that if he needs help, it's a good thing that we're in a position where we can help him. That's all I'm saying."

Polly exhaled noisily and sat back in her chair. "Well, we're not going to solve it tonight, no matter what," she said. "I'd say, give him a call in the morning and see what's up. We can play it by ear from there."

"So you're *not* saying you *won't* do it if we have to."

For the first time since they'd come downstairs, Tim looked at her and smiled.

"I'm not saying anything either way. I'm just saying, let's see what's happening and go from there. If we absolutely have to spend some time in Hilton, then . . . Well, let's just see what's up, first, okay?"

Tim was smiling, but the expression in his eyes was unreadable as he nodded slightly. With a loud grunt he heaved himself out of his chair. Casting a glance at the wall clock, he said, "Well, it's been one hell of a day and night for both of us. What do you say we get to bed?"

Polly nodded. She was still burning with anger that she knew she had to keep bottled up inside.

"At least tomorrow's Saturday, so we can sleep late if we need to," she said. Even as she said it, though, something in the back of her mind told her that sleep wasn't going to come easily, no matter how tired she was.

And she was right.

•   •   •

Even when the dream started, Polly had a vague sense that it was unlike any other dream she'd ever had before. She was curiously aware of her body, lying motionless in bed and, at the same time, she had a most peculiar sensation of being nearly weightless, of floating in the darkness like a lazily drifting helium balloon.

Polly couldn't see much of the bedroom. At least she assumed it was her bedroom. Some of the furniture seemed distorted and unfamiliar, but everything around her was illuminated by a diffuse blue glow that seemed to emanate from all directions at once. The shimmering quality of the light reminded her of *aurora borealis*, the northern lights. Curtains of blue waved as though being blown by the wind. A faint humming sound seemed to be keeping time with the fluctuations of light. It was impossible for Polly to determine if the sound was inside her head or outside.

Worse than that, though, was the sudden feeling she had that she wasn't alone. She couldn't hear or see anyone, and other than the shifting light, there wasn't any hint of motion around her, but the sensation that she wasn't alone was strong, almost overpowering.

Hello, Polly thought, too afraid to speak out loud.

As much as she tried to resist it, an icy shiver ran up her back between her shoulder blades.

Is someone here? she asked.

She wasn't sure if she had phrased the question in her mind or had spoken it out loud as she waited for a reply. Her apprehension got incrementally stronger with each passing second. With absolutely no sense of physical exertion, she called again, loud enough this time to hear the muffled flutter of her own voice in the darkness.

Hello. . . . Is there anybody here?

She was no longer sure where *here* was, but after a moment or two in which her pulse seemed to stop, she heard what sounded like a short, sharp intake of breath.

Was that me . . . or someone else close beside me?

Where are you? Polly asked the darkness.

After another lengthening moment, a response finally came to her, so faint it wafted over her like unseen smoke in the night.

—I don't know where I am . . . I'm . . . just . . . here—

Can you see anything? Polly asked, feeling a sudden flash of desperation. She couldn't really believe that she had actually heard a reply. The words—if they had been spoken at all—were gone as if they had never been, but she had the clear impression that they weren't just thoughts inside her head. Someone was in the room with her.

—I can't see you. As far as I know, I'm the only one here—

It seemed odd to be so acutely aware of breathing in her sleep while she was dreaming, but Polly felt her chest slowly expand as she took a slow, shuddering breath while waiting for a reply. As she breathed, her nose filled with a sharp, cloying aroma that stung the back of her throat. In the strange dissociation of sleep, the smell confused her and seemed to be as much a taste and a feeling as an actual smell. And as hard as she tried to identify it, Polly couldn't quite pin it down. It was a curious mixture that made her think of old, wet leather mixed with a faint trace of . . . what?

Burning leaves?

As her panic steadily rose, the room seemed filled with a misty, gray glow that towered above her like a cresting wave. For a flashing instant, Polly felt like she was being swept away into a churning ocean that would suck her under and drown her in an instant. She struggled, feeling herself being pulled down, and let out a piercing scream as she sat bolt upright in bed.

It was morning.

Polly found herself staring wide-eyed at the bedroom window across from the foot of the bed. The window looked out over the backyard and at the sky, which was overcast with a thin layer of gray clouds. The window was opened about an inch, and a light breeze was shifting the curtain back and forth in a slow, lazy motion.

"Jesus," Polly whispered, covering her face with her hands as she let her breath out slowly.

"Hey! You awake up there?"

Tim's voice carried faintly from downstairs. From years of living in this house, Polly could tell, just by the sound, that he was in the kitchen, probably over by the sink.

"Yeah," she called back weakly, unsure if her voice carried all the way to him. When she took another breath, the curious smell, stronger now, filled her nose, almost making her gag.

"What the hell are you doing down there?" she called out. "What's that smell?"

"Huh? Oh, just frying up some bacon," Tim replied cheerily from downstairs. "I figured we'd better have a good breakfast before we hit the road."

Polly closed her eyes and groaned as she shook her head, but she quickly opened her eyes again. For some reason, she didn't like the way it felt when her eyes were shut, even for an instant. Although she knew better, the only way she could describe it was that it felt like someone was lurking nearby, watching her. She knew she was alone in her upstairs bedroom. Brian was no doubt still asleep in his room. There wasn't—there *couldn't* be anyone hiding nearby.

Still, she had the unnerving feeling that she wasn't alone.

"Damn it all," she whispered as she tossed the bedcovers aside and swung her feet to the floor. She knew with a cold, dread certainty that there was no way she was going to be able to get out of driving up to Hilton with Tim today. Hopefully, after they checked in to see how Rob was doing, that would be the end of it.

But even as she thought this, she had a strong feeling that there was no way that's what would happen. In fact, she was filled with a gnawing premonition that *it*—whatever the hell *it* was—was just getting started.

three

The overcast didn't last long, and by the time Tim and Polly finished breakfast and were in the car, heading out of town, the sun was shining brightly. After a brief but heated discussion, they had agreed to let Brian stay home alone for the day as long as he promised to work on the term paper that was due in American history on Monday. He complained that he had plans to go to the movies with some friends later that night, but Tim insisted that he not leave the house until they were back, even if it ended up ruining his plans. Polly told him that she'd be calling from time to time on the cell phone to check up on him.

The drive from Stonepoint, Massachusetts, to Hilton, Maine, was a good five hours, not counting rest stops. Tim figured that, if they left before eight o'clock, they'd get to Hilton by early afternoon. If they spent an hour or two with Rob at the hospital, maybe checked with the doctor, then headed back around four or five o'clock, they would hopefully be home well before midnight, even if they stopped for a nice meal somewhere along the way.

"You know, I probably should have stayed home to grade those final exams I gave," Tim said while they were gassing up at the Mobile station in Rowley just before getting onto Interstate 95.

Polly glanced over at him but said nothing. She had made that point a few times over breakfast and was trying hard not to let her anger show. As far as she was concerned, Tim should be handling this whole thing on his own and not dragging her along.

Worse than that, though, she still couldn't shake the unnerving feeling that lingered from her dream this morning. Traces of it still teased her with half-forgotten memories and vague, uneasy feelings that she couldn't quite pin down.

Had she actually been speaking to someone in her dream?

Had there been someone in the bedroom with her?

She wasn't positive she had, but no matter what, the dream had left her feeling disoriented and afraid, like there was something important she had forgotten to do or was supposed to do.

For most of the drive, Tim and Polly didn't speak much. The silence in the car was broken only by the whining of the tires on the road and strains from the new Emmylou Harris CD Tim had just bought. Because it was such a beautiful weekend, the traffic into New Hampshire and Maine was heavier than they'd expected. They got slowed down in the bottleneck at the Hampton toll booth and again at the toll for the Maine Turnpike. After that, it was smooth sailing, but Tim kept checking his watch as though he was up against some important timetable.

Polly closed her eyes and leaned her head back on the headrest, trying to let the rhythm of the road soothe her, but her mind kept wandering back to what she had been through at the hospital yesterday.

Was it really just yesterday? she wondered, amazed at how the events seemed curiously distant and, at the same time, so immediate.

She still couldn't fully accept that Heather Olsen was dead, that she had practically died in her arms. The death of a child wasn't something you got over easily, if ever, and Polly knew that this would haunt her for the rest of her life.

As she stared into the darkness behind her closed eyes, she watched as a vague image of Heather's face formed and dissolved and then re-formed in front of her, drifting in and out of view. The little girl's eyes were closed, and she looked peaceful and relaxed, her features perfectly composed, the way Polly remembered her just before the doctor drew the sheet up over her. Then, without warning, Heather's eyes snapped open, and Polly sat up straight with a startled cry.

"Hey, you okay?" Tim asked, reaching out and patting her leg lightly.

"Umm, yeah," Polly said, nodding. "Just drifting, I guess."

She smiled but was convinced that he knew as well as she did that she *wasn't* okay . . . not even close to okay.

How could she be?

The real question was, after yesterday, how could she *ever* be okay?

They stopped for a quick bite to eat at the Burger King in Kennebunk. Polly had suggested that they swing into Portsmouth and find a nice restaurant, but Tim seemed to be in a hurry and blew off the suggestion. She didn't like the way he seemed so anxious about making good time to Hilton, but she didn't bother to ask him if he was nervous about seeing his brother or concerned about getting back home and finishing up the work he had to do for the end of the semester.

Frankly, she didn't care.

She felt completely isolated in her confusion and grief, and she was mad at Tim for not being more sensitive to how much being there when Heather died had affected her . . . *was* affecting her. She was trying to sort out what had happened but wasn't having much success. It only made it worse that Tim seemed to ignore her feelings.

It wasn't like him.

She couldn't understand why he hadn't responded to how deeply disturbed she was feeling, acting like his problems were the only problems. Even if he did pick up on her edginess, he was probably thinking it was because she was angry at him for dragging her up to Hilton on such a beautiful day when she would rather be working in the garden or doing something else—anything else—to get her mind off what had happened yesterday.

"You know, Hilton is really nice this time of year," Tim said.

His voice startled Polly, drawing her out of her own downward-spinning thoughts. She grunted and nodded, but said nothing.

"If we *do* decide to spend some time up there this summer—and I'm not saying we have to—but if we do, I think you'll be surprised by how relaxing it will be to get away from—"

"Everything," she finished for him, positive that he realized there wasn't a trace of humor in her voice.

"Maybe there'll even be time so you can get a garden started up there," Tim said, sounding hopeful.

When Polly glanced at him, all she could think was, *What the hell is wrong with you? Why can't you see what I'm going through?*

But she didn't say anything because the truth was, she wasn't sure herself what she was going through. Having a child die in your arms was bad enough, but connecting it to what had happened four years before to her own child only made it worse.

So if I can't understand what I'm going through, how can I expect him to? she thought. Smiling wistfully, she reached out and touched the back of Tim's hand on the steering wheel. A warm glow lit his eyes when he glanced at her and smiled.

"Thanks for being there for me," he said softly.

His words hit Polly's ears like darts. A sudden coldness gripped her heart. Close to tears, she turned away from him.

God damn you! I wish I could say the same for you!

If the first half of the drive had been mostly quiet, the second half was in chilly silence. For much of it, Polly kept her face turned to the right, away from Tim, as she gazed out at the passing scenery, such as it was. It didn't take long before stand after stand of pine trees lining the highway got boring as hell, but Polly was determined not to look at her husband. She didn't want him to see the tears gathering in her eyes.

They got off the interstate in Lewiston and took Route 4 out through Turner and Livermore, then followed Route 108 through Canton to Peru and, finally, to Hilton. Polly was grateful that the scenery along the way got at least a little more interesting. She had gained a measure of control over her emotions—at least for now—and when they entered Hilton, she was looking around with mild interest. With the window rolled down, she enjoyed the warm stream of fresh air that washed over her. This far north, spring was still several weeks behind what it was in Massachusetts, but the buds on the maple trees that lined the street were swelling as red as cherries, and most of the other trees had sprouted small leaves that glowed with the brilliant green of new growth.

New life . . . new hope.

Polly had to remind herself of that if she was going to enjoy the day in spite of the gloom that had settled inside her.

Usually, whenever they came to town, they would turn off the main road before hitting the downtown area and drive out Ridge Road to Tim's family home, which was on the edge of the forest, close to Watcher's Mountain. Today, however, Tim continued down Main Street, past the small businesses and shops, until he took a right turn onto Bow Street. The Hilton Community Hospital was on the left, just after the old black iron bridge over the Androscoggin River.

"Do you know what room he's in?" Polly asked once

they had parked in the lot behind the hospital and gotten out of the car.

Tim looked at her with mild amusement as he swung his door shut and pressed the key on his key ring to activate the locks. "It's not that big a hospital, hon. I don't think we'll have a problem finding him."

Polly smiled, but her expression froze on her face when she turned and started with Tim toward the hospital entrance. A sudden rush of fear prickled across the back of her neck when she saw the double doorway and thought how much it looked like the doors to the hospital in Stonepoint.

I can't believe it was just yesterday! she thought, struggling to keep the two events separate in her mind.

But she couldn't stop the uneasy feeling that swelled up inside her now. The fear wound tighter and tighter until it was a hard knot in her chest.

Out of habit, Tim took her hand as they walked across the parking lot toward the door. The sun beat down warmly on her face, but with each step, Polly became more and more convinced that she wasn't going to make it to the door. The backs of her legs felt like they were made of rubber. When she and Tim stepped into the gray shadow cast by the building, a terrible shiver raced through her. Points of white light danced like fireflies on the fringes of her vision.

"Tim—" she said, but that was all.

Her throat closed off, like cold hands were squeezing ever tighter.

She looked over at her husband, surprised to see that he appeared to be moving in slow motion. His mouth was moving. He was saying something, but all she could hear was a low dragging sound, like an audiotape being played at the wrong speed. Her vision suddenly tunneled, and she found herself staring into his eyes, surprised by how moist and bright and scary they looked as they reflected a distorted image of herself back at her.

When they got to the hospital doors, the doors opened

automatically. Polly took a tentative step or two inside, but that was all she could manage. Even before the doors whooshed shut behind her, the smell of the place assailed her nostrils like a solidly placed punch.

A surge of panic ran through her when she registered that this wasn't the "typical" antiseptic hospital smell she'd been expecting.

It was much worse.

Her first impression was of a cloying, rotting egg smell, but when she involuntarily sucked in some more air, trying to catch her breath, she detected something else, something that smelled like burning rubber.

She tried to say something but gagged instead. She sensed more than saw Tim beside her as she took another step and felt her ankle buckle beneath her.

Someone—*it must be Tim,* she thought—grabbed her arm to support her, but everything around her was spinning out of control. She was falling, doing cartwheels, spinning head over heels as she spiraled down into a darkness that was saturated with the nauseating smell.

Down . . . down she went.

Wind roared in her ears as she fell out of control, like Alice spinning down the White Rabbit's hole. Darkness closed over her like soft hands as she plummeted downward until, eventually, the sensation ceased, and she found herself drifting in a black, impenetrable void.

Am I dying? she wondered, hearing her thoughts as if they were spoken out loud. *Or am I already dead?*

There seemed to be no sound except for a whooshing of wind rushing around her and a faint, muffled thumping that she knew was her heartbeat.

No. If that's my pulse, then I can't be dead . . . at least not yet . . . but I must be dying. . . .

Polly took a shallow breath.

Yes, I can breathe. . . .

And tried to orient herself.

The sensation of falling had lessened so gradually that she wasn't sure when it had ceased. She couldn't help but wonder if, right now, she was passed out on the floor in the hospital entryway. She found that thought mildly amusing, but the noxious smell lingered in her nostrils, leaving a thick, oily aftertaste that nauseated her.

How can I be passed out and conscious at the same time? she wondered.

This strange feeling of duality seemed vaguely familiar, and it was with a tingling rush of panic that she remembered her dream—*Was it just this morning?*—about being surrounded by shimmering blue light and convinced that someone was lurking in her bedroom nearby, unseen.

As soon as she thought this, Polly had that same feeling . . . that somewhere in the darkness, unseen by her, there was someone who was able to see her and was watching her!

"Hello," Polly called out.

Her voice was muffled in the darkness, as though it were being pushed back at her.

She waited for a reply, her breath withheld, her heart racing. When it came, it was so faint and subtle she realized that she had been listening to it for a long time before she was consciously aware of it. It was almost as if the voice had always been there, and it was only a matter of paying attention to it before she could hear it.

Is there someone here? Polly said, her voice a strangled whisper as fear coiled up inside her.

She expected to hear her own voice echo back to her from the black void. Instead, the voice, stronger now, but still just barely at the edge of hearing, replied,

—I'm here. . . . Where are you?—

But I . . . I'm right here, Polly said, thinking it sounded almost like a child's voice. *I don't . . . I have no idea where I am. . . . I'm lost.*

—Can you get me out of here?—

The voice had a desperate, frightened edge that, for a moment, made Polly forget all about her own fear. She knew for certain that this wasn't her own mental voice speaking to her. This voice had the same curious duality as her dream this morning. It seemed to be simultaneously inside her and outside her and so real that Polly questioned the validity of such a foolish distinction as internal and external. Somehow, she and this voice were beyond such considerations.

I don't know, Polly replied, feeling a sudden surge of protectiveness. The person—if it was indeed a person, and not a figment of her imagination—most definitely sounded like a child, a little girl. *I'm not really sure where we are.*

—I'm in a room—

Polly thought it might be a trick of her imagination, but the voice sounded fainter, as if whoever was speaking was withdrawing from her.

A room? What room? Do you know where you are?

—All I can tell is that it's a room. . . . I can't see any doors. . . . It's just walls, high, white walls . . . and there's a window . . . but I don't dare to look outside—

Why not?

Polly eyes strained as she looked around, trying to pierce the surrounding darkness. How could this person, this voice, be inside a room? It didn't make sense. The feeling of disorientation grew steadily stronger inside her, but she couldn't deny the reality of the voice and the conversation they were having.

Have you looked around the room? Polly asked, feeling a sharp edge of panic. *How do you know there's no way out? How did you get in there?*

—I don't know. . . . I just . . . ended up here—

How long have you been there?

—I don't know, but I'm scared. . . . I can see . . . things. . . . There are things outside the window—

What kind of things? Polly asked.

The tension winding up inside her was almost unbearable now. The surrounding darkness was squeezing in on her, pressing the breath out of her.

—I don't know. . . . I'm too scared to look, but I want to leave. . . . I want to go home!—

And where is home? Polly asked.

It took an immense effort to keep her voice calm. The truth was, she had no idea where she was or what was happening, but she didn't want this person any more upset than she already was.

—I . . . I'm not sure. . . . I don't remember anymore—

Then tell me your name, Polly said softly. *Do you remember that?*

I'm . . . not sure. . . . I think it's—

Even before Polly heard her name, she already knew what it was. When it came, the name blended into the slowly rising scream that issued from deep inside Polly.

—My name is Heather—

"**Hey there, little brother. How the hell are** yah?"

Tim smiled at Rob's greeting as he entered the hospital room. Polly was only a step or two behind him. He cast a worried glance over his shoulder at her. He still didn't like how pale and shaky she looked. It had been a tough half hour in the lobby, taking care of her after she had fainted in the entryway. She'd been quiet and withdrawn ever since. Tim had tried to make small talk with her on the elevator ride up to the third floor where Rob was staying, but she remained distant. Figuring it was equal amounts of embarrassment about what had happened and reluctance to see his brother, he asked if she'd rather wait in the car, but she declined.

"Jesus, man," Tim said, smiling tightly as he walked over to the bed and firmly shook his brother's hand. "You look like hell hit you and ran."

"Umm. Feel like it, too," Rob said with a twisted, half smile that made the lines in his suntanned face deepen.

He was wearing a hospital johnny and was propped up in bed with a white sheet covering him up to his waist. His left leg was encased in a white cast that went from his toes to just below his knee. It lay outside the covers, resting on a pillow at the foot of the bed. There was a black rubber knob on the bottom of the cast.

"Oh, hey there, Polly," Rob said almost as an afterthought.

Tim bristled at the belated acknowledgment of his wife's presence, but he had no illusions. He knew that there was little love lost between the two of them, either way.

Polly nodded a curt greeting but said nothing.

Stepping back, Tim glanced over at the window with its view of the hospital's back parking lot and a wide stretch of the Androscoggin River. The smooth-flowing water reflected the blue arc of sky except for near the shore, where it was darkened by the shade of overhanging trees that lined both banks. A rectangle of sunlight angled across the floor, illuminating dust motes that swirled in the stale air.

"You ought to open the window in here, man," Tim said, waving his hand in front of his face. "Get some fresh air."

Rob shrugged. "I get all the fresh air and exercise I need

at work, until *this* fuckin' thing happened." He gestured at his leg, then grimaced and, glancing at Polly, added, "Pardon my French."

Tim indicated for Polly to take the cushioned chair over by the window, which she did without a word. Then he sat down on the windowsill with one leg dangling.

"So fill me in," he said. "What the hell happened?"

Rob's scowl deepened, and he chuckled softly as though embarrassed.

"It was my own damned fault," he said. "I was standing too close to one of the dump trucks when it was unloading some fill, and some of it caught my leg. Doc says it's broke in a few places."

"Yeah, he called last night and told me," Tim said. "Three breaks in your foot and two in your leg."

A scowl darkened Rob's face. "Just hairline fractures, though. I told him not to call you. It's no big deal. Really. You didn't have to drive all the way up here. I'll be up and about in no time."

Rob's voice was low and even, but Tim detected an angry edge in it. He glanced at Polly, but she seemed not to be paying the slightest bit of attention to either of them. She was staring out the window at the sky, her eyes distant and unfocused as though she were listening to something.

"Doc says he wants to keep me here overnight for observation. They've given me a walking cast, so I'll be getting around in no time."

"So where'd this happen?" Tim asked.

"Ahh. I've been working on the road they're putting in for a housing development out on Ridge Road. Ridge Estates. Can you believe it? They're building, like, a dozen houses in the woods out by the old place where the shortcut used to be."

"No kidding," Tim replied, whistling and shaking his head.

The shortcut was the narrow, winding path through the woods that Tim and Rob had used just about every day of their lives to go to school and back or downtown to meet up with friends. It made their walk only a mile and a half whereas it would have been almost four miles if they had gone all the way around on the road. When they were little, they used to play guns and hide-and-seek in the woods.

"Those woods have a lot of memories," Tim said, eyeing his brother carefully. "It's kind of sad to see something like that happen, you know? But I guess that's progress."

"Umm. Guess so," Rob said, "but what the fuck're you doing, coming up here. You didn't have to drive all this way just to see me. I'm doing fine."

Not feeling too pleased to have Polly hear exactly what she'd been telling him all along, Tim shrugged tightly.

"Hey, I just wanted to see you, make sure you'd be able to get along, all right?" he said. "It might not be as easy as you think."

"Hell, I'll be fine." Rob said with a wave of his hand. He paused and, for a brief instant, looked at Tim like there was something more he had to say. Then he shook his head and finished, "I'm not giving you any shit or anything. I 'preciate that you'd come see me."

"To tell you the truth," Tim said, "Polly and I have been talking about maybe coming up here for the summer."

As he said this, Tim glanced over at Polly again, but she didn't react. Her eyes remained fixed on some distant point outside the window like she hadn't even heard him.

"To Hilton, you mean?" Rob said, sounding skeptical. His body stiffened as he leaned forward and regarded Tim.

"Yeah. We were thinking about taking a family vacation, and I—we—figured that maybe we'd spend some time up here. You know, to give you a hand if you need it."

"I told you, I don't need no fuckin' hand!" Rob said edgily.

Tim was taken aback by the sudden harsh tone he heard in his brother's voice.

"Besides, there ain't enough room in my apartment for—Oh, wait a second—" He snapped his fingers, then shook his pointed forefinger at Tim. "You aren't thinking about staying out at the house, are you?"

Tim nodded slowly. He knew that Polly had assumed Rob would jump at the chance to have him around if for no other reason than to mooch off him now that he was out of work again or, at least, until he could file for worker's comp. She never tired of pointing out that, as long as she had known Rob, he had made a habit of working just enough to get by . . . if that. She was always saying that Rob had perfected freeloading to an art because at least once a year, sometimes more, he would contact his brother and ask for a little help. Sometimes he was looking for advice, but usually it was money. Even if that wasn't the case now, Tim couldn't understand why Rob didn't like the idea of them being around for the summer.

"Well," Tim said, casting another nervous glance over at Polly. "I figured you might just need a little help . . . at least for a couple of weeks."

The hospital room was bright with early afternoon sunlight, but a dark cloud seemed to shroud Rob's features. Tim felt a crackling tension between them that he didn't like or understand.

"Shit, man, I'll be fine," Rob said with another wave of the hand. "Trust me. I don't need you running up here playing nursemaid."

"We won't be playing nursemaid," Tim snapped. "We're thinking of it as a vacation. We just want to get out of the Massachusetts rat race for a bit."

"I'm not so sure you'll want to stay out at the house, though," Rob said with a solemn shake of the head. "I ain't been out there in a year or more, but the last time I was, awhile after Pa died, it was in pretty bad shape."

"I'm sure we can manage," Tim said. "We're just thinking about staying for a month, max."

Rob bit down on his lower lip, making the jaw muscles on the side of his face quickly tense and untense as he stared at his brother while shaking his head slowly from side to side.

"I don't know, man. . . . I just wouldn't recommend it,

is all," he said tightly. "Not unless you like sleeping with spiders and rats. The place is a freakin' disaster."

"I'm sure we can cope," Tim said with a light laugh. "What? Are you saying you don't want me around or something?"

Rob didn't respond right away, and the brief, awkward moment of silence before he spoke communicated so much more than what he finally said.

"No, I think that'd be great . . . terrific. How 'bout you, Pol? What do you think?"

There was a taunting lilt in his voice, and Tim was positive that Rob had already picked up that he and Polly weren't in full agreement on this. For whatever reason, Rob seemed to be trying to use this against him, trying to goad Polly into reacting.

Turning slowly to face Rob, Tim thought Polly still looked absolutely out of it. The color was just coming back to her face. She blinked a few times and shifted her eyes as though it took too much effort to focus on him.

"You're family, Rob," she said softly, "so of course we're willing to help if we can."

Just below that, Tim could hear the unspoken *like it or not,* but he smiled and nodded.

"Look," he said, "school's out in a couple of weeks for Brian, so we figured we'd pack up and be here . . . oh, probably the beginning of the third week of June, if that's all right with you."

"Hey, it ain't up to me," Rob said with a casual shrug that still seemed to be covering something.

"So it's settled, then," Tim said, forcing a smile.

He looked at Polly, but, once again, she seemed not to be paying the slightest bit of attention to them. Turning back to Rob, he couldn't help but be angry at himself for thinking that his brother's smile was completely fake. Tim didn't enjoy feeling like he was forcing the issue on both of them, but he was determined that this was what they would do for the summer.

"Hey, family's family," he said. Hoping to clear the air,

he laughed and, leaning forward, slapped his brother heartily on the shoulder. "And what's family for if you can't count on 'em to help you out when you're down. Right?"

"Amen to that," Polly said distantly.

Tim was bothered by the repressed anger he sensed in his wife. It was obvious that she didn't appreciate that he had committed the family to something like this without discussing it more fully with her beforehand; but there was something else about her: a frightened, almost haunted look in her eyes that bothered him even more.

Still, like he said, family was family, and he was going to be there to help Rob even if both Rob and Polly were against it.

"So," Tim said, clapping his hands together and rubbing them vigorously, "we have to get back home tonight, but we'll get packed up in the next week or so and be back here before you know it. You okay with all of this, Polly?"

Polly looked at him and nodded once, slowly. Her expression was so blank and drained of emotion that it unnerved Tim. With a cold shudder he suddenly realized that he recognized that look in her eyes.

He'd seen it before.

It was the same emotionally devastated look she'd had four years ago when their daughter had died, and there was nothing Polly or anyone else could do to save her.

She looked so empty, so lost, so alone.

Polly licked her lips, then opened her mouth. When she spoke, her words sliced into Tim like a cold razor blade.

"We'll do whatever we have to do for family," she said. Her voice was so soft, Tim almost couldn't hear her. "But first, we have a funeral to attend."

four

The next two weeks were pure hell for Polly.

The worst part was facing Heather Olsen's funeral. When they got home from Hilton late that night, Polly couldn't sleep. She spent several hours tossing and turning in bed, tormented about what she should do about it. In the end, sometime near dawn, she decided not to say or write anything to Heather's parents, at least not until after the funeral. From personal experience, she knew that the pain of going through your child's funeral was more than enough for anyone to bear.

Why make it any harder for them by describing their daughter's last desperate minutes of life?

As it was, she couldn't imagine how she was going to get through the day of the funeral, not to mention the Olsens; but on Monday afternoon, she, Tim, and Brian were there at Rodger's Funeral Home in Gloucester. As they were passing through the line following the service, Polly stepped close to Marlene. Clearing her throat as she embraced the grieving mother, Polly tried to say something—anything—even if it was simply to give Marlene her condolences, but her voice closed off as sharply as if someone were squeezing her throat.

When they got home after the funeral, Polly considered trying to write something to send to the Olsens. She got a pen and paper, and sat down at her desk, but she had no idea how or where to start.

What could I possibly say? she wondered. *Do I tell them not to worry because I'm pretty sure their daughter's not gone . . . that somehow I'm in contact with her . . . and that she's feeling lost . . . and frightened . . . that she's trapped somewhere and can't escape?*

"Some comfort that would be," she muttered under her breath.

Tears filled her eyes, making it difficult for her to see the paper. Finally, she took the several sheets with all her false starts and crumpled them into a tight ball, which she tossed into the wastebasket.

Over the next few days, Polly agonized as she tried hard to put the whole incident out of her mind, but she knew that she never would. It would always be there, branded in her mind, a ragged scar that would never fully heal, just like the grief of Crystal's death. Polly wished she had someone—her husband or her best friend Lois or *anyone*—she could talk to and unburden her mind, but she felt absolutely isolated in her misery. Tim had suggested, just once, and quite offhandedly, that she might want to look into finding a therapist to talk to, but she dismissed it out of hand.

She could . . . she *would* handle this . . . on her own if she had to!

Besides Heather's funeral, other things happened during the next two weeks that didn't make life any easier for Polly.

Rob was released from the Hilton Community Hospital the day after she and Tim had been up to see him, on Sunday. He went home to his tiny, one-bedroom apartment on Linden Street. That night, he called Tim to tell him that everything was going well, great, in fact, that he was getting around just fine with his walking cast and crutches. Rob hinted fairly strongly that he didn't want or need Tim and his family to come to Hilton to play "nursemaid" for him. He used the word almost a dozen times. He insisted that he had friends in town who would help him out. He'd get by.

After the phone call, Polly threw out the suggestion that maybe they should consider some other plans for the summer, but now that Tim had the idea in his mind, he wasn't about to let it go. As they started packing for the month or so they expected to be in Hilton, Polly viewed their plans with a sense of defeated resignation as much as anything else.

Brian never wavered from his position, which was that he figured either way his parents were going to screw up his summer, so he didn't care what they finally decided. As long as he could bring his computer and stay in touch with his friends with E-mail, he'd go along without too much complaining.

Tim's classes at the university were over on Tuesday, the day after Heather's funeral, and Brian's school ended two weeks after that, on Wednesday, June twelfth. That Thursday, Tim rented a small U-Haul trailer after work, and the family started packing up that evening. Closing down the house was a lot more work than they had expected, but Tim threw himself into it with an energy that Polly hadn't seen in quite some time. He appeared to relish the idea of spending time back home, and he kept telling Polly to look at it as an adventure.

The most Polly could say was, at least it was something *different*.

Fortunately for her, during those two weeks she didn't have any more strange dreams, or if she did, she forgot about them before waking. Also, she didn't experience any more episodes of blacking out or hearing voices, either Heather Olsen's or anyone else's.

That was good.

She figured she'd experienced that as part of the trauma of her own grief, and now—hopefully—it was over.

Even so, Polly wasn't sleeping very well. She sensed

there was some kind of pressure building up inside her, and she knew it was beginning to take its toll. She thought she was much jumpier than usual, and very short-tempered, especially with Brian. One night she even threatened not to let him bring his computer to Hilton because he was giving her so much grief about helping her with the laundry. She kept telling herself not to get so worked up about stupid little things, that she could relax and take things as they came, and that worked . . . usually.

Sometimes, though, she just had to go sit by herself in a dark, quiet room until she felt better.

On Saturday morning, June fifteenth, the family piled into the car with the U-Haul trailer hitched on back, and they were on the road by nine o'clock, heading north. It was a little later than Tim had wanted, but it was a sunny, mild day with only a few fair-weather clouds dotting the sky. Polly tried hard to make the best of things, but it wasn't long before the drive began to feel interminable. Although she never said anything to Tim about how she was feeling, he seemed to pick up on her discomfort. Rather than trying to talk to her about it, though, he simply made small talk as he drove and listened to whatever CDs he wanted. Brian slouched in the backseat and kept himself occupied most of the way with his Walkman and Gameboy.

When they were getting close to Hilton, Tim threw out the suggestion that they swing by Rob's apartment first, just to let him know that they were in town.

"Why not just call him?" Polly suggested. Before Tim could reply, she dug into her purse for her cell phone and held it out to him.

After a second or two of tense silence, Tim took it from her, shooting a sour expression her way as he flipped the phone open and dialed the number with his thumb.

"Yo, Rob," he said, smiling and settling back in the car seat once Rob answered. Polly couldn't help but notice the instant change in his tone of voice and demeanor. All of a sudden, he sounded lighthearted and carefree.

What bullshit, she thought, shifting her gaze out the side window to avoid looking at her husband. It was bad enough that she had to listen to half of the conversation.

"We'll be in town in about fifteen minutes," Tim said. "Just wondering if it'd be okay if we swung by your place before we went out to the house."

In the short pause while Rob was talking to Tim, Polly prayed fervently that it wouldn't be okay. As far as she was concerned, she never wanted to see Rob again. She despised the way Tim acted whenever he was around Rob. He seemed to adopt this casual, almost fawning attitude, as though he were struggling too hard to be accepted by his older brother. She figured while they were in Hilton, Tim could spend all the time he wanted to with his brother, just as long as he never tried to drag her along.

"Uh-huh," Tim said after a moment. "Uh-huh . . . Yup."

Polly glanced at him, trying to read what Rob was saying from Tim's facial expression. He was biting down on his lower lip and frowning slightly.

This is probably good, Polly thought, feeling only a slight twinge of guilt.

"Yeah, I see," Tim said. His voice was nowhere near as chipper as it had been just a few seconds ago. "Sure. . . . No problem. . . . Naw, we'll go out to the house and start unpacking. Maybe I'll drop by later this afternoon. . . . Okay. Cool. I'll call you later, then. . . . Bye."

Tim snapped the cell phone off, his face almost blank of expression as he handed it back to Polly. Without shifting his eyes off the road ahead, he said, "He's busy right now. The physical therapist is over, going through his exercises with him."

"Uh-huh," Polly said, nodding slightly and fighting hard to keep from smiling. If she knew Rob as well as she thought she did, it wasn't too hard to figure out what kind of "physical therapy" he was engaged in that couldn't be interrupted.

But Polly's relief evaporated ten minutes later when Tim clicked on his turn signal and slowed for the turn onto

Ridge Road. When she turned in her seat to face Brian, she couldn't help but notice the plume of yellow dust that rose behind the car and U-Haul as they left the main road. The wheels hummed loudly on the rough asphalt. She wished she didn't feel like she was spiraling helplessly into a slow, out-of-control, downhill slide.

"We're almost there," she said to Brian, knowing that she didn't sound nearly as chipper as she'd hoped. Brian hadn't said more than ten words throughout the drive, but as Polly and he made eye contact, an unspoken but unmistakable communication passed between them. She seemed to hear her son's thoughts in her head as clearly as her own: *No matter how much you try to pretend, Mom,* Brian's eyes seemed to say, *this is going to be a really shitty summer.*

"Hey, it's not so bad . . . seriously."

Tim was standing in the kitchen doorway, holding the screen door open with his butt while Polly moved past him and entered the house. The bottom half of the screen was bagged out and caught in the bottom was a collection of dried leaves and hundreds of husks of dead insects.

The old, brown linoleum floor was chipped and dull. It creaked underfoot as Polly took a few cautious steps into the kitchen. Her shoulders were hunched as though she expected any second now for something to come flying at her from the shadows near the ceiling. When she took a shallow breath, a powerful aroma filled her nose.

"Jesus! What is *that?*" she said, gasping as she waved a hand in front of her face. "It smells like . . . like burned brownies."

His hands on his hips, Tim regarded the small, dusty kitchen. His nostrils widened as he sniffed the air a few times; then he looked at her and shook his head.

"Just a little musty," he said. "The place has been closed up for too long. It just needs to be aired out."

"Are you telling me you don't *smell* that?" She winced

and shook her head as she took another more cautious breath. The strange burned smell filled her nose, sticking like molasses to the back of her throat. "It . . . yeah, it definitely smells like burned brownies."

Tim looked at her with one eyebrow raised.

"Weird," was all he said.

Even after a few more breaths, Polly couldn't get the cloying smell out of her nose and throat.

"Maybe something died in one of the cupboards or behind the walls," she offered, although this wasn't a rotting smell. It definitely smelled like something had burned . . . something chocolaty, like brownies. Her lungs ached for a deep breath of clean air, but she resisted the impulse to inhale too deeply until they got some windows open.

"Whatever it is, it's nothing a little Lysol and fresh air won't fix," Tim said with a tight smile as he unlocked one of the windows by the table and ran it open. The lead weight of the old-style window bumped heavily inside the window frame.

Tim's eyes took on a distant glow as he walked slowly around the kitchen, looking all around. Polly could tell that he was feeling nostalgic about his childhood home after not seeing it for so many years, but all she could see was the same dingy, grimy kitchen, which hadn't changed since his parents had died. The walls, floor, and antique appliances would need to be sandblasted to remove the many years' accumulation of grease and dirt.

She took another tentative breath and was thankful that, with the window open, the burned chocolate smell wasn't quite so bad . . . almost tolerable, in fact. Her shoulders were still hunched, though, as she walked over to the kitchen sink. Over the years, its chipped white porcelain had turned a sickly yellow, the color of old bone. A thick black streak ran down the side of the sink where water had leaked over the years from the faucet. She couldn't imagine ever getting it clean enough to trust washing anything in it.

She grimaced as she twisted the cold water faucet. After

a moment, she heard a dull banging sound in the pipes, then a gush of water, brick red from accumulated rust, emerged. It ran like that for a few seconds, then gradually changed to tea-brown until, finally, after a full minute or more, the water ran clear. Polly wondered if she would even dare drink the water and decided that at least for the first few days, she would stock up on bottled water.

"Rob told me that it had taken a bit of a beating," Tim said after completing a cursory inspection, "but you know what? It's not really all that bad. Not as bad as I expected, anyway. Old houses get this way when no one lives in them for a while. We'll get it cleaned up in no time."

Polly looked at him skeptically. "I wouldn't think it'd take too much effort for Rob to keep the place up," she said after shutting off the faucet. "Especially if you guys think you might want to put it on the market."

"Whoa. Don't get me started on *that*," Tim muttered.

Ever since their father had died three years ago, Tim had been pushing his brother to sell the place, but Rob had adamantly refused. Polly didn't see the point of hanging on to the house if Rob was going to let it go to hell like this. Too many times to mention, she had pointed out to Tim that by the time they did get it on the market, the place would have to be condemned.

While they were looking around in silence, Brian appeared in the doorway. After taking a few steps into the kitchen, he stepped back and, wrinkling his nose, shook his head.

"Oh, man! What died in here?" was all he said before walking back outside.

The family spent the rest of the day unloading the U-Haul and carrying boxes into the house. Polly didn't think she was ever going to get used to the smell of the place, but after a while she thought she might at least be able to tolerate it. Maybe Tim was right. They had most of the downstairs windows open, and after they went over everything with some disinfectant, the smell might go away.

But she had her doubts.

That smell, she thought, *whatever it is, it's like an essential part of the house, and we'll never get rid of it!*

They went upstairs to check out the bedrooms. She and Tim were going to use what had once been Tim's parents' bedroom. Brian would be staying in the smaller room that Tim and Rob had shared while growing up.

Polly's first impression of their bedroom wasn't at all good. The green-patterned wallpaper had numerous water stains, especially near the ceiling. She thought the large one over by the dresser looked a little like the continent of Africa. In a few places, large swatches of wallpaper had peeled away from the wall, exposing the rough, glue-stained plaster underneath. The ceiling itself might have been white once, but now it was covered by a thick yellow film with rust-brown splotches everywhere. There was a ceiling light in the center of the room, but the glass globe was missing, leaving nothing but a single exposed light-bulb that had a large, black splotch on it. Of course it didn't work when Tim flicked the wall switch.

"Let's hope it's just the bulb, not the wiring," he said with a nervous laugh.

There were two windows in the bedroom that faced east. Polly walked up to one of them and pulled aside the antique lace curtains. The yellowing fabric was brittle with age and made a faint crinkling sound. It seemed about to crumble at her touch. Looking out through the dirt-crusted window at the yard below, she could see a portion of the driveway that led around to the old barn in the backyard. Over by the trees, at the edge of what had once been a lawn but was now a weed-choked field, there was a small shed that Tim had told her might have been a chicken coop once upon a time, but while he was growing up, it had been used for storing old tools and junk.

"Do you think this bed will do?" Tim asked as he walked over to the bare double mattress. It was on an old iron frame, its metal scroll headboard jammed up against the southern wall. When he pressed down on the bed, the springs gave a loud, rusty squeak that set Polly's teeth on edge.

"Not if I have to listen to *that* every time one of us rolls over, it won't," she said without a trace of humor.

She was still looking out the window, holding the curtains gently apart. Looking down, she saw the pile of dead, dust-covered insects that had collected on the windowsill over the years. There were dried husks of house flies, yellow jackets, honeybees, and a couple of dead spiders whose long, spindly legs looked like broken, black toothpicks.

"The mattress isn't so bad, though," Tim said as he sat down and bounced on it. "Pretty comfortable, in fact. I'll bet if we oil the springs a little, hit it with the WD-40, it'll be all right." He stood up and lifted an edge of the mattress to inspect the old spring coils. "It'd be better than buying a new one or getting our mattress from home and carting it up here."

Polly looked at him over her shoulder and frowned but said nothing. The smell from downstairs wasn't so bad upstairs, but traces of it lingered in the air, even with the upstairs windows open. She didn't like the damp, musty feeling of the house and wondered why she had never noticed it all the times she and Tim had visited when they were married and his parents were still alive. Tim's mother had been a fastidious cleaner, but she had been dead for five years, and the house had gone to hell in the five years after that and the three years since Tim's father had died.

It doesn't take long for a house to go to hell if no one's living in it, she thought as a deep sense of sadness, of years and lives gone by, swept through her.

Tim continued his inspection of the bedroom, opening the closet doors and running his hand along the dusty edges of the furniture that had been left behind. Polly turned back to the view outside the window. She didn't like thinking this way, but she couldn't help but reflect that maybe she was like one of those insects that had gotten trapped between the lace curtains and the window. No matter how hard they had beat their wings against the glass, they couldn't escape. A sour knot tightened in her stomach at the depressing thought that maybe she, too, was going to end up like them . . . dried to a crisp in the killing heat of the summer sun.

A yearning sadness filled her as she looked out at the side yard. Her gaze quickly shifted over to the small shed by the woods when she thought she caught a flickering hint of motion behind the window. The glass was so smeared with dirt its smooth surface seemed unable to reflect much of anything. It looked like a slab of polished, black marble that showed only a hint of the blue sky and white puffs of clouds floating by overhead. But behind the glass, Polly was sure that she could see *something*.

She was positive of it.

"Is there . . ." she started to say, but her voice trailed off as a prickle of gooseflesh raced up her arms in spite of the stifling heat of the bedroom.

Her throat went dry as she stared at the shed window, convinced that it hadn't been a trick of her eye. For an instant, just before she blinked her eyes, she had seen the faintest suggestion of a pale, white face looking up at her as she looked out from the second-floor window.

No! she told herself as a subtle wave of fear raced through her. *It's just the reflection of the clouds off the old glass.*

As much as she tried, though, she didn't really believe herself, and she couldn't stop herself from thinking the next thought.

What if someone's out there, hiding in the shed, watching us?

"Where's Brian?" she asked, her voice high and tremulous.

Rushes of chills went up her back as she turned around quickly to Tim. When she let go of the curtains, they fell back into place with a rough, scratching sound.

"Is he—?"

She cupped her hands to her mouth and shouted, "Hey! Brian!" then fell silent as she waited for a reply.

Glancing back at Tim, she tried to mask her rising anxiety with a smile. "I think he's outside, in the shed," she said. "He shouldn't be poking around out there, should he?"

The floorboards creaked underfoot as Tim walked casually over to the window, leaned past her, and looked outside. After a moment, he straightened up and shook his head.

"The shed door's shut. I can see that it's locked. I don't think he's in there."

Polly looked outside again but couldn't see anything behind the dirty panes of the shed window. She jumped and let out a shrill squeal when she heard the kitchen screen door open and slam shut.

"Brian? Is that you?" Tim called out as he moved over to the bedroom door and stuck his head out into the hallway.

"Yeah! What do you want?" Brian shouted from downstairs, his voice edged with irritation.

"Oh, nothing. . . . Just wondering what you were up to," Tim yelled back.

"What do you think I'm up to?" he shouted. A moment later, they heard the heavy clump of his feet on the stairs as he lugged another box of his stuff up to the bedroom he would be using.

"Guess it wasn't him," Tim said with a casual shrug.

Polly wanted to look out the window again, if only to convince herself that she hadn't seen what she thought she had seen, but she didn't dare. The feeling that there might be someone hiding out there, watching them as they moved in, was almost too much to bear.

And what if I see it again? she thought with a bone-deep shiver.

"Well," Tim said, clapping his hands together and rubbing them vigorously, "I don't know about you, but I'm starving. What say we go into town and get ourselves some supper?"

Tim's face was streaked with sweat and grime from all the work they had done. His jeans were dirty, and his shirt was ringed with sweat.

"What did you have in mind?" Polly asked. She knew she didn't look her best, either, and was hoping Tim wouldn't suggest that they try to find a nice restaurant for supper.

She was satisfied that the U-Haul was empty, but the house was now filled with cardboard boxes that would need unpacking. Of course, finding a place to put everything was another matter, but they could deal with that tomorrow. She had packed a separate box with towels and sheets for tonight, and that was all that mattered.

"I was thinking we could drive into town and pick up some Italian sandwiches at Digby's. I know I could sure use a cold beer about now."

There was a sour knot in the pit of Polly's stomach, but she forced herself to smile. "Sure," she said. "Sounds good to me. Brian and I can get the beds made up while you're gone. And then . . . I hope the hot water heater's still working, 'cause I need a nice, long, hot shower."

"Umm. Sounds good," Tim said, and before he left the room, he winked at her.

"Sending some E-mail?" Tim asked Brian as he entered the bedroom and sat down on the edge of what had been his bed when he was a boy.

"Uh-huh," Brian answered, not bothering to look away from the computer screen.

They were silent for a moment, and the only sound in the room was the rapid click-click as Brian typed something.

"Aren't you glad I thought to have the phone switched on before we got here?"

Brian's face was illuminated by the bluish glow of his

computer screen. He nodded but didn't glance at his father as he continued to tap away on the keys, scrolling through a few lines of text.

"You know—" Tim said.

"Yeah, I know," Brian snapped back. His voice was laced with agitation as he turned to look at his father. "E-mail's a terrible thing. It's the final assault on decorum and grammar."

Tim smiled to himself and shook his head. "That's not quite what I was going to say," he said, "but I don't think you realize how good you have it. I mean, when I was growing up here, we were lucky to have any TV, much less cable and the Internet. The nearest TV stations were in Portland and on Mount Washington. Channel Eight usually came in fine, but I never even saw PBS until I went away to college. And if I wanted to talk to a friend, we either used the phone or went over to their house."

"Or used a tin can telephone that you made yourself," Brian said. "You've only told me about a hundred times, Dad."

"I know, I know," Tim replied, smiling to himself, "but it just reminds me how much we take for granted these days. When your uncle and I were kids, we never even dreamed about cell phones and pagers and all the things you kids have today. It was a simpler time, a simpler life. A lot less hurried and complicated than life is today."

Brian huffed out a short breath and shook his head.

"What do you want me to say?" he asked, his voice still edged with impatience.

"Nothing," Tim replied, shaking his head. "Nothing at all. It's just . . . I hope that, for the time we're here, you can kind of forget about your computer from time to time, and spend a little more time outside, you know? That way, maybe you can experience a little bit of what it was like for me while I was growing up. That's all."

"Yeah . . . sure," Brian said, but then he turned back to his computer and focused on the screen, ignoring his father.

"Well," Tim finally said as he stood up and stretched. "I'm pretty bushed from lugging all that stuff today. I think I'll see if your mother's out of the shower so I can take one."

"Umm," Brian replied as he started tapping the keys.

"We're gonna do some fixing up around here, too, you know," Tim said as he moved slowly toward the bedroom door. "There's a lot of painting and stuff to get done. I'm not saying I'm going to be rousting you at the crack of dawn to do chores, but—"

"You mean I don't have to get up before dawn to milk the cows?" Brian said. Tim wasn't sure, but he thought that Brian was smiling. Was he mocking him?

"No. I'm just letting you know that I do expect you to help me and your mom some," Tim said. "Deal?"

"Sure. No sweat," Brian said distantly.

"Okay, then," Tim answered. "And I don't want you up all hours of the night on the net, either. We aren't going to have cable TV while we're here, so maybe you can think about doing without the Internet for a while, too."

"Whatever," Brian said all the while tapping away on the keyboard.

Tim hesitated at the door and watched his son for a few seconds more as he scrolled through several screens. He tried but didn't succeed very well at seeing himself as he had been all those years ago when he used to live in this house . . . in this bedroom.

Too many things have changed, he thought, unable to stop the sense of sadness for all the years that had been lost.

He wanted to share his thoughts with his son, to try to get Brian to see that, by sleeping in the room he'd slept in as a boy, they were somehow closer to each other, but he knew that he had failed miserably. All Brian cared about was reading his E-mail from his friends and sending back messages, probably telling them what a sucky time he was having this summer, stuck out here in the boondocks.

If he even knows what the boondocks are, Tim thought.

He started to leave, closing the door behind him, but before he left, he said once more, "Remember to get to bed at a decent time."

"Yeah . . . whatever."

Polly had a tough time settling down to sleep that night. The ancient bedsprings were as noisy as she had feared they would be, and the mattress was thin and lumpy. One of the coils kept pushing up in exactly the wrong place so it dug into her back as she lay in the darkened bedroom, waiting for sleep to come. Thankfully, the shower and water heater had worked, and now that she was tucked into the clean sheets she had brought from home, she thought that she might actually be able to drift off.

Eventually.

She might have, too, except for the thoughts that kept drifting through her mind and the burned chocolate smell that lingered in her nasal passages. Even when she pulled the top sheet right up over her nose and inhaled, she could still smell it. She mentioned it once or twice to Tim, but he insisted that the only unpleasant aroma was a kind of stale, musty smell in the house. It bothered her and struck her as rather curious that her sense of smell seemed to have changed so drastically. Even the bleached sheet covering her nose seemed to carry a trace of a different smell. It was strange, and a little bit unnerving.

Worse than all of that, though, was being so sure she had seen someone inside the shed, watching her through the dirty glass. When Tim was leaving to go get the Italian sandwiches, she had gone outside with him to check the building. The door was locked, like he had said, and when he looked in through the window—Polly couldn't quite muster the courage herself to do that—he claimed to see nothing but dusty piles of junk, including an old lawn mower, some rusty garden tools, and a few wooden barrels filled with old boards, wire, and burlap feed bags.

Still, she was *positive* she had seen *something*.

In her memory, now, she exaggerated it until she was convinced that, for just an instant, between blinks of the eye, a round, pale face with dark smudges around the eyes had been staring up at her. The thought gripped her like cold hands, and in the darkness of the room, the face became more distinct and frightening. Sighing heavily, the bedsprings creaking beneath her, she rolled over onto her side and stared at the window. She wondered if she could gather enough courage to get up, go over there, and look outside to see if the face was still there.

Don't be foolish, she told herself. *There's nothing out there.*

But she didn't quite dare close her eyes, either, even though Tim was sleeping soundly beside her.

—I think he's out there—

The voice, speaking so suddenly inside her head, startled Polly. She let out a faint squeal as she jumped in the bed, disturbing Tim enough so he rolled over and mumbled something unintelligible before he started snoring again.

Cold sweat broke out on her forehead. Her eyes were wide open as she stared into the darkness above her and tried to figure out what had just happened. The voice had been so clear it was as if someone was leaning over her bed and speaking into her ear. Even more frightening, it was a voice that Polly instantly recognized.

No! It couldn't have been, she thought, but she couldn't shake the conviction that it had been Heather Olsen's voice.

Are you . . . ? Are you there, Heather? Are you here with me now?

Polly didn't dare blink. Her eyes felt like they were drying out as she stared into the swelling darkness of the bedroom. At the same time, though, she had a peculiar feeling that her eyes were closed, and that somehow she was able to see through her eyelids.

—I don't know where I am—

This time Polly could hear the trembling, almost frantic edge in the voice, and her heart went out to the little girl.

Where have you been? Polly asked, focusing her mind. *I . . . you spoke to me before, but I thought you had gone away.*

—No, I'm still here. . . . I don't know where else to go . . . or how to go. . . . I . . . I'm really scared here—

Polly realized that she hadn't been breathing, so she loosened her shoulders and took a long, slow breath, surprised by how cold the air felt as it entered her throat and lungs—cold enough to make her shiver. She expected to see her breath frost in the air as she exhaled.

Tell me where you are. Why can't I see you?

Polly had detected the fearful edge in Heather's voice and knew that she had to keep up her own courage. She didn't think she was doing a very good job of it.

—I'm still in the room . . . in the white room. . . . I think I saw him—

Saw who? Polly asked.

Even as she thought it, chills raced through her, getting so strong her teeth began to chatter. The sheets made a rough, scratching noise as she pulled them up to her chin, but they didn't keep out the cold. Tim had left the bedroom windows open, and Polly wondered if the temperature had dropped down near freezing during the night.

—I don't know who it is . . . but sometimes I can see him. . . . He's outside . . . right now—

Who is? Polly thought frantically. *Are you sure you don't recognize him?*

—I don't know who he is. . . . I've never seen him before, but he's angry. . . . He's really angry about something—

Do you know what he's angry about? Polly thought. *Is he angry at you? Has he said or done anything to you?*

—No, not yet . . . but he wants to! . . . He wants to hurt me, I can tell! . . . Don't let him in! . . . Please, don't let him near me! . . . Wait a second . . . do you hear that?—

The little girl's voice inside her head was frantic and near breaking.

Hear what? Polly thought, but even before she finished the thought, a dull sound intruded on her awareness. For a heart-stopping moment, she listened intently but couldn't identify the sound. All she knew was that it was a faint, dry, rasping sound, like someone scraping something, maybe metal against wood or dry, hard earth.

—That's him. . . . He's trying to get in! . . . Do you hear that? . . . He's trying to get to me!—

No! No, he isn't! Polly thought. A surge of panic raced through her just listening to the fear in Heather's voice. *There's no one out there trying to get you. You're safe right where you are. Just don't leave now. Don't go outside.*

—No, I'm not safe! . . . He wants to hurt me!—

Wide-eyed, Polly stared into the impenetrable darkness. The voices were in her head. She knew that on one level, but she also knew that they were real and . . . somehow . . . out there, wherever "there" was.

No one's going to hurt you, Heather. I promise you that.

*—How do you know that? ... Can't you hear him? ...
He's digging. ... He's trying to find a way in ... to get to
me. ... Can't you stop him? ... Why can't you stop him?—*

An almost overwhelming sense of desperation and
hopelessness filled Polly. How could she convince Heather
that she was safe where she was? She didn't know that.
None of this made sense. How could she be "talking" to
someone who was already dead? And where was Heather
that, even in death, she felt threatened?

—He's going to get in here! ... I know he is—

As Polly strained to listen in the darkness, the clawing,
scratching sound grew steadily louder until it was like tearing cloth close to her ears. Goose bumps rose on her arms
and legs, and a chill ran up the back of her neck as if someone were touching her with cold, dead hands. A low, quavering cry originated deep in her belly. Polly suddenly
flung the bed sheets aside and sat bolt upright in bed.

"Wha—what is it?" Tim cried out, his voice thick with
sleep.

The old bedsprings squeaked terribly as her husband
rolled over and felt for her in the darkness. Her skin was
bathed with cold sweat, and her throat felt like she had inhaled flame. Violent shivers shook her shoulders as she
gasped for breath.

"Hey ... hey, you're just dreaming," Tim said, his
voice low and comforting. It did little to soothe Polly. The
sound of Heather's voice was still echoing in her ears, but
in the darkness, she noticed something else: a soft, dull
scratching sound that was coming from the wall behind her
head.

"What is that?" she asked, her throat so tight she was
barely able to speak. "What's that sound?"

They listened for a moment in silence; then the sound
came again. Tim grunted and chuckled softly.

"I think we have a little nighttime visitor," he said.

"What?"

Polly could barely breathe.

"There's a rat or mouse inside the walls," Tim said softly. He put his arm around her in the darkness and gave her a reassuring pat. "Remember we used to hear them all the time when we stayed here. Especially in winter."

Polly wanted to tell him that wasn't the sound she meant, that she had heard something else—a muffled scraping sound, like there was someone outside the house, scratching against the window, trying to get in—but her voice failed her. She wanted to snuggle with him and forget all about the dream she'd just had—because she was convinced now that it had to have been a dream—but she was afraid to close her eyes, even in the darkness.

"We'll put out some rat poison tomorrow," Tim said before settling down. Within seconds, he was asleep again, breathing deeply and regularly. The warmth of his breath washed over Polly's face, but the chill still lingered deep inside her. She waited, tensed, in the darkness for the sound to come again, but it didn't. Finally, around two o'clock in the morning, she drifted off to sleep. Six hours later, when she awoke to see the golden light of the morning sun angling across the bedroom floor, she felt as though she had hardly slept at all.

five

Tim was still sleeping soundly when Polly awoke at 8:30. Even though they had a lot to do over the next several days and weeks, she decided to let him sleep in as she got out of bed and tiptoed downstairs. The door to Brian's bedroom was closed. She paused for a moment and listened at the door but didn't hear him stirring. No doubt he would stay in bed until noon if she didn't wake him, but she decided to let him have a little extra time, too, at least for the first day here.

The day was unusually warm, especially for so early in the morning. Sunlight poured in through the kitchen window, turning everything in the room a golden brown as if it were coated with nicotine. Using some of the bottled water they'd bought the night before, Polly started a pot of coffee, then poured herself a glass of orange juice and went out onto the back porch to sit. She was thinking about how pleasant it would be just to enjoy the peace and quiet of the morning, but when she raised her glass and took a sip of juice, she wrinkled her nose and gasped with disgust, almost spitting it out.

The juice tasted terrible.

Frowning, she brought the glass up to her nose and

sniffed it. She hadn't noticed anything peculiar about it when she had opened the container and poured it just seconds ago, but there was no denying that there was something wrong with it. Her brow wrinkled with concentration as she sniffed it a few more times. At first, she couldn't quite place it, but then it hit her.

"Cedar chips," she whispered as she pulled the glass away from her nose. "It smells just like cedar chips."

She swirled the juice around in the glass. There didn't seem to be anything wrong with it. It looked all right, but the thick, piney smell lingered in her nose. She had done enough gardening over the years to recognize the aroma of cedar chips, and that's exactly what this orange juice smelled like.

"Weird," she muttered as she leaned over the porch railing and poured the remaining juice onto the ground.

The morning calm had already been disrupted, so she sighed, stood up, and walked slowly back into the kitchen. The refrigerator was working; she was sure of that, so the juice must have been spoiled when they bought it. She checked the expiration date on the carton and saw that there was still over a week left but was determined to have Tim take it back for a replacement.

"Must just be a bad batch," she whispered to herself.

With the juice carton still in hand, she kicked the refrigerator door shut and was just turning around to pour the remaining juice down the sink when she caught a glimpse of a dark silhouette in the doorway. She jumped and let out a startled yelp, almost dropping the carton.

"Whoa. Kinda jumpy there, aren't yah?" Tim asked, smiling tightly as he walked into the kitchen. He was barefoot and still wearing what he had slept in: plaid boxer shorts and a dark blue UMass T-shirt. His dark hair was tousled from sleep, and he obviously needed a shave.

"I didn't hear you come downstairs," Polly said, still a little flustered. Her pulse was racing, and she made herself take a slow breath just to calm down.

"Gotta get started. We've got a lot to do today," Tim

said as he walked over to her and gave her a quick hug and kiss on the cheek. Still holding the carton of juice, Polly returned the hug with one arm.

"Wanna pour me some of that?" Tim asked.

Polly grimaced and shook her head. "I think it's gone bad. It smells kind of funny."

Tim cocked one eyebrow as he fetched a glass from the cupboard, took the juice from her, and poured a tiny bit into the glass. After swirling it around under his nose like he was sampling a snifter of brandy, he took a noisy sip.

"Hmmm . . . tastes all right to me," he said, smacking his lips. He proceeded to fill the glass and drink half of it with a few noisy gulps. "So, where we gonna start today?"

Polly glanced around the kitchen and tried not to look as hopeless as the sight made her feel. The dingy walls looked like they had been saturated with grease for the last ten years or more. The ceiling paint might have been white once, but now it was yellowed and peeling. The darker paint on the doorjambs, window frames, and cupboards didn't look much better, either.

"I suppose we should start in here," she finally said, hoping that her voice didn't betray the depth of despair she was feeling. As far as she was concerned, the whole house was too far gone to be fixed, at least by them. It would need to be entirely renovated before she'd be comfortable in it. Of course, that wasn't their intention, at least not this summer. All they hoped to do was make it livable for a few weeks, at most. Maybe, if they did a little cosmetic work, they'd at least be able to sell the place . . . that is, if Tim could convince Rob that it was time to put the house on the market.

"First things first, I guess," Tim said before draining the glass of juice. "We should head into town and pick up some cleaning supplies, some paint and stuff."

Polly nodded. "Yeah, maybe they sell biohazard suits at the local hardware store, too," she said, cracking a tight smile. "Think we ought to wake up Brian, or let him sleep?"

"Apparently we don't have to," Tim said as he walked over to the kitchen table and picked up the sheet of paper that was lying there. After scanning it quickly, he handed it to Polly.

" 'Went for a walk down by the river,' " Polly read out loud. " 'Shouldn't be too long. Get some of that clean country air you were talking about, Dad. Brian.' "

Frowning, Polly handed the note back to Tim. She was surprised that she hadn't noticed it earlier, when she had first come downstairs. It had obviously been sitting there all along but, somehow, she had missed it. The thought crossed her mind that Brian might have come downstairs and left the note there while she was out on the back porch, but that didn't make sense. He would have had to sneak out the front door to avoid her, and why would he do something like that?

"Is that okay?" she asked. "Going down by the river, I mean? It's safe for him to be down there, isn't it?"

"Hell, yes," Tim said with a dismissive wave of the hand. "We played down there all the time when we were kids. Swam in it. Fished in it. Remember before we were married? That summer night we went down there and—?"

"All right. All right. That's enough," Polly said, smiling to herself.

She remembered, all right, and she couldn't help but wonder when that level of passion had left their relationship. It had been years since they had made love the way she remembered it had been back then. Now, like all of her friends complained about their husbands, they were once-a-weekers, at best, and it was usually with about as much passion as having a regular oil change done on the car.

"He's gotta be careful," Tim said, "but he's a big boy. He's not going to do anything stupid."

Polly nodded but wasn't convinced.

Sure, Brian was a smart kid and all, but he had lived his whole life in suburbia. She wondered if he would know what to expect out here in the country, in a place where there were mice and rats creeping around in the walls, keeping you awake until all hours. Who's to say there weren't dangerous animals like bears or coyotes in the nearby woods? Or that he might think it was safe to swim in the river and then be swept away by the current?

"You want to come into town with me?" Tim asked.

He was standing by the refrigerator as he poured himself another glass of orange juice. Polly couldn't believe that he could drink it when it smelled like it did, but he seemed not to mind. She thought maybe it had just hit her wrong and she should try it again, but the pine smell still lingered in her nose and made her stomach twist.

"No, I don't think so," she said hesitantly. "I can get started cleaning around here. Plus, that way one of us will be here when Brian gets back."

"He's thirteen years old," Tim said. "He can take care of himself."

Polly nodded. "Yeah, but still . . . I can get some cleaning done while you're gone. It's going to take me an hour or two just to scour the sink."

Tim nodded, looking thoughtful for a moment, then said, "Well, while I'm in town, then, why don't I swing by Rob's and see how he's doing? You wouldn't want to do that, anyway."

"Oh, no. Give me a toilet with five years' accumulation of grime to clean instead, please," she said with a laugh that she didn't really feel.

Tim hesitated, obviously not sure how to read what she had said, but Polly waved him off.

"What do you say I make us a real country breakfast, first," she said. "We've got eggs, bacon, whole wheat toast—"

"But skip the orange juice?" Tim offered.

Polly nodded, "Yeah, skip the OJ for me, but while we eat, we can make a list of the things we'll need for starters. Then, while you're in town, I'll get organized so we can jump right in."

"Sounds good to me," Tim said. He walked over to the cupboard and pulled out a frying pan that had obviously been sitting there for many years. After blowing off the dust, he ran the water in the sink until it was hot and then started scrubbing it.

"Fried or over easy?" he asked.

"One . . . two . . . three . . . four."

Brian counted out loud as the flat stone skipped across the still water's surface. He was standing on the narrow muddy shore of the river, close to where the water ran smooth and dark beneath the overhanging trees. The riverbank rose up almost head high behind him, the slope covered with a dense growth of brush. Birds were singing in the trees, and Brian could hear the soft, rushing sound of the wind in the pines. Out over the water, small, dark birds that Brian didn't recognize darted around erratically, skimming over the water and dimpling the surface wherever they touched it.

The ground by the river's edge was soggy, and the smell of damp earth filled the air. It wasn't entirely unpleasant, but there was a hint of something rotting in the air that made his stomach turn. Brian realized that he was really hungry and wished he'd taken the time to eat something before coming out here. He kicked at the loose pebbles that lined the shore until he found another one that was the right shape. Cocking back his arm, he sent it skipping out across the water.

"One . . . two . . . three," he counted until the rock sank into the swirling, dark depths of the river.

"That's only two," a voice said suddenly from behind.

Brian jumped and turned around quickly. Shading his eyes with one hand, he looked up the steep slope of the riverbank. It took a moment or two for his eyes to adjust to the dim light underneath the trees, but then he saw the young boy in the dense green shadows of the pines. Dappled sunlight and shadow played across him in a dazzling display that momentarily blinded Brian.

"What do you mean?" Brian said defensively. He'd

been a bit taken aback by this boy's sudden appearance but wasn't going to let it show.

"I mean, that was only two skips," the boy said. He had a low, pleasant-sounding voice that seemed to drift on the warm breeze that was funneling from the land onto the water. "You can't count the first one."

"Oh? And why's that?"

"Because you'd have *one* skip even if all you did was throw the stupid rock into the water," the boy said. There was a strong trace of sarcasm in his voice that Brian didn't really like, but he gave the boy a half smile and nodded his agreement.

"Yeah, I guess you've got a point there," he said as he crossed his arms over his chest. Cocking his hip to one side, he stared up at the boy.

The early-morning sun was angled behind the intruder. Yellow bars of sunlight filtered through the bright green of the newly blooming leaves, making it difficult for Brian to see the boy's features clearly. All he could be sure of was that the boy's face and arms were pale, and that he had blond hair and blue eyes. He was short and slightly built, certainly no bigger than Brian, who quickly determined that he could beat up the kid in a fight, if it ever came to that.

But this kid didn't seem like a threat. That much was obvious.

"So what are you doing out here?" Brian asked.

"I could ask you the same thing," the boy replied coolly. "I come out here all the time, and I've never seen you out here before."

Brian ran his fingers through his hair and nodded.

"Yeah, well, that's because I just moved here yesterday," he said. "Only for a couple of weeks. I'm staying with my folks for part of the summer in the house over there." When he pointed in the general direction of the house, the boy glanced over his shoulder, then slowly turned back to face him.

"You mean the old *Harris* house?" the boy said.

There was a funny quality to his voice that Brian couldn't quite pin down. It sounded sort of lonely or even respectful, like the way you would whisper in church or something.

"Yeah," Brian replied. "My name's Brian Harris."

He was still shading his eyes with his hand and craning his neck to look up at the boy.

"Why don't you come down here so we can talk?"

The boy was silent for a moment. Brian could see that he was looking off to one side with a curious, perplexed expression on his face, almost like he was trying to remember something. Then the boy laughed lightly and said, "My name's Josh . . . Josh Billings."

"So, you must live around here, huh?" Brian asked.

"No," Josh said snappily. "I live in New York City and just come up here every day to hang around."

"Very funny," Brian muttered, chuckling as he shook his head.

He wasn't quite sure what to make of this kid. He figured that it wouldn't be bad to make friends with him, if only to have someone to hang out with the short time he was in Hilton. Otherwise, this was going to be one long, boring summer vacation. But there was something peculiar about this kid, almost like he didn't know how to—or didn't want to—even try to be friends. Then again, he was the one who had spoken first. Brian wouldn't have even known he was there if he hadn't spoken up.

"So what do you do around here, for fun, I mean?" Brian asked. He shrugged and slapped his hands against his legs as he looked around. "Doesn't seem like much of a happening town."

The boy laughed again, softly, and shook his head. "Oh, there's stuff to do. . . . You know, baseball, ride bikes, hang out, stuff like that."

Brian nodded and was silent for a moment as they regarded each other. He didn't like that the boy was still standing on the bank so high above him. It made him feel vulnerable, like he was under observation.

"Can you swim in the river?" Brian finally asked. "The water looks kind of dirty to me."

"It's just a little muddy, stirred up from the bottom," the boy replied. "It won't kill you or anything."

"Well, it seems to me like it's gonna be a hot day. What do you say we go back to our houses, get our bathing suits and towels, and meet back here for a swim?"

The boy didn't respond immediately. The woods were filled with the sound of singing birds, but in the spaces when they weren't talking, there was an odd, muffled quality to the air. Brian figured it was just the way things sounded down in the hollow of the river basin.

"I don't know about today," Josh said after a lengthy pause. "I've got some other stuff to do."

"Like what?" Brian asked, half hoping that Josh would ask him to join in with him. He took a few steps forward as if to climb up the riverbank, but then halted, thinking that it might be a little forward of him. Then again, he didn't like standing down by the water's edge with Josh looming so high above him.

Josh glanced upward and rolled his head from side to side as though looking for something in the sky. The wind whispered in fitful gusts that shook the branches, and the shadows played across his face.

"Just . . . stuff," he said at last.

The sunlight cast faint gray shadows under his cheeks and chin, looking like soot smudges. His blue eyes sparkled brightly like polished glass beads, but there was a funny distance in them that made Brian feel uncomfortable.

"So I guess you've gotta get going, then, huh?" Brian asked.

The boy didn't seem to be in any particular hurry. Brian wondered if he was just making excuses or something.

"Yeah, I don't want my dad to be mad at me. He gets real mad if I'm late. I should've been home by now," Josh said with a slight nod. Once again, there was that distant, muffled quality to his voice that bothered Brian. "Maybe I'll see you later."

"Yeah. Okay," Brian replied. "Maybe catch you later, then."

He hoped his tone of voice conveyed that he could care less if he ever saw Josh again. He watched as the boy turned and walked off into the woods. His feet snapped twigs, making faint popping sounds as he whisked through the low-hanging branches. There wasn't a path up there, at least as far as Brian knew, but Josh was out of sight within seconds, lost in the dense screen of foliage. Once he was gone and the silence of the woods descended, Brian was left with the curious feeling that the boy might never have been there at all.

Turning back to the river, he stood there for a long while, watching the birds skim low over the water and wondering if Josh wanted to make friends or not. He couldn't help but feel confused and a little bit ticked off by the boy's odd behavior. Just because Brian was new in the area, that didn't mean he had to be mean to him or snub him or anything.

Who the hell does he think he is, anyway? Brian scowled as he gritted his teeth and shook his head. *Probably just some hick hayseed jerk-off who doesn't know how to relate to people anyway.*

Brian took a deep breath. His nose wrinkled at the dank, rotting smell of the river mud. He looked around on the narrow bank until he found another round, flat stone, then picked it up and winged it out across the water. After waiting until the second skip, he started counting out loud.

"One . . . two . . . three."

Four bright concentric rings spread out across the water's surface, and then the stone sank quietly beneath the dark surface of the river.

"Hey!" he called out, hearing his voice echo from the opposite shore. "I got three, even counting your way."

But there was no answer . . . nothing except for the

singing birds and the rushing sound of the wind in the pines.

"Well, how's that son of a bitch brother of yours doin'?"

Standing beside the hardware store's checkout counter with his pile of paint cans, brushes, rollers, and household cleaners, buckets, and sponges, Tim was waiting for the salesclerk to ring up his purchase when Ray Fuller, the store owner, spotted him. He cringed slightly when Ray shouted a typically boisterous greeting to him from across the store, then strode over and slapped him heartily on the back, hard enough for it to sting. Tim had known Ray pretty much his whole life, having gone to school with him since kindergarten. Ray had taken over the local hardware store from his father, J. Raymond, after his father died back in 1986. He was doing his best to run the store like it was still an old-fashioned hardware store from the 1950s. There was something quaint and endearing about that, but it didn't make up for the fact that Ray, while likable enough, was somewhat of a loudmouth.

"I heard he'd been knocked around pretty bad, but I ain't had a chance to go see him yet. How's he doin'?"

"He's doing just fine," Tim said with a quick nod. "I was just over visiting with him. They've got him in a walking cast, and he's getting along pretty well."

"Glad to hear it," Ray said with a wide smile.

"Good to see you, Ray. How's business treating you?"

Ray winced and pursed his thick lips as if he'd just bitten into a lemon. His heavy jowls jiggled as he leaned to one side, resting a beefy elbow on the worn linoleum counter. The wooden floorboards creaked beneath his weight.

"Strugglin' along as usual, yah know?" he said with a shrug. "They've got that fancy new hardware store over to Rumford, 'n I can't really compete with their prices, but I'm hanging on. Customer loyalty 'n all."

"Glad to hear it," Tim said.

"So, you're up for the summer, I hear. Plannin' on doin' a little fixin' up out at the old place?" Ray said, indicating with a quick nod of the head the supplies Tim had picked out.

Tim bristled for a moment, thinking that it really wasn't any of Ray's business, but then he remembered how fast news and gossip spread in a small town like Hilton. In point of fact, if Ray really cared and wanted to know, he probably could have found out what Tim had for breakfast that morning.

"Yeah. I thought we might clean and paint a bit," Tim said. "The place really could use some remodeling, especially the kitchen and bathroom, but I figure a little touch-up wouldn't hurt, especially if we're ever going to put it on the market."

Ray arched an eyebrow at that. "I thought your brother said he'd never sell the old place. Not while he's alive, anyway. Course, right now might not be such a bad time, what with that new development goin' in out your way. Property values are gonna go up a bit."

"Rob's never going to live out there, that's for sure," Tim said, "so . . ." He threw his hands up. "We'll see if we can get him to change his mind."

"Well, if you need a carpenter, my brother Howie's a damned good one," Ray said. He grunted softly as he leaned forward and, resting his chin on his meaty palm, regarded Tim so long that Tim began to feel slightly uncomfortable.

"So, any more word about what they found out there?" Ray asked casually.

"What do you mean?" Tim asked, momentarily confused.

"Don't tell me you hadn't heard?" Ray said, obviously taken aback. "What they found at the construction site."

Tim slowly shook his head *no* even as a slight chill tickled his stomach. A faint voice in the back of his mind told him to ignore what Ray had said, to forget all about it and just get along with what he and Polly had planned for today. Almost against his will, though, he heard himself say, "What did they find?"

Ray snorted as he scratched the stubble on his cheek, making the flesh jiggle like jelly. "I would've thought for sure Rob would've mentioned it to you. 'S far as I recall, it happened the same day he got hurt out there." He paused and took a sharp breath that made a watery rattle in his throat. "You know where they're building them new houses out your way, right?"

Tim nodded slowly as the coldness in the pit of his stomach grew steadily stronger. He had seen the sign for Ridge Estates. Deep down, he knew that he didn't want to hear this, but he said, "Yeah, there's . . . what? Maybe five or six homes going in there. I haven't really had a chance to check it out yet, but I kind of hate to see it because they're tearing up the woods where we used to play when we were kids. But that's progress, I guess."

"Yeah, well, they found someone out there," Ray said, his voice lowering to a phleghmy growl.

Now the cold was like a spike in Tim's gut. The air in the store felt suddenly too thin to breathe, and a sheen of sweat broke out across his brow.

"What do you mean, *found* someone?" He could hear the tight tremor in his voice as though he were listening to someone else speak.

"Just that," Ray said as he shifted his weight from one foot to the other, making the floorboards creak again. "They were digging out the road with a 'dozer and back-hoe, and they uncovered a body. Newspaper says it was a kid."

"Jesus Christ," Tim said. His voice was barely a whisper. "I didn't hear anything about it."

Ray shrugged. "Not too surprised. It got some attention in the local paper, a course, may have even made the Portland paper, but probably not outta state. Yeah, they turned up some human bones. Skull and everything. Been there a while, I guess. The paper said they were pretty old, anyways."

"I'll be a son of a bitch," Tim whispered as he wiped his hand across his forehead. "Can you imagine that? Someone died out there." His throat made a gulping sound when he swallowed. "Any idea who it was?"

"Authorities ain't sure," Ray said. "Local cops were first on the scene, but they called in the state crime unit right away. Far as I know, though, they still haven't determined the exact age or sex of the person. Just that he's been there a while."

"Christ on a cross," Tim whispered, shaking his head. After a moment, he licked his lips and looked straight at Ray. "But they don't have any idea who it is, huh?" he asked. "Probably someone got lost out there hunting or something. That'd be my guess."

"Could be," Ray replied. "There hasn't been much in the news about it since they found it, but I was talkin' to Dougie Shaw the other day. He was the first cop out there—"

"Christ! Are you telling me Dougie Shaw's a town cop?" Tim asked. "I remember when he was just a snot-nosed little kid who used to get beat up all the time."

"He's been on the force goin' on ten years now," Ray said. "But he was tellin' me and some of the fellas the other day that whoever it was, he had a cracked skull, so they're considerin' it a homicide. Looks like someone gave the poor bastard a good whack on the side of the head 'n then left him for dead out there."

"You don't say," Tim said, more to himself than to Ray.

"Yeah, Dougie says the bones were rotted pretty bad because of the pine trees. You know, they make the soil real acidic, so bones and stuff will dissolve pretty fast. They guess the body's been out there no more 'n thirty years, give or take."

"Is anyone from around here missing?" Tim asked.

"Oh, hell." Ray waved his hand as though shooing a fly. "There's been lots of people gone missin' in the past thirty years. Kids, hunters, husbands 'n wives—even reports of people just passing through disappearing now and then. I figure the cops'll run it down with dental records or whatever. If not"—Ray finished with a who-gives-a-shit shrug—"it can't be all that important if no one's missin' him after all this time. Probably a runaway or something. But I'm surprised Rob didn't mention it to you."

"Umm. Me, too," Tim replied, hearing the tremor in his voice. "Maybe he just didn't want us to worry, you know? I mean, he knows Polly's not too keen about staying out at the old house in the first place. She's . . . ah, she had some trouble after we lost that baby a couple of years ago. Maybe Rob didn't say anything 'cause he didn't want her to worry, living out there."

"Yeah . . . maybe," Ray said. He straightened up and, reaching under his gut, hooked his hands in his belt loops. "Well, I can't spend the whole day jawin' with you. Good to see yah, though." He gave Tim another stinging slap on the back. "Give my best to Polly and your boy."

"Yeah, I sure will," Tim said with a faint smile. He was feeling cold and numb inside as he watched Ray walk to the back of the store. As the thin, gray-haired woman at the register began to ring up his sale, the steady beep-beep-beep of the register scanner became almost hypnotic, lulling Tim.

This could be serious! he thought as he fought against the tightening nervousness that gripped him. *This could be really fucking serious!*

From what Ray had said, all the authorities knew was that someone had been killed and buried in the woods not far from the house. There was no telling who it was or how long ago it had happened. One thing Tim was absolutely sure of, though, was that he wasn't going to mention anything about it to Polly or Brian. For now, all he could hope was that neither of them heard about it on the news or from someone else.

•   •   •

Polly spent the morning doing what she could, cleaning out the cupboards and making at least a first pass over the kitchen countertop, cabinets, and walls with hot water and some Lysol she'd found in the old pantry. The house was hot, even with all of the downstairs windows open and a fan on. She had her hair tied up with a kerchief and was wearing cut-off jeans shorts and a T-shirt, but it wasn't long before her face was dripping with sweat. The rubber gloves she wore didn't help any, but she wasn't going to touch anything with her bare hands any more than she had to before she was positive that it was clean.

A little past one o'clock in the afternoon, she was long past ready for lunch when she heard the crunch of gravel as a car pulled into the driveway. She threw her sponge into the sink filled with water and went to the screen door. Tim backed up the car, parking as close as he could get to the back porch. The car door opened and slammed shut, sounding like a gunshot as he got out.

Something's wrong.

That was Polly's first thought when she saw him. In the bright sunlight, his face looked pinched and pale. She told herself it was only because she was looking out into brilliant daylight from inside the darkness of the house, but she immediately sensed that something was wrong.

Maybe something's happened to Rob, she thought, and she felt a tiny twist of guilt when she realized that she almost hoped she was right.

Or maybe they had an argument about something, maybe about selling the house.

"Hey," she called out cheerily as she eased the screen door open and stepped out onto the porch. Tim had walked around to the back of the car and was opening the trunk.

"Hey," was all he said in response, barely bothering to look up at her.

"Whoa! Looks like you bought out the whole store," Polly said with a laugh as she came down the steps to help him. There were four boxes, cut in half, all loaded with painting and cleaning supplies.

"Probably not even half of what we need," Tim said, grunting from the effort as he lifted one of the boxes. "Is Brian around to help?"

Biting her lower lip, Polly shook her head. "He's not back from his walk yet," she said, not masking the worry in her voice. "I was waiting for you to get back so maybe we could go look for him."

Tim glanced at her, then looked out over the wide, sloping field that led down to the river. The summer air shimmered with heat waves. A solitary crow cawed as it cruised from one tall pine tree to another.

"You're not worried about him, are you?" he asked.

Polly inhaled sharply and held it for a moment.

Of course she was worried about him. Especially since she had lost her baby, she had worried at least a little whenever Brian wasn't around. She didn't need what had happened to Heather Olsen to convince her how fragile life was, how easily it could be snatched away. Besides, it was a mother's job to worry.

"Well," she said, keeping her voice steady only with effort. "He doesn't really know the area. I just don't like thinking that he may have wandered off and gotten lost or something."

Tim noticeably stiffened. He looked like he was about to say something but then thought better of it. She almost asked what was bothering him but let it pass. The important thing right now was to find Brian.

"You want to make lunch while I go look for him?" Tim asked. "Or do you want to come along?"

Polly didn't consider even for a moment. She peeled off her rubber gloves and dropped them onto the back steps on top of the box of supplies.

"Let's go," she said.

They unloaded the remaining three boxes, placing them on the back steps. Tim's expression still looked tight when he slammed the trunk shut. Brushing his hands together, he said, "My guess is he headed down to the river."

"You know the way," Polly said, indicating the field behind the house with a sweep of her hand.

As they started out across the field, side by side, the long grass swished at their knees. Numerous insects erupted up out of the grass, jumping and flying in buzzing arcs to get out of their way. A gentle breeze pressed down the top of the grass, carrying with it a sweet, flowery smell that Polly couldn't identify. The farther they got from the house, the stronger the scent became until it was so thick it was almost cloying.

It was a beautiful June afternoon, and Polly told herself that she should be enjoying it. There was no reason to worry about Brian. He was old enough to take care of himself. He would be fine. But that didn't assuage the hollow feeling in her stomach. Try as she might, she couldn't block out the single, bothersome thought that kept repeating in her head.

Something's happened to him. . . . I just know it!

six

A thin, gray tendril of smoke curled up to the ceiling in the darkened kitchen where Rob Harris sat at the table. The table rocked back and forth as he leaned forward with both elbows resting on the soiled, checkered table-cloth. His eyes stared straight ahead, not really focusing on the burning joint he held between his thumb and index finger. He had already had a first, quick hit, and was taking slow, shallow sips of air through his mouth, feeling the steady beat of his pulse in his neck as his thoughts grew a bit fuzzy. His pulse had slowed down a little since Tim had left, but a slippery coil of tension still twisted deep in his gut.

"This may take care of it," Rob whispered hoarsely as he brought the joint to his lip again and sucked noisily. The orange tip of the joint glowed painfully bright in the dark room as he filled his lungs with smoke. Then he sat back in his chair, held his breath for nearly thirty seconds, and exhaled a thin haze of smoke.

"Then again . . . maybe not," he said.

He narrowed his eyes and smiled as the gauzy lightness of euphoria lifted him a little bit higher. Looking at the ceiling, he let his gaze drift over the random pattern of light brown and yellow stains left by moisture and nicotine. For a minute or two, he got hung up on one particular stain that looked sort of like a face in profile. Snorting loudly, he turned his attention back to the joint in his hands and took another slow, steady hit.

He hadn't been ready for a visit from his brother this morning, and he was still feeling agitated in spite of the marijuana. Over the last several weeks, ever since his accident, he'd gotten into the habit of staying up late at night and sleeping until noon, at least. Now that he was out of work again, what did it matter? At least he would have disability checks coming . . . eventually.

But what does good old Tim do?

Ten o'clock, and he's at the door, ringing the doorbell, and tearing Rob from a peaceful slumber.

"Fuckin' asshole," Rob whispered as he cupped the joint in his hand and took one last hit. This stuff was potent as hell, and he knew that if he wasn't careful, he'd be crawling around on all fours, walking cast or no walking cast.

He licked his thumb and forefinger and extinguished the joint, then carefully laid it down on the table. Lacing his fingers together and cupping the back of his head, he leaned back in the chair, closed his eyes, and replayed their conversation in his head.

"Why didn't you tell me about what they found out there?"

"What? What did they find out where?"

"You know damned right well what they found! You should have told me about it the first time I talked to you after you broke your leg!"

"I didn't think it was all that important."

"Not all that important? What the fuck are you talking about, not that important?"

"Just what I said. It's not all that important."

"And by Jesus, it *isn't*," Rob whispered hoarsely.

He opened his eyes to narrow slits and stared at the joint, lying on the table. For a moment or two, he considered relighting it but decided that would take way too much effort. Then again, feeling the way he did right now, just about anything seemed like too much of an effort. If dragging his sorry ass over to the refrigerator and getting something for breakfast seemed like a nearly insurmountable task, then getting all worked up just because they found a *body* at the construction site where he'd been working certainly wasn't anything to be too concerned about.

No, the only thing worth the effort—if anything—was trying to figure out what Tim was going to do. He was going to be a problem, no doubt about it. For sure, he'd start pushing to sell the family home again . . . like he needed the money!

Then there was Tim's wife.

What about her?

She was a nice enough piece of ass, but saying that she was a little on the unstable side was putting it mildly. Rob could just imagine how she would react if—or when—she heard about them finding a body in the woods so close to the house.

No doubt she'd flip out.

That might not be such a bad thing, though.

Maybe the mistake he'd made had been *not* telling Tim about the discovery of the body. If he had known right away, he might have changed his plans for the summer and never even come back to Hilton. Now that he was here, it might cause complications.

"But just minor complications," Rob whispered with a snicker as he looked at the ceiling.

He suddenly found himself amused by all of this. Shaking his head from side to side, he closed his eyes and started to chuckle softly. Before long, the laughter built up until he was cackling out loud. Wave after wave of laughter filled the kitchen, bringing tears to his eyes and making him short of breath.

Man, it's all too fucking much!

Rob's laughter became so uncontrollable that he had to

double over to keep his stomach from hurting so much. Tears ran down his cheeks, and he could feel his face flush. Heat and pressure were building up inside his head as he leaned back and roared and roared with laughter.

"Oh . . . boy . . ." he said, gasping. His voice hitched on every word. "He . . . thinks . . . it's . . . a . . . *problem*. . . ."

Sitting back to catch his breath, Rob sat there, slouched at the table. Nearly half an hour later, he finally came down enough to find the motivation to rustle up some breakfast. He stood up clumsily and went to the stove, where he tried to scramble some eggs but ended up burning them. Thick smoke filled the tiny kitchen, but it didn't set off the smoke detector because Rob hadn't bothered to replace the worn-out battery. Scowling, he scraped the rubbery, brown eggs into the sink and ran the disposal, then settled for a couple of pieces of toast with jelly. He got the Sunday edition of the *Rumford Journal* from the stoop. Now that his high was a little more manageable, he made a cup of instant coffee and went outside to sit on the steps and read the paper while he ate his toast.

The first section he checked out was the local news. There wasn't anything more about the body they had found at the construction site. Not that he had expected anything. It had been nearly a month ago, and it was old news. Rob had been close by when the excavator turned up the skeleton. Having seen it just before he'd broken his leg, he was pretty sure that the authorities weren't going to be able to identify anything. The bones were brown and rotting, crusted thick with dirt and crumbling. There wasn't much left of the skull, and what there was had been smashed into tiny fragments.

No way they'll ever figure out who it was, he thought.

But even if they did, Rob was positive that they'd never figure out how this person had died or how he had come to be buried out there in the woods.

The bitch of it was, they had *found* him!

That might make things a little more complicated, like

Tim said, but it wasn't an emergency. The only real worry was that Rob wasn't sure what Tim would do.

"Just keep your mouth shut," he whispered as he took a slurping sip of coffee, closing his eyes to savor the taste. "That's all I'm asking of you, little brother. Just keep your fucking mouth shut!"

Still feeling his buzz, Rob looked up at the arc of blue sky. It was beautifully clear except for a few puffy fair-weather clouds that drifted by low on the horizon. The breeze was warm in his face, feeling like a current of water washing over him.

He felt good. Damned good!

Now that the initial rush was over, Rob was left with a warm, mellow feeling that he hoped he could maintain all day. The dull ache of his broken leg felt a little better today. He was even pretty much over being mad at Tim for stopping by earlier and waking him up.

"To hell with it," he muttered as he drained his coffee cup.

There was absolutely *nothing* to worry about.

He folded up the newspaper and tossed it inside the door. Then, grunting with the effort, he stood up and hobbled down the steps to his old Ford pickup truck, which was parked in the side yard. He smiled when he saw the bumper sticker on the rear of the truck. He had put it there so long ago it had started to fade and peel, but it still cracked him up every time he saw it.

FRIENDS DON'T LET FRIENDS
DRIVE CHEVYS

It was a beautiful day for a drive, he decided, so he fished the keys from his pocket and, whistling softly, opened the truck door and climbed up into the cab. It took a bit of effort to swing the left leg up, but he was getting better at moving around with it. He was grateful, at least, that he didn't have a standard shift where he'd have to work the clutch. When he started the engine, he looked in the rearview mirror at the cloud of blue smoke that blew out of the tailpipe. Shifting into gear, he pulled away slowly from the curb.

Why not take a little drive out by the old house, he thought, *just to see if anything's going on.*

He didn't think he'd stop in for a visit. He had already seen more than enough of Tim for one day, and he wasn't too keen about seeing Polly again. He knew she didn't like him, and she wouldn't be too happy if he stopped by without calling first. Besides, he wasn't very fond of her.

"Although she *does* have a wicked ass, I'll grant her that," he said with an evil grin as he glanced at his reflection in the rearview. He needed a shave but decided to hell with it. There wasn't anyone he was trying to impress.

As he drove down Main Street, he rolled the window down and popped a Doobie Brothers tape into the deck, cranking up the volume so everyone he passed by on this gorgeous Sunday afternoon would hear the heavy, pounding beat of "China Grove." He drummed the rhythm on the steering wheel with both hands while singing along with a flat, tuneless voice.

He was feeling good . . . maybe even happy.

There wasn't a thing in the world to worry about, he finally decided; and even if there was, he'd take care of it . . . just like he *always* had.

"Bri-an!"

"Yo! Brian!"

Polly and Tim shouted as they angled across the field, heading down to the river. Their voices echoed back from the trees, but the steady buzzing of crickets and grasshoppers was their only reply.

As they walked, Tim reached for Polly's hand once or twice, but she pulled away from him. This was anything but a pleasant afternoon stroll. She was hungry and tired after not sleeping well the night before, and she despaired of all the work they still had to do to make the house even marginally livable.

Plus, she was worried about their son.

"Bri-an!" she called, so loud it made her throat hurt.

"You know, he may not even have come down here," Tim said as they neared the woods. "He might have headed downtown to check things out."

"Wouldn't you have seen him while you were there?"

"Not necessarily," Tim said with a shrug as they continued walking.

An uncomfortable feeling was creeping steadily up between Polly's shoulders. She hugged herself to keep from shivering as they entered the dark green shadows of the forest. The air was thick with pine resin and filled with birdsong, but Polly thought the shadows under the pines looked particularly dense and threatening. Once or twice, she thought she caught a fleeting glimpse of motion in the deeper shadows, but when she looked, there was nothing there. The wind sighed overhead, making the branches sway. Ink-stain shadows rippled across the forest floor.

It wasn't long before Polly caught the scent of the river: a dank, fetid aroma that filled her nose and almost made her gag. She couldn't help but wonder why her sense of smell was so acute, and almost said something about it to Tim, but she decided not to. Right now, she had enough to worry about wondering whether or not Brian was safe.

After following a narrow, well-worn path for a few hundred yards into the woods, they came to the riverbank. Tim paused and, placing his hands on his hips, looked around.

"Remember when we used to come down here to go skinny-dipping?" he said. A playful smile twitched the corners of his mouth.

Polly didn't reply as she looked at the narrow stretch of flat, black earth. A large maple tree leaned at a dangerous angle over the river, the black latticework of its branches reflected in the dark, smooth-flowing water. At the river's edge, the water had a rich tea color. Polly could see the muddy riverbed that quickly dropped off into black, impenetrable depths. Close to shore, a large, submerged tree branch spread out underwater with only a few sun-bleached tips poking up into the air.

Kneeling down, Tim carefully inspected the hard-packed earth. After a few moments, he looked at Polly and shook his head.

"I don't see any fresh footprints or anything," he said.

"Who died and made you Tonto?" Polly said edgily. "Besides, who's to say he even came down here? He might have stayed on the path." She could hear a faint trembling in her voice but didn't try to hide it. Stronger chills were dancing up and down her back, and there was a sour tightness in her stomach, even though she kept telling herself that it was foolish to worry.

What are the chances that Brian is in any danger? she asked herself; but then she shivered when she asked herself what were the chances that someone as innocent as Heather Olsen would be struck and killed by a car in front of her own home.

Bad things happen to good people all the time, she cautioned herself. It's how you handle them that's the true measure of your character, and she knew from terrible experience that she didn't handle crises all that well.

Cupping her hands to her mouth, she turned to face the woods and called out as loud as she could, *"Brian! Answer me right now!"*

Her voice echoed from the opposite side of the river, but there was no other reply, only the sound of singing birds and the wind rushing through the trees overhead.

"There's a good chance we missed him, and he's already home," Tim said as he straightened up and brushed the dirt from his knees. "What do you say we head back for lunch?"

"And what if he's not there?" Polly asked nervously.

Tim started to say something, then checked himself. Stepping close to her, he put his arms around her and drew her close. As she pressed her face against his chest, she caught the strong scent of cigarette smoke and knew that he must have stopped by and visited Rob when he went into town.

Fighting back the rush of fear that was building up inside her, Polly pulled away from him and took a deep breath. She couldn't decide what to do. Traipsing around in the woods all afternoon wasn't going to do them any good, especially if Brian had already gone home while they were down here.

And if he wasn't home?

Well, that didn't necessarily mean that something bad had happened to him. It just meant that he was off doing something, somewhere. Maybe Tim was right, and Brian had gone downtown to hang out. It wasn't like him to do something like that, but then again, he wasn't home on familiar turf. Maybe he was just wandering around, feeling sorry for himself because he was stuck here for the summer.

"Yeah," Polly said at last. "Let's go back to the house."

Her voice sounded constricted, but Tim seemed not to notice. He smiled as he took her hand, and they started back the way they had come. The shadows under the trees shifted and danced in the corners of her vision, and once or twice Polly thought she caught a glimpse of someone hiding in the brush, watching them pass by; but when she turned to look, she saw only the deep, green shadows.

The warmth of the sun felt good on her back once they broke out of the woods and started back across the field. The long, tasseled grass swayed in the wind. Bees buzzed from flower to flower, and crickets sang a low, steady hum.

Polly suddenly stopped and turned to look behind them. She was sure that she had heard something . . . a voice calling faintly from the woods. It had sounded so far away she hadn't made out the words, but she was positive she had heard something.

"Did you hear that?" she asked, turning to Tim. Her eyes were wide and watery as she stared back at the woods.

"Huh?" Tim said, frowning and shaking his head.

Polly waited for several heartbeats, her ears straining to catch the sound if it was repeated, but she couldn't hear anything over the steady singing of the insects in the field.

"Uh . . . nothing, I guess," she said, shaking her head. "I just thought . . . Forget it."

She let the wind whisk her words away as she turned and started back toward the house. Stinging tears gathered in her eyes, but she held them in check.

Don't worry so goddamned much, she commanded herself. *Everything's going to be all right. Nothing's happened to Brian.*

She wanted desperately to believe that, but she couldn't shake the unnerving feeling that, even though she hadn't seen anything, *someone* was lurking in the woods, watching them every step of the way back to the house.

It never even crossed Brian's mind that his folks might be worried about him. Wasn't he doing exactly what his father had talked about just last night, enjoying the simple pleasure of life in the country?

Whoopee! he thought. *I'm having so-o-o-o much fun!*

Brian had half expected that Josh would come back, but after waiting by the river for half an hour or so, he realized that his new friend, if he could call him that, probably wasn't going to show, at least not today. After walking beside the river for a while longer, Brian realized that he was getting hungry. The best thing to do, he knew, would be to go back to the house—he couldn't think of it as *home*—for lunch. But then he realized that he had a few dollars in his pocket and decided to walk all the way to downtown Hilton and check it out, such as it was.

At a corner store named Patsy's, he bought an Italian sandwich, a bag of potato chips, and a cream soda. He ate, sitting alone on a peeling green bench in the small park beside the town library. While he ate, several kids passed by. They all glanced at him, obviously wondering who the new kid was, but no one spoke to him. Even the group of

boys roughly his own age who went by on bikes and skate-
boards didn't respond when he smiled and nodded a silent
greeting to them.

"Yeah, some friendly town," Brian muttered under his
breath as he balled up the oily wax paper the sandwich had
been wrapped in and stuffed it along with his empty chip
bag into the overflowing trash can beside the bench. He
left his empty soda can beside the trash can, figuring someone would pick it up for the five-cent deposit.

The town library, a small, one-story, gray granite building surrounded by yew bushes, was right behind him. He
considered going to check it out but decided against it.

Too much effort on such a hot day, he thought.

With or without Josh, he thought he should go back to
the river and swim but decided to check out the town instead. After wandering up and down Main Street, looking
in most of the stores to see if there was anything interesting, which there wasn't, he started up Main Street, heading
back to the house the way he had come.

He turned right at the blinking yellow light at the end of
Main Street and started up Route 4. It was at least three
miles to the turn onto Ridge Road, probably more, but the
walk felt a lot longer than that. He wasn't even halfway to
the turn before he was feeling sweaty and tired. With half
a liter of cream soda sloshing around in his stomach, he
began to get painful cramps.

On the iron bridge that spanned the river, he paused for
a rest. Folding his hands together and leaning over the
freshly painted black railing, he looked down into the fast-
flowing water. Swallows fluttered back and forth from
under the bridge.

*I'm gonna have to get myself a bike if I'm gonna be
stuck here all summer,* he thought as he hawked up a ball
of spit and sent it flying into the water. It was hard to believe that this was the same river that flowed so quietly just
a short way upstream. He wondered if right now Josh
Billings was back there at the river, hanging around in the
secluded cove, just looking for something to do.

Brian dallied on the bridge until his stomach began to settle down, then he continued his walk, keeping his pace slow and easy so the cramps wouldn't return. No point in hurrying back to the house, anyway. Once he got there, he was either going to go up to his bedroom and go on-line or else get stuck helping his parents clean the house.

Some choice!

He realized that he was going back to the house only because he was bored out of his mind and there was nothing else to do. Then and there, he decided that it might not be such a bad idea to try to make friends with that kid, Josh. If he was going to be bored out of his mind, he might as well be bored *with* someone.

The sun was shining directly into his face as he started down Ridge Road. Both sides of the road were lined with tall pine trees, but after a mile or so, he came upon the new housing development that was going in. The sign by the road proclaimed: Ridge Estates. Brian had passed it on his way to town but hadn't bothered to check it out then. Now, for want of anything better to do, he decided to have a look around.

The paved road leading into the development was covered with arcing streaks of yellow dirt from the construction vehicles that had passed by. A winding dirt road had been carved out between the trees, and about a quarter of a mile in, Brian could see huge areas that had been cleared of brush. There were mounds of dirt and exposed, scraped rock where the houses would be. Property lines were marked by orange spray-painted stakes and fluorescent flags tied to trees. Several large piles of brush had been stacked up, waiting to be burned or hauled off. It being Sunday, all the earth-moving machinery was standing idle.

Brian's first thought was that, if he had been just a little bit younger, this would be a cool place to come out and play. Like any kid, he had once been fascinated by construction vehicles, but seeing the real thing was always a little intimidating to him. When he saw the slashes on the trunks of trees and the gashes on boulders, he realized just how powerful and destructive these machines could be. He could just imagine hearing his mother, warning him to be careful and not get too close.

He scuffed his feet in the dirt, raising dust in his wake as he wandered down the dirt road, casually looking around. One house was already under construction. Its basement was a large, gaping, cement-lined hole in the ground with stacks of lumber beside it. Workers had started putting up the floor joists, covering over about half the basement.

The road ended in a wide *cul-de-sac*. From the looks of things, there were going to be at least five or six houses down here when everything was finished. They looked like they were going to be fairly large, fancy houses, too. Brian couldn't help but wonder who would want to spend so much money to live way the hell out here. He was about to walk over to the house under construction when he heard the crunch of tires on gravel behind him.

Turning, he saw a battered red Ford pickup truck moving slowly down the road toward him. When it entered the wider cleared area, about fifty yards away from Brian, it skidded to a stop. The dust that had risen in its wake slowly drifted away on the beeze like yellow smoke.

Brian froze, not knowing whether to turn and run or just continue his casual perusal of the development, acting like he belonged here. It wasn't as if he was doing anything wrong as long as he didn't monkey around with any of the machinery.

But what the hell's this guy doing here?

He cast a nervous glance at the truck. It just sat there, idling irregularly and spitting out puffs of blue exhaust from its rattling tailpipe. The sun was reflecting off the windshield, so Brian couldn't see the driver's face, but he could tell that the person was watching him.

He could feel it.

The guy was just sitting there. His knuckles were illuminated by the sun as he gripped the steering wheel. His

shoulders and face were nothing more than a vague silhouette, lost in the sun's glare.

Brian wondered if this might be one of the construction
workers, coming back to check on the site or maybe pick
up some tools he'd left behind. Or maybe it was the person
in charge of the development, dropping by to make sure
everything was secure and that none of the local kids were
playing around on the machinery.

No, Brian decided, it couldn't be the developer. He
wouldn't be driving a beat-to-shit pickup truck like that
one. He'd have a fancy car to impress prospective buyers.

*So who is this guy, and what's he doing? What the hell
is he waiting for?*

Tension mounted inside Brian as he considered what he
should do. He wanted to turn and run, but he didn't want to
look suspicious, either.

So he just stood there, staring back at the truck. After a
while, Brian saw the window on the driver's side slide quietly down, shifting like a sheet of dark ice. A cigarette butt
flew from the window, spiraling end over end in the air before landing in a tiny shower of sparks on the dirt road near
one of the brush piles.

Okay, Brian thought as the tension coiled inside him.
*It's not anyone who works here . . . not unless he doesn't
care about maybe starting a fire.*

The driver pumped the accelerator a few times, making
the engine race. A thick, black cloud of exhaust rose into
the air and was whisked away by the wind. Cold trickles of
sweat ran down Brian's sides from his armpits as he
glanced over his shoulder, looking for the quickest way out
of there. Off to the right, he saw what looked like a winding path that led deeper into the woods. As long as whoever this was stayed in his truck, he'd be okay, he thought.
Turning around slowly, still trying to look like he wasn't
up to anything, Brian started across the clearing to the
path. It was hard to resist the urge to break into a run.

Once again, the driver revved up his engine, letting it
roar like he was at the start of a race. The truck jerked for-

ward a few times, skidding in the dirt like a bull getting ready to charge.

Brian's shoulders were knotted up with tension, and a cold, twisting feeling filled his gut. Pressure began to build in his bladder. He could feel the truck driver's eyes boring into his back the closer he got to the woods.

What the fuck is his problem?

The driver continued to rev his engine. When he was about twenty feet away from the woods, walking faster now, Brian took one last look over his shoulder at the truck.

It was still sitting there. Still idling. Still chugging thick exhaust into the sky. He tried not to imagine the face of the unseen man, glowering at him as he watched him move away.

Finally, unable to take the pressure any longer, Brian broke into a run. Within seconds, he entered the woods. His sneakers slapped the hard-packed ground as he followed the narrow, winding path farther into the woods where the shadows were deep and cool. Twigs snapped underfoot, and branches whipped his face and arms, but all he cared about was getting away from the construction site. When he finally dared to look back, he could no longer see the pickup truck. He continued to run because all he could imagine was that the driver had gotten out and was now chasing after him.

Tightening fear made him run all the faster. His breath burned in his lungs, and running over the uneven ground made his bladder feel like it was about to explode, but he ran as fast as he could.

The path was narrow, with trees pressing in on both sides, blocking out the slanting afternoon sunlight. Up ahead, Brian could see that it curved around to the left. He knew this would eventually bring him back onto Ridge Road. He only hoped he would exit the woods near enough to the house so he could make it home without any trouble.

Trouble? What kind of trouble did he expect? He hadn't

done anything wrong, but he couldn't shake the feeling that the man in the truck was going to come after him.

What if he knows about this path? Brian thought. *He must, and if he does, then he knows where it comes back out on the road.*

The thought filled Brian with fear.

Maybe he'll drive down the road and wait for me to come out of the woods. Maybe he's already there, waiting!

A faint whimper escaped Brian as he ran. The wind burned his throat. The ground was uneven, and there were several low spots that were filled with muddy water, but Brian splashed through them, not thinking about anything except getting back to the house.

Where I'll be safe!

At last, through the dense screen of foliage, he saw the flat expanse of the road up ahead. He slowed to a jog and then drew to a halt. Leaning forward and placing both hands on his knees, he tried to catch his breath. His throat felt like it had been singed with fire.

He listened but didn't hear anything except the chorus of birdsong coming from the woods. Crouching low and moving as silently as he could, he crept closer to the road, scanning all around as he went. Images from dozens of horror movies played in his mind, and he cringed, expecting the shadowy man to burst suddenly from the woods and attack him with a long, sharp blade.

"Cut it out. You're just being a jerk," he whispered hoarsely to himself. He was trying to gather his courage, but he couldn't relieve the tension that made him feel ready either to run or fight if he had to.

But I won't have to. I'm safe.

He felt foolish, getting so scared, but he ducked to one side of the path and kept himself hidden as much as possible as he leaned forward and looked out at the road.

The air above the pavement shimmered with afternoon heat, but there was no one in sight in either direction.

No rusty, red pickup truck.

No shadowy, knife-wielding figure.

Brian was still trying to catch his breath, so he waited a few minutes while his pulse slowed and he started breathing more evenly.

"Okay, okay," he whispered to himself. "There's nothing to worry about. Jesus, stop acting like a jerk!"

He knew he had overreacted, but even so, he couldn't figure out what the driver in the pickup truck had been up to.

Why did he just sit there like that? Was he watching me? Or didn't he even realize I was there?

No, he had known Brian was there. Brian was positive of that. Why else would he have revved his engine the way he had, as if challenging him or trying to scare him.

Well, he did a good job of that, Brian thought as he wiped his hand over his sweat-slick face. His sneakers were soaked through and caked with mud. They squished with each step as he broke cover and moved cautiously up the embankment and onto the road.

Still nothing in either direction. No cars, no trucks, and no knife-wielding maniacs.

Brian took a deep breath and forced himself to loosen his clenched fists. His mouth and throat were dry as dust as he looked down the tree-lined road. The driveway leading up to his father's house was no more than a hundred yards away. He knew he could make it easily. He was safe.

Inhaling sharply, Brian started down the road, moving at a fast pace, but not running.

What was he afraid of?

He hadn't done anything wrong.

That guy, whoever he was, wasn't after him. Probably just some local jerk . . . maybe a teenager who'd gone out there with his girlfriend and a six-pack and condom to have a little fun, and who didn't want anyone else around.

Brian was about halfway between where the path joined the road and the driveway to the house when, from behind, he heard the sputtering sound of an engine. His heart gave a quick, heavy throb in his throat when he turned and saw the red pickup coming down the road in his direction.

"Jesus Christ," he whispered.

Brian darted across the road, feeling a little foolish for running away like this as if he had done something wrong or was in some kind of danger. Fists clenched and arms pumping steadily at his sides, he started running toward the driveway. He was pretty sure he could make it to the yard before the truck caught up with him, but the hairs on the nape of his neck bristled as he listened to the truck, getting closer behind him, its cylinders sputtering irregularly. Another quick glance over his shoulder showed him that the truck was gaining on him.

Fast!

He might not make it in time.

Pouring it on, Brian bent his head down and ran as fast as he could. He tried not to think that as soon as the truck was right behind him, it would swerve across the opposite lane and run him down. He didn't want to imagine the loud clunk his body would make as it bounced off the hood of the truck, adding one more dent to the rusted metal before sailing off into the puckerbrush that lined the side of the road.

His feet slapped hard against the asphalt, sending little jolts of electric pain up the backs of his legs. His lungs were burning from the exertion. He cringed as he listened to the truck getting louder and louder the closer it got, but he didn't dare turn and look again because he was afraid he might stumble and fall, making it all the easier for the driver to run over him.

No, he's not going to run me over!

"Fucking bastard!" Brian whispered through gritted teeth as he ran. "What the *fuck* is your problem?"

The truck was almost on top of him now. He could practically feel the heat of its engine bearing down on him. In his mind, he imagined it was a charging bull with heated breath blowing like a furnace over the back of his neck. Sweat ran down his face, stinging in his eyes.

The turn into the driveway wasn't far away now.

Only a hundred feet or so.

Brian was suddenly convinced that he wasn't going to make it. His body strained with the effort. His arm and leg muscles felt like they were going to rip loose. Random, panicked thoughts filled his mind as he imagined his mother or father finding him squashed on the roadside . . . his friends back home in Massachusetts gathering at his funeral . . . his room back home, in his real home, empty and deserted.

The truck's engine raced louder as the driver shifted gears, gaining speed, zeroing in on him. Brian wanted to scream or cry or simply just disappear.

This isn't happening! he thought with a tug of desperation. *This can't be happening to me!*

He was at the limit of his endurance. In a few more steps, he was either going to make it or fall face first onto the side of the road, and the truck's tires were going to squash him into the pavement.

Maybe it will be quick and painless, he thought, but even if it wasn't, he knew with a dread certainty that he was going to be dead soon.

But he was closer.

The driveway was only twenty feet away.

Brian stared straight ahead at it, reaching for it with outstretched, clawing hands like a drowning man who was grasping for the shimmering glow of the sky above the surface of the water as he sank deeper and deeper.

No, goddamn it! I'm gonna make it! I'm gonna make it!

He strained forward. He almost couldn't believe it when he made it to the driveway entrance and drew up to a skidding halt. He made sure he kept the large maple tree at the foot of the driveway between him and the approaching truck. It wasn't far behind him, now, but Brian was surprised to see that it hadn't swerved across the lane in an attempt to run him down. In fact, it hadn't veered from its lane at all. It was just racing down the road, perhaps a little fast for a country road, but nothing out of the ordinary if the driver was a local who knew the road well.

"Son of a bitch," Brian whispered hoarsely as he leaned

forward with both hands on his knees and watched the truck speed by in a swirl of dust and exhaust. He caught only a fleeting glimpse of the driver through the now-closed side window. It was a man in silhouette who was staring straight ahead at the road. He didn't even bother to glance at Brian as he went by, but once he was past, he tooted the horn a couple of quick blasts and raised his hand as though in friendly greeting.

"You son of a bitch!" Brian yelled as he straightened up and shook his fist at the rapidly receding truck.

He thought to notice the driver's plate number so he could report him to the police, but the driver really hadn't done anything wrong except maybe make Brian look and feel foolish.

As the truck sped away, its cloud of smelly exhaust lingered in the air. Brian watched it go, and before it was out of sight around the bend in the road, he noticed the peeling bumper sticker stuck to the rear fender of the truck.

It read:

**FRIENDS DON'T LET FRIENDS
DRIVE CHEVYS**

seven

"Where have you been? Good Lord, look at your sneakers!"

When Brian showed up at the house late that afternoon, Polly was so mad she was trembling. She couldn't believe that, after disappearing for most of the day without leaving word where he was, he had the gall to show up looking like he did and acting as though he had done absolutely nothing wrong.

"What do you mean?" he said, shrugging as he looked at her, all innocence. "I was just out."

Polly noticed the tiniest little catch in his voice, but she let it pass. He certainly looked guilty, like he knew he'd done something wrong, but he wasn't going to admit to anything.

Not yet, anyway.

"Well *you* can clean those sneakers yourself," Polly said, pointing at his mud-crusted sneakers. "*I* certainly will not! And you know better than to track mud into the kitchen like that. I spent a good part of the day scrubbing this floor on my hands and knees."

"Sorry. I'll clean 'em. Don't worry," Brian said, lowering his gaze and seeming a little more contrite. "I was just out for a walk in the woods, and I . . . I didn't even notice that they'd gotten so bad."

He paused again, like he knew he was lying to her or trying to hide something.

"Well you *should* have noticed," Polly snapped.

She wished she could control her anger, but she was still angry at him for disappearing for so long. It would be foolish to tell him how worried she and his father had been, at least right now. It would sound phony, like she was trying to guilt him into confessing something. Besides, he knew better. They had always emphasized to him how important it was for him to let them know where he was going and what he was doing. Just because they were away from their usual routine for a few weeks didn't mean all the rules that applied at home had been suspended.

"Your father and I have been working really hard here all day trying to get this place cleaned up, and you . . . you're off doing . . . *what?* Off gallivanting in the woods, and then you come home with your new sneakers looking like *this!*"

She sighed and shook her head in frustration.

Brian raised his eyes, blinking rapidly as he looked straight at her. For a flickering instant, she thought he was going to say something, but then he lowered his head again and, letting his shoulders slouch, sighed.

"I . . . I'm really sorry," he said, so softly she could hardly hear him. "I won't do it again, I promise."

"You're darned right you won't!" Polly said, almost a snarl. "We'll be eating in an hour or so, and after supper I want you to help us with the cleaning. I figure you can get started by taking a bucket of water and Lysol and wash the living room walls and ceiling."

"Ahh, come on, Mom," Brian said, holding his hands out with a pained, persecuted expression.

But Polly wasn't buying any of it. He knew the rules.

"You take those sneakers outside right *now*," she said. "Your father turned on the water to the outside faucet, so you can rinse them off there and then leave them on the back steps to dry."

"And what am I supposed to wear?" Brian asked.

Polly sniffed and shook her head. "You should have thought about that before you went wallowing around in the mud. Besides, you're not going anywhere tonight. You're helping us. Understood?"

Again, Brian opened his mouth and almost said something; then he nodded his agreement before turning around and going back outside. The screen door slammed shut behind him. Polly stood there, staring outside until she realized there was someone standing behind her, watching her. She turned around quickly and saw Tim in the living room doorway. There was a faint smile of amusement on his lips.

"What?" she snapped, still angry.

Tim sniffed and shook his head.

"A little hard on him, don't you think?" he said mildly. "I mean, it's not like he's a five-year-old."

"My point exactly," she said. "And I don't care *how* old he is, while he's living with me, he can't just take off on his own without letting one of us know what he's up to."

"He *did* leave a note," Tim said.

"Yeah. Saying he was going for a walk. Big deal. No mention of where he was going or how long he'd be gone. Sorry, Tim, but that just doesn't cut it."

Tim's smile tightened. Like her, he was wearing yellow rubber gloves for scrubbing, which he now peeled off and dropped into the sink before walking over to her and giving her a big hug.

"I know," he said softly as he pulled her close and nuzzled against her neck. "You were worried about him all day long, and this is just your way of letting him know that you care."

"Oh, cut it out," Polly said, feeling a rush of anger directed at him. "I'm really mad at him, okay? And yes, I was worried. You mean you weren't?"

"Not really," Tim said. "But then again, I grew up around here. If anything feels safe to me, it's here."

At first, Polly resisted her husband's hug, but after a moment she allowed him to draw her closer. Moaning softly, she ran her rubber-gloved hands up his back, hearing the faint squeaking sounds they made as she clung to him. Unaccountably, her eyes began to fill with tears that threatened to fall. She tried to convince herself that it was from the fumes of all the cleaning agents they had been using all day, but she knew better. She had been wound up and close to tears all day, worrying about Brian. Now that he was home safely, she could let herself feel everything she'd been holding back.

At least to herself she could admit that she had been more than worried about her son while he was gone. She had been close to hysterical because she had been absolutely convinced that something terrible had happened to him. She had felt it in her bones. Throughout the day, as she and Tim had worked at cleaning the house, she hadn't been able to stop thinking that soon she and Tim were going to find out exactly what the Olsens were going through after losing their daughter. Cold, heavy dread filled her mind, squeezing all life and hope out of her. Before long, her tears were falling as she desperately hugged her husband, praying that she could lose herself in the safety and security of his embrace.

But Brian's home. He's safe and sound, and that's all that matters.

She squeezed her eyes tightly shut as tears rolled down her face. She was so choked up with pent-up emotion her throat closed off, making it difficult for her to breathe or swallow.

—But he saw him—

The voice spoke in her head so suddenly and so clearly that she easily could have mistaken it for Tim if it hadn't been for the lilting, little-girl tone which Polly recognized immediately.

A wave of dizziness swept through her, filling her head

with hissing, twinkling lights that flashed in the darkness behind her closed eyes. For a terrifying moment, Polly felt curiously detached from her body, as if she were floating and tumbling in a dark void with no up or down, no left or right. She was vaguely aware that she had lost muscle tone, and her body was sagging limply in her husband's arms. She tried to move but found even the slightest motion impossible.

He saw who? she thought, struggling desperately against the rushing waves of vertigo that were pulling at her, trying to suck her down.

—He saw him. . . . I don't know who he is . . . but he's out there. . . . He's one of the ones I can see . . . outside the window . . . outside the white room—

Sour nausea churned in Polly's stomach. Her tears, hot and searing, ran down her cheeks as she squeezed her eyes tightly shut and tried to concentrate. The voice inside her head seemed distant, faint. Instead of hearing it, it seemed almost like she *saw* it . . . like a candle that was almost burned out, sputtering as it struggled to stay lit.

Tell me who he is! Polly heard the thought like an angry shout inside her head. *Tell me what happened! What did you see outside the white room?*

—I don't know. . . . I'm not sure. . . . I've never seen him before. . . . I don't recognize him . . . but I can tell that he's dangerous . . . and he's angry. . . . I can feel it like . . . like poison in his heart—

"Are you all right? Pol?"

Tim's voice cut through to her, making Polly jump. She concentrated for a moment, wondering where he was. He sounded so close, but that other voice—Heather's voice—while fainter, seemed much closer.

No, I'm not all right, she thought.

She was so confused she wasn't sure if she said it out

loud or not. The darkness was swelling like a storm-tossed ocean all around her. Vibrating tiny points of light hissed with loud static. Something seemed to shift, but Polly was so confused she couldn't determine if it was the darkness around her or something inside her. Suddenly she felt herself falling as the darkness deepened and closed in on her. The next thing she knew, she felt like she was lying down on something hard and looking up at a dark silhouette that hovered over her.

"Polly?"

The voice was distorted, full of echo, and the face leaned closer. She couldn't see it clearly enough to recognize, but there was something familiar about it. Behind the head and shoulders were bright, shimmering lights that rapidly shifted through the spectrum. Spikes of blue and violet light predominated, radiating above and behind this person's head like a halo.

For a dizzying instant, Polly thought that she might have died and that this was an angel, come to escort her to the other side of life. She had the curious sensation of not breathing and not needing to breathe, as though the light that surrounded this person was all she needed to enervate her mind and soul.

But after a strange, timeless moment, Polly became aware of the steady thundering of her pulse. As she stared upward, she finally recognized that it was Tim who was leaning over her.

"Jesus, Polly," he said. His voice sounded much more like him. It was no longer so distorted. "Are you all right?"

Polly's lungs burned from lack of oxygen, so she couldn't answer him right away. Her lips felt like they were cracked and peeling. They stuck to her teeth when she tried to speak, no matter how much she licked them. As her vision gradually cleared, she saw the expression of concern on her husband's face.

She realized that she had passed out.

She wondered how long, but there was no way of

telling. It could have been only a few seconds or several hours.

"Can you stand up?" Tim asked. He sounded really worried about her.

Polly felt his hands slide around behind her back and begin to lift her. She wanted to stand up on her own, but all the muscles and bones in her body seemed disconnected.

"Come on. Let's get you outside so you can get some fresh air," Tim said.

Somehow—she wasn't sure how—Polly found herself standing up. With Tim holding her tightly, moving like people doing a carnival three-legged race, they made their way to the kitchen door. The brightness outside stung her eyes. Her vision was swimming with tiny amorphous shapes that looked like a crazy whirl of one-celled animals.

"Whoa! What happened to Mom?"

That was Brian's voice. Polly was thankful that she recognized it, and as soon as she did, an almost overwhelming sadness filled her. The love she felt for her son filled her like the strong, steady blast of the sun's warmth. She wanted to say something to him, tell him how much she loved him and worried about him, but she still couldn't get enough air into her lungs to speak.

"Probably was breathing ammonia fumes too long," Tim said as he half dragged her down the porch steps and into the sunlight. A cool breeze curled around her, sending chills through her body, but she could feel herself reviving.

Her legs felt board stiff as she walked, a little more under her own power, over to the weathered wooden chairs under the apple trees by the side of the house. She was trembling inside as she cautiously lowered herself into one of the chairs and leaned back. Looking up, she saw the confusing riot of green leaves dancing against the clear blue of the sky.

"Feeling a little better?" Tim asked, his voice still edged with concern.

Polly tried to reply but could only make a deep grunt in the back of her throat as she nodded.

"Man, oh *man,* you gave me a scare," Tim said, followed by a nervous chuckle.

Polly looked at him and smiled weakly, then raised her hand and touched him lightly on the face.

Yes, she thought, *he's real.*

She knew that she wasn't imagining all of this and that she hadn't died. She had just blacked out for a moment. The more she thought about it, the more it made sense that she had been breathing fumes from the cleaning agents all day. No wonder she had passed out.

"Want a glass of water?" Brian asked.

Polly rolled her head to one side and saw him standing close by, a pinched, worried expression on his face.

Now maybe he knows a little bit how much I worry about him, she thought.

"Yeah," she said. "Some water would be nice."

She was surprised by the strength of her voice. At most, she had been expecting her voice to be a raw whisper. Without another word, Brian turned and darted back into the house.

"You're probably not feeling up to cooking supper tonight, and I know I sure am not," Tim said, "so what do you say we clean ourselves up and head into town for supper. Pizza and beer at Corsetti's sounds good to me."

Polly forced a smile and nodded weakly.

"Umm. Sounds good to me, too," she said.

A moment later, Brian was back with a glass of water. She smiled when she saw that he had even taken the time to put some ice and a wedge of lemon in it.

"Thanks, honey," she said. Holding the glass with both hands, she took a quick sip. The cold wetness felt indescribably good as the citrus flavor exploded in her mouth, but there was something else; the hint of another taste lingered on her tongue after she had swallowed the first mouthful. At first she couldn't quite identify it, but with the second swallow she realized what it was.

The water tasted like it had garlic in it.

Frowning, she glanced at Brian. She wanted to ask if

this was bottled water or if he had gotten it from the tap, but she didn't want to hurt his feelings. If this was from the tap, no wonder it tasted funny. But she still felt guilty about yelling at him earlier, so she let it pass and, smiling wider, took another sip even though it almost gagged her.

"There . . . I'm feeling better now," she said huskily as she leaned forward and placed the glass carefully on the ground by her feet.

Leaning back in the chair, she looked up at the sky through the leaves. The bright blue hurt her eyes. There was still plenty of daylight left, and they could get a lot more cleaning done if they got to it, but she'd had enough for one day. It wasn't like they were in a race or anything to get the house cleaned. They'd do what they could and screw the rest. Chances were, Rob wasn't going to agree to putting the house on the market, anyway, so why bust their asses cleaning up the place? Just as long as it was livable for a few weeks. That was all they needed.

"What do you say to pizza in town?" Polly asked Brian.

His smile looked a bit thin as he nodded his agreement.

"Does this mean I'm off the hook?" he asked. Polly was relieved to see that his smile seemed a bit more genuine.

"Yeah," she said, reaching out and touching the back of his hand. "Sorry for losing it. But you *really* can't just disappear like that. You have to let us know what you're up to."

"I know . . . I know," Brian said.

"Come on, then," Tim said as he clapped his hands together. "It *is* our vacation, after all, so what say we have ourselves a night out on the town?"

"Whew! Running a little rich, I'd say," Tim said as he waved his hand in front of his face. Coughing softly, he switched off the ignition and stepped out of the old car.

The barn had instantly filled with thick, billowing blue smoke that was shot through with golden sunbeams that streaked through the dirty windows and the cracks in the wall. Five or six barn swallows chirped loudly as they darted about in the rafters overhead, disturbed by the sudden sound and smoke.

When they had gotten back from having supper at Corsetti's, everyone had agreed that they'd done enough cleaning for one day. It was time to relax. Brian had wanted to go up to his bedroom to check if there was any E-mail from his friends back home, but Tim had suggested that they see if, working together, they could get his father's old relic out in the barn to start up.

That was pretty much the last thing Brian wanted to do, but he didn't see an out; so for the last hour or so, he and his father had been tinkering under the hood of his grandfather's old car. After checking the fluids, they had topped off the radiator and battery with water, tightened a few loose connections, and then his dad had turned the key.

For a few seconds, the car had run, but certainly not smoothly. The engine had knocked and sputtered as it spewed thick exhaust from the tailpipe. All cylinders weren't firing, that was for sure. Brian was glad he had been ready for it and had covered his face with both hands just before his father turned the key.

"That's to be expected, I guess," Tim said as he swung the car door shut and walked around to the front of the car. The hood was raised, and he leaned forward, looking intently at the engine as though it would give him the answers he needed. "The surprise is that it turned over at all."

The exhaust stung Brian's eyes, making him blink rapidly, so he walked over to the open barn door and stuck his head outside to catch a breath of fresh air. Remembering what had happened to his mother earlier with the cleaning chemicals, he wasn't about to let himself get asphyxiated.

"How long do you think it's been since it's even been started?" Brian asked, followed by a light cough.

Bracing both hands wide on the fender, his father leaned over the engine and studied it. It was obvious that he had no idea what to do next to make the car run any better. The cylinder heads were caked with oil, and the distributor cap and leads were corroded. He didn't bother to look back at Brian when he said, "Maybe Uncle Rob gave it a crank or two every now and then, but I'll bet this baby's been sitting here for three or four years, at least. Grandpa stopped driving it five or six years ago. Maybe I should have it towed to the station to get a tune-up."

Brian grunted. "I don't see why you'd even keep it," he said. "The thing's a piece of junk."

Tim straightened up and glared at him, an expression of absolute shock on his face. Huffing as he folded his arms across his chest, he looked from his son to his father's old car, a 1973 Olds Cutlass Sierra. When the car was new, the blue paint had been beautiful, but it had long since faded to a dull shade of robin's egg blue. The side panels and fenders were so badly pitted with rust they looked like the surface of the moon, and there was a spiderweb crack in the center of the rear window. The roof, hood, and trunk were thick with bird droppings from years of having been left uncovered in the barn. The tires had little—if any—tread left, and clots of spiderwebs hung in the rusty wheel wells. The dashboard was littered with dirt and the husks of dead insects.

"Piece of junk?" Tim finally said, his voice rising. "You call this . . . this work of *art* a piece of *junk*?"

"Yeah, I think I just did," Brian said with a twisted half smile.

"Why, my boy, this car is an American *classic*. In another couple of years, in fact, just about the time you'll be getting your driver's license, it'll be an antique."

Brian sniffed with laughter, not quite sure if his father was being funny or serious. Maybe a little of both.

"Tell you what, then," Brian said. "From now on, you can drive this, and I'll drive the SUV, okay?"

"I'm tellin' you, they don't make cars like this anymore." Tim slapped the flat of his hand against the side panel. Brian tensed, half expecting the car to cave in from the impact.

"Umm, and maybe it's a good thing, too," Brian replied. He rubbed his eyes, still burning from the exhaust.

"No, seriously. This car was made back when they built them to last. Course, when *I* was growing up here, we had an even better car. My friends and I had this old Chevy. I think it was a '48 or '49—"

"Nineteen forty-nine or *eighteen* forty-nine?"

"Nineteen forty-nine, wise guy," Tim said with a chuckle. "A big old green thing that we kept out in the woods. We'd lug out five-gallon cans of gasoline, fill it up, and roar up and down the old dirt roads."

"Great," Brian said, totally unimpressed.

"Yeah, well, you can't do stuff like that nowadays," his father continued. His eyes had taken on that same distant focus he'd had last night in his bedroom, when he was waxing nostalgic about his childhood.

"Hell, if you did something like that today and something happened, if one of your friends got hurt or whatever, there'd be lawsuits flying all over the place."

"Hey! What's burning out here? Is everything all right?"

His mother's voice startled Brian. Both he and his father turned to see her standing in the doorway of the barn with one hand covering her nose and mouth while she waved the other in front of her face.

"It smells . . . terrible."

"Yeah, well, we managed to get it started," Tim said. He snapped his fingers as if he'd just performed a magic trick. Brian couldn't miss the look of genuine pride on his father's face, but that expression quickly faded when his mother, still covering her nose and mouth with one hand, moved closer to the car and looked at it.

"Tell me, why in the world would you want to drive a piece of junk like this in the first place?"

"That's exactly what I was saying," Brian interjected, laughing. He quickly wished he'd kept his mouth shut when he saw how crestfallen his father looked.

Frowning deeply as he stared at them, his father sadly

shook his head. "This is a great car," he said, "and who knows? We might need it sometime. You never know."

Polly regarded him in silence for a lengthening moment, then chuckled softly to herself.

"Right," she muttered. A faint smile played at the corners of her mouth. "Getting that rust bucket to start is pretty good, I'll grant you that, but if you ever get this thing to pass inspection, *then* you'll be a miracle worker."

Without another word, she turned and walked out of the barn and headed back into the house. Brian saw his father open his mouth as if to say something, but then he turned back to the car. Arms folded across his chest, he stood there staring at it for a long time.

"Women," he finally muttered, as much to himself as to Brian. "They just don't understand."

"Yeah," Brian said, nodding in agreement, but truthfully, he wasn't sure he understood, either.

The night wind billowed the bedroom curtains in and out, in and out. From somewhere deep in the woods, a whippoorwill sang its lonely song. Tim was sound asleep in bed beside Polly, but like the other nights so far in the old house, she found that sleep wouldn't come, at least not easily. She flirted around the edges of it, dipping down and then startling herself awake with a jump and silent cry. She'd started thinking about maybe buying some sleeping pills to help her drift off.

She had no idea why she was feeling so tense, but she sighed and yawned and settled her head in the pillow, trying to relax her shoulder muscles. No sooner had she closed her eyes and started taking deep, calming breaths, though, but she would realize that her shoulder and back muscles were all bunched up again and she'd open her eyes and look around the darkened room.

"Jesus, this is ridiculous," she whispered into the darkness.

She wanted to get out of bed and go downstairs, maybe

brew a cup of herbal tea to see if that would help settle her, but she stayed where she was, not quite finding the energy—or daring—to get out of bed.

Her gaze kept being drawn to the bedroom windows where the sheer curtains billowed in and out . . . in and out. A strange image filled her mind, and she found herself imagining that the house was a living creature, and that the curtains were its lungs. The creature was softly and steadily breathing the warm night air in and out . . . in and out.

In a vague, dreamy sort of way, Polly realized that she was flitting between wakefulness and sleep. She found it relaxing and elaborated on the idea that the house was a living thing. Before long, she found herself thinking that the hall outside her bedroom was the living house's throat. As the wind sighed gently in and out of the open windows, she imagined that she could hear a deep, sonorous voice, whispering to her from out of the darkness.

That thought was mildly disturbing, but Polly let herself go with it. She floated as though suddenly weightless and drifted about on the night wind that circulated through the dark house. From somewhere downstairs, she heard a muffled banging sound and thought that maybe the kitchen screen door was blowing back and forth in the breeze as the house breathed.

A curious chill raced through her as she pricked her ears and tried to listen more intently. She wanted to hear what the voice that was dancing on the wind might be saying. While she had the distinct impression that words were being said, she couldn't begin to make sense of them. Her slight feeling of discomfort intensified, taking hold of her when she thought that maybe the house really had something to say to her . . . something that she *needed* to hear.

Or is that Heather's voice? she thought as another, stronger spike of fear jabbed her.

She hadn't heard Heather speak inside her head since last night and wondered if maybe she had gone away. Now the thought struck Polly that maybe Heather's voice had blended with the voice of the house or had actually become the voice of the house.

Subtle, tingling currents of apprehension ran through her, and she imagined that the voice on the wind was simultaneously inside her head and outside her, and that it was her fault for not listening more carefully and understanding what it was saying to her.

Faint, hollow whistling sounds swirled all around her. In Polly's mind, the sounds mixed with her other senses until she imagined that she could see the sounds as shimmering blue lights that flickered across her retina, and that she could feel them twisting around inside her like slow-moving currents of cold water, and smell them as faint, indistinct odors that had a vague and unnerving familiarity.

She shivered and cuddled deeper under the covers. The sheets felt cold and damp with sweat. She reached out to touch Tim's hand but couldn't feel it, even though she could hear him snoring beside her.

Or was that the house, breathing and whispering to her in the night?

Are you still here, Heather?

She closed her eyes and concentrated hard on reaching out to the little girl. In a small corner of her mind, she knew that it was ridiculous to think she could communicate with the dead girl, but another, larger part of her seemed to accept it as totally natural.

Can you hear me, Heather?

Although it continued to rasp and hiss in the darkness, the voice inside the house didn't reply.

Polly had the curious sensation that, although she knew her eyes were closed, she could—somehow—still see as if her closed eyelids had become transparent. She watched the gauzy curtains drift lazily in and out . . . in and out, and all the while the voice in the dark whispered secrets to her that she didn't understand on a conscious level, but which she sensed she did understand deep inside her mind.

What are you trying to tell me?

The feeling that something was wrong grew steadily

stronger inside her. She realized that the night or the house or *something* was hiding nearby, lurking in the darkness and shadows, and that something had eyes and was watching her.

Right now!

She could feel and smell and see the chilling gaze brushing against her skin like ice.

Someone or something was probing her with a cold, unblinking stare, and Polly was suddenly convinced that this hadn't just started. She was suddenly positive that it had been going on for a while—ever since they first arrived at the house. It was only now, when her defenses were down and she was drifting in that weird borderland place between sleeping and waking that she could even begin to feel it.

And see it and smell it and touch it!

Wake up! she commanded herself as her sense of imminent danger grew stronger.

Wake up! Right now!

A soft, strangled cry filled her throat, but she could barely make a sound as she struggled back to consciousness like a swimmer who had dived too deeply and who was now reaching up to the sunlit surface that glittered impossibly high above her. She wasn't at all certain that she had enough air in her lungs to reach the top. Cold, iron bands squeezed her chest, making her ribs ache. A cold, clammy sensation gripped her like huge, unseen hands that wanted to drag her down deeper into the blackness and hold her there until it was too late.

No . . . no! . . . NO!

Polly wanted to cry out. She wanted desperately to resist this powerful downward pull with everything she had, but her body felt strangely drained of strength . . . limp . . . useless. The thought crossed her mind that if she let herself go, if she didn't struggle and let herself sink down deeper into the darkness, she would hear the voice more clearly. She might even be able to understand what it was saying to her.

But she also knew that, if she let herself go that deep, it might be too far. She might be too far gone to come back. She might die.

No! . . . NO! . . . I don't want to die!

Tingling rushes of fear swept up her back and clutched her throat. Her arms and legs stiffened as though paralyzed by a powerful electric current. Her back arched, and her heels and elbows vibrated as they pressed down hard against the mattress, making the old bedsprings squeak terribly. Then, without warning, something inside her made a loud snapping sound. Polly's eyes shot open, and she found herself lying on her back, staring up at the gray square of the bedroom ceiling.

Her throat was raw and burning as she took a ragged breath of the warm night air. Slick tracks of tears were running from her eyes. A terrible sour taste that seemed horribly familiar filled her mouth. For several heartbeats, she just lay there, staring in horror at the gray shadows that shifted across the bedroom ceiling and walls. She was immobilized by the fear that the night shadows would gradually solidify and become three-dimensional, and then reach out for her. Cringing back on the bed, she waited to feel their cold, insubstantial touch. She wanted to cry out but couldn't.

After a few moments, her panic began to subside, and she managed to take a deep, calming breath.

"Jesus," she whispered, listening to the rasping sound of her voice. It sounded odd in the darkness and frighteningly close.

Every muscle and joint in her body ached, and she was surprised to find that she could move at all as she tossed the sweat-damp bed sheet aside and swung her feet to the floor. She cowered, imagining that something cold and dead and rotting would reach out from underneath the bed and grab her ankles, but that didn't happen as she shifted her weight forward and shakily stood up. The loud creaking of the old bedsprings didn't seem to bother Tim, who slept on undisturbed.

Polly was trembling terribly inside. She felt weak and completely wrung out as she walked to the bedroom window and knelt down on the wooden floor. The coolness of the wood penetrated the thin fabric of her nightgown and chilled her as she leaned forward. Her breasts pressed against the windowsill as she pulled aside the curtain and looked outside.

Bluish silver moonlight cast ink-wash shadows across the lawn. The trees that bordered the yard swayed gently in the night breeze, their branches and leaves rustling softly. They looked like black lace against the star-dusted sky. Crickets were chirring softly in the darkness, and from deep within the woods there came the solitary song of a whippoorwill.

Closing her eyes, Polly rolled her head from side to side as she inhaled deeply, letting the moist, earth-smelling night air fill her lungs. Almost against her will, she opened her eyes and shifted her gaze over to the small shed in the side yard. The shingles looked chalk white in the moonlight, and the trailing vines cast black, twisting shadows that looked like veins against the wood. The single window was slate black except for in the upper right-hand corner, where it caught and reflected back a distorted image of the moon.

Polly shivered, remembering the pale face she had seen—or thought she had seen—in that window. She found herself wondering if that face might still be there, staring at her, its dead eyes reflecting the pale glow of the crescent moon.

A subtle thrill ran through her body as she looked out at the silent, peaceful night. She sucked in a quick breath, held it for a moment, then let it out slowly.

"Talk to me," she whispered. She couldn't help but feel as though she were saying a prayer. "Talk to me . . . please. . . . I promise you I'll listen."

eight

The rusty key felt heavier than it seemed it should as Polly bounced it up and down in the palm of her hand. She was standing on the back steps, her body turned a little to the left so she could see the old shed that stood across the driveway on the fringe of the woods.

She and Tim had spent the morning washing the kitchen ceiling and giving it a fresh coat of white paint. It looked like it was going to need at least one more coat if not two to cover up the grease and water stains. While the first coat was drying, Tim had decided to drive into town to have lunch with his brother. He had asked Polly to come with him, but she had no wish to see Rob and had decided to stay at the house.

Brian had helped them in the morning, but after lunch she had given him permission to take off. It seemed as though when he wasn't up in his room chatting on-line with his friends back home, he was moping around the house, acting lonely and bored. She had hoped that he'd make friends with some of the local kids, but that didn't seem very likely. Not if he didn't get out. She tried not to feel a stirring of resentment at Tim for his decision to return home for the summer because it put Brian in such a lousy situation. She hoped he would make the best of it.

But with Brian gone, that left her alone at the house, and the old shed with its sagging roofline, vine-covered walls, and blank, dirt-glazed window seemed to beckon her to come over and have a little look inside. It made her nervous, but her curiosity also drew her to it.

She shivered, remembering how the shed had looked last night as she gazed down at it from her bedroom window. That seemed so long ago, now, like it was in a dream. She could only recall remnants of what she had been thinking as she drifted off to sleep last night . . . something about the house being alive and breathing and trying to talk to her or something. In the harsh glare of daylight, none of it made much sense, but she was still left with a strange, disoriented feeling.

One thing she did remember clearly was looking at the shed and seeing the distorted reflection of moonlight in the glass. She remembered how when they had first arrived here she had thought she had seen a face in the window, staring at her. Just the thought of it made her shiver.

It was foolish, of course.

She knew that. It didn't make sense that anyone would be lurking about in the shed. Tim had shown her that the door was locked, and they had both walked around the shed to make sure that there weren't any holes in the wall or a broken window out back where someone could have gained entry.

Still, there was something about that shed that drew her to it.

As soon as Tim left for the afternoon, she had started thinking about unlocking the door and having a look inside if only to assure herself—finally—that there was nothing to worry about. It was just an old, falling-down shed that should probably be torn down or burned after the many years' worth of accumulated junk in it had been carted off to the dump.

The sun was warm on her face, and Polly felt damp rings of sweat in her armpits and around her neck as she walked down the steps and started across the gravel driveway to the shed. She licked her upper lip, tasting the salt, and realized just how nervous she was. Her hand holding the key was tightly clenched, and she had to purposely relax her grip so the rusted metal wouldn't cut into the palm of her hand.

She knew there was no reason to be afraid.

It was foolish.

There was nothing out there.

She was simply letting her imagination get the better of her, running away from her. She couldn't deny that she was still feeling vulnerable, especially since what happened at the hospital with Heather. She was feeling fragile inside and wished, if she couldn't talk to Tim about it, then at least Lois was around so she could unburden herself.

But it's just your imagination!

She could already hear Tim and Lois saying it to her.

There wasn't anyone hiding out there, and there isn't now!

For her own peace of mind, though, she had to take one quick look inside. She hadn't mentioned anything to Tim, knowing what his reaction would be. Ever since she lost her own baby, he had seemed a little worried about her mental stability. It was nothing overt, but from time to time he would suggest that she might want to see someone, a therapist she could talk to. Now, after seeing what had happened to Heather, he seemed even more tentative about her stability. The last thing she wanted was for him to know how upset she was about this shed. She would never even consider asking him to come out here with her.

She had to face it on her own.

As she approached the building, her breath came in sharp, shallow hitches that hurt her chest. Sunlight glaring off the gray, weathered shingles stung her eyes. Dried vines from last summer were intertwined with this year's new growth that was crawling up over the sides of the building and onto the roof like green, grasping hands. Wasps and yellow jackets hummed and bounced around the eaves. Polly could see several of their small paper cone hives in the blue shadows under the roofline.

You don't have to be doing this, she told herself.

But on a deeper level, she knew that she did.

It was always better, she believed, to confront what was bothering her head-on rather than turn away from it and let it fester and grow. Once she had proven to herself that there was nothing here to worry about, she could put it behind her and forget about it. After that, if she ever thought she saw a face or caught a hint of motion behind the window, she could dismiss it as nothing more than her overactive imagination.

Still, her hands were sweaty and trembling as she fit the rusty key into the lock and started to turn it. The lock, an old-fashioned hasp model, was rusted as badly as the key, and it didn't turn easily. Because her hands were slick with sweat, she almost lost her grip on it as she gritted her teeth and twisted it as hard as she could. At first the lock didn't seem to want to yield. She was thinking that maybe she should get a can of WD-40, but then, with effort, the tumblers inside the cylinder began to turn with a low, grinding sound.

Leaving the key in the lock, Polly stepped back, took a deep breath, and wiped the sweat off her brow with the back of her hand. She was aware of the tension that coiled up like a snake inside her. The droning buzz of the wasps overhead and the chirring of crickets in the grass created a peaceful, lulling effect, and she tried to convince herself that there was nothing weird or scary about what she was doing. It was a beautiful, sunny, summer afternoon, and she was just going to have a quick look inside the shed to make sure there was nothing inside.

Yeah, but remember what curiosity did to the cat?

She quickly dismissed the thought and, after rubbing her hands on her pants legs to dry them, she took hold of the key once again and gave it another savage turn. Her hands trembled from the effort. Finally, after the key twisted a full 180 degrees, the lock made a dull clicking sound. Smiling, Polly pulled down hard on it, but the shackle remained frozen where it was.

Maybe the lock was broken or rusted shut forever, she thought. If nothing else, this proved that no one could have been in there in a very long time. And if she was going to get in today, she might have to resort to breaking down the door.

"You *son* of a *bitch*!" she hissed. She gripped the body of the lock tightly with both hands like she was praying and, twisting it from side to side, yanked down as hard as she could on it.

The shackle didn't move by much, but it sprang open just enough so a gap appeared between it and the body of the lock. Rusty grit chafed her hands as she pulled harder. With a bit more pressure, she finally was able to pry the lock open enough to get it off. She left it hanging on the latch as she took hold of the old porcelain doorknob, turned it, and pushed the door inward.

A rank, musty smell billowed out with the hot air that blew into her face. Keeping one hand on the doorknob for safety, Polly leaned forward into the shed and sniffed. There was something . . . an indefinable smell in the air that teased her with its familiarity, but as familiar as it was, she couldn't quite place it.

It was as hot as an oven inside the shed. Up near the rafters, Polly could see more wasp nests as well as numerous mud nests made by hornets. Sooty clots of cobwebs were draped in every corner of the ceiling and walls, especially by the window, where the sill was littered with the dried husks of dead insects. A fat-bodied wasp buzzed and bounced against the dirty panes of glass, trying to get out.

Poised and tense, Polly took a few tentative steps into the shed. On one side, the small room was filled almost to the ceiling with piles of rusted and rotten junk, including two old lawn mowers, an engine block propped up on sawhorses, several old mattresses, and a collection of oil drums and wooden boxes that had been used to collect just about everything from old newspapers and rags to antique tools and metal and wood pieces that Polly didn't even recognize. *Some of these things may be worth money to an antiques collector,* she thought, but she didn't see anything that interested her.

The floorboards were gray with age and rotting. They snapped and creaked beneath her weight as she edged farther into the shed. The heat inside the building was almost suffocating. In one spot in the far corner, she saw that someone had replaced several floorboards, but even those looked like they had been there for a while. A thick layer of dust and dirt covered everything. Looking closely at the floor, Polly could see that there weren't any fresh footprints. That allayed her fears at least a little.

A curious sensation filled her when she turned and looked back out at the open doorway. Outside, it was a glorious summer day, but inside the shed there was a dark, muffled stillness that created a weird illusion, making the outside world look impossibly far away. Polly felt almost as though she had entered another dimension or was looking at a screen projection. She experienced a brief moment of panic when she thought that maybe now that she was inside, she might not be able to get back outside.

"Jesus, don't be ridiculous," she whispered to herself, but even the sound of her own voice in the close confines of the shed had an odd effect, almost as though she were listening to someone else talk.

Finally, she was satisfied that there was nothing in here of any interest, not unless Tim wanted to take a look at this stuff. Some of it might have sentimental value for him, but she could care less. They should cart it all off to the dump. As she was turning to leave, one of the old garden tools that had been leaning against the wall fell over with a loud clatter. Polly jumped and let out a squeal, but then she chuckled to herself when she saw that it was just an old pitchfork.

She moved quickly back outside, feeling relieved once she was back in the sunshine. After easing the hasp of the lock closed, she gave it a hard shove to lock it again.

See, that wasn't so bad.

She hesitated a moment, still feeling like there was some unfinished business. Even as she started across the lawn, heading back to the house, she felt like there was still something wrong.

She had no idea what it was.

Maybe it was just that odd, dissociated feeling she had gotten while looking out from inside the shed.

Or maybe it was the feelings of nostalgia and loss she got from seeing the detritus of another life, now long past, collected there and waiting for the junkyard.

Or maybe it was as simple and sad as that she was feeling lonely and lost inside herself, that sadness and grief had permanently altered the way she felt about life.

Her plan for the rest of the afternoon was simply to get a glass of lemonade and sit in the shade in the backyard and take it easy. Maybe she'd read a little or take a nap. But as she opened the back door and stepped into the cool of the kitchen, another thought struck her.

Maybe she was feeling strange because Heather hadn't spoken to her last night.

She had almost gotten used to hearing the dead girl's voice inside her head as she drifted off to sleep, and now— maybe—she found it troublesome because last night, although she clearly remembered hearing a voice whispering to her, it hadn't been Heather's.

What if something was wrong with Heather?

And then an even more terrible thought struck her.

What if Heather really had been in danger in the white room, and what if now something's happened to her?

"So who have you told?"

Tim was sitting in a rickety chair across the kitchen table from his brother. They each had a bottle of beer in hand, and Rob had a cigarette in his other hand. It sent up a thin, blue curl of smoke. Glaring beams of sunlight shot through the cracks and holes in the yellowing window shade. The tablecloth was dirty and sticky to the touch. Rob probably hadn't washed it in weeks if not longer.

"What do you mean, who have I told?" Tim asked, squinting against the smoke as he shook his head. "I haven't told anybody anything."

"Bullshit," Rob snapped.

Leaning back in his chair, he took a swig of beer and swallowed it noisily, all the while glaring at Tim across the table. He was wearing a white T-shirt that was yellowed with age and full of holes, and jeans with the left leg cut off to accommodate the cast on his leg. He hadn't shaved in a few days, and his hair looked oily and matted, like he'd just gotten out of bed, even though it was well past one o'clock in the afternoon.

"Why would I tell anyone?" Tim said with a helpless shrug.

Rob smiled but said nothing as he raised the cigarette to his mouth and took a long, slow drag, filling his lungs with smoke and then blowing a gray cloud up at the ceiling.

"Then tell me what your boy's doing out there, snooping around?" Rob asked after a lengthy pause. He took another drag and casually flicked the ashes into the jar lid on the table that served as an ashtray.

"Well, I seriously doubt he was *snooping* around," Tim replied with another defensive shrug. "He was just checking the place out like any kid would do."

"Yeah, right," Rob said, sounding unconvinced. He narrowed his eyes until they were little more than glowing slits. The lines in his tanned, weathered face looked deeply etched, and Tim found himself wondering if he looked as old as his brother. They were only two years apart, after all, but he didn't think he had aged nearly as much as his brother had.

"For Christ's sake. You can't make such a big thing of it," Tim said. He shifted uneasily in his seat, then took a sip of beer, trying his best to look casual and unconcerned. "It's not that big a deal."

"Oh, I can make a big deal out of it, all right, little

brother," Rob said. His voice was thick with menace as he reached up and thoughtfully scratched the side of his face with his thumbnail. The stubble on his cheek made a loud rasping sound, like sandpaper. "You ain't mentioned any of this to Polly, have you?"

Tim snorted a laugh and waved a hand at him.

"Come on," he said. "Why would I do something like that? Look, as far as I'm concerned, it's all past history. Long past. Dead and buried."

"Not anymore it ain't," Rob said gruffly.

He snubbed the cigarette out in the jar lid and shook another one from the pack on the table. He left it hanging in his mouth unlit as he stared at his brother long enough to make Tim feel uncomfortable.

"So what's going on with that, anyway?" Tim finally asked, hoping that his voice didn't betray how uncomfortable his brother was making him feel.

"Whaddayah mean, what's going on?" The unlit cigarette bounced up and down as Rob spoke. "What do you think I'm gonna do, call the state police and ask 'em how's it going? As a concerned citizen, I'd like to know if you've made any identification on those bones you found? Shit, no!"

"But I haven't seen anything about it in the news," Tim said. "I wouldn't have even known about it if Ray Fuller hadn't mentioned it to me when I was in the hardware store."

Rob scowled and shook his head.

"In fact," Tim continued, "I'm kind of wondering why you didn't say something about it to me when I called you. That's the least you could have done."

Rob laughed so loud he almost spat the cigarette from his mouth. Taking the butane lighter from his pants pocket, he lit up and inhaled deeply.

"The least I could have done?" he echoed. "Man, I know you too well. That's why I didn't tell you about it." He was almost snarling. "I'm surprised you ain't been blabbing about it to everyone since you got here."

In spite of the anxiety he was feeling, Tim couldn't help but smile. He got up from his chair, walked over to the kitchen sink, and snapped up the window shade. The sudden blast of direct sunlight hurt his eyes as he looked out at the view from Rob's kitchen window.

It wasn't much. Just the side of another run-down apartment building and a fenced-in backyard with an overgrown lawn and a rotting picnic table. Across the street, down a grassy slope, he caught a glimpse of the river that flowed through town, but most of it was obscured by foliage.

"It doesn't ever bother you? What we did that day?" he asked. His voice was soft, almost dreamy in spite of the horrible thoughts he had.

From behind him, he heard Rob chuckle softly, but the laughter ended in a deep, rasping cough. Tim turned to look at his brother, and he didn't like what he saw. It was hard for him to admit it, but Polly was right; Rob was pretty much a loser, but there was something more, something lurking just below the surface, like a shark, something dangerous and deadly.

"*Bother* me?" Rob said before taking another drag and exhaling noisily. "Why the fuck should it *bother* me? First of all, we don't even know for sure who this was they found."

Tim squinted and pressed his hand against his forehead as though trying to massage away a migraine.

"Well we don't," Rob said, sounding more agitated now. "'N we probably never will. It could have been anybody out there!"

"Yeah, but what are the chances?" Tim kept his voice as low and level as he could. "Seriously, Rob. What are the fucking chances?"

"You still don't get it, do you, little brother?" Rob practically spat the words. "You're the big, fancy college teacher, but I still have to do all the real thinking for you, don't I?"

At a loss for words, Tim just stood there and stared back at his brother.

"Well, let me tell you something," Rob said. He had the cigarette in a clenched fist and jabbed it in Tim's direction. "We don't have to do or say or think *anything*! You got that? Not a single goddamned thing! Because even if it *is* who we think it is, there's no fucking *way* they can connect either one of us to anything! Not if we keep our fucking mouths shut! You got that?"

Tim tried to reply but couldn't. His throat had closed up. Cupping his chin with his hand, he took a deep, shuddering breath and tried to think of something to say, but his mind was a complete blank.

"Yeah," he finally said, yielding to his brother's forcefulness. "Okay."

"I mean it!" Rob said. "I'm abso-fucking-lutely right! You keep your goddamned mouth *shut*!"

With that, he drained the beer from his bottle, dropped his cigarette butt into it, then got up and limped over to the refrigerator. The rubber peg of his walking cast dragged on the linoleum, making a low chattering sound that set Tim's teeth on edge.

"You ready for another?" Rob asked as he opened the refrigerator and bent down to grab another beer.

"No. No thanks," Tim muttered. Even though his throat was really parched, he knew that more beer wasn't going to make him feel any better. "I usually don't have anything to drink before supper."

Rob smirked and shook his head as he twisted off the bottle cap and tilted his head back to take a long swallow from the bottle.

"Well, like they say," he said, wiping his mouth with the back of his hand, "it's five o'clock somewhere." He drained half the bottle in a series of noisy gulps. "'N speaking of supper, when the fuck are you 'n Polly gonna have me out to the house for a nice, home-cooked meal, huh? I would've thought for sure, me being the invalid 'n all, that you'd invite me over before now."

"We're still cleaning the place up," Tim said. "It wasn't in the best shape even back when Pa was still alive."

Rob grinned, making the skin around his eyes wrinkle.

"Hold it right there," he said, raising his hand and jabbing a finger at Tim. "Don't get started now about when are we gonna sell the old place, okay? I don't want to hear it."

"But—"

"Ut-ut! I said I *don't* want to hear it."

There was a light, almost mocking tone in Rob's voice, but Tim could see something besides humor in his brother's eyes. There was a cold and dangerous look in his brother's glance, and Tim realized with a sudden sinking feeling in his gut that he was the only person in the world who knew how truly dangerous his brother could be. And for the first time in his life, Tim found himself thinking that, in order to keep their secret, even he might not be safe. A cold, tingling shiver raced up the back of his neck.

"Fine, fine," Tim said, nodding. "I won't mention it again."

For now, anyway.

"I ought to get going, anyway."

He finished his beer, which had gone warm and flat, then rinsed out the bottle at the kitchen sink and left it on the counter to dry. He could see the boxes of empties stacked in the entryway and knew that his effort was wasted, but what the hell.

"And as for supper," he said as he fished in his pocket for his car keys, "let me talk to Polly about that and see when she thinks we might be ready to entertain."

"Entertain," Rob said, laughing. "I love it!"

"Yeah . . . well, I'll drop by tomorrow 'n see how you're doing," Tim said. "Take care."

Rob said nothing as Tim walked out the door and closed it quietly behind him. As he stepped out into the warm afternoon sunlight, he couldn't shake the cold, twisting feeling of dread that filled him. The one thing he was sure of was that he could never, *never* tell *anyone*—not even Polly—that he and Rob knew exactly who had been buried out there in the woods. Worse than that, they knew exactly how he had come to be buried there. And no matter how much it tormented him, he knew that it was a secret that would have to die with him . . . or else!

—Something's burning!—

The thick, acrid smell of smoke filled the room and stung Polly's eyes as she bolted upright in bed and stared into the darkness that filled the bedroom. She saw—or thought she saw—a thick veil of smoke suspended in the air above her, but the ambient light in the bedroom wasn't enough for her to be sure. On the fringes of her vision, she could see it a little more clearly than when she looked straight ahead.

Choking panic rose up inside her as she looked from side to side, all the while sniffing the air and trying to determine whether or not it really was smoke she was smelling. After last night, she didn't want to overreact and wake up the rest of the family until she was positive they were in danger.

But what if it's too late once I'm sure?

"Tim . . . Tim," she whispered. Her voice rasped in the darkness as she gripped her husband's shoulder and gave him a gentle shake.

Tim grunted and rolled over, smacking his lips as he exhaled noisily.

"Huh? . . . Yeah, what is it?" he murmured, still more than half asleep.

"Something's burning," Polly whispered, trying hard to keep the rising panic out of her voice. She widened her nostrils and sniffed again and again. The oily smell of smoke lingered like a bad aftertaste in the back of her throat, but it wasn't nearly as strong as it had been when she had first awakened.

"Hold on a second," she whispered. "I'm going to turn on the light."

Rolling onto her side, she felt around in the darkness until she found the switch on the lamp by the bedside and flicked it. The sudden blast of light brought tears to her eyes. She kept blinking them until they adjusted to the brightness. She glanced quickly around the room, surprised not to see a blue pall of smoke hanging in the air. In fact, the room looked perfectly normal, even though the smoky smell still clung to the inside of her nose. She cleared her throat, hoping the aftertaste would go away, but it didn't.

Shielding his eyes with the flat of his hand, Tim sat up in bed, leaning on one elbow, and looked at her. His hair was tousled and matted from sleep, and he had a blank, confused expression on his face.

"What the hell's going on?" he asked, sounding only a little more conscious.

Polly felt suddenly silly for overreacting so quickly.

"I . . . I'm not sure," she said, trying to remember exactly what had happened. "I was sound asleep, and then I . . . I thought I smelled something burning."

She decided not to mention that what had pulled her out of a deep slumber wasn't the smell of smoke at all. It was a voice—Heather Olsen's voice—whispering to her in the night.

—Something's burning—

The more she thought about it, the clearer the memory became until she was positive she had sensed someone standing, unseen, by her bedside, leaning over her, and whispering into her ear.

Tim sniffed loudly as he looked at her with one raised eyebrow.

"Well, I don't smell anything," he said.

She could hear the irritation in his voice, but he was doing a fair job of keeping his anger in check.

"No, I . . . uh, I don't either," Polly said, her embarrassment growing stronger. "Maybe I was just dreaming or something."

"Yeah . . . maybe," Tim mumbled. He rolled away from

her onto his side. "Or maybe you farted, and that's what you smelled."

"Oh, you're hilarious!" Polly said, swatting him playfully on the shoulder.

But he didn't seem at all amused as he yanked the bed sheets up over his head and said, "And put out the light, for Christ's sake. I'm trying to get some sleep."

Feeling absolutely deserted, Polly looked at the rounded lump that was her husband. He was already asleep again, his shoulders rising and falling with the steady sound of his breathing. Sighing to herself, she flicked the light off and just sat there in bed, looking around the room. At first she couldn't see much, but as her eyes adjusted to the darkness, once again she was sure that she could see a faint, glowing blue haze up by the ceiling.

Jesus, forget about it!

She squeezed her eyes tightly shut and lay back down, snuggling under the covers, but she couldn't forget about it, and she knew that sleep wasn't going to come easily.

The cloying smell lingered in the darkness, seeming to grow stronger by the second now that the light was out. After a while, when she was unable to stand it any longer, Polly tossed the bedcovers aside and stood up beside the bed. Her hand was trembling as she reached for the light, but then she thought better of it. Feeling around in the darkness, she made her way to the bedroom door.

In the hallway, she paused for a moment and sniffed the air again, convinced that the smoky smell was getting stronger—strong enough to sting her eyes. The stairway leading down to the living room loomed like a black slab of marble in the night. Polly slid her bare foot forward until she felt the drop-off of the first step. Keeping one hand on the banister and the other on the opposite wall, she started down, taking each step slowly and carefully.

She wanted to turn on the hall light but didn't, deciding not to chance disturbing Tim or Brian.

Yeah, even if you fall and break your damned fool neck, she thought.

The stairs creaked softly beneath her weight. The sound set Polly's teeth on edge, and she could imagine all too easily the rusted nails pulling out of the old wood and weakening their hold every time someone went up or down them. Finally, at the foot of the stairs, she paused and felt around on the living room wall until she found the light switch and flicked it on. She squinted in the light, looking around frantically to see if there was any smoke wafting in the air.

There's nothing wrong, she told herself when she saw that everything looked normal. *You're just overreacting. That's all.* And even though she could see that there was nothing wrong, she couldn't forget the voice she had heard from the depths of sleep.

—Something's burning—

It was useless to sniff the air. She had done that so much she couldn't tell if she was smelling the closed, musty air of the house, the damp night air, or something else.

Like smoke!

She made her way cautiously through the dining room and into the kitchen, all the while looking around. She jumped when she caught a glimpse of her own reflection in the window. For a few seconds, she was paralyzed and just stood there, staring at the distorted, ghostly image of herself. Her heart was racing as she thought how pale and insubstantial she looked.

Like a ghost.

"Jesus, just get over it," she whispered harshly to herself. "There's nothing wrong!"

Still, she checked all the appliances in the kitchen, making sure that the toaster oven, microwave, and coffeepot were all switched off. She was about to turn and go back upstairs to bed when her gaze shifted over to the door that led down into the cellar. The varnish on the solid oak door was yellowing with age and peeling. The old-fashioned doorknob, made of cut glass, caught the light and reflected it back in small, shattered prisms of color. The brass skeleton key was sticking out of the keyhole.

Polly hadn't ever really noticed the door before, but now, for some reason, she fixated on it.

What if something's burning down in the cellar?

A dizzying rush of fear ran through her. Maybe the furnace was malfunctioning or the ancient hot water heater had caught fire and was smoldering away. Maybe that's what she was smelling.

Her first impulse was to unlock the cellar door and have a look down there if only to prove to herself that there was nothing wrong, but she didn't do it.

It wasn't that she couldn't do it.

For some reason she felt unaccountably nervous about opening the cellar door, especially now, in the middle of the night. For a long time, she just stood there in the middle of the kitchen, staring at the cellar door key and wishing she could gather the courage to open it.

Jesus, what's the big deal? Just go over there and do it!

Her legs felt weak, and tension coiled up like a writhing snake inside her as she moved over to the door and grasped the doorknob with one hand and the key with the other. Both were cool and slippery to the touch, but she gritted her teeth, tightened her grip, and turned the key slowly.

The lock clicked faintly. The sound set her teeth on edge. She held her breath as she slowly twisted the doorknob. The hinges squeaked loudly as she pulled the door slowly open. A cool, damp, earthy smell wafted up the darkened stairwell, washing over her face. The smell almost gagged her as she reached blindly for the wall switch and brushed it with the palm of her hand.

The lightbulb at the bottom of the stairs came on, but it was barely strong enough to illuminate much. Holding her breath like she was about to dive into cool, deep water, Polly looked down the stairs and tried to see if there was a blue haze of smoke down there. Her vision was hazy and unfocused. She took another quick, shallow breath and swallowed, feeling a dry rawness in her mouth. Licking her lips didn't help. An icy rush of fear rippled through her when, from down in the darkness, she heard a faint, rustling sound.

Craning her head forward and trying not to choke on the damp, earth-smelling air, she stared at the dense shadows at the foot of the stairs, wishing she had the courage to go down there to investigate. She couldn't determine if the sound she was hearing was really coming from down there or if it was the rushing of blood in her ears. Her nerves tingled as though electrified, and the longer she stayed there at the top of the stairs looking down, the louder the rustling sound became until at last she was convinced that there was a voice—no, not one voice, but many, and they were all hissing and whispering in the dank darkness of the cellar.

The tightness around her throat grew worse until it almost choked her. When she took another breath, she heard a distinct click in the back of her throat. Her chest ached as though a great pressure was squeezing in on her, making it almost impossible to take a deep enough breath. And all the while, the hissing sounds from down below grew steadily louder, sounding more and more like whispering voices.

No! That can't be!

Polly was frozen where she stood. She knew she didn't have the courage to go down there and check it out, but she also didn't dare move. She wanted to close the door, lock it, go back upstairs to bed, and forget all about it. She wished she could believe that it was just her imagination getting carried away, but she was positive that she could feel an indistinct presence, lurking down there in the chilled dampness. Suddenly, she squealed and jumped back when she saw something—a shadow darker than the darkness—shift across the cellar floor. It wasn't much, just the slightest hint of motion, but she couldn't help but think someone was moving around down there just at the edge of the light.

And it was waiting for her down there in the darkness.

As her panic mounted, the ragged whispering sounds grew steadily louder, and Polly was sure now that she could see several shadowy forms shifting back and forth just out of sight in the darkness below.

A sheen of sweat had broken out on her forehead and was trickling down her face and neck. She couldn't stop shivering as she strained to listen to the faint rustling sounds, trying to determine if they were in fact voices or if they were something else.

But what?

Maybe it's those rats Tim was talking about, scurrying about in the darkness and scrambling to safety now that the light is on.

She wished she could convince herself that was all it was, but the elusive sounds didn't stop. Like the shifting shadows, they remained just at the edge of perception, teasing her with the rhythms of whispered words and sentences that she couldn't make out.

Stop it! You're just scaring yourself! There's nothing down there!

She wanted to believe that she was just overtired from working so hard on the house or that she had been under too much pressure lately and was imagining all of this, just like she had imagined those other things like when she saw someone in the old shed watching her . . . or hearing Heather's voice inside her head.

That's all it is! It's all in your imagination! It has to be!

Finally, she couldn't take the tension any longer and—somehow—found the strength to move. Taking a few, halting steps backward, she shifted her hand to the light switch and turned off the light. The squeaking sound of the door's old hinges set her teeth on edge, but the sound wasn't loud enough to block out the whispering voices—*No! They're not voices!*—coming from down in the cellar.

Her body was damp with sweat, and she was trembling. She realized that she'd been holding her breath too long and let it out before taking a long, slow breath. The dank smell wafting up out of the cellar gagged her. White spots of light drifted like fireflies in front of her eyes.

Just close the door and leave!

It seemed to take forever for her to swing the door shut, and all the while, she couldn't look away from the thickening darkness at the foot of the cellar stairs. She was convinced now that it was taking on shapes that looked vaguely human. Finally, with what seemed like her last ounce of strength, Polly slammed the door shut. She jumped and almost cried out when she heard the latch click. Her hands were shaking terribly as she turned the key, locking the door. Breathing short, shuddering gasps, she was about to walk back upstairs to bed when something banged once—hard—against the cellar door.

The impact was hard enough to make the door bounce against the frame and knock the key onto the floor.

Startled, Polly fell backward, sprawling on the floor and almost paralyzed as pure terror ripped through her. Her ears were ringing so loudly she could barely hear herself whimpering as she started scrambling crablike across the floor, away from the door. Her gaze was riveted to the door. She thoroughly expected to see the wood suddenly explode inward as something—*whatever the hell was down there!*—burst into the kitchen and attacked her.

She kept backing up until she banged into the edge of the old stove hard enough to knock the wind out of her. Trembling with fear, she cringed on the floor, her hands covering her mouth as she stared in terror at the cellar door, waiting . . . waiting for something to happen.

But the sound never came again.

The kitchen was so quiet the silence hummed in her ears. The night wrapped around her as she listened to the rapid *whoosh*ing of blood in her ears.

Jesus, just calm down! she told herself, but deep tremors kept running through her, making her feel hollow and fragile. She wanted to scream at the top of her lungs, but her throat closed off so no sound escaped. Intense, burning pressure filled her bladder.

That was just something falling on the cellar steps when I slammed the door shut, she told herself, wishing she could convince herself of it. *A broom or a hammer or a paintbrush we left on the stairs fell. That's all it was.*

And she almost believed herself.

After several minutes of sitting there on the floor, waiting for something terrible to happen, she slowly rose to her feet. Her body ached, and her back was sore where she had bumped into the stove, but the cellar door remained closed, and nothing happened.

Nothing's going to happen. Everything's fine.

Slowly, she inched her way over to the cellar door, picked the key up off the floor, and slid it back into the keyhole, drawing her hand away quickly like she might catch fire. Casting several nervous glances over her shoulder, she walked from the kitchen through the dining room and living room to the stairs. The whole time, she couldn't stop wondering if what made that thumping sound might be lurking just behind the closed cellar door. Frightening images rose in her mind, but she tried to push them away.

Moving quickly, she went up the stairs, unable to dispel the feeling that something was following close behind her, nipping at her back. By the time she slipped back into bed, she was shivering terribly. Tim was still snoring away as she turned off the light and lay down in the dark. She was sure that she wouldn't be able to drift off to sleep. She couldn't stop wondering if it was possible for a shadow to become so dense, so thick that it would be able to knock against a door hard enough to make a sound and knock a key out of the keyhole.

Clutching the bed sheets to her chin, she lay there shivering in the darkness for at least an hour or two. Finally, as she drifted off to fitful sleep, she was aware of a voice whispering to her just on the edge of hearing. As she dipped deeper into sleep, she thought she could make out what the voice was saying. By then, though, she had sunk too deeply into sleep to react when it whispered, *Something's burning.*

nine

In the clear light of day, with the sun shining brightly and birds singing loudly from the fringe of woods in the backyard, Polly thought that what had happened to her the night before seemed almost kind of silly, really. She did experience a slight tingle of expectation when she walked into the kitchen and looked over at the cellar door. The key was still in the keyhole, and she remembered hearing the thump against the other side of the door, so hard it knocked the key onto the floor. But the memory had a distinct sense of unreality to it, as if she had dreamed most if not all of it. Anything she hadn't dreamed must certainly have been a product of her overactive imagination. As if to prove to herself that she wasn't afraid, once Tim came downstairs for breakfast, she walked over to the cellar door, unlocked it, opened it, and looked down the stairs.

As soon as she opened the door, a cool, damp breeze with a familiar smell washed over her face, making her shiver.

"What are you doing?" Tim asked, rubbing his eyes with his thumb and forefinger as he yawned. His bare feet scuffed softly on the linoleum as he walked over to the refrigerator and took the can of Maxwell House from the freezer.

"Huh? . . . Oh, nothing," Polly said quickly, glancing at him over her shoulder. "Just checking something."

The cellar walls, floor, and foot of the stairs were lit with a dull, gray glow of sunlight. The moist, earthy smell that filled Polly's nostrils seemed to intensify, and she had the momentary impression that she was looking down into deep, silent water.

But there was nothing really threatening about it.

She looked at the top of the stairs but didn't see anything there that might have made that sound against the door last night. There were no tools, and as far as she could see, nothing had fallen down the stairs. Still, she told herself that there had to be a logical explanation for the thump she had heard. Of course, there was a good chance it might never have even really happened, or if it had, that it was something she had done. Maybe she had kicked or bumped against the door without even realizing it and frightened herself.

No matter what, there was nothing there now.

Tim shook his head and let out a low groan as he opened the top of the coffeemaker and scooped coffee into the basket. Then he went to the sink and started filling the carafe with cold tap water.

"Hey. Aren't you going to use bottled water for that?" Polly asked as she leaned against the cellar door, shutting it firmly behind her. Once it was closed, she cringed a little, half expecting to hear another *thump* from the other side, but it didn't happen. Her hand hardly shook as she turned the key, locking it.

Tim looked at her and sleepily shook his head. "Doesn't really make a difference that I can tell," he muttered.

"Well *I* can," Polly said. Moving close to him, she took the carafe from him and dumped the water down the sink before refilling it, this time from the Poland Springs bottle in the refrigerator. She noticed that her forearm was sprinkled with goose bumps but let it pass.

There is *something down there,* a voice in the back of her mind whispered, but she tried to ignore it.

Once the coffee was brewing, she placed some strips of bacon on a paper plate and popped it into the microwave, then started frying up a few eggs for each of them.

"You going to wake up Brian?" she asked as she shifted the eggs around in the pan.

"Naw," Tim said with a wave of the hand, "let him sleep. Teenagers need extra sleep."

Polly started to protest but then let it drop. Tim was right. Brian was bored enough as it was living here, so what was the harm if he wanted to snooze away ten or twelve hours a night? He'd get back on schedule once they were back home, she'd make sure of that.

"We going to tackle some more of the painting today?" Polly asked. "Or is today a day off?"

The eggs were sizzling in the frying pan, sending up faint wisps of steam. Polly gave them a quick swirl, then got four pieces of bread and dropped them into the toaster.

Tim had poured himself a tall glass of orange juice and was leaning back against the counter, sipping slowly and staring blankly down at the floor. He was bare-chested and still wearing his pajama bottoms, and he looked like he still wanted to be asleep, too. Polly walked up to him and, sliding her arms around his waist, pulled him close, and kissed him full on the mouth. Usually, their morning kisses weren't much more than a quick brush across the lips, but this kiss lingered. Polly sighed deeply as she pressed against him and slipped her tongue between his lips, darting it playfully between his teeth.

Tim reached out blindly and placed his juice glass on the counter behind him, then wrapped both arms around her and held her. Their kiss grew heated, passionate. Polly felt herself melting, being almost smothered in the warmth of his embrace. Any lingering thoughts about what might have been happening down there in the cellar last night instantly vanished.

After nearly a minute, Polly broke the kiss off and,

leaning back but staying in his arms, looked him straight in the eyes and grinned.

"What are you . . . Oh, you devil," Tim said with a laugh when he caught the mischievous glint in her eyes.

His own eyes widened as Polly shifted her hand down below his waist and grabbed him, giving him a firm but gentle squeeze. She groaned softly when she felt him stiffen in her hand. The eggs were sizzling away on the stove, and the microwave timer went *bing*, but she ignored them as she ran her other hand behind his back, over the mound of his butt, and started tugging his pajama bottoms down, exposing him. She made soft, pleasurable sounds as she started rubbing him up and down. Dropping down to her knees, she opened her mouth to receive him.

Tim let out a long groan of satisfaction as he leaned back against the counter, bracing himself with both hands and rolling his head from side to side, letting her do whatever she wanted to do. Polly sucked on him gently, feeling a wonderfully sensual connection as he hardened even more inside her mouth. After a while, she released him and looked up at him with a wide grin.

"I like a little sausage with my eggs," she whispered, her voice husky with emotion.

She stood up, quickly unzipped the shorts she was wearing, and slid them down her legs. Smiling, Tim grasped her hips and slowly turned her around until she was facing the table. Then he gently pushed her forward, spread her legs, and entered her from behind.

Polly closed her eyes, reveling in the pleasure of feeling him thrust deep inside her. Waves of dizziness and ecstasy swept through her as they moved together in rhythm. It wasn't long before their passion built to a crescendo. Polly could feel that Tim was about to release. Slow, warm, sensual waves rippled inside her as heated blood rushed through her veins. Suddenly, she spasmed in orgasm just as Tim let out a deep, shuddering breath, then shivered and grunted loudly as he exploded inside her. He clasped her tightly and then started running his hands up and down her sides, pulling her hard against him.

Exhausted, Polly leaned forward onto the table, her arms shaking and almost unable to support her. Smiling wickedly, she glanced at Tim over her shoulder, then turned around to embrace him with a passionate hug.

"You're good, mister," she whispered. "*Damned* good."

Tim ran his fingers through her hair and was about to say something when suddenly he jumped and pulled away from her. Polly watched as he waddled awkwardly over to the stove, his pajama bottoms tangled around his knees. Blue smoke was rising from the pan, and the smell of burning eggs filled Polly's nose, making her stomach twist with nausea.

"Shit! . . . *Shit!*" she muttered as she pulled her shorts up and straightened her blouse.

Tim let out a howl as he grabbed the hot pan and slid it off the burner. It was already too late. The eggs were ruined. Just then the toast popped in the toaster, and she knew that the magic moment had broken.

"I'm sorry," Tim said.

He stood at the sink, looking almost comically helpless with the pan of burned eggs in his hand and his pajamas around his ankles. Polly kissed him quickly on the cheek before taking the pan from him. Using the spatula, she scraped the ruined eggs into the garbage.

"You didn't do anything wrong," she said. "In fact, you did everything right."

But she was feeling like the magic moment had passed. For the first time in—she couldn't remember—they had been spontaneously passionate, screwing like newlyweds in the kitchen. She started to chuckle as she turned on the tap and ran water into the pan. It was still hot enough to sizzle and splatter, but she squirted a few drops of dish detergent into it and washed it out.

She could feel Tim's gaze on her back as she grabbed four fresh eggs from the carton and cracked them into the pan.

"I'll take a rain check for game two tonight," he said, looking at her with genuine fondness and lingering lust in his expression.

Polly smiled back at him, but for some reason she found herself feeling a little irritated. She wasn't sure why. Maybe it was just because their sexual encounter had been interrupted, but she felt like there was something more.

Maybe it was because the raft of blue smoke from the burning eggs was hanging in layers up by the ceiling, looking for all the world exactly like the smoke she had imagined seeing in the bedroom last night.

And then a thought hit her, sending a cold shiver up her back.

Maybe that's what it was last night . . . a premonition.

Still flushed from their early-morning sexual encounter, she set to work making breakfast and tried her best to push any negative thoughts from her mind. Still, she couldn't help but sniff the air from time to time, trying to determine if that was the same smoky smell she had smelled last night.

—Something's burning—

She consoled herself with the thought that Tim had been so responsive to her. She now realized that, ever since they had moved to Hilton, she had felt more than a little alienated from her husband. Maybe that—like so much else—was just her imagination, but she didn't like feeling as though they were drifting apart. What they had just done cast everything in a new light. She felt a warm glow deep in her belly and thighs, satisfied that, by doing something different this summer instead of staying at home in Stonepoint, they were beginning to rekindle feelings she had feared were dulled if not actually dying or already dead.

They were mostly silent but smiled contentedly as they went about preparing breakfast. Polly thought Tim seemed almost a little embarrassed about what they had been doing, but she let him know how much she appreciated it by lingering glances and touches throughout the morning. She was surprised at herself, actually. It wasn't like her to be quite so sexually aggressive. As she stirred the new batch of eggs, she wondered what had come over her. It was almost as if she was fearful that she was losing her husband and was trying to be different and outrageous just to try to keep connected to him.

And what if I just got pregnant?

She felt a twinge of guilt that they hadn't used birth control. It wasn't very likely that she would get pregnant, and Polly tried to dismiss the idea out of hand, but the soft, glowing warmth she felt deep inside made her think more than once that morning that maybe they had done it. It didn't take her long to decide that, if she really had gotten pregnant just now, it wouldn't be such a bad thing after all.

It might, in fact, be exactly what she needed.

After breakfast, Tim helped by clearing the table and washing the dishes and frying pan. Then they both changed into grubby work clothes and set to work painting. They had decided not to be too ambitious. This was, after all, supposed to be a vacation. Now that they had a first coat of paint on the ceiling, their goal was to get a fresh coat on the kitchen walls. Tim got the painting supplies he'd bought and spread them out. Polly was a little upset when she realized that he had gotten oil-based paint for the walls instead of latex.

"What's the deal with this?" she asked, pointing to the label on the can of beige paint.

"Oh, yeah. Ray down at the hardware store said he thought oil base would cover better."

Polly frowned and shook her head. "Maybe," she said, "but do you know what a pain in the ass it is to clean up? You just use water with latex."

Tim started to protest but fell silent. He looked a bit defensive as he took the paint can from her and ran around the edge of the lid with a screwdriver to open it. Taking one of the stirring sticks, he started mixing the thick paint. The oily smell was strong. It reminded Polly of something, but she couldn't quite place it. Not wanting to argue, she spread newspaper on the floor and got the brushes and rollers ready. Tim put *Pet Sounds* into the CD player and started singing along tunelessly as he worked. Polly was still feeling a little off, maybe wishing that they had spent a little more time with their romantic interlude, but she started painting the edge work, determined to make the best of the day.

The work went faster than Polly had expected. Once most of the trim work was done, Tim got the roller and started covering the wall with long swatches of fresh color. Polly could see right away that they were going to have to give the walls another coat. The surface they were covering was browned from years of accumulated grease and dirt. There were thick clots of cobwebs in the corners of the ceiling, and there had been a water leak just above the back door, but that covered over a lot easier than the oily mess above the stove. In just under three hours, just about the time they heard Brian's feet thump on the floor upstairs, they had finished the first coat.

"Oil base is going to take a lot longer to dry, too," Polly said, still feeling a little miffed at her husband. "We probably can't do another coat till tomorrow."

He didn't argue with her. Although they had the kitchen door and all the downstairs windows open, the thick paint smell was making her feel nauseous, so they went outside to clean up the brushes.

"Let me show you something my father used to do," Tim said as he took the paintbrush from her. After filling an empty coffee can with water from the hose, he put both of their brushes into it.

"Hate to tell you this, buddy," Polly said, "but that kind of paint doesn't clean up with just water."

"I know. But it doesn't have to," Tim replied, sounding smug. "The water keeps the brushes from drying out, so all we have to do tomorrow is shake out the water and start painting again. Saves on cleanup time."

"How about the paint roller? You soak that overnight, too?"

Tim studied it for a moment, then braced it between his knees and squeezed it tightly until he was able to wiggle it off the handle. His hands were coated with beige paint that dripped down to his elbows. Taking the paper bag the painting supplies had come in, he folded it a few times around the roller and tossed it onto the ground.

"They're cheap enough to just use and throw away," he said with a weak smile. "I'll pick up a couple more when I go in town to have lunch with Rob."

"You're going in town again today?" Polly asked, a little crestfallen.

Tim bit his lower lip and nodded. "Yeah. Aren't you forgetting why we're even here?" His voice had an edge to it that Polly didn't like. "I thought the whole purpose of coming to Hilton was so we could help him out."

"That doesn't mean we can't have a little fun of our own," Polly said. "I mean, just you and me. Besides, how much help does he need?"

"You should see his apartment," Tim said, rolling his eyes. "I should take a day or two and clean the place for him."

Polly could feel the flinty coldness in his glance as she looked at him. As exasperating as it was, she knew there was no point arguing with him once he'd made up his mind, so she didn't say anything more.

"Why don't you come, too?" Tim said, his eyes brightening expectantly. "We could find a nice little restaurant and have lunch, just the three of us."

"No thanks," Polly said, not wanting to consider it for even a second. She shook her head, avoiding eye contact with him. "I'll be fine, eating here with Brian."

A chill seemed to settle between them, and they didn't speak to each other as they cleaned their hands with splashes of turpentine, then washed up using the outdoor hose. It wasn't long before the water was running ice cold, and Polly was shivering. Her hands had a funny, tingling feeling in them, like her skin was stretched too thinly. They smelled terrible, too. She kept sniffing them as she walked back into the house to see what Brian was up to. She found him leaning against the counter wearing nothing but boxer shorts while he ate a bowl of cold cereal.

"Looks good," he said, indicating the kitchen walls with a casual flick of his head. Then he went back to chomping cereal.

Polly felt a rush of anger and almost asked him when he might see his way to helping them a little, but she checked herself, knowing that it wasn't Brian she was angry at.

No, she was angry at her husband. She might try to deny it, but even in spite of their lovemaking this morning, something seemed to be hanging over them like a storm cloud. Maybe she was just mad because Tim was spending every damned afternoon with his brother. Or maybe it was something else.

Maybe she was still feeling too tense and wired about staying in Tim's old family house. Night after night, she wasn't sleeping well. She was seeing and hearing and smelling things that just didn't seem right. And she still couldn't stop thinking about Heather Olsen's death and connecting that to her own loss four years earlier.

The truth was, when she was honest with herself, she felt like she was a bit of a wreck, mentally and emotionally. Maybe Tim was right. Maybe she should just learn how to relax a little and come to lunch with him and Rob.

Then again, Rob was a whole other issue that she didn't even want to begin thinking about.

She had never really liked him, not from the first day they met, and she didn't see how anything was going to change that. Sure, she felt sorry for him because of his broken leg, but that didn't change the essential fact that she didn't like or trust him.

And she knew that he didn't like her, so she figured it would be best for everyone all around if she and Rob kept their distance.

"Have a good lunch," she called out.

Without a backward glance over her shoulder, much less a good-bye kiss, she strode into the living room and sat down on the couch to wait until she heard Tim's car start up and pull out of the driveway. Almost without noticing, she reached up and wiped away the tears that were forming in her eyes.

Just how close are you to having a breakdown? she wondered as she stared straight ahead, not even noticing the view out the living room window.

The field behind the house was buzzing with the sound of insects as Brian made his way toward the woods and the narrow path that ran along the riverbank. He had given up on the idea of hanging around downtown in hopes of meeting any of the local kids. The few he had seen the last time had studiously ignored and avoided him, except for one little girl who had smiled a greeting at him. He hoped vaguely that Josh might show up. From what he'd said before, it seemed as though he spent quite a bit of time down by the river. If he was a loner like Brian, maybe he'd want to make friends.

Or maybe not.

The kids in this town sure didn't seem all that open to welcoming new people.

The knee-high grass swished against his legs, and grasshoppers leaped out of his way, buzzing and exploding all around him like tiny shrapnel. The sun was hot on his shoulders, and there was a curious moist smell in the air that got steadily stronger the closer he got to the river. When he entered the leafy shade of the trees, a teasing chill ran up his back. He had the distinct impression that he was leaving one world behind and entering an entirely different one. Looking back over his shoulder, he stared for a moment at the house. Through the heat haze, it seemed almost to be an illusion against the pale blue sky. He turned back and walked deeper into the woods.

"Hey, Josh!" he called out, cupping his hands to his mouth.

His voice echoed back from the opposite side of the river with an odd, reverberating flatness. He waited a few seconds for a reply but heard none, only the chattering songs of the birds darting from branch to branch. The river flowed smoothly, its dark, rippled surface reflecting back the blue sky and the trees along its margin. Several swallows darted along the surface, snapping up insects.

"Yo! . . . Josh!" he called again.

He didn't really expect an answer. Josh had struck him as a pretty strange kid who probably wouldn't answer even if he could hear him. Brian picked up a stick and slashed at the brush as he wandered along the winding, muddy path beside the river. If he had been a few years younger, he would have pretended he was an Indian tracker as he scanned the ground for some sign that someone—Josh, maybe—had passed by recently. All he saw was a scattering of small animal tracks that he guessed were either a skunk or raccoon.

The river was no more than a hundred yards wide at the point where it curved in a wide bend and flowed toward the town. Brian thought of the day not long ago when he had walked home from town and spent some time leaning over the bridge railing, watching the river flow. He hawked up a wad of mucus and spat into the water, watching the little dimpled ring that quickly smoothed over and disappeared.

He took a deep breath, telling himself that he should enjoy just being alone in the peace and quiet of nature. Whistling softly, he walked along the river path, occasionally glancing at the swirling, muddy water and the dark weeds he could see fanning out below the surface. As he rounded the bend and the riverbank path opened up into a wide, flattened beach area, a strong fishy smell suddenly assailed him. It was strong enough to make him stop short and turn his head away as he gasped for breath.

"Jesus! What the fuck—?" he muttered, looking around.

It wasn't just a fishy smell. It was something else . . . something stronger . . . almost, he thought, like a rotting body. Maybe an animal had died by the river or some creature had drowned and washed up on shore and was decomposing in the summer heat.

Choking and coughing, Brian picked up his pace, practically running until he thought it was safe to take another deep breath. The smell lingered in the air, but it wasn't nearly as bad as it had been.

Up ahead, he saw an old tree leaning over the river. Several of its limbs were submerged, their black branches looking dark and dangerous below the surface of the water. Brian paused for a moment to catch his breath. When he glanced at the river, he caught a glimpse of something that made his flesh crawl.

Just below the surface was a pale, round, white object. His first impression was that it was a sunken ball stained with dirt and muck that had gotten caught on a submerged branch. When he looked closer, though, the white ball took on the vague features of a face.

Panic jolted Brian and made him cry out as he jumped back, stumbling so he almost fell. The stick he'd been holding fell from his hands, and a tight pressure gripped his chest.

No way! That can't be what I thought it was!

He tried taking another deep breath, but the rotting, fishy smell was much stronger. It gagged him, and he gasped for breath. Tiny white lights danced around the fringes of his vision. His legs felt all rubbery as he backed away from the river's edge, feeling equally terrified and intrigued by what he had seen . . . or thought he had seen.

"That can't *really* be someone underwater," he whispered to himself, but he knew it could. Accidents happen. Someone could have fallen into the river and drowned. It was a hot day. Maybe some kids had been swimming upstream, and one of them had been swept away by the current or banged his head against a rock or something and was caught up on the submerged branches.

What if it's Josh?

The thought filled Brian with dread. He tried to bring back a clear image of the face he had seen underwater to see if it matched with what he remembered of Josh's face, but he couldn't. He had been so surprised when he had first seen it that his only reaction had been to get the hell away from it. All he could remember now was that he'd had the clear, instant impression that it looked like a person underwater whose sightless eyes were looking up at the sky.

Brian knew that he should go back and check it out, but he was filled with such dread he wasn't sure he would be able to do that.

What if it really is a dead person? What if it's Josh?

As scary as those thoughts were, he suddenly had to know for certain.

Taking a deep breath of the warm, fetid air, he started back to the edge of the river. He saw the stick he had dropped and picked it up again, even though he knew it wasn't much security. If there was a dead person in the river, he wasn't going to have to defend himself. The worst that could happen was he would get scared and run away again. Once he was sure, he knew he should run back home and call the police to report it.

The water slid by in thick, black ripples that shimmered like oil along the edge of the riverbank. The fallen tree leaned far out over the water. It was still alive. The branches, even the ones that dipped down and touched the river's surface, had fresh, green leaves. Below the surface, the branches looked white and slimy with tangled weeds and other debris.

And that's all it is, Brian tried to convince himself. *Some crap got tangled in the branches underwater and it just* looks *like a human face.*

Maybe . . .

Then again, maybe not . . .

His hands were trembling so badly he could hardly control them as he approached the fallen tree. His freshly cleaned sneakers made loud sucking sounds in the black mud of the riverbank. He placed one foot on the wide trunk of the tree, making sure the footing was good. Grasping a branch for support, he leaned out over the water and looked down.

The water was dark and muddy. It eddied in little swirls around the tree branches, making it almost impossible for him to see very clearly below the surface. Some of the bark had been peeled away from the submerged branches. They looked like rotting bones in the murky water, but as Brian looked around, he couldn't see anything that might have looked like a face.

I must've just imagined it, he thought, but he wasn't convinced. He had definitely seen *something.*

But what?

The tree trunk bounced beneath his weight as he took a few more cautious steps out onto it, all the while peering into the river's depths. Leaning forward, he dipped the stick he was holding into the water and probed around. He could feel the submerged branches and the muddy river bottom, but he didn't see anything.

Maybe it was farther out, he thought, moving still farther out onto the tree. He didn't think it could be this far out. It was tough enough seeing into the water even close to shore.

Maybe whatever it was broke free and floated away. My weight on the tree trunk shook it loose.

There was that possibility, Brian thought, but he knew that the most likely explanation was that there hadn't been anything there in the first place except rotting tree branches covered with slime and whatever debris they'd caught over the years. Maybe he'd been blinded momentarily by the sunlight reflected off the water and had just imagined seeing a face.

But he wasn't convinced.

He didn't usually imagine seeing things. He was sure there had been something there, he just didn't know what.

Sunlight and shadows dappled the leaves and branches that brushed against his face and arms as he made his way even farther out onto the tree trunk. It bent beneath his weight, its branches dipping into the water, disturbing the smooth surface. Looking carefully on either side of the tree, he tried to see into the murky depths but couldn't see anything that looked even remotely like a human face.

Forget about it, he told himself, but the memory of the image played in his mind, teasing him with its gruesome suggestion that he had seen a dead person underwater.

He was aware of what a beautiful day it was with birds chirping in the woods and sunlight sparkling on the water, but suddenly he felt the hairs at the nape of his neck prickle as if a chilled wind was blowing across his back. He realized with a start that he felt like he was being watched.

Someone's close by, hiding in the woods, watching me!

Brian swallowed, his throat making a loud gulping sound as he looked over his shoulder, trying to catch whoever it was. The feeling was palpable, and he couldn't dismiss it as just his imagination working overtime.

"Christ, you're being a jerk," he whispered harshly to himself, but that didn't make the feeling go away.

The woods suddenly seemed hushed with expectation and danger. The hot summer air crackled with energy, like the odd stillness just before a thunderstorm breaks loose. Looking down at the water again, Brian poked around a little more, but then in frustration, he cocked back his arm and flung the stick away. It *whoosh*ed like a flying arrow as it ripped through the branches and then plunked into the water almost in midstream. He watched as it was swept away by the swift current.

He was just turning around to go back to the shore when he caught sight of a dark shape on the far shore. The figure was motionless and blended into the deep shadows of the surrounding pines, almost invisible, but Brian knew that someone was lurking there, watching him.

He froze. His hands tightened on the branches for balance as he stared across the water. His first thought was that it must be the same person who had chased him down the street in the truck the other day, the truck with the FRIENDS DON'T LET FRIENDS D R I V E   C H E V Y S bumper sticker.

Maybe the guy was nuts and was stalking him, he thought as fear twisted in his stomach.

Don't let him know that you know he's there, he cautioned himself, but it was already too late. He had revealed himself by his reaction. The good thing was, there was a river at least a hundred yards wide separating them. If this person—whoever it was—really was after him, he could get away easily before the person could swim the river to his side.

As Brian stood there, paralyzed and looking out across the water, the dark shape shifted forward. Brian was hit with a flash of recognition.

It's Josh!

The boy had stepped out of the deepest shadows and was staring at Brian, his face slack, expressionless. His skin looked eerily white in the shifting shade, and it struck Brian as odd how the sunlight seemed not to touch the boy where he stood, almost like it shined right through him.

With a tentative grin, Brian raised a hand and waved to Josh, but as he did, his left foot slipped on the wet bark, and he started to fall. He still held on to the tree branch with his other hand, but his grip wasn't good enough. He dangled out over the water, his feet splashing in the water as he scrambled to keep his balance. There was a loud snap as the branch he was hanging on to broke, and he fell backward into the river. The broken end of the branch raked a gash along the inside of his forearm.

Brian's back slapped hard against the water, and then its cold embrace closed around him. He had just enough time to suck in half a breath before going under. The daylight was closed off by the thick, brown water. Flailing wildly, he struggled to the surface and opened his mouth to call for help and to inhale, but all he got was a mouthful of foul-tasting water that choked off his cries.

His frantic efforts churned the water around him, frothing up a thick, white foam. Brian was a good swimmer, so he tried to control his fear as he scrambled to grab hold of the tree trunk, but it was slick and kept slipping out of his grasp. His jeans and T-shirt were sodden, and their weight hampered his efforts. They seemed to pull him down. Choking and gasping for breath, he kicked and flailed wildly, trying to keep his head above water. He saw the blood streaking down his arm and panicked all the more.

As he struggled to find something to grab onto, a sharp pain bit into the back of the calf muscle of his left leg. His first thought was that he had jabbed himself against one of the submerged branches, but as he tried to pull away, something encircled his leg just below the knee and began to squeeze tightly. A fresh rush of panic seized him as he tried to kick his leg free and found that whatever was holding him was holding tightly. When he paused a moment to catch his breath, it started to pull him under.

Brian screamed.

Wide-eyed with fear, he looked across the river to the far shore. He could still see Josh Billings standing in the shadows, absolutely immobile.

"Help . . . help me. . . ." he gasped, but his plea ended with a loud gargling sound as the muddy water filled his mouth. He was slowly being dragged under the water as if someone had grabbed hold of him and was pulling him down.

Brian's fingernails raked across the tree trunk, but he didn't catch anything that would hold. Then something as cold and strong as a bear trap closed around his other ankle. Brian let out a loud, gurgling scream as he thrashed back and forth, but it felt as though his efforts only tangled him more. No matter how hard he tried, he couldn't get free. A violent tug started pulling him away from the tree and deeper down. The water covered his mouth as he craned his neck back and struggled to stay above the surface. His nostrils filled with a rotting fish smell that clogged his throat.

With a mighty burst of effort, he lunged forward and hooked his arm around one of the tree branches. The steady downward pull grew even stronger, but he kept his head above water and hung on. For an instant, his panic subsided. Just enough for him to clear his mind and think through what had happened.

It was obvious that his legs were tangled up in the submerged branches of the trees. Thrashing around was only making it worse. He told himself he had to settle down and think this out. It was like that kids' toy, the Chinese finger trap. The harder he pulled, the worse it would get. The submerged branches clung to him like cold, grasping hands, and it was only by remaining calm and working this out that he would get free.

Wincing with pain, Brian tossed his head back and gulped in a lungful of fresh air. When he looked over at the opposite bank, he was shocked to see that Josh was still standing there. He hadn't moved.

"Jesus! . . . Help me!" he called out, his voice echoing from the opposite shore.

Spikes of pain ran in sharp, tingling jolts up both legs, making his hips and stomach ache. His grip on the branch was tentative at best. Tree bark dug into the cut on his forearm, bringing tears to his eyes. His arms and shoulders were trembling from the effort of hanging on, and he wasn't sure how much longer he could cling to the branch before he lost his grip and went under.

Stay calm. . . . Just stay calm.

He knew that giving in to panic was the worst thing he could do, but he also couldn't understand why Josh wasn't doing anything to help.

Can't he see me?

Doesn't he hear me?

Does he even know what's going on?

Or is he just plain stupid and mean, and doesn't care if I drown?

Clinging desperately to the branch, Brian blinked his eyes to keep the water out of them. His breath came in ragged, shallow gulps that burned his throat and lungs. His muscles felt rubbery and loose, filled with a deep ache. Whenever he tried to move, the pressure around his leg and ankle would tighten, and he would feel himself being pulled under again.

"Help . . . me," Brian called out feebly.

His only answer was the soft rustle of wind in the trees and the gentle sound of water lapping against the shore.

Jesus, I'm going to die here. . . . I don't want to die!

But he was so drained with exhaustion he almost embraced the idea of just letting go and going under. He was caught. For all he knew, his leg might be skewered on one of the underwater branches. He might be cut and bleeding to death and not even realize it because he was in shock and couldn't feel the pain as he slowly bled to death underwater.

"No, goddamnit!" he whispered, gritting his teeth as he somehow found the energy to tighten his grip on the tree branch and pull himself up a notch. "I'm *not* giving up!"

Holding on tightly, he moved his leg very carefully, twisting it first one way, then the other. Whatever he was snagged on certainly had a tight hold on him. No matter which way he wriggled, he couldn't free himself, but at least it was no longer pulling him under. His teeth chattered from the cold water, and the gentle breeze blowing over the river's surface only made it worse, raising goose bumps on his exposed arms. He stared at the blood streaming down his forearm and saw to his relief that the cut wasn't so bad. Just a scratch, really.

At last, near collapse, Brian realized there was only one way out of this. He had to dive under and try to free himself. Tilting his head way back, he stared up at the blue sky through the green canopy of leaves as he sucked in a deep breath and held it. Then, knowing it might mean his death, he let go of the branch and ducked under the water. He tried to control his panic as he reached down to his feet. Keeping his eyes tightly shut, he felt around for whatever was holding him. The slick, barkless branches beneath the surface felt like a net that was tangled around his feet. His chest began to ache for air, but he kept feeling around, trying to extricate himself and didn't resurface until his chest felt like it was going to explode. Finally, with a roaring intake of fresh air, he thrust his head above the surface.

"What the fuck?" he muttered when he realized that he wasn't any closer to being free.

If anything, the underwater branches had an even tighter hold on him. He tried not to imagine that they were hands, thin, rotting, skeletal hands, that were reaching up from the dark depths of the river and pulling him down, down to a watery grave.

His strength was ebbing fast. The cold water felt smooth and clammy as it flowed over him, tugging him away from the tree trunk. His mind clouded over, and his vision blurred. He knew that he wasn't going to get out of this unless he started thinking clearly. After sucking in another deep breath, he dove under again. He fought hard to free himself, but the branches that held him were thin and slick with river slime. They kept slipping from his grasp and bending without breaking as he savagely twisted them back and forth.

I don't want to die like this! . . . Please, God, I don't want to die like this!

It seemed to take forever, and Brian began to think that any second now, his air was going to give out, his lungs would collapse, and he would surrender to the dark, oily embrace of the water. He remembered that putrid smell in the air along the riverbank and tried not to imagine that days or weeks from now, once his bloated corpse rose to the surface, he would wash up somewhere downstream, and the terrible stench of his rotting body would fill the air.

No! . . . That's not gonna happen!

Still fighting his panic, he violently yanked his left leg up. The branches clung so tightly he could feel his sneaker being pulled off, but he was so intent on getting free that he didn't care.

Then, miraculously, his left leg was free.

He broke the surface of the water, took another quick breath, and went back under to work to free his other leg. The underwater branches were as supple as vines as they twisted around his calf muscle. The harder he pulled, the tighter they got. Then, just when he thought he was going to have to resurface for another gulp of air or die, his leg slipped free, and he shot up to the surface.

Gasping and coughing water out of his lungs, he grabbed the tree trunk and held on to it tightly. The horrid taste of river water gagged him. His stomach convulsed, but he didn't throw up. Heaving a heavy sigh, he rested his cheek against the rough bark and clung on as he took several deep, even breaths. After a while, his pulse began to slow down. He was cold and shivered wildly, but he was free! Looking over his shoulder, he laughed when he saw that his sneaker had washed up on the shore about twenty feet downstream. His smile instantly melted when he turned and looked to the opposite shore and saw that Josh was nowhere in sight.

"You *bastard*," he whispered as he pulled himself along the tree trunk and floated back to the shore. When his feet touched the slick clay river bottom, he let out a loud groan and lunged forward to sprawl face first on the hard-packed mud of the riverbank.

Foul-smelling water ran in streams down his face and neck. His body was coated with slime and mud, but he didn't care. The sun beat down warmly on his back, driving away the death-cold chill of the river. For several minutes, he just lay there, amazed that he once again could feel the heat of the sun and hear the birds singing in the woods. It was amazing to think that the whole time he was struggling for his life, everything else in the forest had just gone on as always without any regard for him.

Brian's wristwatch was fogged over with moisture, but by the position of the sun, he guessed it was late in the afternoon. He laughed softly to himself, feeling a peculiar timeless quality to the forest. He was hardly able to believe that he was still alive, and it wasn't very hard to imagine that all of this might be a dream or hallucination he was having even as he sank deeper and deeper into the black river mud.

Uttering a small cry, he rolled over onto his side and sat up, taking in a deep breath of the pine-scented air. The dead fish smell was gone. Shivering inside, he looked up at the blue arc of sky above the trees.

"No, goddamnit, I'm not dead! I'm alive!" he whispered, hearing the hoarse strain in his voice.

He ran his hands over his chest, feeling the slick, greasy texture of his shirt. Looking down at his legs, he saw that his jeans were caked with drying mud and algae. He wasn't sure what he was going to do next. He knew he should head back to the house and get cleaned up, but his mother would pitch a fit if she saw him like this. He had to figure out some way of sneaking back to his room without her seeing him. If she ever found out what had happened, he'd be grounded for the rest of the summer. Then again, being stuck here in Maine was just as bad as being grounded. He wasn't going to make any friends, not even with good old Josh, who'd just stood there like a zombie watching him go under!

After thinking it through, Brian decided that he would clean himself and his clothes as best as he could before heading back to the house. His mother and father weren't expecting him to help work on the house today, so he could take all the time he needed before he went back. Rolling his head from side to side, he tried to massage the tension out of his neck and shoulders. After a while, he got up and walked up to the grassy slope by the river. Letting out a long sigh, he lay back on the grass and closed his eyes with only one thought on his mind.

I'm alive! . . . I can't believe it, but thank God I'm alive!

ten

"What could possibly happen in the clear light of day?" Polly whispered to herself as she let go of the doorknob and placed her left foot on the first step leading down into the cellar.

Unfortunately, it wasn't the clear light of day down there in the cellar. Even with the light on at the foot of the stairs, the dank air was suffused with a gloomy, gray glow. The top step creaked as she shifted her weight onto it, and a cool dampness washed over her face and arms, raising goose bumps. She placed her right hand on the banister and the other hand on the opposite wall for balance. The crumbling yellow plaster was damp and gritty to the touch.

She knew that she didn't have to be doing this.

She could just as easily close and lock the cellar door and never look down there again. The family's vacation time wasn't turning out at all the way she had hoped it would. She wouldn't be surprised if Tim decided to leave in a few days.

So why not just forget all about what might be down here?

She asked herself this question over and over, but that didn't stop her from placing her foot onto the next step down and shifting her weight forward. The banister was worn as smooth as marble with age and use. Her grip on it tightened when the stairs snapped so loudly it sounded like a small firecracker going off.

Polly paused and sniffed the air. It had a moist, earthy smell tinged with a cloying brackish aroma that made her think of stagnant well water. That impression was intensified when she took another step down, and the cool air of the cellar wafted around her, making her feel as though she were wading deeper and deeper into a pool of fetid water.

Polly noticed something curious about sounds down here, too.

The farther she went down the stairs, the more muffled the air seemed, as though it were too dense to transmit sounds clearly. Even the creaking of the old stairs sounded different, somehow, like the roaring crackle of a fire in the distance. She sniffed the air, her breathing sounding unusually loud.

Running her hands over her bare arms, she glanced over her shoulder at the small rectangle of kitchen she could still see. It looked impossibly far away, and she couldn't shake the disorienting feeling that she was slipping into another world, another dimension.

Don't be ridiculous, she cautioned herself, reaching out and grabbing the banister again. *You're just going to scare yourself.*

Widening her nostrils, she sniffed the air, trying to determine if there really was another smell she could just barely detect or if she was imagining it. The shadows were densest at the far end of the cellar. In the corner of her eyes, she thought she caught flittering hints of motion. In the ghostly gray light, she could almost imagine that she saw rafts of dust or thin smoke hovering near the ceiling, assuming vague, indistinct shapes.

Is that it? Do I smell smoke?

The memory of a faint voice whispered in her head.

—*Something's burning*—

She sniffed the air again, almost chuckling at the image of Smokey the Bear, sniffing a forest fire.

Upstairs, the refrigerator suddenly kicked on. Polly squealed and jumped, then listened for a moment to the low, steady rumble transmitting through the kitchen floor. She was surprised at how foreign such an ordinary sound seemed. It made her feel as though it—or she—didn't belong there.

Maybe that's it? A chill rippled up her back. *I'm the intruder here!*

She was about halfway down the stairs when she stopped again. Keeping her hand firmly on the banister, she leaned forward and looked from side to side, scanning as much of the cellar as she could. The rusting hulk of the old oil-burning furnace was in the corner next to the rusting black tank of the water heater. Motionless clots of black cobwebs draped down from between the floor joists of the ceiling. A thick coating of dust covered everything, and the old cement floor was pitted and crumbling, especially near the walls where there was obvious water damage.

There was only one window at the far end of the cellar, next to the bulkhead door which had several planks and sheets of plywood nailed across it, sealing it shut. Beyond the furnace was a narrow doorway that led into a small room. Polly thought it might once have been used as a root cellar.

She still couldn't shake the feeling that she was intruding on a silence that was best left undisturbed, but something compelled her to keep moving down until finally she was standing at the foot of the stairs.

"There, see? It's not so bad," she whispered.

But even the sound of her own voice was grating in the dense, gloomy silence. Once again, she sniffed the air. The odd smell was stronger now but still teasing and unidentifiable. It lingered in her nose like . . . like . . .

What?

She wasn't sure, but it stirred deep, intangible memories and sent another wave of chills racing up her spine. Her sneakers scuffed the cellar floor loudly, the sound oddly amplified by the silence as she moved from the foot of the stairs toward the furnace. Tim had come down here when they first arrived to make sure the furnace and hot water heater were working. She thought she could see traces of his footprints in the dust on the floor. There were other markings on the floor that she knew weren't Tim's, but she wasn't sure who or what might have made them.

Her heart was pulsing light and fast in her neck as she made her way through the semidarkness. A few times, she raised her hands to brush away cobwebs that hung down too low. Afraid of what she might see, she couldn't quite bring herself to look up at the denser shadows near the ceiling.

As she got closer to the hot water heater and furnace, she became aware of a high-pitched buzzing sound. For a moment, she thought it must be coming from the furnace or the water heater, but when she looked in that direction, the sound receded. It seemed to be playing tricks on her, getting incrementally louder or fainter whenever she turned her head to one side or the other. She realized that she couldn't pinpoint the source of the sound and wondered if maybe it was in her head. Listening, she could hear the soft, steady *whoosh*ing of blood in her ears, keeping pace with her pulse.

Moving past the furnace, she approached the narrow doorway that led into the smaller room. Her heart skipped a beat, and a sharp tightness gripped her throat when she saw that the walls inside the room were painted white.

"Oh my God," she whispered hoarsely.

The color had yellowed over the years, but it was unmistakably white. The wall to her right was covered by a rack of shelves that ran from floor to ceiling. Each shelf was made of two wide pine planks that ran side by side. They were covered with several dozen antique preserve jars. On the far wall, there was a small window that had been boarded over, but daylight made its way through some of the cracks, casting the room with an eerie, milky glow. It was bright enough for Polly to see that the canning jars were full of fruits or vegetables that had gone bad over the years.

"Jesus," Polly whispered, not quite daring to reach out and touch any of the jars. The outsides of the glass were coated with dust, but she could see some of the contents.

In the weird half light of the room, she saw twisted strands of black and dark red material suspended in the thick, amber syrup.

"Weird," she whispered, her voice hushed with awe.

She had no idea what was in the jars. It could be tomatoes, beets, or peaches, maybe even beans or peas that had discolored as they rotted over the years. Curious, Polly reached out and brushed away the dust on one of the nearest jars. After a moment or two, she found the courage to pick it up and examine it. Tilting it from side to side, she watched, feeling both fascinated and repulsed as the dark-colored strands shifted slowly back and forth in the heavy syrup. It reminded her of a lava lamp, only a lot grosser.

Tim's mother had been dead for five years, but Polly had no doubt that she had put up these preserves, so they had been down here at least that long. Tim's father never would have bothered. If it wasn't on an aluminum foil tray that came out of the freezer and heated up in stove, he would have had nothing to do with it.

Polly felt an odd sense of loss as she stared at the long-neglected jars. Someone had worked so hard to put up all of this food, and now here it was, wasting away into rotting, putrid messes that wouldn't even qualify as some kid's science experiment. Bending down, she looked at more of the jars, trying to determine what was in them. She jumped and let out a sharp cry when she bumped a jar on the bottom shelf.

A stringy red and black . . . something . . . floated in the jar. It looked more like flesh than vegetable matter. She had no idea what it was, but her first impression was that it looked like a bloated, black leech that had attached itself to the side of the jar. One spot that was white with mold actually looked like tiny teeth inside a sucker mouth.

Polly's stomach churned with a rush of nausea, but she was fascinated and couldn't look away. Shifting closer, she reached in and pulled several more of the jars forward to inspect them. Each one looked more and more disgusting than the last. In one of them, there was a tangled pink thing that looked like fresh ground meat that had gone bad. It floated at the top of the jar, a black, bubbly mass of rot. The lid was bulging up as though pressure was building up inside, pushing it up.

"Oh, my God," Polly muttered as she carefully placed the jar back on the shelf and wiped her hand on her jeans leg.

But as repulsed as she was, she didn't stop. Reaching back even farther on the shelf, she grabbed another jar and pulled it out. When she saw what was inside it, her jaw dropped. The only sound she could make was a strangled gasp. At the bottom of the jar, looking like a pickled egg, was what looked like a large, pickled *eyeball!*

Polly was so caught by surprise that she didn't have enough strength to stand up. Drawing her hand back quickly, she propelled herself away from the shelves so hard she slammed her back into the opposite wall. A jab of pain shot through her shoulders, but she barely noticed it because her gaze was riveted to the contents of the jar.

There's no way! That can't be what it looks like!

Over the years, the object had spread out, flattening against the bottom of the jar. It was angled a little to one side so it looked sort of cross-eyed. The liquid in the jar had turned to a rich amber yellow that looked as thick as oil. Tiny bubbles, like little pearl beads, rose slowly through the liquid and collected on the surface under the lid.

The cool air in the cellar room suddenly felt too thin to breathe. Spots of light shot across Polly's vision, and the steady muffled thud-thud of her pulse was as loud as a drum in her ears.

Polly wanted to get up off the floor and get the hell out of there, but she knew she didn't have the strength. She couldn't tear her gaze away from the jar and its horrible contents. In her imagination, she couldn't help but think that the eyeball was looking back at her and could see her! She wanted to scream but couldn't catch a deep enough breath to make a sound.

Somehow, though, she found the willpower to tear her gaze away from the jar and look at the narrow doorway that led back into the cellar. It was so close, all she had to do was lunge at it and she would be out of there, but she couldn't make herself move. Every muscle in her body seemed frozen, all except for her eyes, which shifted back to the horrible collection of canning jars.

The eyeball was still there, and although she tried to convince herself that it couldn't really be an eyeball, that it had to be something else like a rotting tomato or something, it looked exactly like an eyeball.

"It's gotta be an optical illusion," Polly whispered, and she couldn't help but laugh nervously at the morbid pun.

When she looked at the rest of the jars, especially the ones on the back of the shelf, she saw now that there were other things that looked like body parts floating in the rancid juices. One jar in particular caught her attention. Suspended in the middle was a dark, twisted mass that looked like a small, deformed embryo. Its tiny, clawed hands were raised slightly against the inside of the jar, almost as though just before it died it had been scratching against the glass in a futile attempt to escape.

Polly's mind filled with an audible *whoosh*. She knew that she had to get out of there!

Some sick bastard has preserved body parts and fetuses!

Bracing both hands against the cold floor, she shifted forward and tried to rise. Waves of dizziness swept over her, threatening to pull her down, but somehow she managed to get to her feet. Trembling with fear, she took a lurching step toward the doorway, toward freedom. Her chest ached from lack of fresh air. She cringed as she reached out and grabbed on to one of the shelves for support.

I'm not gonna make it!

Her left leg buckled beneath her, and she started to fall forward. Her shoulder hit hard against the top edge of the shelves. Pain as clean and sharp as an electric shock shot down her arm. The canning jars on the shelf rattled from the impact, and as she pressed against the old shelving, trying to regain her balance, one of the planks snapped with a loud crack.

Polly screamed as the jars slid forward in horrible slow motion, clunking with a dull sound against each other. Several of them fell over onto their sides and started rolling toward the edge of the broken shelf. When the first one hit the cement floor, it exploded with a thick, wet slapping sound. Polly screamed again when she felt something thick and wet splatter against her leg. The liquid instantly saturated her pants leg, making the cloth feel heavy. It felt almost as if a tiny hand was wrapped around her ankle and squeezing to hold on. Her throat closed off, and the only sound she could make was a high, strangled squeak when she looked down and saw the gelatinous red mess that had splattered her sneakers and was soaking into her pants.

It's blood!

The other jars were still rolling around, clattering against each other on the broken shelf. Before Polly could react, another one fell behind her and exploded open with a dull pop. She spun around and looked down as the gory contents seeped out onto the floor in thick, black and red clumps. Something was sticking up through the goo—a thin shard that Polly told herself had to be a piece of broken glass, but it was opaque and gray, and it looked more like a sliver of old bone than glass.

"Jesus, no! . . . *No!*"

Afraid that she was going to pass out, she spun around quickly. As she did, her hand inadvertently scooped several more jars onto the floor where they broke. The dense, noxious smell of rotting food—*or worse!*—filled the air, gagging her and making her cough. One of the jars that didn't fall broke open like a cracked egg when it rolled against the narrow board that supported the front of the shelf. A thick, stringy glob of red fluid laced with small, black chunks dripped in a looping strand over the edge of the shelf. It hung suspended in the air for a moment or two before its weight made it drop to the floor with a sickening plop.

Polly wanted to scream again but couldn't. Not daring

to breathe the terrible stench that filled the room, she sucked in a shallow breath and held it as she darted for the door. She was unaware that her hand brushed through the noxious fluid until she was back out in the main part of the cellar. Then, when she paused to get her bearings, she noticed that the fingers of her left hand felt sticky. She screamed so hard her voice broke when she held up her hand and saw the thick smear of red that dripped halfway up her forearm.

Her stomach twisted sourly when she glanced back into the room and saw the hideous mess. It looked like a slaughterhouse. The floor and walls were splattered with dark red fluid that Polly knew had to be blood. Holding her hands out in front of her, she ran for the cellar steps, suddenly fearful that there was something terrible behind her, pursuing her.

She skinned her knuckles when she grabbed one of the support beams and pivoted around to the stairs. Her legs were weak and trembling as she raced up the stairs two at a time until she pitched forward, practically falling into the kitchen. Whirling around, she slammed the cellar door shut and leaned against it, her chest heaving, her lungs burning from the sudden burst of effort.

She screamed and covered her face with both hands when she heard and felt a heavy *thump* against the door. It hit hard enough to make the wood bounce against her back, but then a sudden, dense silence settled onto the kitchen.

What the hell is that down there?

Polly was trembling violently as she pressed her back against the door, determined that if there was something down there, it wasn't going to get the door open . . . not without coming through her.

"Stop it," she whimpered. "Please . . . leave me alone."

She had no idea why she said that or who she was saying it to, but she couldn't ignore the feeling that there was something—a terrible threat to her and her family—lurking down in the cellar.

Tears gathered in her eyes and ran down her face. Her hand was shaking as she tried to wipe them away, but more came, spilling down her cheeks.

The banging sound against the door didn't repeat, so finally, after several minutes, Polly calmed down enough to find the courage to twist the key in the lock and step away from the door. She backed up slowly, her gaze riveted to the old oak door. She tried to convince herself that it was ridiculous to think there was someone down there. How could there be? No one was going to burst through the door and attack her. Still, she couldn't shake the horrible fear that *something*—she had no idea what—was waiting down there in the cool, damp darkness.

Just waiting . . .

Still trembling, she edged her way over to the wall phone, picked up the receiver, and quickly dialed the number to Tim's cell phone. A sickening aftertaste filled her mouth as she swallowed and listened to the phone ringing at the other end of the line . . . once . . . twice . . . three times . . .

"Come on, Tim! Pick up!" she whispered heatedly.

But the phone kept ringing, eight . . . nine more times before she finally realized that Tim wasn't going to answer. Still staring at the cellar door, she hung up the receiver and told herself she had to calm down.

That *couldn't* have been what she thought it was down there!

She had panicked, that's all.

And in her panic, she had mistaken the canning jars filled with rotten fruits and vegetables for something else. Something it couldn't possibly be.

That's what it had to be.

There was no logical reason why anyone would preserve what looked like human body parts and distorted embryos in glass jars down in the cellar. When Tim got home, she would have him go down there and check it out, but for now, she wasn't about to go down there and look around. As far as she was concerned, the cellar door was locked shut forever. She wouldn't go down there even if her life depended on it!

Once she had calmed down a bit, she walked over to the sink, ran the water until it was cold, and splashed her face. A shiver ran through her, but it wasn't nearly as bad as what she felt whenever she thought about what she had seen—no, what she *thought* she had seen—down there.

Still feeling shaky, she went to the refrigerator and grabbed a bottle of spring water, twisted the cap off, and took several gulps, draining nearly half of it. The cold water felt good, rushing down her parched throat, but it didn't come close to washing away the horrible taste that still clung like glue to the back of her throat. She forced herself to take deep, even breaths, but she still couldn't calm down. The memory of that eyeball—*But it couldn't really have been an eyeball!*—wouldn't go away, and she couldn't shake the feeling that someone, somewhere was still watching her.

Shivering wildly, she looked around, straining to hear if there were any unusual sounds in the house.

The silence was dense.

Even the faint song of birds outside seemed muffled and much farther away than she knew it was. She had the unnerving thought that she might be dreaming all of this, that she was trapped in a terrible nightmare and would wake up soon—if she could.

"No, I'm awake," she whispered hoarsely as she slapped her cheek a few times just to make sure.

But the creepy feeling she'd had down in the cellar, although lessening, wouldn't go away. It hovered at the edge of her awareness, making the hairs on the back of her neck stir. The *whoosh*ing sound of her pulse in her ears grew steadily louder, and she realized that it wasn't over. She was having a panic attack, and it wouldn't stop.

A low whimper escaped her as she turned and looked around the kitchen, trying to determine where—if any-where—the danger she sensed was lurking. The kitchen walls seemed to be closing in on her. Even with the windows open, the air felt stuffy and close, too hot to breathe.

I've got to get out of here!

She didn't know where Tim was. She had no idea why he hadn't answered his cell phone. There was no reason for him not to unless he had switched it off accidentally. But he was somewhere in town, and if she could get to town, she could find him.

Either that, or she could wait here until either he or Brian came home.

The feeling that she was being watched wouldn't go away as she walked into the living room and looked around. Everything appeared to be normal until she happened to glance out the living room window at the row of apple trees that lined the field. The view through the old gauzy curtains wasn't very good, and there were deep shadows beneath the trees, but Polly had a quick, clear impression that she saw someone—a person—standing under the trees with his face turned toward the house.

"Jesus," she whispered, dropping down into a defensive crouch.

Had he seen her?

Was he watching the house, waiting for her?

Who could it be, and what was he doing out there?

Trying to keep out of sight, in case someone really was watching the house, Polly made her way closer to the window and pulled the curtain aside. She peeked out around the window frame, squinting at the bright wash of sunlight that lit the grass and leaves. Still, beneath the apple trees was as dark and shady as early evening. Polly wasn't entirely surprised to see that there was no one out there. A steady, silent wind rippled through the long grass, pressing it down, but watching it through the closed window gave her the impression of watching a movie, not real life.

Suddenly, a hint of motion at the top of the window frame drew her attention. When she looked up, she thought she caught a fleeting glimpse of a face, leaning out over the edge of the roof and looking down at her. It was gone an instant before she could register it, but she was sure she had seen a small, pale face. It couldn't have been a passing cloud or a trick of her eye.

Cold, clenching panic hit her in the stomach, filling her with an irresistible urge to run.

But where?

The cellar certainly wasn't safe, and she didn't want to go upstairs alone if there was someone lurking outside the house. She was filled with a terrible sense of danger.

Where can I go?

"Just get the fuck out of here," she whispered to herself, wishing that she could find at least some measure of courage in the sound of her own voice as she hurried to the back door.

Brian used a stick to fish his sneaker out of the river. Then, moving downstream a short distance, he found a place along the riverbank where the sun shone brightly. The mud and slime that covered him from head to foot was shrinking as it dried, making his skin feel tingling and tight.

Kneeling by the river's edge, he washed up as well as he could. The whole time he held on to a tree branch, not wanting to risk falling into the river again. He shuddered whenever he thought about how close he had come to actually drowning. The memory of his feet getting tangled in the underwater branches—and how, in his imagination, he had pictured thin, skeletal hands, grasping for him and trying to pull him under—filled him with fear. He decided never even to contemplate swimming anywhere except someone's swimming pool where it was safe.

After rinsing his clothes out, he spread them over some branches in the sun. Wearing nothing but his underwear, he lay down in the sun and closed his eyes, hoping to rest. He stared at the dense field of red that shimmered behind his closed eyes. It wasn't long before the powerful heat of the sun drove the lingering chill out of his bones. With birds chittering in the trees around him, he drifted off to sleep. Sometime later, in a half-dreamy haze, he became aware of the soft tread of footsteps on the forest floor. He stirred but didn't fully wake up as he listened to the footsteps approach. Then, without warning, a flash of panic made him utter a low cry, sit up, and look around.

The sudden blast of sunlight hurt his eyes, making them water as he glanced all around. He was positive that he had sensed danger. Even the birds seemed to have stopped singing, and the chilly tension had returned.

Someone's around here . . . watching me!

Shifting patterns of sunlight and shadow in the forest confused his eyes. In the deepest shadows under the trees, he thought he saw figures, moving in and out of sight, but whenever he looked directly at them, he realized that it was just a trick of shadows and leaves waving in the breeze.

"I know you're there," he called out.

His voice echoed faintly from the opposite shore, and he sat huddled as he waited for a reply.

"It's no sense hiding. I know you're there."

After a few tense seconds, he heard the crunching of leaves and twigs behind him. He wheeled around into a defensive crouch, his fists raised, ready to protect himself if he had to. He felt foolish and vulnerable being caught out in the woods wearing just his underwear. His jaw dropped in astonishment when Josh appeared from the brush. A wide smile split his face. "Hey, man, how's it going?" Josh asked.

Brian didn't answer him. Then, as if realizing for the first time that Brian was wearing nothing but his underwear, Josh frowned and said, "Is everything all right?"

A sudden flash of anger filled Brian. Seeing Josh in the direct sunlight, he couldn't help but remember the figure he had seen on the opposite shore the whole time he had been struggling to save himself from drowning.

"No," Brian said softly through gritted teeth. "Everything's *not* all right! What the fuck were you doing a little while ago?"

Josh took a step back and folded his arms across his chest, a perplexed expression on his face. Even in the bright sunlight, his skin looked as pale as paper, especially for someone who seemed to spend a great deal of time outdoors.

"What do you mean, what was I doing?" Josh asked with an innocent shrug. "I was . . . with some friends, and I'm just heading home."

"You weren't out here a while ago? Maybe half an hour or so? You didn't see me fall into the river?"

Again, Josh shrugged innocently. "No. Honest. I was just heading home." He paused, and a faint smile twitched at the corners of his mouth. "So that's what happened, huh? You fell in?"

Brian wasn't sure if he should be embarrassed or disgusted, but he nodded slowly and said, "Yeah. I thought I saw something floating in the river, and when I went to check it out, I kinda slipped in."

It seemed foolish to him now, embarrassing. He tried not to think about the pale face he was sure he had seen under the water.

Josh nodded and took a single step forward, then scooched down. "You have to watch out for this river. Its currents can be pretty tricky. Every summer, at least three or four people drown in it. Usually summer people, you know? Campers and canoeists who don't know what they're doing. Some folks claim it's because there's an Indian curse that the river will claim a certain number of white folks every year, but I just think it's people who don't know what they're doing."

"Which I guess I'm one of," Brian said with a tight chuckle.

He was feeling really self-conscious, standing there in his underwear, talking to Josh. Trying to look as casual as possible, he wandered over to the trees and collected his clothes. They were still damp and funny smelling. They clung to his skin as he slipped them on. Even in the hot sun, a chill ran up and down his spine, but he pretended not to notice.

"So," he said as he sat down on the ground and started lacing on his sneakers. "What are you doing now?"

"Oh . . . like I said, just heading home," Josh replied.

He seemed innocent enough, but there was a funny tone in his voice that Brian couldn't help but notice. He wasn't sure what it was about Josh that bothered him. Maybe it was just that he sounded so aloof or vacant when he talked about himself, but there was a strange kind of emptiness about him that Brian didn't like.

"Well, I'd ask if you wanted to do something, maybe go play tennis or something, but I should probably get back to the house myself and get cleaned up." Brian finished lacing his sneakers and stood up. "I'm just hoping my folks aren't around. My mom will pitch a fit if she sees me like this."

"Umm," Josh replied, nodding his head slowly up and down.

For some reason, Brian had the impression that he was only half listening to him, that he had something else on his mind that was distracting him.

Maybe that's why he seems so out of it, Brian thought. *He's just a self-centered asshole.*

Brian was pretty sure he already knew the answer even before he asked the question, but he decided to go ahead and ask it anyway.

"Maybe after I get cleaned up we can hook up and do something?"

"I'd like to," Josh replied, his face looking almost sad, "but I got some stuff I have to do later."

"Yeah? What kind of stuff?"

Brian wasn't sure why he felt like pressing Josh. The more he thought about it, the more convinced he was that it had to have been Josh he had seen standing on the opposite shore in the shadows, watching as he struggled to save himself. Josh could pretend all he wanted to, but

Brian knew he had seen *someone,* and he was sure that it had been Josh.

"Just . . . stuff, you know?" Josh said with a tone almost of resignation as he shrugged. There was a dull glow in his eyes that Brian found unnerving. It confused him, but the more he thought about it, the more he decided that he didn't really want even to try to be friends with this kid. There was something really weird about him. No wonder he didn't have any friends and was always wandering around alone out here in the woods.

He's a fucking jerk! To hell with him!

"Well," Brian said, brushing the seat of his pants, "Catch you later, then."

"Yeah . . . later," Josh said with a nod.

His voice sounded even fainter as he looked not at Brian, but past him, as though focusing on something far off in the distance.

Thoroughly disgusted, Brian turned and started walking away. His sneakers were still soaked. They made funny, squishy sounds as he scrambled up the riverbank to the trail. His clothes were stiff and scratchy against his skin, and he was already thinking about how he was going to get into the house without his mother or father catching him. If they saw him like this, especially after the last time, he'd have a lot of explaining to do.

Before starting down the trail, Brian looked back to wave one last time to Josh. He wasn't at all surprised to see that the boy was nowhere in sight. The only sounds that filled the forest were the chirping of birds and the soft, slow hiss of the dark, flowing river.

Polly opened the screen door and stepped cautiously out onto the back porch. A warm breeze, heavy with the scent of pine, washed over her, but it did nothing to dispel the chill that coiled up inside her.

Someone's watching . . . watching the house and watching me!

She shifted her gaze to the row of apple trees but saw no one there, nothing but sunlight and shadow playing across the grass and dark tree trunks. As she walked out into the driveway, she cast a furtive glance at the house, looking up at the roof as though half expecting to see someone squatting up there, glaring down at her.

You imagined it. That's all it was. There wasn't anyone up there. How could there be?

Her feet crunched the gravel of the driveway as she walked slowly toward the barn. She was fighting hard to keep down her rising panic, but the sound set her teeth on edge. It wasn't hard to imagine that—somewhere, if not in the shed on the other side of the driveway or up on the roof or lurking in the trees—somewhere close by, *someone* was watching her!

She wanted to scream, but she forced herself to remain calm as she walked straight to the open barn door and the old car that was parked inside.

I'll drive into town. It doesn't matter if I see Tim or not. The important thing is just to get the hell out of here!

She wasn't sure if she was going to make it. Every shadow, every shifting branch, and every blade of grass waving in the wind seemed threatening. Polly cringed, expecting at any moment that something was going to leap out at her. Even the cool, shadowed recesses of the barn seemed fraught with danger.

What if the car doesn't start? What if the key isn't in it?

Polly didn't care that the car wasn't registered or inspected, as long as it started and she could drive into town. She had to get away, at least until her husband got back home. After that, she would think about what to do next, but she was sure that she was going to ask if they could leave the house and Hilton, Maine, and head back home.

As Polly approached the Olds, she realized that she was biting down on her lower lip hard enough almost to draw blood. Her throat felt dry and raw, and she was prepared for disappointment as she walked up to the driver's side and looked inside.

The keys were there!

She breathed a sigh of relief even as the shadows in the barn seemed to condense and shift closer to her. Her hand was slick with sweat and almost slipped off the pitted chrome door latch as she grabbed it tightly and pulled.

The door latch clicked.

The instant she pulled the car door open, a dense mildew smell blew into her face, making her gasp and choke. The smell was so strong that it stung the insides of her nose and coated the back of her throat with a sickly taste that felt like it would never go away.

Deal with it, she told herself as she slid onto the seat. The old seat springs creaked beneath her weight. The fabric was hot against the back of her legs.

Just start it up and get the hell out of here!

The interior of the car was as stifling as an oven. Polly thought it was somewhat strange, since the car had been in the shade of the barn all day. She glanced at her reflection in the rearview mirror, caught for a moment by her wild, glazed eyes. Her forehead was beaded with perspiration that dripped down the sides of her face. She thought she was moving a little too sluggishly, almost as if she were in a dream as she reached out for the key and turned it slowly.

For a few heart-stopping seconds, the engine made a loud grinding sound but didn't catch. It sounded like a stubborn car trying to turn over on a frozen winter morning.

"Come on, you bitch!" she muttered, feeling her frustration rise.

She stopped for a second, sat back in the seat, took a deep breath, then tried again. After a few noisy cranks, the engine kicked in with a rattling roar. A thick cloud of exhaust blew out the back, looking like dense cannon smoke in the still air. Overhead, the barn swallows chirped as they darted about. Polly heaved a sigh of relief as she shifted the car into reverse, rested her right arm over the back of the seat and, looking over her shoulder, backed out into the driveway. One of the spark plugs was obviously fouled, making the car run with a jittery sputter, but it didn't die on her.

What the hell are you doing?

She looked at her reflection again, almost frightened by what she saw in her own eyes.

You look like a crazy woman!

It suddenly dawned on her that she might be overreacting, but the panic she had felt earlier was still fresh in her mind. She couldn't ignore the urgent need to run. Tim was nowhere around and not answering his cell phone, and Brian still hadn't come back from wherever he was, so there was no one here to talk to or help her.

She wondered if she could just be making all of this up because she had been so wound up lately, but she was positive that it was more than that. It wasn't just that she felt funny whenever she was in the house alone. She didn't feel comfortable there even when she was with her family. It was just that the bad feelings were much more intense when she was alone.

But it's not just me!

A deep shudder ran through her.

It's not! There's something wrong with that house!

She cut the steering wheel to the right and swung the car around so she was facing the road. Even from within the safety of the car, she felt like she was in danger. She had no idea what she was afraid of, but the threat was real and palpable. She didn't need Heather Olsen's voice to tell her that!

She wiped the sweat from her face with the flat of her hand, then gripped the steering wheel tightly and shifted into Drive.

The transmission made a loud clunk sound but caught. She glanced at the fuel gauge and saw that the tank was nearly empty, but there was enough gas to get to town. It was so hot in the car that she was tempted to roll the window down, but even that seemed to be inviting danger. Instead, she reached for the controls and slid the bar over to Vent. As soon as she turned on the blower, a loud buzzing sound filled the car as dozens—hundreds of small, brown pellets shot out of the vents.

Almost blind with panic, Polly took her foot off the brake and stepped down hard on the gas. The car roared and sputtered as it jolted forward. Its underinflated tires scruffed loudly on the gravel and skidded, raising a cloud of dust in its wake. The motion was so sudden that Polly screamed as she fought to control the car, but then she felt a needle-sharp sting on the side of her neck that made her howl even louder.

The blower was still running, still shooting out dust and small brown objects. In a flash, Polly realized that a swarm of yellow jackets was angrily buzzing as the air vent blew them out of their nest and into the car.

With one hand gripping the steering wheel, Polly swatted at the yellow jackets with the other, but there were too many of them. She felt at least another six or seven stings on her arms and face, and she watched like a helpless observer as the car swerved back and forth, barely staying on the driveway.

Polly couldn't take it any longer. Reaching out blindly for the door handle, she pulled it up as she stepped down hard on the brakes. The tires skidded loudly on the driveway, and the car heaved around to the right, spinning a full 180 degrees. When it finally lurched to a stop, Polly threw the shift into Park and pulled the door handle up hard. Her hands were so sweaty she lost her grip, and in that brief space of time, two more yellow jackets found their mark and stung her, one on the forearm and the other behind her left ear. Whimpering softly, she yanked the door handle up as hard as she could with one hand while waving her other hand wildly in front of her face.

That seemed only to agitate the yellow jackets. There was a buzzing brown flurry of activity around her head as she shouldered open the door and fell out onto the driveway.

"Jesus!" she shouted as another wasp darted at her, and she swatted it away with the palm of her hand.

Unmindful of the pain, she crawled over the gravel on her hands and knees to the lawn. When she was at least thirty feet away from the car, she stopped. The house was on the opposite side of the driveway, and she realized that the old shed was close by. She could feel its ominous presence, but she hardly cared as she collapsed face first onto the grass and exhaled loudly. For a long time, she just lay there, hugging the ground and cringing as she waited to feel the sharp pain of more stings.

But none came.

She pressed her face down hard into the grass and smelled the sweet, moist aroma of the soil. She could still hear the angry, droning sound of the agitated hive, but it was so distant it seemed dreamlike. Squeezing her eyes tightly shut, she flattened herself against the ground and took a deep, steadying breath through her nose. After a few minutes, she heard the car sputter and then die with a soft chuffing sound. That left just the buzzing of the yellow jackets and the soft sighing of the wind in the trees behind her.

Feeling suddenly sleepy, Polly wondered if it was the effect of getting several bee stings. She groaned softly as she rolled over onto her back and stared up at the sky. There wasn't a cloud in sight. The wide arc of blue vibrated with intensity.

She couldn't believe that she was still alive.

A few stings were nothing. She wasn't allergic to wasp or bee stings, so she knew she'd be all right. Still, she felt an overwhelming tide of weariness weighing her down. The sun caressed her face, and she closed her eyes to stare at the swirling field of shimmering red behind her closed eyes.

"Jesus . . . Jesus . . . Jesus," she whispered as she scratched the burning sting on the back of her neck.

Without any resistance, her consciousness slowly slipped away, and she drifted off to sleep.

eleven

"I think I might be losing my mind."

Polly was close to tears as she and Tim sat side by side on the porch steps. They were so close that their shoulders and hips were pressing against each other. She appreciated the warmth of his body, but she was feeling so fragile she wished he would put his arm around her. Tim seemed to be shying away from her, though, and that left her feeling alone and empty even with him beside her.

Maybe it was because her neck, face, and arms were covered with big dabs of mud. Tim had told her that mud was the best remedy for bee stings, but she wasn't so sure. She thought it probably would have been better to go to a pharmacy in town and get something for the stings. But Tim had insisted nature's remedy was best, so he had run the garden hose and mixed up a handful of mud in the palm of his hand, then carefully dabbed the mud on every sting.

That had been nearly an hour ago. Now, as the mud dried and hardened, it was cracking and pulling at her skin. Beneath the mud, the dozen or more yellow jacket stings felt like burning match tips were being held against her skin.

"I don't think you're losing your mind," Tim said.

There was just a trace of impatience in his voice. He clamped his hand over her knee and squeezed tightly.

"But if you think you need to talk to Dr. Finch again . . ."

He let his voice trail away, and Polly cringed at the memory. When she had lost the baby four years ago, she had spent about a year in therapy. It had helped, but this time it felt different. Before she had been dealing with grief and loss. This time, she felt . . . *threatened* was the first word that popped into her mind.

Besides the pain, Polly was also humiliated that she had lost her self-control so badly. Blinking back the tears, she looked at her husband. She couldn't help but wonder if it was just her imagination or if Tim really did seem more distant to her. She tried not to think it, but she couldn't help herself. If there was a distance widening between them, how and when had it started?

She wanted to think that things hadn't really gotten weird until they moved into the old house, but she knew that wasn't true. The memory of the day Heather Olsen had died in her arms was still as fresh in her mind as if it had happened yesterday. But the truth was, long before that she hadn't really felt like herself. Not for a long time.

Maybe as far back as when Crystal died trying to be born.

The memory sent a pain tingling through her that was much sharper and deeper than any yellow jacket sting. An icy cold hardness centered in her chest weighed down her heart and made it difficult for her to breathe.

"I just . . . I just don't *feel* right," she said in a shattered whisper. "I don't feel like myself anymore. I'm not even sure I know what my real self *is* anymore."

"Then maybe seeing Dr. Finch is a good idea," Tim said softly. Looking at her with a tight smile, he took her left hand into both of his and held it tightly. "I think you're doing just fine," he said in a low voice. "But you know better how you're doing."

Polly could see that he was trying to help, but for some

reason, his words angered her. She felt almost as if he were patronizing her. She slid her hand from his grasp and, squeezing both hands into tight fists, punched her thighs once, hard.

"No, I'm *not* doing fine," she said. "That's what I'm telling you."

She would have shouted it, but her throat was still raw from screaming when the yellow jackets had attacked her.

"I'm not doing fine at all! Ever since we got here, I've been . . . I've been—"

Her voice choked off, ending with a strangled sob as she leaned forward, covered her face with both hands, and started to cry. Her body shook as grief and pain and unnamed fear ran through her. Finally, Tim slid his arm around her shoulder and pulled her up hard against him, but Polly thought it was too late for that.

"There, there," he whispered in her ear.

His words did nothing to soothe the anguish she was feeling. With her eyes tightly closed and her hands pressing against her face, Polly couldn't have felt more isolated, more alone. She wished there was someone she could talk to, if not Tim, then Lois or *someone* who might understand what she was feeling.

"Why didn't you answer your cell phone when I called?" she asked, her voice muffled by her hands. "I called and it just kept ringing and ringing."

"I'm really sorry about that," Tim said softly, still rubbing her shoulder, "but Rob and I went out for lunch, and just out of habit, I switched the phone off in the restaurant and just forgot to switch it back on."

"So where *were* you?" Polly asked, still not taking her hands away from her eyes. "It was around three o'clock when I called. You can't tell me that you were at the restaurant the whole time."

Tim was silent for a long moment, and in that silence, Polly imagined all sorts of things that she didn't even want to contemplate. Her first thought was that he might have been with someone else . . . not his brother, but someone else . . . maybe a woman he used to know when he lived here. . . ."

Stop it! Don't think like that!

But that was the first and seemingly most natural assumption to make when a husband seems distant and less communicative than usual. He's having an affair or at least fucking someone else.

"I . . . uh, I dropped Rob off at his place around one o'-clock, I guess, and after that I just drove around." Tim's voice didn't sound at all convincing. "I haven't really had a chance to . . . you know, check out the town since we got here, and I was feeling nostalgic, so I just drove around, kind of mulling over old memories."

Polly wanted to ask him what kind of memories but was afraid of what he might say.

No! Don't think like that! That's not what this is about!

When she took a deep breath between her fingers, a powerful smell filled her nose with such intensity it almost gagged her. She hadn't cleaned up yet, so her hands were still dirty, but the smell reminded her of something else. She couldn't identify it, but after sniffing a few more times she finally got it.

Vinegar!

"What the fuck," she muttered as she inhaled again.

Now that she had identified it and was expecting it, she couldn't miss it. Her hands were imbued with the acidic tang of vinegar.

"What, you don't believe me?" Tim asked.

His voice sounded far away, but it brought her back at least a little bit to where she was and what she was doing. She looked at him and smiled, trying hard to focus, but she couldn't stop wondering why her hands would smell like vinegar. She hadn't touched anything with vinegar in it or used it in cooking. Even when she was scrambling around on the ground, she had just been crawling in the grass. The smell could have come from something in the old car, possibly, but if that was it, she would have noticed it by now.

Both she and Tim were silent for a long while. The afternoon sun felt warm on her shoulders. In the fields and woods, she could hear the steady buzz of insects and the warbling of birds. All of this should soothe her, she told herself. Wasn't that what moving to the country was all about? Finding peace and harmony with nature?

So why was she feeling so tense, so shattered, like there were only thin fragments of her real self left, and they were hanging together with the most tenuous of connections?

—*Old bones*—

The words popped into her mind with such clarity that, for an instant, Polly thought Tim had spoken them, but she instantly realized that it had been a girl's voice, whispering softly, like the wind in her ears. She covered her face with her hands again and concentrated on hearing the voice.

It had been a while since she had heard Heather's voice, so she wondered if that's who it was or if it was someone else. In an odd way, Heather's "voice" had become such an integral part of her own mind that she sometimes had trouble distinguishing between the two voices in her head.

"What did you say?" Polly whispered into the cup of her hands.

Her warm breath rebounded onto her face. She could feel the sweat and grime grinding into her skin as she stared into the swelling darkness.

"I asked if you didn't believe me," Tim said. His voice sounded hollow and maybe a bit defensive.

I don't mean you!

Polly wanted to shout that at him, but the fear welling up inside her was getting stronger, almost unbearable, and it kept her silent.

—*Old bones*—

The voice whispered again, softer now, almost lost in the hushed silence that surrounded her.

"Look, Pol . . . I honestly don't know what to tell you,"

Tim said. "If you really want to see a doctor, then maybe you should."

"No, it's not that . . . it's not that at all," Polly whispered. It took a great effort to say this and not start screaming.

"Then do you want to leave here?" Tim asked. "Is that it? Do you think we should go back home?"

Twisted, tortured emotions filled Polly with such intensity that she couldn't speak. She couldn't even cry out or whimper. She felt so wrung out, so useless and spent, so full of tangled emotions that she couldn't even identify that she was left feeling dry and empty.

Beside her, Tim took a deep breath. She could hear a slight shudder as he exhaled. His arm was still around her shoulder, and he pulled her tightly against him, but she was feeling so dissociated that she could easily imagine her body was as light and lifeless as a scarecrow stuffed with straw.

She knew, with a dreaded certainty, that her husband was not being entirely honest with her. She wasn't sure what, exactly, he was keeping from her, or why, but there was a distance between them, something that they had lost and might not ever be able to recover. The thought filled her with aching misery.

Maybe that's what was ripping her apart, she thought, and maybe there was something more. It might just have something to do with this old house because the truth was, whatever had been bothering her before had gotten much worse since they arrived in Hilton.

Keeping her eyes covered with her hands and staring into the darkness, Polly got a mental image of a high stone wall that was separating her from her husband. It was tall and thick, practically impenetrable. She pictured herself, sobbing as she clawed at the unyielding stones, trying to get through to him.

That was bad enough, but what filled her with an even deeper anguish was the feeling that she was no longer sure if she had the will or the energy to try to break through that wall.

Maybe that's what insanity is. . . .

The hollow, black feeling inside her grew so intense it seemed to fill up every square inch inside her.

Maybe going crazy is when you simply no longer have the will to fight back . . . when you get so tired of fighting that you finally lose your fear of the end.

Staring into the darkness and feeling herself being pulled into it, Polly wished desperately she had enough strength left to cry.

"Old bones."

She whispered the words so softly that she wasn't even sure if she had spoken them out loud or just thought them. The darkness in the bedroom was so intense that she was confused for a moment as to whether or not her eyes were open or closed. A blanket of black vibrated all around her with such intensity she could almost imagine that it was making a low, steady humming sound.

"What did you say?"

Tim's voice, coming so suddenly and clearly out of the night, startled her, making her jump. She clasped the bed sheet to her chin, feeling its cool, damp touch against her bare skin. Her brow was slick with perspiration that chilled her, and a scratchy dryness gripped her throat. The yellow jacket stings felt like hot coals beneath her skin.

"I . . . I didn't say anything," Polly said, surprising herself with the sound of her own voice.

"Yes you did."

She heard and felt the old bedsprings creak loudly as Tim rolled over to face her. The room was pitch black, and she knew that he couldn't see her, but she couldn't shake the feeling that he was watching her intently. Shivering, she shifted her gaze over toward the window and looked at the faint, dusky gray night sky framed by the curtains. The air in the room was cooler than she would have expected after such a hot day. It hurt her ribs when she inhaled.

"You said 'old bones.' What did you mean by that?"

Tim's voice had a certain intensity that she didn't like. She wanted to reach out to him, to feel his reassuring touch, but the wall she had imagined between them earlier that day seemed to still be there. She knew it was really just herself holding back, not letting him in, but she sensed that there was a reason to mistrust him almost as if a voice inside her head was telling her to.

Is mistrust *the right word? Do I really mistrust my husband?*

"I was just . . . probably just talking in my sleep," Polly said, hoping that would satisfy him, and he would go back to sleep. Talking to him in the dark like this gave her a strange, unnerving feeling that she didn't like. She could easily imagine that none of this was really happening, that she was dreaming even now. It had started, she remembered, when she heard a voice—*Was it Heather's voice*—whispering in the darkness?

—Old bones—

"No. I was just dreaming," she muttered softly as she rolled onto her side away from him, hoping he would get the message that she wasn't up for a conversation right now. The tone of his voice, though, had made her think he wanted more than conversation. There was an edge to it that she only heard whenever they were having an argument. She couldn't see what they could possibly be arguing about right now. All she wanted was to be left alone.

"Why would you say something like that?" Tim asked.

The impatient edge was still in his voice, making him sound almost cruel. Polly felt as though she suddenly was in grave danger.

"I was just mumbling in my sleep," she said hoarsely. "That's all it was. I don't even remember what I said."

That was a straight-up lie because she knew *exactly*

what she had said . . . or thought. She was still a little confused as to whether or not she had even spoken out loud, but the words *old bones* echoed in her memory like the ringing sound of metal striking against metal.

—Old bones—

Once again, she heard and felt the mattress creak as Tim rolled over. A second or two later, the bedside light snapped on, flooding the bedroom with a harsh, yellow glare. Shielding her eyes with one hand, Polly looked over her shoulder at her husband. He was bare-chested and sitting up with his back against the headboard, his arms folded across his chest.

"I want to know why you said that," he said sternly.

Squinting into the light that was shining behind his head, Polly tried to focus.

How much can I tell him?

It bothered her that she even had to ask herself that question. If she was worried that she might be going a little crazy, then how would it sound to him if she told him the truth?

He would think she was going a *lot* crazy.

She didn't want him to worry about her or wonder how close to the edge she was. She wanted to deal with whatever was bothering her on her own, but it was getting too hard to do that. She needed someone to talk to, and it hurt her to think that someone wasn't her husband.

"I . . . I'm not sure," she said.

She cleared her throat and looked away from him before she could continue.

"I was sound asleep, and I heard . . . I thought I heard a voice say 'old bones.' I don't know why."

Tim was silent for a long while, but she knew he hadn't gone back to sleep. The only sound in the room was the harsh sound of him breathing through his nose. Polly could feel the hard, steady thumping of her heart in her chest, and she couldn't help but wonder how much she could trust him. There was an edge to him, a hostility that she had never seen before.

"Do you know anything about what happened in town?" Tim finally asked.

Biting her lower lip, Polly looked at him and shook her head quickly.

"What do you mean?"

Tim sighed and, making a fist, pressed it against his mouth. He looked lost in thought, but Polly saw something deep in his eyes that worried her. It took a moment or two for her to realize that it was fear she saw there.

Is he hearing the voices, too?

"You know that construction site up the road heading back to town?" Tim asked.

Unable to speak, Polly nodded. She noticed that his voice was shaking.

"A few weeks before we came here . . . the same day Rob broke his leg, in fact, they found some bones buried out where they were excavating."

"Old bones?"

Polly heard the catch in her voice, and for a dizzying instant, she wasn't sure if she had said the words out loud or simply thought them.

"Yeah," Tim replied. "Old bones. They found some old bones buried out there. Human bones."

Polly's throat made a wet rattling sound as she inhaled sharply.

"They're sure they're human?" she said. "I mean, maybe it was just . . . you know, probably some animal that died in the woods and was covered over or something."

Tim chuckled, but there was no humor in it. The gleam in his eyes looked more malicious as he regarded her silently for a moment.

"It was an animal all right," he finally said, "an animal named Mark Dufresne."

A sudden dash of chills hit Polly in the stomach like a solidly placed punch.

I don't want to hear this. It's going to be bad . . . really bad.

She knew that she had already heard more than she wanted to, but it was almost as if someone else was controlling her voice when she asked, "How do you know who it is?"

The twisted smile on Tim's face got wider. His eyelids fluttered a few times, and then he winced as though he'd had a sudden pain in the center of his head. His eyes had a steady, glazed look that terrified her. Even when he was looking straight at her, she had the impression that he was focused on something far, far away.

"I know," Tim said softly, "because I helped put him there."

It was the third week of October, and—so far, anyway—junior high school had been going really well . . . until today, anyway.

Timmy had gotten caught goofing around in seventh-grade science class, and Mr. Doyle hadn't been the least bit amused. Of course, Timmy claimed it wasn't fair that he was the only one to get detention. It wasn't like he'd been fooling around all by himself. But he was the one Mr. Doyle had caught with his arm cocked back, ready to flip a spitball at Brittany Dahms, so he was the one who had to stay after school for detention.

That wasn't so bad, though. It wasn't all that serious an infraction. His parents probably wouldn't even find out about it. And even if they did, he could probably slough it off. Mr. Doyle had a reputation for being a hard-ass. He'd had Timmy's older brother, Rob, in class two years earlier, and Timmy's dad didn't have much good to say about the man. Besides, Timmy was a good student, overall. Certainly much better than Rob had been. So he might get a lecture from his father about how in junior high it was starting to count as far as getting into college was con-

cerned. He might even be grounded for a day or two, but there wasn't much chance that he'd get a lickin'. Those days were long past unless he really screwed up, like Rob had been doing so far this year.

After he got out of detention, though, Timmy was a little nervous about the walk home. Standing outside the back door of the school, the parking lot all but deserted, he considered what he should do. He could take the shortcut through the woods, like he always did, but that was something he was a little nervous about.

He'd never taken the shortcut home alone. He'd always been with either his big brother Rob or some of his friends. And he wasn't too keen about taking it now . . . especially so late in the afternoon. Then again, if he went the long way around Ridge Road, he might not get home until almost dark. Then he'd have some explaining to do.

So even though it made him feel really nervous, especially approaching Halloween time, he decided to take the shortcut.

Alone.

After all, what could possibly happen?

He was twelve years old. It wasn't like he really believed all those stories the kids told about the path being haunted or that there were drunken killers lurking in the woods, just waiting to pounce on an unsuspecting kid . . . especially if he was walking the shortcut.

Alone.

Those were just stories the older kids told to scare the little kids. He had absolutely nothing to worry about.

Still, as he slung his book bag over his shoulder and started walking away from the school, apprehension coiled deep inside him. He followed Bristol Street down to the Crosbys' lumber yard and walked around *the back of the building to the stretch of woods where the path began.*

It's not too late to go all the way around, *he told himself, but he knew that would be chickenshit of him. Besides, it would add about four miles to his walk home, so he braced himself as he plunged into the woods.*

The leaves had already passed their peak for color and had started to fall. The forest floor was spread with a carpet of reds, yellows, and browns that dazzled the eye. Bare branches stood out starkly against the sky, swaying and creaking in the wind as evening approached. The brisk chill in the autumn air sent shivers up Timmy's spine as he entered the woods. The shortcut was a well-beaten path that wound through a dense grove of maples first, then dipped down to a winding stream that flowed eastward into the river that ran through town. Beyond the stream, which was about the halfway point, the woods changed to a dense pine forest. The path there was a thin, curling yellow line strewn with fallen pine needles. On hot summer days, when Timmy and his friends cut through here on their way downtown to buy sodas and ice creams, the air was thick with the scent of pine resin.

When he left for school that morning, the temperature had been warm, almost an Indian summer day, so Timmy was wearing a summer-weight jacket. Over the course of the day, though, it had gotten much chillier as a cold front moved in from Canada. His teeth were chattering, and a sprinkling of goose bumps covered his arms as he walked along the well-beaten path between the maple trees. Brief gusts of cold wind made the yellow and red leaves chatter. He tried not to think that they were skeletal hands, applauding with a dry, rattling sound of old bones. Through the branches overhead, he could see the sky, bright blue with puffy white clouds moving fast to the east. Crows cawed in the distance, and blue jays sang their annoying song as they flashed through the trees. The tension Timmy felt inside got steadily worse the farther he went.

It's not too late to turn around, go back and take the road.

Long, blue shadows rippled across the uneven ground, and the sound of his feet scuffing loudly through the dried leaves set his teeth on edge. He was afraid it would block out the sound of someone sneaking up behind him, so he kept pausing and looking back, not sure who or what he expected to see stalking him.

Timmy kept trying to convince himself that he wasn't really afraid.

It was always good to be cautious in the woods. You never knew when you might encounter a fox or a raccoon, maybe even a deer or bear.

But those were the least of Timmy's worries.

What he was really nervous about was the people he might encounter in the woods at this time of day.

While he knew that there weren't really any bands of killers and outlaws hiding out here, there was always a chance that he might bump into one of the town drunks staggering home from the bar, or maybe "Twitchy," the man who passed for Hilton's village idiot. His real name was John Andersen, and he was famous for going around town asking people if they wanted to hear the chicken sounds he could make. He'd then make them, no matter what the person said.

"Forget about it," Timmy whispered to himself, hoping to boost his courage. But even the sound of his own voice seemed faint and lost in the expanse of the surrounding woods. Licking his lips, he looked ahead to where the shortcut started to dip down to the stream.

That was the halfway point.

He was almost there.

He began to feel a swelling of pride that he had actually done this because it was the first time he had ever dared to take the shortcut alone. So his dad was right about one thing: Junior high meant that he was growing up. With the midpoint in sight, he didn't feel nearly so bad about taking the shortcut alone.

Still, Timmy had close to a mile to cover, so he hurried along the path, feeling the faint heat of the late-autumn sun prickle on his face. Up ahead, the pine forest on the other side of the stream looked dark and foreboding. The green shadows shifted as the breeze swayed the branches. Timmy knew the path that wound through the pines as well as anybody. He couldn't remember the first time he'd walked here. But he still felt nervous as he approached the stream. It was as dark as night under the pines, even at midday.

He wasn't home free yet.

But he'd be fine.

It might get a little creepy in the shadows of the pines, but he'd be all right. He thought maybe he'd jog the rest of the way. It'd be good to get a little exercise after sitting in school all day, he told himself, so he started to run, following the path with an easy, loping jog. His book bag bounced against the small of his back, and he felt good when he inhaled deeply of the cool, dry air.

His feet thudded the ground with an easy rhythm, sounding like a strong, steady drumbeat. As he neared the narrow, slow-moving brook, he clenched his fists and picked up some speed on the down slope. Being careful not to slip on the muddy bank, he grunted out loud when he reached the edge of the flowing water and then sprang into the air, his arms raised up over his head.

The stream wasn't wide. No more than six feet, even with the spring runoff, but ever since he was a little kid, Timmy had made it a challenge to leap over it like it was a raging river.

He landed with a loud thump on the opposite side of the stream, and—like he always did—started danc-

*ing around and pumping his fists above his head like
an Olympic gold medalist.*

"What a fuckin' pussy!"

The voice broke the silence of the woods so suddenly and so loudly that Timmy was startled. He let
out a surprised yelp as he turned around to see who
had spoken. Standing in the densest shadows of the
pine tree, his arms folded across his chest as he leaned
against the tree trunk, was Mark Dufresne. Everyone
called him "Cunna" because his thick, full lips gave
his face a fishlike look. His eyes were deeply set and
dark beneath his perpetually furrowed brow.

Timmy's jaw dropped in surprise. He felt embarrassed at getting caught acting like a little kid. He
started to say something, then caught himself.

It wouldn't pay to insult or even speak to Cunna out
here alone in the woods. He reveled in his reputation
as town bully. Several of Timmy's friends had gotten
bloody noses or cut lips from the boy but, so far, anyway, Timmy had managed to avoid any confrontations
with Cunna. He felt a sudden dread that today his luck
had finally run out, and it was going to be his turn to
get beaten up by the town bully.

"You know, you look like a fuckin' little fairy boy,
prancing around like that," Cunna said.

An unlit cigarette dangled from his lower lip and
bobbed up and down as he spoke.

"Is that what you do out here? You and your little
faggot friends? You come out here to mince around
and blow each other?"

Once again, Timmy wanted to say something, at
least to defend himself, but he knew that it would be a
fatal mistake. He knew that Cunna was just itching to
beat up on someone and was egging him on, trying to
get a rise out of him. He'd best keep his mouth shut
and try to get away without a beating, but he felt certain that Cunna was going to do something to him, no
matter what he said or didn't say.

So far, though, Cunna hadn't made a move.

He was standing off to one side, about ten or fifteen feet from the trail. Timmy couldn't help but wonder where he had come from and why he hadn't noticed him before he spoke. It seemed almost like he was hanging around out here just waiting for someone— for him!—to come along.

Timmy was frozen with fear, not sure what to do next. He knew that, if he started to run now, the older boy would easily catch up with him before he could get even halfway to the road. His heart skipped a couple of quick beats. The coldness of the autumn air seeped into his body, penetrating his stomach and bowels as Cunna casually pushed himself away from the tree and started walking toward him.

"I . . . I don't want any trouble," Timmy said.

He wished he didn't hear the high, irritating squeak in his voice, but maybe if Cunna knew just how scared he was of him, that would be enough, and he'd leave him alone without a beating.

Then again, maybe not.

Cunna did nothing but smile as he drew closer. His hands were clenched into fists at his sides, and he was flexing his arms up and down like he was lifting weights. The veins and muscles of Cunna's summer-tanned forearms rippled like thin, metal rods beneath his skin.

"Trouble?" Cunna said, his voice dripping with menace as he mocked Timmy's tone of voice. "You should have thought about that before you turned me in to Principal Wallace, not after."

"Wha—? I didn't say anything about you to any-one."

A strange lethargy invaded Timmy's body. He found it almost impossible to take a deep enough breath. His chest felt like it was encased in cement, and a heavy, leaden feeling weighed down his hands and feet, root-

ing him to the spot. He couldn't have run away now if he had wanted to, and oh, Lord, did he want to!

"You squealed on me, you pig-fucker . . . about that firecracker in the boys' room last year," Cunna said menacingly. "I just haven't had a chance to talk to you about that till now."

"I didn't squeal on you about anything!"

Timmy heard the sharp note of desperation in his voice, but he didn't care if Cunna knew how afraid he was. That was what he wanted, for the younger kids to be afraid of him.

Well, if that's what he wanted, that's what he was getting.

Hot pressure filled Timmy's bladder, and his eyes were stinging like he was about to cry as he watched Cunna move steadily closer.

"Oh, and now what? The little pussy's gonna start crying?" Cunna said in a singsong voice. "Poor little baby."

He stopped only a foot or two from Timmy, so close that he could feel and smell the older boy's hot, rancid breath on his face. The smell made him dizzy. His vision blurred as his tears gathered and then spilled over, running in slippery tracks down his face.

"I owe you this, ass-face," Cunna said, and in a flash, his fist jabbed out like a striking cobra, connecting solidly with Timmy's chin.

The blow was hard enough to rock Timmy back on his feet. His teeth slammed together as a jolt of pain flashed like electricity down his neck and shoulders. Thick, vibrating darkness started to nibble at the edges of his vision, and his legs got all wobbly, then collapsed under him and he fell. His butt hit the pine needle–covered ground hard enough to send another stab of pain up his tailbone.

Timmy was blubbering now, unable to hold back the tears. The pain was bad enough, but the fear that Cunna wasn't finished with him, that he was just get-

ting started, rooted Timmy to the ground. Cunna loomed above him, a huge silhouette against the dark, swaying pine trees. All Timmy could see was the boy's smiling face and his clenched fist as he cocked his arm back and then swung at him again.

Pain exploded in a spray of fiery white stars across Timmy's vision. A loud crunching sound reverberated deep inside his head, and before the sound had faded, it was replaced by a high-pitched ringing. The coppery taste of blood filled his mouth, almost gagging him. He had no idea what was up or down as he tumbled over and hit the back of his head hard against the ground.

In a flash, Cunna dropped onto Timmy's chest, straddling him and pinning his arms down with his knees. Timmy heard a soft, piglike grunting laugh as Cunna alternated left-right-left-right punches to his face. Timmy thrashed about and tried to turn away to protect his face, but it was no good. Cunna had him and was raining down blow after blow onto his face and shoulders. He almost choked on the blood and snot that filled his mouth and throat.

Swept away in a hurricane of pain, Timmy went numb as he stared into the darkness that vibrated at the fringes of his vision. It deepened and spread out, narrowing his focus until all he could see in a tiny pinpoint of light was the twisted, malicious, big-lipped face of Cunna Dufresne.

But then—suddenly—the weight on Timmy's chest lifted, and the dark shape that had been looming above him pulled away.

Timmy had the brief impression that Cunna had somehow sprouted wings and flown away, but he didn't care what had happened. All that mattered was that he could breathe again. Shuddering with sobs, he rolled over onto his side, coughing and spitting out globs of blood. Only vaguely did he register the sound of angry voices. Then, through tear-filled eyes, he *looked up in amazement and watched as someone whose back was to him picked Cunna up in his arms and flung him onto the ground. After a confused moment or two, Timmy realized that it was his brother, Rob.*

"You wanna pick on someone your own size, asshole?" Rob yelled as he circled around Cunna, waving his clenched fists in front of him like an old-fashioned prizefighter.

Timmy could see his brother's face, and he couldn't believe the savage fury in his expression. Rob's face was flushed bright red, and his eyes were bugging out, making him look like he was totally insane.

Cunna, lying on his back, tried to scramble away with an awkward crab walk, but he didn't get far. Rob leaned down and grabbed him by the shirt, practically lifting him off the ground. Cunna's feet flopped around wildly, kicking up clumps of pine needles and dirt as he tried to get away, but it didn't do any good. Rob held him up for a moment or two, then he brought his clenched fist down hard on the top of Cunna's nose. A thick jet of blood shot out of Cunna's nose and splattered across the front of Rob's white T-shirt.

"You son of a bitch!" Rob shouted, his face contorted with anger as he threw Cunna down onto the ground. "Look what you did! You messed up my nice, clean shirt!"

With lightning speed, he jumped onto Cunna, pinning him down with the weight of his body. Cunna's breath was expelled in a loud whoosh, and Timmy heard a snapping sound that had to have been a couple of Cunna's ribs cracking.

Timmy watched, unable to move or say anything as his older brother reached out to one side and picked up something from the ground—a fist-sized rock that was lying by the edge of the stream. Holding Cunna down with his left hand, Rob drew his right hand back and then brought the stone around quickly. It looked almost as if he had thrown the rock.

There was a loud, sickening crunch.

Cunna grunted, but the sound abruptly ended with a gurgling groan. Cunna's feet were still kicking up pine needles and dirt, but the top half of his body had gone limp. He just lay there, taking his punishment. Timmy saw that the bully's face was a bloody crater as Rob cocked his arm back for another swing.

"No! . . . Stop!" Timmy yelled as he scrambled to his feet, but he fell silent when Rob turned to him with a cold, ferocious gleam lighting his eyes. A thin string of saliva looped down from his bottom lip.

"The motherfucker deserves it," Rob said, his voice low and thick with phlegm.

Timmy was frozen where he stood.

It all seemed like a dream.

He had never seen his brother look so . . . so insane before. Sure, as brothers, they'd had their squabbles, but this was way beyond anything like that. Rob looked like he'd gone totally out of his mind. A sick, twisted grin split his face as he sat back, his knees straddling Cunna's chest. Gripping the rock with both hands, he held it high above his head and then brought it down as hard as he could into the center of the bloody mess that had been Cunna Dufresne's face.

The impact made a loud, wet, smacking sound that was punctuated by a crackling that Timmy knew was the bones of Cunna's skull caving in.

"Jesus! Rob!" he shouted.

Panting heavily, his face dripping with sweat in the cool air, Rob swung himself off Cunna like a man dismounting a horse. He let the bloody rock drop from his hand. It rolled down the slight slope until it came to rest in the fast-flowing stream, which washed the blood away in scarlet swirls. Cunna's body twitched a few times and then lay perfectly still. The blood run-

ning from his smashed nose and mouth whistled and bubbled with escaping air.

For a long time, what seemed like several minutes, Timmy just stood there with his mouth hanging open. He couldn't believe that what he had just witnessed had really happened. Everything around him—the slanting rays of sunlight shining through the pine trees, the sound of the wind whistling through the branches, the distant twitter of birds, and the gentle babble of the brook—everything had a weird, surreal cast. A thick wash of blood dripped down over Cunna's right ear onto the ground and spread out in a wide, dark puddle that turned to black as it mixed with the pine needles and dirt.

Timmy was still gaping in absolute disbelief. At first, when he tried to speak, his breath caught like a hot coal in his throat. He couldn't stop staring at the bloody mess that, just moments before, had been Cunna Dufresne's face. A sour taste flooded his throat, and he thought he was going to throw up.

Finally, he dared to look into his brother's eyes and somehow found the strength to mutter, "Jesus Christ, Robbie! You . . . you killed him!"

"Yeah," Rob said, smiling at him with an insane gleam in his eyes. "Kinda looks that way, don't it?"

twelve

"Jesus Christ, Tim! He actually *killed* him?"

It was almost two o'clock in the morning, and Polly and Tim were sitting at the kitchen table where Tim had just finished telling her everything that had happened almost thirty years ago. They had come downstairs into the kitchen to talk so they wouldn't disturb Brian. While he was telling his story, Polly had set about brewing some herbal tea for them, but it wasn't long before that had been all but forgotten.

"I mean I . . . I just can't *believe* it," she muttered.

Polly leaned back in her chair and shook her head in amazement while staring wide-eyed past her husband to the black rectangle of night sky outside the kitchen window. She thought she could see the first hints of dawn in the east, but she knew that morning was still hours away.

"I know, I know," Tim muttered, looking down at the floor and shaking his head solemnly. "I couldn't believe it either."

When Polly swallowed, her throat made a loud gulping sound that in other circumstances might have struck them as funny.

But not now.

Not when her husband had just admitted to being an accomplice to murder. She realized that she had been clutching her teacup tightly with both hands. The tea had long since gone cold. Releasing the tension in her grip, she tried to control the shaking in her hand as she carefully placed the cup on the table and took a breath.

"What the hell did you do about it? I mean . . . Jesus *Christ,* Tim! That was a human *being* he killed!"

"I know," Tim said. He looked drained of all emotion as he stared off into the distance and vacantly nodded his understanding. "You don't think it's haunted me my whole life?"

"Jesus Christ," Polly whispered, staring at him in utter amazement.

She felt unable to process what she had just heard. How could she even begin to accept what Tim had told her? The man she loved, the man she had lived with for almost twenty years—*twenty years!*—the father of her son and her daughter had been involved in . . . in a *murder!*

It was beyond belief.

"And you . . . How could you keep this from me? . . . All this time?" she said, her voice breaking on practically every word.

Tim looked at her, his eyes softened by the yellow glow of the overhead light. His face looked pale; his lips thin, almost bloodless. She could see that his hands, clasped on the table in front of him, were white-knuckled and trembling.

"I . . . What could I say?" Tim asked. "How could I confess to something like that to you . . . to . . . to anyone?"

He gave her a tight, helpless shrug.

"How *couldn't* you?" Polly shouted as she pounded the table with a clenched fist. "I'm your *wife*, for God's sake! And it's not like . . . like you *did* it! *You* didn't kill this . . . this Cunna kid! Jesus Christ, Tim! I can't believe you would keep this from me!"

Polly was trembling deep inside as she stared at her

husband. She had to resist the urge to get up and run out of the room. How could she even pretend that she knew this man if he'd been keeping a secret like this from her all these years? She hated to think it, but ever since Crystal died, maybe even before then, she had sensed a distance growing between them. It was almost amusing that she had actually been worried he might be having an affair. Now, something like an affair seemed so totally insignificant, it was foolish compared to the fact that her husband had been a partner in . . . *murder!*

"So what did you do?" she asked shakily. "You didn't just leave him out there in the woods, did you?"

Tim opened his mouth and started to say something, then fell silent and shook his head. She could see that he was struggling to frame his response carefully.

"No, we . . . we went home and cleaned up, and then we went back later that night and . . . took care of things."

"Took *care* of things?"

Tim sighed and looked down at his hands on the table, unable to maintain eye contact with her for long. A dense, terrible silence filled the kitchen as she stared at him, but she had no idea what she wanted to hear him say.

"My mouth was cut pretty bad, and my nose was bleeding all over my shirt. I had some serious bruises on my face and neck, too, and Rob's T-shirt and pants were covered with blood. We washed up in the stream as best we could, but even then, Rob had to sneak back into the house and change his clothes before our mom or dad saw him."

Tim took a quick sip of his tea and winced, but Polly wasn't sure if it was because the tea was cold or because of what he was confessing to her.

"Then, late at night, we snuck out of the house, got a couple of shovels from the barn, and went back out into the woods and buried him. We smoothed everything over as well as we could. Fortunately, it rained the next couple of days, so all the tracks were pretty much wiped away."

"Oh, my *God!*" Polly whispered, covering her face with her hands as a bone-deep shudder ran through her.

"So I figure that has to be Cunna they found buried in the woods out where they're excavating for that new development," Tim said.

Polly sat there staring at him blankly. Her thoughts were lost in a dizzying swirl until she got a moment of clarity.

"You have to tell them," she said firmly. "You have to go to the police and tell them everything you know."

Tim looked at her skeptically for a moment, then tossed his head back and snorted with laughter.

"Oh, yeah, right. And have them lock up me and my brother for murder? I don't think so."

"You're not saying you're just going to let it be, are you?"

Polly stared at him, absolutely flabbergasted.

"You can't pretend that it didn't happen! That they didn't find him! They'll figure it out sooner or later, anyway."

"I'm not so sure," Tim said, running the flat of his hand across his mouth. "And even if they do, then what?"

"Then they'll investigate, and if they figure it out, they'll nail you as an accomplice to murder, that's what!" Polly shouted. She couldn't believe they were even having this conversation.

"They won't figure out a thing," Tim said, although the tone in his voice indicated that he wasn't entirely convinced of that himself. "They'll probably just write it off or else just figure whoever it was died out there in the woods of . . . you know, natural causes."

"With a smashed skull?" Polly said. "Jesus, Tim, I don't think so."

"But I don't see the point in confessing to it after all these years." Tim's voice was raw and close to breaking. "There's no statute of limitations on murder, you know. So if this were to come out, I could end up in jail just as easily as Rob could. Is *that* what you want?"

"No, of course not," Polly snapped. "But I don't want you and me having to live the rest of our lives knowing that you were involved in a murder and that my brother-in-law is a *killer*!"

They fell silent for a long time and just sat there, neither one of them daring even to look at the other. When Polly glanced out the window at the night sky, she was confused for a moment by the faint reflection she and Tim cast in the glass. For just an instant, between blinks of her eyes, she thought she saw a face outside the window, pressed against the glass, looking in at her. She jumped and let out a scream, but in that instant, the illusion disappeared.

Tim got out of his chair and walked over to her. Kneeling in front of her, he held her hands in his and pulled her close. Polly closed her eyes and inhaled, luxuriating in his warmth, but deep inside her chest, it felt as though cold, thin hands had taken hold of her heart and were squeezing . . . squeezing.

"I don't know what else to do," Tim said softly. His breath was hot against her neck. "I didn't then, and I don't now. It's just that . . . I've been so afraid, my whole life, that something like this would happen and we'd be found out."

"You can't just pretend it didn't happen," Polly said tightly. "That's a dead boy they found out there, and you have to tell the authorities what you know."

Tim took a deep breath and held it for several seconds. Polly's heart was pounding hard in her chest, and the cold, slimy feeling inside her spread into her stomach and bowels.

"I can't do that," he said in a hoarse whisper. "I can't betray my own brother and turn him in. I couldn't see him go to jail. I just couldn't!"

"Even knowing that he killed someone?" Polly said.

She drew away from his embrace and looked straight at him, but Tim dropped his gaze and looked down at his hands holding hers. He was still kneeling in front of her, but Polly thought he looked weak and pathetic. A surge of anger filled her, and she had all she could do not to slap him across the face so he would see how serious this was.

"I can't believe you!" she shouted.

She tore her hands from his grasp and, twisting to one side, stood up and moved quickly away from him. He stayed where he was, kneeling on the floor and looking at her with an imploring look.

"You could help the police solve this, and you're not going to do it?"

Tim was pale and trembling as he looked at her and slowly shook his head no.

"I can't," he said. "I was there, Pol. I'm just as guilty as Rob is. Do you want me to go to jail for murder, too?"

Shaking his head sadly, Tim stood up and brushed his knees. When he took a step or two toward Polly, she retreated, keeping a safe distance between them.

"Of course I don't want you to go to jail," she said, her voice breaking with emotion, "but . . . Jesus, Tim, your brother is a killer!"

"So what you're saying is, my brother doesn't matter? Just because he doesn't live the kind of life you think he should, it doesn't matter if he's carted off to jail?"

Tim suddenly no longer looked like a broken man. His face was flushed with anger.

"I'm just saying that you shouldn't . . . You don't have to protect him," Polly said patiently. "If you know who this is, then you should report it to the authorities."

Tim was gnawing on his lower lip as he leaned back against the counter and thought for a moment. Polly didn't like the hurt and fear and anger she saw seething inside him, but she knew that she had to get him to see beyond that. Finally, Tim let out a sigh and looked at her with pleading eyes.

"They're going to find out eventually," she said, lowering her voice. "When this kid, Cunna, disappeared, there must have been a search for him and everything."

Tim closed his eyes and shook his head like he wanted to ignore what she was saying.

"They're going to put two and two together eventually," Polly said. "They'll date the bones, or maybe use dental records or whatever to figure out who he is. They may already know who he is."

"Okay, and then what?" Tim's voice was trembling but filled with defiance. "They still won't know how he got there, and as long as you and I and Rob don't say a fucking thing, they'll *never* connect it to my brother or me."

Polly started to say something but then stopped herself. What could she possibly say?

If her husband already didn't realize that he had a moral and legal obligation to reveal what he knew, then nothing she said was going to make a difference.

Murder was murder. Even if it happened thirty years ago, even if it was in self-defense, they had found a dead boy in the woods, and someone was going to be held accountable for it. If Tim went to the authorities now, both he and his brother would probably be charged with murder, at least until the investigation cleared him.

"There's no way they can connect it to me," Tim repeated in a low, shattered voice. "As long as we don't say anything to anybody, we can just . . . just forget it ever happened."

Polly looked at him, feeling absolutely confused and conflicted. She loved Tim, she knew that much, but she couldn't begin to grasp how she was supposed to reconcile the affection and devotion she felt for him with what she now knew about him. As for Rob, knowing what she knew now only solidified her feelings about him. That he was a murderer fit in perfectly well with her conception of him as a loner and a loser.

Neither she nor Tim spoke for a very long time. Polly was aware of the faint tick-tock of the clock in the living room. Floorboards creaked in the night, and outside, the wind hissed in the darkness, sounding like voices faint with distance. A pressing sense of danger filled Polly, and she couldn't help but think, now that she knew the truth about her husband and her brother-in-law, something far worse was going to happen to them.

Without another word, she walked out of the kitchen

and trudged slowly up the stairs and back to bed. Thankfully, Tim stayed downstairs. She shivered as she slipped back into bed. Sighing deeply as tears filled her eyes, she lay down and stared up at the gray square of the ceiling. She knew that sleep wasn't going to come easily, if at all, but as she lay there in the dark, she couldn't stop thinking that she wished she would be sound asleep by the time Tim finally came back up to bed.

Rob knew who it was as soon as he heard the car pull into the driveway, but he walked over to the kitchen window, limping awkwardly with his walking cast, and looked out just to make sure. He frowned when he saw Tim stepping out of his car. He must have caught sight of him in the kitchen window, because he smiled broadly and waved a cheerful greeting.

"Yo," Rob called out as he waved back.

He didn't feel any particular pleasure seeing his brother. In fact, Rob was beginning to think old Timmy-boy was getting to be a bit of a pain in the ass, dropping by every fucking day right around noontime. It wasn't like he was a goddamned cripple. He was getting around just fine with his walking cast. In fact, he'd been out for a drive by the old homestead the other night, just to have a little look around.

When he heard the heavy tread of Tim's feet on the stairs, Rob limped over to the kitchen door to unbolt the lock. He gave his brother a twisted half smile as he swung the door open.

"Wanna beer?" Rob asked without preamble as Tim entered the apartment.

"No . . . no thanks," Tim replied. He placed the bag of Chinese carryout he'd picked up on the way into town onto the counter. "I brought some cashew chicken for you. Hope that's okay." With his back to Rob, he opened the bag and began lining up the containers on the counter.

Rob instantly bristled. Something was wrong. He could

tell, just by the way Tim was acting, like not even bothering—or *daring*—to look at him while he unpacked their lunch.

"You know what?" Rob said after clearing his throat, "I don't think I need you dropping by here every day like I'm some kind of invalid. No offense."

Tim glanced at him over his shoulder but still didn't look him straight in the eyes.

"I'm getting around pretty good, now," Rob continued. "In fact, if you wanna know what's bugging my ass the most, it's wondering why you ain't invited me out to the house yet for a home-cooked meal. Why is that?"

Finally, Tim turned and looked at him. He had a box of fried rice in one hand, and Rob could tell that it was hot and burning Tim's hand, but he didn't react. He just stared back at him with his mouth partway open, making him look like an imbecile.

"Haven't really had a chance," Tim replied. There was a weak, almost frightened tone in his voice that confirmed Rob's suspicion that *something* most *definitely* was wrong.

"Haven't really had a chance, huh?" Rob echoed in a mocking tone as he took a few steps toward the counter. "'N why's that, Timmy? Huh? Could it be because your wife ain't exactly my biggest fan? Is that why you ain't had a chance?"

Tim shook his head in denial, but Rob knew better.

That was exactly what was wrong. He knew, sure as shit, that Polly didn't like him. His opinion of her wasn't any better, either. As far as he was concerned, she was an uptight, frigid little cunt who was so full of bullshit she didn't know how obvious she was in her dislike of him.

Fuck her! And fuck Tim, too, for that matter!

Tim got a fork and two plates from the dish drainer and started scooping rice onto them. The sound of the fork scraping the plate set Rob's teeth on edge. He clenched his fists tightly and squeezed them, fighting back the sudden urge he had to punch his brother in the face.

"Here you go," Tim said as he turned around and placed

Rob's plate on the kitchen table. He took another clean fork from the dish drainer and put it on the table beside the steaming plate of rice and cashew chicken.

"Will you stop talking to me like I'm a fuckin' baby or something?" Rob said.

He was trying hard to control his rising anger, but there was something in his little brother's demeanor that was really getting on his nerves. Just his body posture seemed . . . wrong. His shoulders were all hunched up, the way he used to get when they were kids and he was afraid that Rob was going to beat on him for some bonehead thing he'd done. Tim's whole attitude seemed somehow off kilter. It was almost as if . . .

"Jesus, you told her, didn't you?"

The question popped out of him so fast it surprised even him, but not as much as it obviously surprised Tim. He jumped and almost dropped the second plate of Chinese food, which he was carrying over to the table.

"What—?" Tim said. His voice was so high-pitched he sounded almost like a cackling hen.

Rob snapped his fingers and then shook an accusatory finger at him while giving him a long, steady stare. Tim's face visibly whitened, and his hands were shaking as he put the dish down and drew the chair away from the table so he could sit down.

"You went and blabbed to her," Rob said. The madder he got, the lower and steadier his voice became. "I can tell by your face." He shook his head, snarling with disgust. "Why you miserable, little mother*fucker*!"

He placed his fingertips under the edge of the plate and flung it off the table. Fried rice, chicken, and cashews went flying. Some stuck to the ceiling, but most of it splattered against the cabinets and streaked across the floor in a wide smear. Tim let out a surprised yelp as he jumped back, shielding his eyes with his forearm.

"What the hell are you talking about?"

"What I'm talking about is, you couldn't keep your fuckin' mouth shut, could you, little brother? You told her everything about what happened out there, didn't you? *Didn't you?*"

Tim's lower lip was trembling as he stared back at Rob. He looked like a scared little kid, the nerdy little brother Rob had threatened and intimidated throughout their childhood . . . the little brother who would give Rob his lunch money if he even raised a clenched fist.

"Jesus *Christ*, man!" Rob shouted. He brought his fist down so hard on the table he made everything on it jump and rattle. "Are you a fuckin' *moron*? Do you know what's at stake here?"

Tim was wringing his hands together as he tried to stare down his brother, but he quickly looked away. It wouldn't do any good, no matter what he said. Any denial would sound so hollow Tim knew better than to try to lie his way out of this.

"Why'd you do it?" Rob said almost sadly. "Why the fuck did you *do* it?"

"It . . . it's not a problem," Tim replied. "I was just . . . She already knew about it. She'd figured it out."

"Oh, really?" Rob asked, glowering at his brother and privately enjoying the way Tim shied away from him as though he was afraid he was going to get slugged. "And just how did she figure it out? Huh? Tell me that!"

Tim's mouth kept opening and closing, making him look like a fish out of water, gulping useless air.

"It was really weird, man," he finally managed to say. "She was talking about it in her sleep . . . about old bones. She kept saying 'old bones,' and I was sure that she knew all about it."

"Jesus *Christ*, Tim!" Rob shouted as he pounded the table again. "Do you know what you've done?"

Tim didn't say a word. He just stared back at his older brother with a dazed, blank expression. After a moment or two, Rob got up and hobbled over to the sink and grabbed a sponge. Keeping his leg with the cast straight out, he bent down and started cleaning up the gobs of fried rice and chicken. Springing from his chair, Tim ripped a few paper towels off the roll by the sink and joined in to help. The brothers worked quietly for a minute or two. Rob enjoyed it because he knew that Tim was still twisted with fear and guilt for what he had done . . . and worry about what Rob might do about it.

"You can . . . ah, eat mine," Tim said as he opened the bottom cupboard and threw the bunched-up paper towels into the trash can. "I'm not really hungry, anyway."

"Thanks," Rob said, wanting to see his brother stew in his own guilt a while longer.

Once the floor and cupboards were clean, Rob grabbed a beer from the refrigerator, popped the top, and sat down heavily. The effort of cleaning the floor had taken it out of him more than he would have thought. A sheen of sweat had broken out on his forehead, and his pulse was thrumming in his neck. His hand shook slightly as he leaned back and took a long gulp of beer. Smacking his lips with satisfaction, he put the beer down and pulled Tim's plate over in front of him.

"Sorry about the mess," he said as he picked up a forkful of rice. "You sure you don't want half?"

Tim had his lips compressed as he shook his head tightly.

"No. Seriously. I'm not hungry."

"Suit yourself," Rob said and, without another word, he set to eating, shoveling the food into his mouth in huge scoops.

As he ate, he was conscious of the tension in the room. Tim just stood there, watching him eat, but he didn't care. He'd seen this coming for a long time, and he was mentally prepared for it. The only real surprise was that Tim hadn't spilled his guts to his wife before now. Rob had always thought he had told Polly about it a long time ago.

Now that he knew for certain that she knew, well he would just have to take whatever precautions he would need. He couldn't leave any loose ends.

It was as simple as that.

•   •   •

"You *what*?"

Polly's face flushed with anger. She knew that she should keep her voice down. They had just finished washing the supper dishes. She was sitting in the living room, and Brian was upstairs, "chatting" with some of his friends back home over the Internet. She didn't want to disturb him *or* herself. She had slept so poorly last night that she hadn't done any work on the house today. Instead, she'd taken the day off to sit in the shade out back, read a little, and doze a lot. Her plans for this evening hadn't been very ambitious, either. She was thinking she'd just watch a little TV or read some more, then go to bed early. Maybe, if she felt like it, she would do some more painting in the morning, but she no longer really cared one way or another. As far as she was concerned, they should start packing up first thing tomorrow and get the hell out of this house and this town. She didn't care if she ever saw either again.

"I invited Rob over for supper." Tim gave her a tired, helpless shrug. He was standing in the living room doorway, leaning on the door frame as though he didn't quite dare enter the room. "What's so bad about that?"

"What's so *bad*?" Polly could feel her eyes bugging out of her head as she turned to face her husband squarely. Lowering her voice even more, she whispered, "Do you think I actually *want* to have a"—she dropped her voice even more—"*killer* over to my house for supper? Are you nuts or something?"

"Jesus Christ, Pol," Tim said, also trying to keep his voice down. His face was flushed, but she wasn't sure if it was from anger or embarrassment. "He's still my brother. What happened back then happened. The way Rob looks at it, it was one less pimple on the ass of the world."

"Oh, sweet," Polly said. She curled her upper lip with disgust and almost felt like spitting.

"Whatever," Tim said. "What's done is done. It happened almost thirty years ago, and there's nothing we can do about it, anyway."

"Yes, there is," Polly said. She glanced up at the ceiling, hoping Brian couldn't hear them. Lowering her voice to a soft hiss, she said, "You can tell the cops what you know, and you can hope that only Rob will get charged with the crime. Until then, I don't even want to see him."

Tim glared at her. His hands were shaking, and his face looked drawn and pale in the feeble light of the living room. Polly almost felt sorry for him. She wasn't used to seeing him appear so shattered and indecisive, but what else could she do? How was she supposed to react? It wasn't every day you found out that your husband was involved with a murder.

"Look," she said, scooting her feet off the footstool and standing up to face him. "You know what the right thing to do is." She walked over to him and placed a hand on his shoulder, but he pulled away from her as though she had given him an electric shock.

"It happened so long ago," he said. "How do you think it's going to look to the authorities?"

Polly ran her teeth over her lower lip as she thought about what to say. "I honestly don't know, but you have to do something. Maybe you could make an anonymous call to the police, and they'll just arrest Rob."

"You don't think Rob would turn me in, too?" Tim asked.

Polly could see the genuine fear in his eyes, and she didn't need to ask if he thought that was a real possibility. Of course it was. From what she knew about Rob, it was not only possible but likely that if he were arrested, he would twist everything around so much Tim might end up taking the rap instead of him.

"So what are you going to do?" she asked, moving closer and trying to hug him if only to give him a measure of reassurance that he didn't have to mistrust and fear her like he mistrusted and feared his older brother.

Tim was silent for a long time. Whenever they looked at each other, he would look away first and stare off into some middle distance.

"I don't know," he said weakly. Polly saw the tears

forming in his eyes. "I think all I can do is what I've been doing all along . . . and that's just to . . . forget about it."

"But you *can't* forget about it," Polly said. "It's so obvious that it's eating you up inside. All these years, it's been bothering you that you *know* there was a dead boy buried out there in the woods . . . a person died, and you didn't do anything about it . . . not one single thing to help put his soul to rest."

—He's still out there—

Who is?

—I don't know who it is. . . . I can't see his face, but I know he's out there . . . and he's angry—

Who is he angry at? Is he angry at you, Heather?

—No . . . not me . . . at you . . . you and your husband—

Why is he angry at us? We didn't do anything to him. Did we do something that got him upset?

—I don't know. . . . I just know that I can . . . hear him. . . . He's outside the room right now . . . sneaking around. . . . I can hear him. . . . I can hear his footsteps. . . . It sounds like one foot is dragging. . . . I can hear his foot dragging—

I think I know who that is, Heather, but you don't have to worry about him. He can't hurt you.

—I know that. . . . He doesn't want to hurt me. . . . He wants to hurt you . . . and your husband . . . and your son—

No, he doesn't. Not really. He's a sad, angry man, but I really don't think he'd do anything to hurt any of us. We're his family.

—He's hurt the others. . . . He's a bad man . . . and he wants to hurt you. . . . Especially you. . . . He likes to hurt people. . . . That's the only thing he really likes . . . scaring and hurting people. . . . He enjoys it when he scares them first, and then he . . . he hurts them—

Well, don't you worry, Heather. I can take care of things, and I promise you, he won't hurt you or me or anyone else.

—It's already too late for that. . . . He's already outside the white room. . . . He's out there right now . . . and he's going to do it. . . . He's going to hurt all of you—

I promise you he . . . won't!

Polly woke up with a violent start. Her body was shaking and slick with a cold sweat. Her hands trembled out of control as she clutched the bed sheet to her heaving chest. Every breath felt like fire in her throat. Her pulse was racing so fast she thought she could hear it skip a few beats.

Tim grunted in his sleep and rolled over onto his side, away from her.

Good, Polly thought. *Keep right on sleeping.*

She couldn't remember what had awakened her, but whatever it was, she didn't want to face dealing with Tim right now.

She could handle it alone.

After all, it had just been a dream, but she couldn't recall what she had been dreaming. She had the distinct impression that she had been . . . somewhere . . . in a room . . . maybe down in the cellar of this house. And she'd been talking to . . . someone. But who?

She couldn't remember. She thought it was possible she had been talking in her sleep, but the fragments were slipping away now. Even as she tried to recall them, they dissolved in her mind like gossamer threads, leaving nothing but a vague feeling of unease.

A soft, warm breeze fluttered the curtains as she threw the sheet aside and got out of bed. It was only when her feet hit the floor that she inhaled and smelled something . . . unusual.

"What the . . ."

She straightened up and widened her nostrils, sniffing the night air.

The smell was strong but at first unidentifiable. It had almost a sour tang to it, a little like orange or lemon peels, but it was oilier than that. The smell coated the back of her throat with a sticky taste that almost gagged her.

The curtains scraped softly against the windowsill. From far off in the woods behind the house came the hollow fluting of a whippoorwill. The sound raised goose bumps on her arms and prickled the hair at the nape of her neck.

It's nothing, she told herself, *forget about it.*

But she couldn't stop sniffing the air as she started toward the bedroom door. She had taken no more than a few steps when the night was suddenly shattered by an ear-piercing wail. Polly jumped and felt a sudden, urgent pressure in her bladder. The high-pitched wail remained steady, and after a heart-stopping moment or two, Polly realized that it was the smoke alarm down in the kitchen.

She dashed out into the hall, snapping on the light before running down the stairs, taking them two at a time. She heard a scramble of activity behind her and knew that Tim and Brian were both up, but she was already down the stairs and halfway to the kitchen. As she burst into the kitchen, two things immediately caught her attention.

One was that the base of the coffee machine was glowing bright, cherry red and sending up a plume of hazy, gray smoke. The white plastic had melted into a thick goo that ran in bubbling puddles across the countertop. A napkin that had fallen from the dispenser and landed too near the coffee machine had been smoldering and had just started to flame.

The other thing Polly noticed was that the kitchen back

door was open partway. She could see a narrow wedge of black night sky outside and feel a warm draft curling around her ankles. But she barely registered this as she grabbed the fire extinguisher out from under the kitchen sink, pulled the tab, and then aimed the horn at the burning napkin and let it blast. A cyclone of white flame retardant blasted the counter, instantly smothering the flame. Being careful not to burn herself, Polly grabbed the plug and yanked it from the wall socket.

"Jesus! What's going on?" Tim shouted breathlessly as he burst into the kitchen. Brian was only a step or two behind him. A dense gray cloud of smoke hung in the air like a cotton blanket. Polly placed the fire extinguisher on the floor and waved her hand in front of her face.

"Someone left the coffeepot on," she said, scowling as she looked at the melted mess on the counter.

"Brian. Get the door and windows open so we can clear the air," Tim snapped as he moved closer to Polly. "Son of a bitch," he exclaimed when he saw the remains of the burned napkin. The center of the napkin was still white, but one edge was scorched black. Tiny bits of ash swirled in the air.

"How the hell do you think that happened?" Tim asked, incredulous.

Polly glanced at him, then at the narrow opening of the door. Brian hadn't gotten there yet. He was still working on unlocking the windows by the table and running them up.

A slow shiver ran through Polly as she moved to the back door and opened it just enough so she could see outside. The steady drone of crickets singing in the field filled the night. Off in the distance, the whippoorwill was still crying its mournful cry. The shiver inside her got so strong she felt like she was standing outside in the middle of winter. She jumped and let out a little squeal when Tim came up behind her and placed a hand on her shoulder.

"What?" he asked as Polly turned to him, wide-eyed.

"Huh?" she managed to say. "Oh. Nothing . . . nothing."

Grasping the door by the handle, she started waving it back and forth like a bellows, hoping it would waft some of the foul-smelling smoke out of the house. Brian got a fan from the living room and turned it on, setting it on a chair so it blew directly out one of the windows.

Tim was over by the counter, using a thick wad of paper towels to clean up the melted, charred mess. Polly shivered as the night air and smoke swirled around her. The smell was so strong in her nose and throat that she thought she might never get rid of it.

Why did the smoke smell like citrus? she wondered.

"We've got to be more careful," Tim said, wrinkling his nose at the burned plastic smell. "These fumes could've killed us."

Polly looked at him, feeling a deep, subtle fear as fragments of the conversation she'd been having in her dream swirled through her mind.

"Yeah," she said in a distant, dreamy voice.

She thought it sounded as if she were talking in her sleep, but her voice also had a tinge of utter hopelessness as well.

"We have to be a *lot* more careful."

thirteen

"A little late in the season to be gardening, don't you think?" Tim called out as he walked through the knee-high grass over to the edge of what had once upon a time been his mother's vegetable garden. In spite of years of untamed weed growth, the edges of the garden were still clearly defined by the cut-off turf and rounded mounds of earth.

Polly was wearing a wide straw hat, faded cut-off jeans shorts, and a loose cotton blouse, which she had tied up at the waist with a knot, Daisy Mae style. For the last half hour or so, she'd been digging in the garden patch with an old clam-digging fork she'd found in the barn. The tines were rusty and bent, but they did the job. Every forkful of soil she turned over had at least one, sometimes more than one earthworm squiggling around in it. *Employees,* she always called them, being careful not to hurt any of them if she could help it.

"This is amazingly good soil, and I'm surprised how much of this stuff has self-seeded over the years," she said as she straightened up and wiped the sweat and dirt from her forehead on the back of her gardening glove. "I've found some pumpkins, a few tomato plants, and tons of dill and some other herb. I think it might be basil. I thought if I cleared away some of the other weeds, I might be able to get a few of these veggies to grow."

"My mom always did have a pretty good garden," Tim said with a faint smile. "She liked gardening, maybe even more than you do, if that's possible."

Polly chuckled, relieved to find that they could still relate so easily, in spite of the shared secret they now had.

"But I thought we were going to paint today," Tim said, squinting into the sun. "The kitchen walls sure could use another coat."

"Tim, the whole damned house needs a coat of paint, inside and out," Polly said. She laughed as she said it but could also hear the slight trace of exasperation in her voice. "I, for one, don't really enjoy being inside on a day like this. Besides, I'm sick and tired of painting and cleaning. It's not like it's going to make any difference, anyway."

"Neither is gardening," Tim replied, his slight scowl deepening so his brows shaded his eyes. He might have been squinting because of the sun. "I thought you said you wanted to move back home soon. We certainly won't be here in time to harvest."

"I do want to leave. As soon as possible," Polly said, "but things have a right to live."

The truth was, working out here in the fresh air and hot sun, breaking up the thick, rich clumps of black soil was making her feel better—*much* better than she had since they moved to Hilton. Sure, she missed their house back in Stonepoint, and she wondered if Mrs. Gonzales next door was watering her garden as she'd asked. She would pack up and be gone today if Tim said he was ready to leave, but this was supposed to be their family vacation, and he'd been adamant about sticking around to help his brother out, so she figured she would have to make the best of it. She tried not to think about what Rob had done back when they were kids. All it did was cause agitated thoughts and bad dreams.

And voices . . . you're hearing voices and seeing things.

"You look like you're heading into town again," Polly said, trying to shift her mind away from such thoughts.

She hoped her disappointment didn't show too much. It took a great deal of effort not to say something about how much she didn't like her husband even visiting with his brother. The guy was a creep, pure and simple. Broken leg or not, she would just as soon let him rot away by himself. To hell with helping him out!

Tim nodded, his scowl deepening as he glanced over his shoulder, back at the house. So much was passing between them unsaid that it hurt Polly. After stewing about it all night, wondering what—if anything—she could or should do about what she knew, she had finally decided to let it drop. The decision galled her, and it was working on her conscience like a burrowing worm, but what helped her make her final decision not to do anything about it—as hard as that was—was knowing that they couldn't trust Rob. When it came down to it, he wouldn't hesitate for an instant to implicate Tim in the murder of Cunna Dufresne. He'd sell his brother out in a flash and with no regrets. That was the kind of person he was, so Polly knew she couldn't do anything because it would put her husband in jeopardy.

"Is Brian up yet?" Polly asked, trying her best to keep her mind off such worries. Gardening always seemed to help.

Tim bit his lower lip and shook his head.

"Yeah, I think so. I heard him clumping around in his room. Probably on the Internet again, chatting with his buddies."

"Any chance you could ask him to come out here and help me?"

Polly didn't really need the help, but if Tim was going into town—as usual—it'd be nice to have some company. She still felt uncomfortable about the figure she had seen—*thought* she had seen—under the apple trees and hanging over the edge of the roof, and she didn't want to be alone. Besides, it would do Brian some good to get out in the fresh air and sunshine. He might even help willingly.

"I'll see what I can do," Tim said as he turned and started walking back to the house.

Polly watched him go until he was on the back porch steps. Then she turned back to her work. Placing the tip of the fork just in front of one of the scraggly tomato plants, she stepped down hard. The fork sank several inches into the rich soil, but then one of the tines scraped loudly against something, a buried rock, she guessed.

"Damn!" Polly muttered, stepping back and wiping her forehead with the back of her glove again.

The old joke about New England fields being best for raising a crop of stones and boulders was absolutely true. She figured that over the years Tim's mother must have worked this garden deeply and well, so this was either a buried stone that had been too big and deep to dig up and move, or else, due to the frost heaves, it had shifted closer to the surface over the years while the garden went untended.

Polly withdrew the clamming fork and started probing around in the soil, searching for the edge of the buried rock. Placing her foot on the fork and gritting her teeth, she stepped down, prepared for the fork to fetch up again.

It didn't.

The tines plunged into the soft ground right up to the hilt, so fast it jolted Polly and rattled her teeth.

"What the heck," she muttered as she took a step back and glared at the freshly turned soil.

She guessed that the bulk of the rock must be to the other side, so she probed on that side, digging as deep as she could. Once again, the fork went all the way into the earth without meeting any resistance. She was working far enough away from the tomato plant she was hoping to save, so she drove the fork into the ground as deeply as she could and then levered it up with her body, raising a huge clump of dirt, turf, and wriggling worms.

And something else.

Sticking out of the soil like a long-buried, rotting branch was a dark yellow cylinder crusted and streaked with black dirt. One end of the object had a rounded knob. The other end was broken off with jagged points. The break looked fresh, and Polly wondered if she might have just broken it while digging it up. The surface of the object was pitted and looked light and spongy. As she bent down and brushed her gloved fingers along the length of it, she realized that she was holding a piece of buried bone.

"Oh my Jesus!"

She dropped the object and backed quickly away. After a moment, once the initial surprise had passed, she knelt down and, hooking her arms over her knees, stared at her find.

There was no doubt that it was a bone. It had long since been stripped clean of flesh. When she finally dared to reach out and pick it up, she was surprised how light it felt, as if it had a hollow core. The texture was slick and spongy. She found that she could easily make an impression on the surface just by pressing it. After inspecting the broken edge, she determined that she had broken it while digging it up. She gingerly brought the piece of bone up to her nose and sniffed it. She had been expecting a strong, earthy smell, and the bone did indeed smell like freshly turned earth, but she caught another smell as well—a hint of something that she couldn't quite identify.

Turning the bone over in her hand, she kept sniffing it, knowing that she recognized the smell but unable to place it.

And then, at last, it hit her.

It was the same smell she had smelled last night, when the coffeemaker had burned. The old bone had an oily, citrus smell.

"That's not what bones are supposed to smell like," she whispered, but in fact, she had no idea what a bone that had been buried in the earth was supposed to smell like. Whatever it was, she found the smell intriguing, almost intoxicating. Narrowing her eyes, she sniffed the bone again, then rubbed her gloved fingers together and sniffed them. Her gloves had also been imbued with the strange, elusive citrus smell.

And then a frightened thought hit her.

What if this is a human bone, like the one they found out at the construction site?

The thought of it filled her with nausea. Her stomach roiled, and a thick, sour taste flooded the back of her throat. For a few panicky seconds, she thought she was going to throw up. She tilted her head back and took a deep breath, filling her lungs with fresh air. Although the smell still clung to her nasal passages, she felt a little better.

Staring at the bone where she had dropped it, she was unable to believe that she had touched it . . . and actually smelled it!

What was I thinking?

"Gross," she whispered, her breath raw in her throat.

From behind her, she heard the screen door open and then slam shut. Looking back at the house, she saw Tim walking out to his car, which was parked in the shade of the barn. With the heat haze shimmering over the field, he looked much farther away than she knew he really was. He looked almost like a mirage.

"Tim . . ." she called out, although her voice wasn't much more than a faint warble.

She watched as he opened the car door. Everything seemed to be moving in hazy slow motion. A rush of panic ran through her like a blast of cold water. A distinct sensation of unreality swept over her. She felt totally isolated, like she was trapped inside a translucent bubble, able to see the outside world but separate from it. The sense of helplessness and desperation was almost overwhelming. When she tried to call out to her husband again, her voice broke.

"Tim!"

Her cry was loud enough now so he paused, the car door open, and turned slowly to look at her. His face was a blur in the gray wash of the barn's shadow. Above him, the sky was a vibrant, cloudless blue. Sunlight poured down onto the house and side yard, but Polly was having trouble focusing on Tim.

"Tim!" she called again, louder.

She could taste her rising panic. Her leg muscles felt too weak to support her as she started moving slowly toward him. She wanted to run, but the knee-high grass whipped at her legs and tangled her feet. The sound of insects all around her seemed to intensify into a deafening hum as the summer sun beat down on her mercilessly. She raised her arms feebly.

"What's the matter?" she heard Tim call out.

He sounded so far away that, even though she could see him, the panic inside her spiked all the higher. Sweat ran down her face, stinging her eyes. She could taste the salt at the corners of her mouth and could feel the blood draining from her head. She felt dizzy, and she staggered.

"It's . . . I found something," she gasped.

Tim hesitated a moment, then broke into a run, but Polly thought he looked so far away she was sure he would never get to her before she dropped.

The grass whisked around her legs like a heaving, green ocean. She felt like she was caught in the undertow and being dragged backward, no matter how much she struggled to move forward. A sudden gust of wind blew her straw hat off.

But Tim rapidly closed the gap. His expression was grim and determined. When they finally met, Polly collapsed into his arms. He held her tightly as she panted heavily, trying to catch her breath.

"What is it?" he asked, frowning as he held her away from him so he could look her in the eyes.

"I found . . . something . . . out there," Polly gasped.

"What?" Tim asked, his expression suddenly hardening.

"Come and see," was all Polly could say as she took him by the hand and led him back to where she had been working. She was grateful for the simple security of a human touch, but it didn't remove the chill rushing inside her. She wondered why she didn't feel safer now that Tim was with her.

"That," she said simply once they reached the edge of the old garden.

She pointed at the yellow, decaying cylinder of bone lying on the ground where she had dropped it.

"Hmm," Tim said softly.

His knees popped as he bent down and gingerly picked up the bone. Turning it over carefully in his hand, he inspected the knobbed edge first, then the broken end. "Yeah. It's a bone, all right."

"Do you think . . . ?"

Polly had been about to ask him if he thought it might be a human bone, like the remains they found out at the construction site, but she let her question trail away and just stood there, staring at him.

"You know what I think this is?" Tim finally said. He swung the bone, smacking it into the open flat of his hand. "I think this might be Daisy."

Polly raised one eyebrow as she looked at him.

"When I was growing up, I had a collie named Daisy," Tim continued. His eyes took on a distant cast as he studied the bone. "She was the best dog in the world, let me tell you. I was off to college, at Orono, when she died. My mom called and told me she and Rob had buried her out in the field." Putting his hands on his hips, he scanned the immediate area, looking like a pioneer scouting out where to build his cabin. "And I'll bet you this is where they buried her."

Polly licked her dry lips and swallowed noisily before speaking.

"I don't know," she said, shaking her head. "It looks kind of big for a dog bone, don't you think?"

Tim frowned with concentration as he turned the bone over and over in his hand. The spongy material made a faint rasping sound as he rubbed it.

"You find anything else? Any other bones?" he asked.

Pursing her lips, Polly shook her head.

"No. Once I found that one . . . I kind of freaked."

"Umm, I don't blame you," Tim said, nodding solemnly. Pacing back and forth, he carefully inspected the ground where Polly had been working, but finally he stopped and looked at her.

"My guess is it has to be Daisy," he said, nodding with determination. "Either that, or else maybe it's an old deer bone or something. The soil around here's pretty acidic, so nothing's going to last very long once it's buried out here."

Polly looked at him, wanting desperately to suggest that maybe they should have someone look at it—a professional, just in case he was wrong.

What if it isn't a dog or a deer bone? What if it's human?

But she didn't dare say that out loud. A strong chill ran through her, and she practically screamed out loud when a faint voice whispered deep inside her mind.

—Old bones—

"Are you sure?" she asked, cringing at the quavering sound her voice made.

Tim was still looking at her, his eyes bright but steady and cold.

"Yeah," he said flatly. "I'm positive. I mean, what else could it be?"

Polly wanted to tell him what she was thinking, but she left his question hanging between them in the hot, still air. He knew what she was thinking. She could see it in his face. Trickles of sweat ran down the inside of her blouse. She wiped her forehead with the back of her hand, then picked up her straw hat and adjusted it to shield her eyes.

"So what do we do?" she finally asked.

Tim shrugged. "Well, if it's Daisy, I want to make sure she stays buried. She deserves that much."

Polly wanted to ask him how he could show more respect for a dead dog than for a human being, but she watched silently as he took the clamming fork and began digging in the soft earth. He turned over scoop after scoop until he had a narrow trench about three or four feet deep.

"Good old dog," he whispered as he carefully laid the bone down in the hole and then, using his hands, scooped soil back over it. Once it was covered, he patted the soil down and pressed it firmly. "Let's hope she rests in peace."

Polly didn't say anything, but the voice in her mind—so faint now that she couldn't even be sure if it was her own thoughts or the hushed voice of Heather Olsen—kept whispering . . .

—*Old bones. . . . Old bones*—

It was well past midnight.

The sky was overcast, and there was a slight chill in the air that made Tim shiver as he carefully eased open the kitchen door and stepped out onto the back porch. Holding the edge of the screen door, he eased it gently shut behind him so it wouldn't bang. The yard was alive with the steady chirring of crickets. A gentle breeze whispered with a snakelike hiss in the grass and leaves, and off in the distance, he could hear a whippoorwill singing.

There were no lights on in the house because Tim had sneaked out of bed once he was sure Polly was asleep. He didn't want to wake her up.

No way . . . not now, he thought as he tiptoed down the back steps to the grass.

With no moonlight, the backyard was lit only by the hazy, gray glow of the night. Deep shadows shifted under the eaves of the house and inside the gaping door of the barn. The trees in the backyard looked like huge ink splotches against the night sky.

Feeling his way carefully in the darkness, Tim walked over to the barn without tripping over anything. He had purposely left a shovel just inside the doorway, and he

smiled grimly as he gripped the handle and then turned toward the field beside the house.

You're crazy to be doing this, he told himself, but he
wasn't about to turn around and give it up.

Polly had been visibly upset by the bone she had found
while working in the garden, but he had to follow through
with this if only to settle his own mind. Resting the shovel
on his shoulder like a soldier carrying a rifle, he crossed
the driveway and started out across the field.

The grass was damp with dew, and it wasn't long before
his sneakers and pants legs were soaked. The song of
crickets rose louder, seeming to come in swells that fell
silent only in his immediate vicinity as he crossed the field.
Even in the darkness, it wasn't difficult to find the old garden. After reburying the old bone, he had left the clam-
digger's fork stuck in the ground to mark the spot. He was
glad that Polly hadn't noticed it and put it back in the barn.

When he reached the spot, he bent down and felt around
on the ground until he was sure that he'd found the spot
where he'd reburied the bone. After casting a quick glance
up at the second-floor bedroom window to make sure no
lights had come on, he placed the tip of the shovel on the
ground, positioned his foot, and stepped down.

The shovel blade made a loud rasping sound as it bit
into the soil. The sound set his teeth on edge, and he
looked back at the house again to make sure the sound
hadn't carried in the night and disturbed Polly. The windows were open, and he could just barely make out the
faint, gauzy white curtains, swaying back and forth in the
night wind.

Licking his lips, he gripped the handle of the shovel,
pressed it into the loose soil, and turned over the first spade-
ful. It looked blacker than the rest of the field, and the rich,
earthy smell filled his nose. Secure, now, that he wouldn't
disturb his sleeping wife, he set to work, quickly turning
over the soil as he dug down deeper in the area where Polly
had found the bone. He knew why he was out here, but he
tried not to think too much about it as he worked.

It wasn't long before he was winded from the effort. Sweat coated his face and chest and ran down the sides of his neck, making his T-shirt cling to his skin with a clammy touch. The gentle night wind chilled him, raising goose bumps along his forearms, but he worked steadily, methodically digging in a line that ran parallel to the edge of the old garden. Other than a few stones he turned up, he didn't hit anything for the first fifteen minutes or so of digging. Then, with a sudden jolt, the shovel blade hit something and made a loud grinding sound. He knew, just by the feel, that this wasn't a rock.

"Oh, Jesus," he whispered as he dropped down onto his hands and knees, unmindful of the damp ground, and felt around. His hands brushed over something that felt spongy and hollow to the touch. He strained to see what it was, but the night was too dark. When he pried the thing free of the dirt, he held it up to the night sky to see if he could make out what it was.

Even without much light, he saw that it was another bone, maybe the other end of the piece Polly had broken in half while she was digging. Tim brushed his fingers along the jagged edge, shivering inside.

He didn't like what he was doing, just as he didn't like what he was thinking, but he was positive that the bone Polly had showed him earlier that day hadn't belonged to his dog or to a deer. He hoped Polly hadn't seen through his reaction and figured out what he really thought it was. He hadn't said anything because he didn't want her to freak out.

Besides, he didn't want to jump to any conclusions. Not yet. Not until he checked it out.

Placing the piece of bone on the grass to one side, Tim continued to dig, turning over several more scoops of dirt. It wasn't long before he developed a steady rhythm to the work, chopping into the dirt and turning it over with a mechanical ease.

After fifteen more minutes of working, he hadn't found anything else of interest. He was beginning to think that solitary bone might indeed have been a fluke, that maybe it was a dog or deer bone, and there was nothing else out here. But he kept on working with a strong, steady pace until the shovel blade struck something else, something that he knew wasn't a stone just by the sound the blade made scraping against it.

His hands were trembling, and his breath came in short, raw gulps as he knelt down and thrust his hands into the loose soil until he found what he was looking for. It was rounded and felt soft to the touch. He managed to grab a corner of it and wriggle it free.

"Oh, Jesus. . . . Oh, shit," he muttered as he rubbed his hands across the rough, rounded curve of the object. "Please . . . no!"

He was shaking all over as he scraped away the crusted dirt, revealing a small rounded object a little smaller than a basketball. Bringing it close to his face, he tried to see what it was, but all he saw was something black against black. He had to rely solely on touch because he hadn't thought to bring a flashlight. Cupping the object in his hand, he shifted it back and forth until the fingers of his right hand jabbed into a round, dirt-filled socket. A heavy choking sensation grabbed his throat when he felt a little to the side of that hole and found another, identical hole.

Eye sockets!

His stomach clenched. He retched once and tasted vomit in the back of his throat. He knew without a doubt that he was holding a skull, and it wasn't a dog's or a deer's skull.

It was definitely a *human* skull!

Waves of nausea washed through him.

No! . . . It can't be what I think it is! he thought. *It can't be!*

But he knew that it was.

A tightening feeling of dread bordering on outright terror gripped him. He was filled with revulsion and didn't know what to do, whether he should throw the skull away or rebury it or what.

Who is this? And why is he buried out here?

His gaze shifted back to the house and the dark rectangles of the upstairs windows. He wanted to deny it, but he knew that Polly had to at least suspect what was really buried out here. How could she not know? He had seen it in her eyes.

Worse than that was wondering what he should do about it. Someone—he had no idea who—had been buried out here.

The police and crime investigators would have to be involved, just like they were involved with the bones that had been uncovered at the construction site. It was an unattended human death, so it would have to be handled as a crime until the exact cause of death was determined.

And then what?

Then, whoever buried this person here would be discovered. It wasn't very difficult for Tim to figure out who had done this.

It had to have been Rob!

The dense night seemed to close in around him. The sound of the crickets grew maddeningly louder until he thought the sound would drive him insane. As he stood there in the night, holding the rotting human skull with both hands, Tim decided what he had to do.

He would rebury these old bones and leave them in the ground where no one else would find them before they rotted away to nothing.

He had to do that because—otherwise—the investigators would no doubt figure out what had happened to Cunna Dufresne, and then . . . then both he and Rob would be charged with murder.

Whatever or whoever was buried out here in the field was only going to make it worse!

Skritch . . . skritch . . . skritch . . .

Polly thought the steady, rhythmic sound was footsteps. She leaned forward in the darkness, straining to hear more clearly. The sound was faint, muffled, but it had a definite pattern. As she listened, it became clearer.

Skritch, thump . . . skritch, thump . . . skritch, thump . . .

There's someone walking around outside.

A wave of fear tickled up her back.

Or is it something in the wall? Rats, like Tim said?

Skritch, thump . . . skritch, thump . . . skritch, thump . . .

Her fear spiked higher as she imagined *someone* sneaking around outside the house, scratching at the windows, tapping on the walls, and clawing at the doors to get in. Her mind filled with ghastly images of bloated, white faces that appeared out of the darkness and then dissolved back into inky blackness. Their eyes were blank, and their mouths hung open in long, silent screams.

Polly realized that she was sitting up, staring into the darkness, but something felt wrong.

What she was sitting on was hard, unyielding. It didn't feel like the bed. She reached out and felt on either side of her. Her hands touched a hard, flat surface. It certainly didn't feel like a mattress.

What the hell is going on?

Could she have fallen out of bed? Was she sitting on the floor?

She reached out as far as she could all around her, but even behind and in front of her, she couldn't feel anything except for a cold, flat, hard surface.

Where the hell am I?

—You're here . . . with me—

The voice whispered softly out of the darkness, filling Polly with clutching fear.

Heather?

—Yes . . . I'm right here—

Polly lurched forward until she was on her hands and knees. The darkness was filled with the harsh sound of her own breathing and something else: *Skritch, thump . . . skritch, thump . . . skritch, thump . . .*

Are we safe here?

Polly was trying to fight back the almost overwhelming sense of desperation that filled her.

Skritch, thump . . . skritch, thump . . . skritch, thump . . .

—*He's out there. . . . Can't you hear him?*—

Polly couldn't even tell if her eyes were open or closed. She had no physical sensation of vision. She took a breath and smelled a hint of citrus . . . or was it the smell of old bones?

The darkness surrounding her was total, absolute. She grew dizzy and was almost swept away by a plunging feeling of vertigo. Even when she put her hands down flat on the floor—*Why isn't it the mattress?*—the feeling didn't subside.

Skritch, thump . . . skritch, thump . . . skritch, thump . . .

Do you know who it is? Who's out there?

Polly's throat made a loud hitching noise when she tried to take another breath.

—*He wants to hurt you. . . . I told you that. . . . He wants to hurt all of you*—

Polly fell silent, unable even to phrase in her mind what she might want to say. As she stared into the impenetrable darkness, a dim, white light began to glow all around her. It began so subtly that Polly was only aware of it once the surrounding walls began to come into view, materializing out of the darkness like a slowly developing photograph.

Where the hell am I?

By increments, the light got steadily brighter. Polly listened to her pulse racing in her ears. It was almost, but not quite, loud enough to drown out the steady *skritch, thump . . . skritch, thump . . . skritch, thump* that filled the night.

The dull, white glow stung, bringing tears to her eyes as she looked around. Off to the left, she could see a small figure, huddled on the floor. The details of the figure were lost in shadow, but she had the distinct impression that there was a little girl, cringing in the corner of the room.

What room? This isn't the bedroom!

As the light steadily brightened, it illuminated sharp, angular walls that stretched high overhead until they were lost in deep shadows. The light brightened, and the walls gradually blended from dense gray to a milky white that reminded Polly of curdled milk. She was gripped by a feeling of being trapped. The air in the room—*What room is this?*—seemed too thin to breathe. She gasped for breath even as something that felt like cold, clammy hands encircled her throat and began to squeeze.

No! This is impossible!

Panic rose in strong, steady pulses until she thought she couldn't bear it another second.

Tears filled her eyes, blurring her vision as she stared at the tiny figure on the floor in the corner of the room.

It *was* a little girl!

And as much as she tried to deny it, Polly realized that she did look familiar.

It's Heather Olsen!

Heather had her knees drawn up to her chest. Her hands covered the bottom part of her face, and her eyes, wide with terror and unblinking, stared back at Polly.

This can't be happening! This has to be a dream!

Heather tilted her head to one side. Her vacant stare drilled into Polly, freezing her soul. The depth of fear inside her eyes was too terrible to contemplate.

—It's happening. . . . I'm here . . . and, now, so are you—

The words filled the white room, thrumming like hammer blows in Polly's ears, but Heather's face remained immobile. She never blinked, and her lips didn't seem to move. The parchment whiteness of her skin seemed to blend in with the white walls as the light kept getting steadily brighter. For a moment, it looked like just her eyes were hovering in midair and staring at her.

—And he's out there . . . the man who wants to hurt you . . . all of you. . . . He's outside . . . right now—

What can I do? Why does he want to hurt us?
Polly's fear opened up like a black pit inside her. She could feel herself being sucked into it.

—I don't know what you can do—

Heather's voice had a dull, hollow tone that seemed to be coming from several sources at once. Her dark, terror-filled eyes swelled, widening as the room brightened. Polly thought crazily that Heather's eyes were the source of the white light.
Skritch, thump . . . skritch, thump . . . skritch, thump . . .

—That's him. . . . He's outside now . . . Can't you hear him?—

Yes, I can. Those are his footsteps, and it sounds like . . . like one foot is dragging behind him.

—That's why the rest of them are so upset. . . . He hurt them . . . all of them. . . . And now he's going to hurt you . . . all of you—

Skritch, thump . . . skritch, thump . . . skritch, thump . . .
The room was filled with bright light now. The white walls shimmered with a glow that blinded Polly. The small figure slumped in the corner was almost lost in the glare. Heather's features melted away until nothing remained except her wide, staring eyes.

—You tried to help me. . . . Now I want to help you—

Polly swallowed, and a thick, acidic taste filled her throat, making her gag. She wasn't sure she could speak, but she carefully formed the words in her mind.

Tell me what I can do to stop him.

—I don't know. . . . I only know he's there because I can hear him . . . walking around outside. . . . Listen. . . . That's the sound of his footsteps—

Skritch, thump . . . skritch, thump . . . skritch, thump . . .
But what can I do to stop him?

—The white room is a safe place. . . . He can't get to you while you're here. . . . Stay here with me. . . . You're safe in the white room—

Before Polly could respond, the white light in the room suddenly exploded, obliterating everything in sight with a roaring concussion. Polly let out a wild shriek as she lurched forward. Her hands raked the air in front of her as if she were falling and trying desperately to catch onto something—anything—to save herself.

"*Jesus!* You scared the *shit* out of me!"

In her panic, Polly didn't immediately recognize her husband's voice. She sat there blinking in the bright light as her eyes tried to adjust. After a moment or two, she saw that Tim was standing in the doorway of the bedroom, his hand still on the wall light switch.

Squinting, Polly stared at him, unable to speak because her racing heartbeat was squeezing her throat with every pulse.

"I—"

That was all she could manage. She put her hands down to her sides and, unbelieving, felt the cushioned softness of the bed mattress. It squeaked beneath her as she shifted her weight. She could see that the walls of the bedroom were the way they were supposed to be: a dull beige wallpaper with a faded design and dark painted wood trim. Not bright. Not white. The walls didn't stretch up over her head at impossible angles.

"What's the matter?" Tim asked. He walked over and sat on the edge of the bed, taking her hand in his. "Nightmare?"

Polly licked her lips and nodded, feeling an iron stiffness in her neck. She squeezed his hand so tightly her own began to tremble. When she tried to take a breath, she heard a high wheezing sound in her throat.

"Yeah," she managed to say. "I . . . uhh . . . guess so."

She tried to fight the feeling of desperation as she looked at him, but the coldness that gripped her heart wouldn't go away. She wanted to tell him what had happened, but she knew that she couldn't just as surely as she knew that it hadn't been just a dream.

It was more than a dream.

She had *been* there . . . in the white room . . . with Heather.

She had seen her, and spoken to her, and Heather had told her that she and her family were in danger.

And Polly now knew with certainty who she was in danger from.

It's Rob!

"Your hands are ice cold," Tim said softly.

He started rubbing the backs of her hands, but Polly just sat there, staring at him and nodding numbly. She could barely register what he was saying and doing because of the fear that filled her, but she looked down at his hands holding hers and noticed that his fingernails were crusted with dirt.

"Why are—" she started to say but then stopped herself.

Tim looked at her, frowning with concern, but she wouldn't finish the thought. She couldn't because she knew, if she started talking now, she would blurt out that she knew that his brother was a threat to them . . . to the whole family.

She knew this because a dead girl named Heather Olsen had told her.

fourteen

The afternoon was overcast, and judging by the darker clouds that were blowing in from the west, Brian was sure it was going to start raining soon. He didn't care, though. He had no interest in going outside or taking a walk down by the river, and he certainly wasn't going to waste his time hanging around downtown Hilton.

What a joke that was!

If this was what passed for civilization, no wonder the kids around here all seemed so weird.

The nearest movie theater was probably thirty miles away, and he hadn't seen a decent bookstore or anything else that interested him in town. The one small computer store he checked out had prices that were almost double what they were back home. If it wasn't for the Internet and E-mail, he'd be going totally crazy by now. As it was, he felt frustrated and angry about being stuck in this hick town. Sometimes late at night he heard his parents talking—arguing, really—about when they should go back to Stonepoint. His mother was getting pretty insistent that they should leave soon, so Brian felt confident that they wouldn't be here much longer. It was just a question of how long.

Too bad we can't leave today . . . right now!

He never said anything about his feelings to his folks. There was enough tension between them as it was.

He'd spent most of the afternoon up in his bedroom, surfing the net. Around three o'clock, he figured he needed a break and came downstairs. He found his mother in the living room. She had a book open on her lap, but it was obvious that she hadn't been reading. She was just sitting there on the couch, staring out the living room window at the apple trees that lined the field. She barely acknowledged his presence when he walked by, saying a quiet "Hi" to her. All she managed was a quick half turn and slight nod before turning back to the gloomy, gray view outside the window.

When he walked into the kitchen, his father was sitting at the kitchen table with pretty much the same blank expression on his face. His hands were wrapped around a steaming cup of coffee, and he, too, looked like he was just sitting there, staring straight ahead out the window; but he brightened when Brian came into the room.

"Hey, how's it going?" he asked.

Brian instantly detected the forced cheeriness in his voice. His first thought was that it sounded like his father was hiding something from him. He smiled in return, nodded, but said nothing. If he said anything right now, he was sure it would be to ask why didn't they pack up today—close the house, and head back home.

Brian took the two-liter bottle of Pepsi from the refrigerator and drained what was left in it with two or three huge gulps. The carbonation stung his nose and brought tears to his eyes, but it felt good. When he walked over to the kitchen sink to rinse out the bottle to throw it into the recycling container, he suddenly froze.

A battered Ford pickup truck was just pulling into the driveway. As it rumbled past the kitchen window, Brian saw the peeling sticker on the rear bumper.

FRIENDS DON'T LET FRIENDS
D R I V E   C H E V Y S

"Oh, *shit!*" he whispered.

He turned quickly to see what his father's reaction would be. His father had heard the truck, too, and was getting up slowly from his chair to go to the back door.

Brian panicked.

Even though he knew he was perfectly safe with his mother and father nearby, he couldn't help but feel afraid.

Oh my God! The asshole's back!

He felt a sudden urge to run.

What the hell is he doing here? Is he still after me?

Brian wanted to believe that the guy in the truck hadn't really tried to run him over the other day, that he'd just been goofing around, maybe just trying to give him a little scare, but he certainly had felt threatened.

So who the hell is he?

Brian stood there, frozen, because he knew that he was about to find out. His father was at the screen door, now, holding it open with one hand. From the side, Brian could see that there was a wide smile on his father's face.

What the fuck? He knows *this guy?*

The tension winding up inside him got even stronger, almost unbearable.

What the fuck is going on here?

Moving slowly, Brian edged toward the door, poised and ready to run for his life if he had to. Looking past his father, he saw a man who looked maybe a few years older than his father getting out of the truck. He moved with an awkward gait, and when he came around the back end of the truck, Brian saw why. The man's left leg was in a cast up to his knee.

In that instant, he recognized his uncle.

"What the hell are you doing here?" his father called out.

The comment struck Brian as strange. His father waved a greeting as he stepped out onto the shadowed coolness of the porch, but he seemed to be more than a little irritated that his brother was here.

Brian didn't follow his father outside. The screen door

slammed shut with a bang loud enough to make him jump. Brian still couldn't figure out what was going on.

Was his dad happy to see Uncle Rob or not?

He couldn't believe it had been his uncle who had tried to run him down! Maybe he'd been so scared he'd made a mistake, but no. He clearly remembered seeing that particular truck. He especially remembered seeing the bumper sticker on the back, which must pass for country humor.

But maybe someone else had been driving his uncle's truck that day.

If it had been his uncle, even if he'd just been trying to give him a little scare and not really kill him, it didn't make any sense.

Why would his uncle even *pretend* to try to kill anyone?

"I don't think you should be out driving," Brian heard his father say.

Uncle Rob sniffed with laughter and said, "Don't you worry 'bout me. I'm gettin' around just fine."

Together, the two men started up the steps to the back door. The sound of their feet on the porch filled Brian with rising apprehension, especially the alternating heavy clump of his uncle's walking cast.

He figured his uncle must not have recognized him that day out at the construction site. That was the only possible explanation. Why else would he chase after him in his truck and try to run him down?

Brian held his breath as the rusty spring on the screen door squeaked, and his father stood back, holding the door open for his brother to enter first. As soon as Uncle Rob came into the kitchen and saw Brian standing there, a wide smile spread across his face.

"You probably don't even recognize Brian," his father said as he stepped inside the house and eased the screen door shut behind him.

Narrowing his left eye like he was sighting down a gun, Uncle Rob stepped forward and extended his hand for Brian to shake. Brian noticed that the man's hand was rough and calloused—a working man's hand, not at all like his father's.

"Oh, I think I might've seen him around town some," Uncle Rob said with a faint chuckle. "Haven't I?"

Cringing inside, Brian shrugged and said, "I dunno . . . maybe."

"'S been quite a few years, though," Uncle Rob said. "You sure have grown."

Brian flinched when his uncle clapped him hard a few times on the shoulder with his other hand. There was a twinkle in his eye that Brian couldn't miss. A sudden coldness filled his stomach when he realized that maybe Uncle Rob *had* recognized him that day out at the construction site. Maybe he had tried to run him over on purpose.

"So how's it going, Uncle Rob?" Brian asked weakly.

He quickly let go of his uncle's hand and then involuntarily wiped his own hand on his pants leg.

"Been better," Uncle Rob said, smirking as he thumped the cast heavily on the floor. "But I'm doin' all right now. Keepin' myself out of trouble, anyway."

Yeah, I'll bet you are. . . . Tried running over any other kids lately? Brian thought but didn't say.

All three of them turned when they heard Polly approach from the living room. She stopped in the doorway, a cool, neutral expression on her face that seemed to tighten when she made eye contact with Uncle Rob.

"Hey, Pol. Look who dropped by," his father said.

Once again, Brian heard the forced cheerfulness in his father's voice. He still had no idea what was going on here. Neither of his parents seemed really glad to see Uncle Rob, but they were welcoming him almost like they were afraid to let him know that they didn't want to see him. His mother was trying to maintain a neutral expression, but it subtly shifted into a slight, almost imperceptible sneer. Knowing her as well as he did, Brian read her reaction as one of thinly veiled disgust.

He figured it was an adult thing and none of his business. All he wanted to do was get away from them, go back up to the privacy of his bedroom and be by himself.

"How about a beer?" his father asked.

Before Uncle Rob could reply, he opened the refrigerator door and grabbed two bottles of Shipyard.

"Hey, the good stuff," Uncle Rob said as he seated himself at the kitchen table. Brian noticed that his mother seemed to flinch every time the cast scraped across the linoleum.

"Well," Brian finally said with a nervous shrug. "I . . . uh, I've got some stuff to do up in my room. Nice to see you, Uncle Rob."

"Yeah, you, too," Uncle Rob said with a wink.

Brian didn't miss the mocking tone in his uncle's voice as he turned and left the room. A thin sheen of sweat broke out on his forehead as he walked quickly through the living room, then dashed up the stairs, taking them two at a time. A cold, prickling sensation swept across the back of his neck, and he couldn't help but feel as though someone was watching him from behind the whole time. He was trembling and out of breath by the time he entered his bedroom and swung the heavy oak door shut behind him.

"Jesus *Christ*, that was weird," he whispered.

For several seconds, he stood there with his back against the door, panting heavily until his racing pulse began to slow. Once he had calmed down a bit, he walked over to his desk by the window, sat down heavily, and switched on his computer.

Staring out the bedroom window as he waited for his computer to boot up, he saw that the storm clouds were closing in fast. The sky had gotten noticeably darker since he'd been downstairs. A few raindrops had begun to patter against the window. Within seconds, as he watched, the sky opened up, and the downpour began in a low, rushing hiss.

Try as he might, Brian couldn't stop thinking about what had just happened downstairs. It was confusing and downright scary. He kept realizing that his teeth were clenching and his shoulders were bunching up with tension. He kept shaking himself, trying consciously to relax; but no matter what he did, he still felt wire tight.

Jesus, just calm down!

He took a long, shuddering breath and eased back in his chair while he watched the trees down by the river bend to the sudden gusts of wind and rain. His computer had finished clicking through its initial setup and was on his opening page, but he was so lost in thought that he hardly noticed.

You'll be out of here and back to civilization soon, he told himself, *so—Jesus Christ!— just forget about it.*

After a few social pleasantries, which Rob thought were forced and phony, Polly excused herself and went back into the living room, leaving Rob alone in the kitchen with his brother. He finished his first beer before Tim had taken more than a few swallows of his own and was patiently waiting for him to offer another. The only outward sign of the agitation he was feeling was that he couldn't stop himself bouncing his leg nervously up and down. He kept glancing at the kitchen doorway as though he suspected that Polly—or maybe Brian—was lurking just around the corner, eavesdropping on them.

"So what brings you out here today, any-who?" Tim asked.

He was trying to look so casual, Rob thought, leaning back in his chair with his thumb hooked through a belt loop and sipping his beer, but Rob could see right through him. He knew that Tim and Polly didn't want him here, and that really pissed him off.

Whose fucking house is it, anyway? He'd spent more time here than Tim had since their old man died!

"You know," Rob said, "I figured—what the fuck? You've been stopping by to see me every day. . . . I figured it was time I returned the favor."

Rob shrugged, all the while rolling the empty beer bottle between the palms of his hands, wondering when—or if—Tim was going to get the hint that he wanted another. They both looked out the window as the sudden downpour of rain rattled against the glass.

"You probably should've called first," Tim said, lowering his voice and leaning forward as he flicked a quick glance toward the kitchen doorway.

"Hold on a second," Rob said, glowering. "Are you telling me I have to *call* first to come over here? This is as much my house as yours, you know."

"I know, but we've been"—Tim shrugged tightly, looking really nervous. Rob liked that—"under a little bit of pressure, you know?"

"No, not really," Rob said, fighting hard to suppress a smirk. "Why don't you tell me about it."

Rob was here for one reason, and one reason only: to make sure, short of outright threats, that his brother and his wife were going to keep their mouths shut about what they knew because if they didn't . . .

Well, he knew that he would do whatever he had to do to keep them quiet. Some part of him was still hoping it wouldn't come to that.

"You know . . . Polly's not feeling very well," Tim said.

Rob could tell that his little brother was holding back something, but he knew Tim well enough to know that, given time, he'd spill his guts to him.

That was the whole fucking problem!

It was sad, really, the way Tim couldn't keep his goddamned mouth shut. The truth was, he was genuinely surprised that Tim hadn't told his wife about Cunna Dufresne long before now.

That is, if he hadn't. Most likely he had told her, years ago, and was just using recent events as an excuse to get everything out in the open.

Finally, Rob couldn't stand it any longer, so he waved the empty beer bottle back and forth like he was ringing a bell.

"Hey, you got another one?"

"Oh, yeah . . . sure."

Tim scrambled to his feet and fetched another beer from the refrigerator. There was a stilted awkwardness about him that Rob was thoroughly enjoying. He didn't like the way Tim was treating him like an intruder in his own family home, like he didn't even belong here. No doubt that was partly Polly's influence, but whatever, it really pissed him off!

"Thanks," Rob muttered as he took the beer from his brother, raised it, and guzzled down about half of it in a few big swallows. Smacking his lips and wiping his mouth with the back of his hand, he smiled and nodded with satisfaction.

But it was satisfaction for what he was doing here as much as anything else. He had easily read the confusion and fear in Brian, and that was good. It would keep him off balance, too. Although he hadn't recognized him that day out at the construction site, he realized soon enough who he was when he saw the kid take off into the woods and then come out on Ridge Road not far from the house.

Ultimately, it didn't matter who he was. No one should be poking around out there. The fact that it was his nephew didn't change a goddamned thing.

"You know," he said, shaking with laughter at his private thoughts, "I was kinda hopin' you'd ask me to stay for supper." He noticed that he was bouncing his right leg up and down and made himself stop. "I mean, those lunches you been bringin' me are fine 'n all, but there's nothin' like a home-cooked meal, you know? 'Specially on a rainy, crappy day like this."

Rob almost laughed out loud as he watched the conflicting thoughts and emotions play across his brother's face. He could see that Tim was nervous just having him in the house, but it was also obvious that he was scared shitless about even suggesting to his wife something like asking him to stay for supper.

"It's just . . . I'm not sure this is a good time . . . today, especially," Tim whispered. Once again, he glanced nervously over at the doorway.

"Hey, if it's a problem, I'll just have another beer or two with you 'n hit the road," Rob took another long drink. "It's no sweat."

Tim started to say something, then stopped himself and swallowed hard. He seemed to have forgotten the beer in his hand. Lowering his gaze, he ran his hand across his forehead and sighed.

"No . . . no. It'll probably be all right. It's just—"

His gaze went to the window again, and Rob turned to look outside as well.

It was still raining hard. Raindrops bounced on the driveway, making it look like it was dancing with energy. Across the field, the trees were swaying back and forth in the wind, and a cool, moist breeze was blowing the lacy curtains in as rain splattered against the screen.

"Make sure the windows are closed up there," Polly hollered from the next room just as Tim got up and went to the window and lowered it enough to keep the rain out but not enough to cut off the cooling breeze.

"Maybe it'll cut the humidity," Tim said, like he was just trying to make conversation.

Rob quickly finished his second beer and placed the empty down on the table. As if on cue, Tim got him another one and popped the cap off before sitting back down. Rob was satisfied to see that he still had that tight, worried expression, like a trapped animal.

Gotta make sure he knows who's in charge here.

"Yeah," Tim said after a long moment of silence. "Let me see what Polly thinks, but I don't see where it'd be a problem. We don't have anything fancy planned."

"Ahh," Rob said, with a dismissive wave of his hand, "I don't need anything fancy. I'm pretty easy to please."

"Maybe we should run into town, first," Tim said. "There's not a lot of beer left, and maybe we could pick up a few steaks or something."

"Umm. Sounds good to me," Rob said. Once again, he

found it almost impossible not to let the smirk he was feeling show. "If you don't mind, though, I'd just as soon hang here and rest my foot. It starts to tingle when the weather changes like this."

Tim hesitated, but only for a moment; then he nodded before getting up and walking into the living room.

As he listened to the hushed buzzing of voices in the next room, Rob let the smile spread across his face. Reaching behind his back, he adjusted the heavy object he had wrapped in a handkerchief and stuck under his belt in the small of his back. It was starting to hurt.

After a minute or so, Tim came back into the kitchen. His mouth was set in a firm line, and it looked to Rob like he'd just taken a load of shit from Polly. It was a real struggle not to laugh out loud.

"Yeah," Tim said with a quick nod. "You can stay for supper. I'll just zip into the Star Market and get some steaks."

"And beer."

Tim nodded. "Right. And beer. Anything else you think we need?"

Rob winced and leaned forward in his chair to relieve the pressure of the gun that was pressing into the small of his back.

"Here. Take my truck," he said. He shifted to one side and fished the keys out of his jeans pocket. Tim took them and smiled tightly.

"You know," Rob continued, "I was thinking maybe, it being such a shitty day 'n all, we could have a little fire in the fireplace after supper. I think there's still some firewood down in the cellar." He heaved himself out of the chair and stretched as he stood up, being careful to turn and face Tim so he wouldn't see the bulge in the small of his back. "Maybe while you're in town I'll see if there's anything down there worth burning."

Tim hesitated, his expression unreadable for a moment, but then said, "Yeah. Sounds like a good idea."

"Real cozy *family* time," Rob said.

By the expression on Tim's face, he was sure that his brother hadn't picked up on the irony of his comment. He couldn't help but smile, though, because things had fallen into place even better than he had expected. There was this little matter about a gun he didn't want to have in his possession, so while he was here and Tim was out of the house, he'd hide it down in the cellar. Even better was the thought that, if the gun ever was found, it might be connected to Tim, not him.

Now that would be interesting!

But while he was down in the cellar, besides hiding the gun, maybe he'd think of something else to do to fuck with Tim and his family. It never hurt to cover your tracks. Rob was a firm believer in that.

Polly was *furious!*

Her hands were clenched so tightly into fists her knuckles turned bone white. Her whole body was shaking as she sat hunched on the couch and stared out at the rain-swept yard.

You shitty, rotten bastard!

She couldn't believe Tim had dumped something like this on her. The last thing she wanted was to have Rob in the house, and now he was leaving her alone with him while he went in town grocery shopping. She clenched her teeth and punched the arm of the couch hard enough so it hurt. She could have asked to come with Tim, but that would have looked weird. So instead, she was trapped in the house with a man she knew was a murderer!

You shitty, rotten bastard! I'll never forgive you for this, Tim!

She turned around quickly and stared at the kitchen doorway when she heard Rob's truck start up. As Tim backed around, the crunching of the tires on the wet gravel driveway set her teeth on edge. All she could think was, as soon as Tim's gone, as soon as we're alone, Rob's going to come in here and want to talk. She couldn't imagine what she would have to say to him or how she could even look at him.

He was a killer, and the sound his cast made, dragging on the kitchen floor when he walked, sounded exactly like the sound she had heard last night—outside the white room—of someone creeping around in the dark.

Jesus! Stop thinking like that. Rob's not going to do anything to me! He's not that crazy!

Still, she felt vulnerable.

She considered calling out to Brian and asking him to come downstairs on the pretext of helping her get supper ready, but she couldn't bring herself to do that. So far, Rob had remained in the kitchen, and like an ostrich with its head buried in the sand, all Polly wanted to do was pretend that he didn't even know she was here. She'd be safe if she didn't move or say anything. She jumped when she heard him get up and start walking, thumping his walking cast on the linoleum floor.

Skritch, thump . . . skritch, thump . . . skritch, thump . . .

Cold pressure began to build up in Polly's chest.

Turning away from the kitchen doorway, she cringed as she thought about what would happen next. The hair on the back of her neck prickled as she waited to hear him enter the living room.

Leave me alone! Please! Just leave me alone!

Skritch, thump . . . skritch, thump . . . skritch, thump . . .

Polly had to fight the urge she had to get up and run. She was afraid to turn around because he might already be standing in the doorway. The sound of his heavy tread resounded through the house, mixing with the terror of her nightmare—*No! It was more than a nightmare!*—the night before.

Heather had warned her about this.

All along, she'd been trying to tell her that there was someone outside the white room—a bad man who was angry at Polly and wanted to hurt her and her whole family.

This can't be happening! Polly thought.

She wished desperately that this was all a dream, and that she would wake up soon.

The heavy tread of footsteps in the kitchen stopped. Tensed, Polly listened to the steady patter of rain on the roof. Blood rushed in her ears with a muffled whisper as she waited . . . waited . . .

Then, very faintly, she heard a faint click that made her jump and almost cry out.

The cellar door! He's unlocked the cellar door!

The memory of what she had seen down there filled Polly with a terror like she had never experienced before. She tried not to think about it, but the mental images of jar after jar filled with bloody organs and viscera filled her mind. Tim had gone down there and cleaned up the mess, and he'd told her it was nothing but rotting vegetables and fruit, no matter what she thought she had seen.

But I know what's really down there!

Whimpering softly, she clapped her hands over her ears, closed her eyes, and tried to catch her breath. A great weight seemed to be pressing down on her.

Skritch, thump . . .

Polly could tell by the sound that Rob had started down the cellar steps. Closing her eyes, she tried not to but couldn't help but picture him, one hand clasping the railing for support as he slowly descended into the cellar. Like a spirit drifting in the night, she could feel herself being drawn along with him down into the damp, gloomy darkness. Terror took hold of her and tightened its grip until she could barely breathe. She was swept up with vertigo and could feel herself falling . . . falling backward in a slow, dizzying spiral. When she opened her eyes and looked around the room, frantic to find something to anchor her vision, everything around her was pulsing with light and energy.

"No . . . please," she whispered in a shattered voice.

She could hear and practically smell her desperation. That only made the helpless feeling of vertigo worse. The fringes of her vision vibrated with a pulsating blackness that throbbed with frightening energy.

She felt trapped . . . imprisoned . . . as if she were in a small room that had no doors . . . no windows . . . no exit!

"*No!* " Polly whispered, her voice sounding strangled, as if someone had their hands wrapped tightly around her throat.

"You say something?"

Rob's voice came from deep below her, faint but penetrating through the floor.

Polly tried to answer him, but she couldn't breathe as her vision closed down around her. Her pulse was racing with a high, papery flutter in her neck and temples. Every needle-sharp throb penetrated her skull, making her wince.

Don't come upstairs! Please! Just leave me alone!

The house was filled with a hushed silence that was broken only by the steady hissing of the rain. Frantic with fear, Polly looked around the living room as if a means of escape would suddenly appear to her, but she was in such a grip of terror that she was rooted to the couch, unable to move.

She lost all sense of time.

Everything around her seemed to be collapsing in on her, telescoping inward until all she could see was a tiny, white hole in the center of her vision. The whole world looked and felt impossibly far away.

I'm dying!

She was surprised that the thought didn't carry as much terror as she had thought it would. In fact, death seemed to be the only thing that would give her the release she needed. She could feel herself fading, falling farther and farther away as the tiny pinpoint of white light in front of her diminished, growing smaller . . . and smaller . . . until it was finally . . . *gone.*

"Hey, Lucy, . . . I'm home," Tim called out in a lousy Ricky Ricardo imitation as he entered the kitchen and slid the two bags of groceries he was carrying onto the counter. He wiped the rain from his eyes, shook off his slicker, and hung it on one of the pegs by the door.

The house seemed unnaturally quiet. His brother wasn't in the kitchen where he had left him.

Is he in the living room visiting with Polly?

That didn't seem very likely. He knew that Polly would have done everything short of throwing his brother out of the house to stay away from him. Tim was just starting toward the living room when he heard a loud crash from down in the cellar. For the first time, he noticed that the cellar door was open. He moved quickly to the top of the stairs.

"Hey! Everyone all right down there?" he shouted.

He couldn't imagine that Polly was down in the cellar, not after the scare she'd had the last time she'd gone down there.

"Huh? Oh, you're back already," Rob called out cheerily from below.

Tim started down the stairs, noticing as he put his weight on the first step that the stairs creaked loudly. Involuntarily, he grabbed the handrail as he leaned forward and peered down into the gloom of the cellar.

"What the hell are you doing down here, anyway?" he called out.

A second later, Rob's smiling face appeared from around the corner as he came forward.

"Just having a little look around," he said. "Man, there's a bunch of shit down here. You know what we should do is get a Dumpster and cart all of this out of here. No one's ever gonna miss it."

"Umm," Tim replied with a quick nod. "You're probably right, but I think Polly wanted to look it over first. See if there was anything worth saving. Antiques or whatever."

"Nothin' but junk 's far as I can see," Rob said. "I found some firewood, though, and a stack of old newspapers, so we can get the fire started later."

Rob was still smiling, a little too much, Tim thought, as

he started toward the cellar stairs. His arms were loaded with wood that had probably been chopped and split ten or more years ago. It looked as gray and hard as iron.

"You want some help with that?" Tim asked, taking a few more steps down. Rob shook his head and started up the stairs quickly. As he turned to go back into the kitchen, Tim noticed that the stairs creaked terribly beneath their combined weight. It sounded as if every rusty nail in the old wood was pulling out.

"This stuff's pretty old. Probably be a bitch getting it lit," Rob said as he pushed past Tim and entered the kitchen. Knowing how Polly felt about the cellar, Tim made a point of shutting the door and locking it behind them.

"Speaking of Polly, where is she?" Tim asked, looking around.

Rob shrugged.

"Hey, Pol! I'm back," he shouted.

He cast a questioning glance at his brother, then moved past him into the living room. For just a second, he froze, and his heart skipped a beat when he saw Polly slumped on the couch. She was lying in an awkward position that wasn't at all natural. One foot was on the floor. The other was cocked to the side, half off the couch. Her torso was twisted around making it look like she had turned to break a fall.

"Jesus! Polly!" Tim shouted as he rushed over to kneel by her side.

Polly rolled her head from side to side and groaned. She winced, and her eyelids fluttered rapidly like she was trying to blink something out of them. When she finally managed to open her eyes, Tim saw that they were bloodshot and unfocused.

"Huh? Oh, hey . . ." she said in a raw, dry-sounding voice.

"You take a nap or something?" Tim asked.

He was trying to keep it light, but he didn't like the way his wife was acting. If he didn't know better, he might have thought she'd had a little too much to drink. Even after she shook her head and eased up into a sitting position, she looked really out of it.

"Yeah, I . . . I guess I did," she said, sounding distracted, almost wistful.

"You want a glass of water or something?" Tim asked.

This wasn't like Polly at all, and he was worried. Her eyes still seemed unfocused, and she seemed distracted, spaced out.

"No . . . I . . . I'll be all right."

She shook her head and rubbed her eyes vigorously.

"Just give me a second. What time is it, anyway?"

"A little after five o'clock," Tim replied after glancing at his watch.

"Hmm," Polly said as she smacked her lips and shook her head.

Her face looked pale in spite of the summer tan she'd gotten working and sitting outside over the last few days. She jumped and seemed to go even paler when she looked at Rob, who was standing in the doorway with a load of firewood cradled in his arms.

"I just get so sleepy on days like this," she said.

Her voice still sounded far away, and if he hadn't been looking right at her, Tim might have suspected that she was talking in her sleep. He knew she was covering up something, maybe not wanting to talk about it because Rob was here.

"I just picked up some really nice steaks from the store," Tim said. "We were thinking about grilling them up for supper."

"Oh," was all Polly said, as if she didn't quite register what he was saying.

"Picked up some corn on the cob, too, and was going to make a tossed salad. Sound good to you?"

For a second or two, Polly just sat there, staring blankly ahead as though she hadn't even heard him. When she looked at him, the expression on her face made Tim think she almost didn't even recognize him. She licked her lips a few times and shifted her focus past him to some middle distance.

"You sure you're feeling all right?" Tim asked, really concerned.

Polly didn't react at first. She seemed to consider the question as though it had deep and profound implications. Then, very slowly, she nodded her head, but it bothered Tim that she still didn't look him directly in the eyes.

"Yeah, I . . . I'm just feeling a little wrung out," she said sleepily. "Maybe I'm coming down with something."

Tim placed his hand on her forehead. Her face was flushed, but he was surprised to find that her skin felt perfectly normal.

"You feel okay to me," he said. "Maybe after you have something to eat you'll feel more like yourself."

Something he said must have gotten to her because suddenly she jumped as though she'd gotten a mild electrical shock. When she looked at him, her eyes had a frantic fire dancing deep within them that Tim found totally disconcerting.

With a heavy sigh, Polly shifted forward and stood up from the couch. She seemed a little unstable on her feet, and Tim stood close beside her, ready to catch her if she started to fall.

"No, you know what? I think I'll just go upstairs and lie down for a while." She took a step forward and dipped to one side but quickly caught her balance. Without a backward glance or another word, she walked up the stairs and was gone.

"Well, I guess that leaves just you 'n me," Rob said.

Tim glanced at him and felt an unaccountable surge of anger at his brother. He was smiling and acting as though everything was fine and they didn't have a care in the world. It was obvious that he could care less about how Polly was feeling.

"Us and Brian," Tim said a little distantly.

He couldn't stop thinking about Polly and wondering if

he should send Rob home and go upstairs and make sure she was all right.

"I'll . . . uh, call him down once supper's ready. Maybe Polly will feel like eating then, too."

The only response from Rob was a little sniff of laughter as he walked over to the fireplace and dumped his load of wood onto the hearth, where it fell with a loud clatter.

"Why don't you go get started cooking up them steaks. I'm starved. While you're doin' that, I'll see if I can get this fucker lit."

For a heartbeat or two, Tim stood there, watching as his brother set to work arranging the firewood on the grate. He considered again telling him that maybe this wasn't the best time for him to visit, that he'd have to take a rain check, but then decided against saying anything.

Rob might take it the wrong way.

As worried as he was about Polly, Tim knew his older brother well enough to know that he didn't want him to take anything the wrong way.

No.

That was the last thing he wanted.

fifteen

I know I'm not asleep right now. . . .

It had been hours since Polly had come upstairs.

After changing into her nightgown, she had slipped into bed, but all she did was lie there, unable or unwilling even to close her eyes, much less drift off to sleep. The only sounds were the steady patter of rain on the roof and windows, and the faint beelike buzzing of Tim and his brother talking downstairs. She knew that Brian was still in his bedroom, no doubt chatting over the Internet with his friends, but she couldn't hear the click-click-click of his keyboard through his closed bedroom door.

Just as well.

She wasn't anywhere near tired enough to go to sleep, but she didn't have the energy to get up and go downstairs, either. The thought that she might be clinically depressed crossed her mind, but there was nothing she could do about it right now. She would have to wait until they got home before she could call the therapist she had seen after Crystal died.

Earlier that evening, she had smelled the steaks broiling and had heard Tim calling Brian down to supper. When he tiptoed into the bedroom to check on her, Polly had closed her eyes and exaggerated her deep, steady breathing. After whispering her name a few times, he had crept quietly back out of the room, shutting the door behind him.

Polly wasn't sure why she faked being asleep.

Maybe it was just to avoid spending any time downstairs with Rob. She told herself that was why she was upset and not feeling well; but deep down inside, she had to admit that it was more than that, even though she couldn't identify exactly what it was.

But something was bothering her on a deep level.

As she lay there in the gathering darkness of evening, she was distracted by the faint sounds of conversation still going on downstairs. Every now and then a burst of laughter would set her nerves on edge. Time after time she closed her eyes and tried to contact Heather and speak with her, but she didn't hear that or any other voice inside her head. She concluded that even if Heather Olsen wasn't literally inside her mind, there was some aspect of herself, some subconscious areas of her mind that she had tapped into only after being there when Heather died in the hospital. And these new aspects of her mind were giving her insights into her life and the things going on around her that were astounding and sometimes frightening.

She wondered, as she had many times before, if she might be going insane. Maybe she was cracking up from all of the stress in her life. Or maybe she had lost it back when Crystal died, and she was just too far gone to realize how crazy she was. Or—worst-case scenario—maybe she had a brain tumor that was putting pressure on her brain, causing these auditory and sometimes visual and olfactory hallucinations.

How else could she explain some of the things she had heard and seen since they moved into this old house?

The figures lurking in the shadows . . . the face she had seen in the shed window . . . the bloody body parts she had seen in the old preserves down in the cellar . . . the face she had seen peering at her over the roof edge . . . and the strange voices and smells that came to her late at night. What was causing them?

Polly had no idea, but she worried about it.

However she explained it, even if Heather's voice really was just an auditory hallucination resulting from a brain tumor, over the last few weeks she had realized that she had come to rely on "talking" to Heather.

Only now, Heather wouldn't answer her.

Had she gone away?

Had she left the white room?

Or had she never really been there, other than as a psychological delusion?

Polly realized that she probably had to be sleeping—or else drifting in that odd twilight zone between sleep and wakefulness—to "hear" Heather's voice or to get those curious smells. She wondered why, ever since that terrible day in the hospital, some things smelled so different to her. She worried that it might be another symptom of a brain tumor that was affecting the olfactory center of her brain . . . either that, or else another delusion brought on by grief and stress.

Tears filled Polly's eyes, and she lay trembling in the darkness. Even long after she heard Rob get into his truck and drive off and later, when Tim came upstairs and slipped quietly into bed trying not to disturb her, she couldn't stop thinking, *Something's really wrong with me!*

Maybe once they left this house, once they got back home, she would make an appointment with her doctor and talk to him about this. She might need to have some X rays or MRIs done, if only to put her mind at ease. Or maybe she'd be better off seeing a psychotherapist first. She knew she'd been doing better lately. That's why she had gone to volunteer in the hospital in the first place, but she could still be depressed about losing her baby. Being there when Heather died might have triggered an even worse depression that was so deep she didn't even realize it.

Or maybe she was just making it all up; it was all in her mind.

Tim was sleeping soundly beside her. She glanced at the luminous dial of the alarm clock and saw that it was well past midnight. She rolled over and closed her eyes tightly, willing sleep to come, but it wouldn't. When she took a deep breath, the strong aroma of chlorine filled her nose and throat, almost gagging her.

"Jesus!" she muttered as she flung the bedcovers aside. Swinging her feet to the floor, she sat up on the edge of the bed and looked around the dark bedroom.

Cautiously, she sniffed the air again. Although the smell of chlorine wasn't nearly as strong as the first whiff she'd caught, it was still there, drifting in the dark like an unseen, noxious cloud.

"What the hell," she muttered.

After glancing at Tim to make sure he was still asleep, she got out of bed and tiptoed downstairs into the kitchen. She knew her way well enough not to need to turn on any lights. She let the darkness and the silence of the night settle around her as she felt her way to the kitchen table, pulled out a chair, and sat down.

Her stomach growled with hunger, but she didn't move to get anything to eat. She wanted just to sit there in the darkness and absorb the night. The rain had passed, and there was a clean, fresh scent drifting on the night air.

Maybe that's all it was, she thought, sniffing the fresh, ozone-laced breeze that blew in the open window.

It could be that's all it was, but Polly sensed that it had to be something more.

"It's a sign, isn't it?"

She felt oddly dissociated from the soft rasp of her voice in the dense darkness.

"I get these weird smells when something's going to happen. They're like a . . . a premonition, aren't they? That's what it is, isn't it?"

She didn't expect anyone to answer her from the darkness, and she wasn't sure if she was disappointed or relieved when she heard nothing, not even a voice whispering inside her head. Even if Heather's voice was the result of a brain tumor, she realized with a sad, scared twist in her gut that she had come to depend on "hearing" and "talking" to the girl.

But there was another possibility she hadn't considered. It was something that Polly wasn't sure she even wanted to contemplate, but she had to consider it even if it meant that she truly was crazy.

Maybe . . . just maybe she really *was* in contact with Heather Olsen.

Was it possible that Heather's spirit really had entered her somehow at the moment of her death?

Could she really be in touch with the little dead girl who was trapped in some limbo state in the afterlife?

Whimpering softly in the darkness and covering her eyes with both hands, Polly leaned forward with her elbows resting on the table and sobbed softly.

I'm going nuts. . . . I'm losing my fucking mind!

Warm tears flowed from her eyes and filled the cups of her hands. Her breath hitched painfully in her chest.

—Down in the cellar—

The voice was as soft as the flutter of a butterfly's wings in the darkness, but it was loud enough to make Polly sit bolt upright in her chair and look around the dark kitchen.

Is that you, Heather?

—In the cellar . . . there's safety there . . . in the cellar—

The words sent a wave of cold up Polly's back. Instantly, her mind was filled with images of the bloody remains she had seen—no, not seen . . . imagined!—in the canning jars in that little room. Her heart started racing, and her breathing came in fast, shallow gulps.

—The white room—

"Yes," Polly whispered out loud.

She trembled as she recalled that the stone walls in the smaller room in the cellar had been painted white.

"Yes, it's a *white* room."

The kitchen filled with a dense silence broken only by the high, wheezing sound Polly made as she struggled to catch her breath and calm herself down.

I can be safe in the cellar. . . . Safe from what?

As if in answer, she heard a dull thump outside the window. Looking up quickly, she saw a dark silhouette, black against black, moving swiftly away from the house. Her heart skipped a beat as she strained to hear the faint sound of footsteps.

Polly's hands clenched into fists as she rose slowly and moved to the window. Crouching down low, she eased the curtain aside and peered out into the night. Her vision seemed to pulsate in time with her heartbeat, and she tried to convince herself that she had just imagined hearing and seeing anything, but then she saw the distinct outline of a person against the night sky, standing under the apple trees in the backyard.

No! That's not there! I'm not really seeing that!

Her breath cut off with a sharp gasp that felt like a knife blade sliding in under her ribs. Try as she might to convince herself otherwise, she knew there really was something there. She could see him!

Shifting her focus a little to one side made it easier for her to see him. Tingling with fear, she watched the figure, just standing there, looking at the house. She had the unnerving feeling that he—*Yes, it's definitely a man!*—could see in the dark. He could see her, crouching by the open window, staring out at him.

Who is it? What does he want?

She tried to convince herself that he couldn't really see her, not unless he had eyes like a cat. Her breathing slowed slightly, but she still felt as though she couldn't get enough air into her lungs. Sweat ran in little tickling streams down her sides from her armpits. It took a conscious effort to loosen her clenched fists as she prepared to run to the stairs and call out to Tim if the figure started moving toward the house.

So far, though, he just stood there, watching the house, no doubt looking for signs of activity inside.

—He's right outside the white room . . . right now. . . . I can hear him—

"No," Polly whispered, so softly she knew the man couldn't hear her, not at this distance. "He's right *here!*"

Look outside, Heather. Look out the window of the white room and tell me if you recognize him. Can you do that?

—I don't dare to. . . . He wants to hurt you. . . . He's mad, and he wants to hurt you—

How do you know that, Heather?

—I can feel his anger. . . . It's like a disease that won't go away. . . . He enjoys hurting people. . . . That's why there are so many of them who are angry at him. . . . They're waiting—

While this conversation was going on, Polly remained at the kitchen window. The figure was perfectly motionless. She began to doubt that it was even a real person out there. It could be a trick of the eye. But then, after what seemed like at least ten or fifteen minutes, the figure turned and started walking away over the crest of the hill. It was only then that Polly saw that he walked with a distinct limp, as if his left leg were in a cast!

Can you see him, Heather? Look outside the window and tell me what you see!

—I don't dare to—

You have to! It will only get worse if you don't face your fear. That's what will make it all go away, if you face it head-on!

—I can't. . . . I don't dare to—

The figure had disappeared over the crest of the hill like a slow-moving cloud that got smaller and smaller until it was gone, swallowed up by the night. Once she was sure he was gone, Polly let her breath out and took a normal, deep breath. Her body felt wrung out with exhaustion, and she wanted to cry.

He's gone, she thought, but she didn't feel the relief she thought she should because she knew that it wasn't over.

He might be gone now, but he would be back.

She had no idea what Rob was doing out there this late at night, but she knew he was up to something. And she knew that he would be back because—like Heather said—he wanted to hurt them.

All of them!

"So what do you think he's doing, creeping around out there late at night? Can you tell me that?"

It was late in the morning, a little past ten o'clock. Tim had slept in later than usual, but the rain had passed, and it was a beautiful, sunny morning, and he was in no mood for any kind of confrontation. "I have no idea," Tim replied. "How do you even know it was him?"

"I *saw* him, for Christ's sake! He was *limping!* I don't think there are too many people around town with casts on their left legs!"

Tim stiffened his shoulders because he knew that Polly wasn't going to let this drop.

"Well then, maybe he forgot something and came back to get it or . . . or . . . I don't know."

"He didn't come to the house," Polly said. Anger made her face flush. "At least not that I know of. He was just creeping around out there in the backyard like he . . . like he . . . I don't know! But if *you* don't confront him about it, then *I* certainly will."

"Jesus, just calm down, will you?" Tim took a deep, calming breath. "I'm sure it wasn't anything serious. I'll talk to him about it when I go over this afternoon for lunch, all right?"

"No, it's not all right!" Polly shouted, shaking her fists in frustration. "I want you to go over there right *now* and confront him about it. He scared the fucking *shit* out of me, Tim! I thought we were being broken into or something. Jesus, Tim, he's a . . . a . . ."

She stopped before she said it, but Tim knew that she had been about to call his brother a murderer again. A chill worked its way up his back as he scratched his cheek and tried to collect his thoughts.

"I'll do it. I promise," he said. "Let me have a little breakfast, and I'll drive over and talk to him."

"I won't put up with this . . . this *terrorizing,*" Polly said, shaking a finger at him. She lowered her voice, but her face was still flushed with anger. "I *mean* it! You tell him, if he comes sneaking around here after dark again, I'll call the fucking cops, and I'll tell them. I'll tell them all about what happened to Cunna Dufresne!"

Tim eyed her seriously. He wanted to tell her that she'd better calm down and watch what she said. He knew that Rob, even more than most people, wasn't the kind of person who reacted well to threats.

"I mean it!" Polly said. "I'll get a gun, and if he or anyone else comes creeping around here after dark, I'll shoot first and ask questions later."

"Okay, okay," Tim said, nodding. "Jesus, just calm down, will you?"

He was struggling to keep his temper in check, but he knew that he had to if only because Polly was so irate. He could feel his wife's angry stare boring into his back as he shuffled over to the refrigerator, took out the carton of orange juice, and poured himself a tall glassful. He stared blankly up at the ceiling as he gulped more than half of it down. All he could think was, the time had finally come.

He had to face up to his older brother and tell him to leave them alone.

"And another thing," Polly said, more calmly. "We're packing up and going home."

"But I thought you wanted to—"

Tim cut himself off when he saw that she was deadly serious.

"I'm not going to spend another night in this house if I don't have to," she said evenly. "While you're in town, I'll get the boxes and suitcases out of the attic and start packing."

Tim knew better than to argue with her. He nodded his agreement and then finished drinking his orange juice as an uncomfortable silence settled over the kitchen. He rinsed his glass at the sink and put it upside down on the dish drainer, then he grabbed his keys from the peg by the side of the door.

"And don't tell him we're leaving," Polly said with iron in her voice.

Tim looked her in the eyes and saw the wild, irrational fear lurking there. He nodded again, slowly.

"I don't want him to know that we're leaving. We'll just pack up and get out. He won't know we're gone until he comes sneaking around again at night and finds the house empty."

Tim considered for a moment, then shrugged.

"Sure . . . Okay. . . . Whatever you say," he mumbled.

"We'll be out of here by tomorrow afternoon at the latest," Polly said emphatically. "And as far as I'm concerned, I never want to see this goddamned house or town ever again!"

Fifteen minutes later, Tim had driven off, leaving Polly alone in the house except for Brian, who as far as she knew was still asleep upstairs. She figured that she'd wake him up if he slept past noon, but until then, she had no idea what to do with herself. She certainly didn't want just to sit around the house stewing about what had happened last night. Then again, she didn't feel like doing any more painting or cleaning in the house, either.

What was the point if they were going to be leaving tomorrow?

If she had her way, they'd pack up and be out of here by tonight, so it didn't make any sense to go outside and do any gardening, either, especially not after turning up that old bone the other day. She shivered as, very faintly, in her memory, she heard a voice whisper.

—Old bones—

She shivered again and tried to keep her mind on the positive, like getting back to her own home and her familiar routine, but she kept coming back to thoughts that were disturbing, like, *What if Rob isn't home when Tim gets there? What if he's gone somewhere for the day? What if he comes back here before Tim gets home?*

These thoughts sent waves of panic rippling through Polly. She was trembling deep inside as she quickly went through the entire downstairs, making sure that all of the doors and windows were closed and locked. For the first time in her life, she wished that Tim kept a gun in the house. At least today, anyway, and until they were safely back home in Stonepoint. She would feel a lot more secure if there was a loaded gun within reach.

"No! Jesus! Screw that," she whispered to herself.

She couldn't believe that she was so wound up and nervous that she was thinking like that. Wanting a gun was just another aberration due to the stress she was under. That's all it was. The truth was, she felt so threatened and exposed in this house she *had* to get out.

"You will," she whispered softly, cringing at the sound of her own voice in the stillness of the house.

But until they left, she had to do *something* while she waited for Tim to come back. She could always go up into the attic and get down the boxes and suitcases for packing, but she wasn't sure she wanted to go up there alone. Maybe after she calmed down a little she'd get Brian out of bed and ask him to help. More than anyone else, he would be glad that they were leaving here.

She had told Tim to be brief and firm with Rob, and then come back home to help her start packing. Just to be on the safe side, she had told him to make sure he kept his cell phone switched on and within easy reach at all times. If she called him and didn't get an answer, her next call would be to the police to have Rob arrested.

As she paced the kitchen floor, Polly began to regret not going into town with Tim. She could have waited in the car while he went inside. It probably would have been safer and a lot easier on her nerves than just waiting around here, cell phone or no cell phone. Finally, she couldn't stand it any longer and went upstairs to start packing. Brian's bedroom door was closed, so she rapped on it lightly before turning the doorknob and easing the door open.

"Hey," she called out as she peered into the room.

The shades were drawn, and the only illumination was the flickering computer screen. Brian sat hunched over the keyboard with his headphones on. Even from twenty feet away, Polly could hear the loud, tinny music blasting into his ears.

"Oh, hi, Mom," Brian said, smiling as he looked up. Simultaneously he slipped the headphones down around his shoulders and turned down the volume.

"You know, you're going to damage your hearing if you play your music that loud," she said.

"Huh—? What—?" Brian replied, cupping his hand to his ear and leaning forward.

"Oh, very funny, wise guy."

Polly couldn't help but smile. Just relating to her son like this made her realize—if she needed a reminder—that she had been getting much too wound up lately. She'd been too self-involved, too introspective. She really had to get out of the rut she'd been in for four years, now, and get on with her life.

"We're packing up," she said.

The smile that spread across her son's face filled her with joy and determination that she was doing the right thing.

"I want to be on the road by this time tomorrow."

"Cool," Brian said.

He looked almost as if he thought she was putting him on.

"I'm going to get the boxes out of the attic. I sure could use some help."

Brian nodded, then glanced over his shoulder at the computer screen.

"I'm in the chat room with Croz and Ricky," he said. "Let me finish up with them, and then I'll come and help you."

Polly nodded as he slipped his headphones back on. She waved her hands to get his attention and indicated once again that she wanted him to lower the volume. He nodded but still hadn't done it as she eased the bedroom door shut. Taking a deep breath, she turned and walked down to the end of the corridor to the attic door.

"Okay," she whispered after taking another breath. She patted the cell phone in the hip pocket of her jeans, then reached for the doorknob and turned it.

The instant the attic door opened, a warm, piney-smelling draft of air washed down the stairs and over her. Sunlight was streaming in through the single window that looked out over the driveway. She could see motes of dust, spiraling in the updraft as she started up the stairs.

Each step creaked underfoot, setting her teeth on edge. And with each step, the temperature rose until at the top step she was dripping with sweat. The air was hot and stale and felt too thin to breathe. Polly was grateful that the boxes they had used were near the top of the stairs. An eerie silence filled the amber-lighted attic. She found it unnerving, like stepping into an old-fashioned photograph.

Polly couldn't help but think how different the house seemed, now that she was determined to leave. When they had arrived, she had been so full of hope that this would be a nice, relaxing way to spend at least a part of the summer.

They had been here—what? only about ten days, but now it seemed like a lifetime ago. Polly shuddered as she inhaled and looked around at the accumulation of junk in the attic. Once she'd had hopes of sorting through all of this to see if there were any valuable antiques squirreled away up here. There certainly must be things from Tim's childhood that he would be interested in seeing again, but she no longer cared. If anything had been up here the whole time they had been married, then Tim certainly wasn't going to miss it now. Let it stay stuffed away up here, slowly rotting in the hot, dry air.

A faint buzzing sound drew Polly's attention to the window overlooking the driveway. At first she didn't see the insect that was causing the sound, but when she took a step or two closer, she saw a single yellow jacket bouncing and buzzing against the dirty glass.

A thrill of fear ran through her when she remembered the incident in the old car, when the yellow jackets had swarmed her. The stings had healed quickly, thank God. Only one on the back of her neck still itched every now and then. Polly's first impulse was to go over to the window and swat the little bastard, if only to get a little revenge.

She laughed to herself at the thought, but the sound seemed strangely muffled in the stifling air of the attic.

Just get the boxes and get the hell out of here!

She could hardly care about the trapped insect. The thing was going to die up here, trapped against the window and fried in the glaring heat of the sun. By tonight, it would join the other empty shells that littered the windowsill.

When Polly leaned over and picked up a handful of the flattened cardboard boxes, she raised a cloud of dust that blew up into her face and made her cough. She couldn't avoid inhaling some of the dry dust, and she turned red-faced as she coughed.

"Jesus," she muttered, wishing she had made Brian come up and get all of these.

Once she had an armload of boxes, she turned to go back down the stairs, being careful not to trip over anything. Her gaze shifted back one last time to the window. As she watched the yellow jacket bounce futilely against the dirty window, she sniffed the air and smelled . . . *something*.

She wasn't sure what, but it was more than just the dry piney smell that she had first noticed in the attic. It was . . . *bleach . . . chlorine bleach!*

Once she identified it, the smell got much more intense, stinging her nostrils and burning the inside of her throat.

Polly gasped for air and covered her nose with her hand. That made her lose her grip on the boxes, and they went sliding onto the floor, fanning out like a pack of huge playing cards.

"God*damn* it!" she shouted, and for good measure, she gave the pile of boxes an angry kick that scattered them even more.

Heaving a sigh of frustration, she got down on her hands and knees and started gathering them up. The smell of chlorine was so strong now that it made her eyes water. She knew she either had to get down from the attic right away or else open a window. When she glanced at the window, her panic rose higher. Where there had been only one yellow jacket before, there were now three . . . no, four yellow jackets, buzzing loudly and bouncing against the panes of glass.

"What the hell . . . ?" Polly muttered.

As she sat there on the attic floor, she watched in amazement as several more yellow jackets buzzed from somewhere up near the rafters and joined the others that had gathered at the window. Within a few seconds, there were more than a dozen insects. The sound of their buzzing rose louder and louder until it was like a whining drill in her ears.

Polly's only thought now was to get the hell out of here.

She could wait and have Brian do the job later, or Tim could do it once he got home. Just as she turned to start down the stairs, she noticed a gust of wind blowing up the stairway into her face like a draft in a chimney. The heavy oak door creaked and then swung shut with a loud bang that made Polly squeal and jump.

She leaped to her feet, slipping on the cardboard and almost falling as she started for the stairs. With the door closed, the attic seemed suddenly to get much darker. When she glanced back at the window, she saw why. More than half of the window was covered with swarming yellow jackets. Even as she watched, more joined them, their bodies blocking out the sunlight and filtering it to a dense, amber glow.

"Brian!" Polly called out, trying to keep the panic from showing in her voice.

She didn't dare to move, afraid that any motion might draw the attention of the yellow jackets. Her fear rose to an almost unbearable pitch as she stared at the window and saw something move beyond the glass. It wasn't just the bodies of the insects that was blocking out the sunlight.

There was smoke!

A thick, black column of smoke was rising up in front of the window.

Jesus, the house is on fire!

Rising slowly so she wouldn't draw the attention of the yellow jackets, Polly moved cautiously toward the window, straining to see where the smoke was coming from. When she was about six feet away from the window, the swarm of insects was so thick she could barely see through it, but down on the ground, across the driveway, she could see orange tongues of flame flickering inside the old shed. Thick smoke that looked almost liquid roiled out from under the eaves. It wasn't long before pale orange flames swept up the outside of the building.

Polly suddenly remembered the cell phone in her hip pocket. She grabbed it and quickly flipped it open. Her hands were shaking uncontrollably as she dialed 911. When she put the phone to her ear, all she heard was a loud, steady blast of static. Frustrated, she hung up and dialed 911 again but got the same result.

Pure panic gripped her.

How was she going to get help?

As far as she knew, Brian still had his headphones on with the music blasting in his ears. His bedroom window faced the opposite side of the yard, so he wouldn't even notice the smoke . . . until it was too late.

She looked carefully at the cell phone and saw that the Low Battery light wasn't on. The phone should work. It didn't make sense that she was in "cell hell" and couldn't get a call out. Maybe there was something about the roof, some tin roofing or something that was blocking her signal.

Her legs almost gave out on her as she half ran, half slid down the steps to the door. Pressing her weight against the door, she gripped the doorknob and shook it. Somehow it was locked or jammed on the other side. It barely turned as she wrenched it violently from side to side.

"Brian! Brian!" she called out as she banged against the door with both fists.

Behind and above her, she could hear the steady droning of the yellow jackets. The sound was getting steadily louder, and their bodies blocked out the light like a cloud that had passed in front of the sun.

Fear, rage, and frustration filled Polly, tingling like electricity all along her nerves. Spittle flew from her lips as she swung her fists repeatedly against the unyielding door. Her pulse was hammering in her ears, and her breathing was nothing more than a shrill, high whistle. Every breath filled her nose with the sharp sting of chlorine, so strong now it made her dizzy.

"Jesus, Brian! Open the door! Come on, Brian!" she

wailed, but she knew that it would do no good. He had his headphones on and couldn't hear her.

Fearful that the fire would spread to the house, she knew that she had to get out of the attic. She tried calling 911 again and got nothing but static again. Running back up the stairs, she looked around until her gaze fixed on an old, heavy bureau that stood beside the chimney. Heedless of the danger of the yellow jackets, she ran to the bureau and started pushing it across the floor to the edge of the stairway. Once she had it in place, she gave it a hard shove. It made a terrible noise as it tumbled down the stairs and smashed against the door.

The impact hurt her ears, but Polly was relieved to see a large crack running up the surface of the door by the doorknob. She dashed down the stairs again and, pushing past the bureau, leaned her full weight against the door.

The wood groaned as it sagged outward, and then the air was filled with the sound of splintering wood. With a sudden, loud snap, the door gave way, and Polly spilled out into the hallway.

Her hands were shaking so badly she was afraid she would drop the cell phone as she flipped it open and—this time—got a dial tone. She quickly pressed 911 and waited for an answer. Brian's door swung open, and he looked at her with a perplexed expression on his face.

"What the—"

"The shed's on fire," Polly shouted to him and into the cell phone at the same time. "Yes . . . yes," she said, forcing herself to calm down as she started down the stairs with Brian only a pace or two behind her. "We're at the Harris place out on Ridge Road. . . . No, I don't think the house is in danger yet. I'm going to check now, but it could spread quickly. . . . Yes. . . . Thanks."

"What's going on?" Brian asked from behind her as they made their way through the living room and kitchen and out the back door. She didn't answer him as she hurriedly dialed Tim's number. He answered on the second ring.

"Yeah," he said.

In the background, she could hear the steady hum of his car, so she knew that he was driving.

As she spoke, Polly walked out onto the driveway, her gaze fixed on the old shed which was now engulfed in flames. The thick column of black smoke rolled and twisted into the still air. The loud crackling of flames sounded like strings of firecrackers going off as the dry wood was consumed. Even standing more than fifty feet away from the blaze, Polly found the heat too much to bear. Shielding her face with her arm, she and Brian backed away.

"The shed's on fire," Polly shouted into the phone. "I was up in the attic, getting the boxes to pack, and I saw it out the attic window."

"Jesus, are you and Brian all right?"

"Yes, yes, we're fine, but the shed's going to be gone. It already is."

Polly backed even farther away from the heat as the flames billowed up with a roaring rush. The leaves of the trees nearby were seared brown and curled up.

"I'm heading back right now," Tim said. "Did you already call the fire department?"

"Of course I did," Polly snapped. "They're—I can hear the sirens now."

Off in the distance, the faint warbling wail of two or more sirens rose and fell, getting louder by the moment. The heat of the fire intensified when the roof collapsed in, raising a shower of twinkling orange sparks. Polly glanced worriedly at the house, wondering if the intense heat would ignite the old shingles on this side of the house or if some live sparks might drift up onto the roof and start burning there.

"Jesus," she whispered when she looked up at the attic window. On the third floor, she could still see the writhing mass of swarming yellow jackets, but for just an instant, the mass of insects seemed to take on the appearance of a face. The illusion dissolved the instant Polly blinked her eyes, but she was left with the distinct impression that there had been someone up in the attic, looking down at her.

With sirens blaring, the town fire trucks pulled into the driveway. Within seconds, the firemen unspooled their hoses and started dousing the trees and grass around the burning building.

"Not much worth saving," one of the firemen said as he walked up to where Polly and Brian were standing. "At this point, we might as well let it just burn down and make sure it doesn't spread."

Polly stared at him numbly and nodded, not knowing what to say or do. There was nothing she could do. Covering her mouth with her hand, she stood there silently and just stared into the roaring blaze until she saw Tim's car speeding down the road toward the house.

Then her legs gave out, and she sat down hard on the grass by the side of the house and began to cry.

sixteen

"**Spontaneous combustion, that's what done it.**"

Polly and Tim exchanged concerned glances, then looked at the burned paint brush handle that Larry Dunbar, the town fire marshal, was holding out to them. There wasn't much left of the handle—just a charred piece of charcoal—but the metal collar that had held the bristles in place had survived the flames, and clinging to it were shreds of burned cloth that flaked away to black powder when Larry lightly touched them.

"You been doin' some paintin' 'round here?" Larry asked, glancing past them toward the old house. His fire helmet shaded his eyes, but they could see that his face was streaked with sweat and ash.

Again, Polly and Tim exchanged glances as they both nodded.

"Oil-based paint, no doubt," Larry added with a curt nod. He seemed like the kind of man who enjoyed playing detective, especially when he knew he was right.

"Yeah," Tim said, "but we didn't wrap any of the brushes up in cloth. I always leave them in a can of water and just shake the water off when I want to use them again. Saves cleaning them with turpentine all the time." He raised an eyebrow as he looked at Polly. "You didn't do anything with any of the brushes, did you, Pol?"

Polly bit down on her lower lip and shook her head tightly. He saw something in her eyes, a distant look like she mistrusted him or something, and he didn't like it.

"Well *someone* did," Larry said authoritatively as he folded his arms across his chest. The rubber of his heavy black raincoat looked like wet sealskin. "I seen this kinda thing a hunnert times or more. You leave a brush wrapped up in a towel, even a paper towel, 'n it can burst into flames like that—" He snapped his fingers so loudly Polly jumped. "'Specially if it's bein' kept outside in a shed in heat like this." For emphasis, he puffed out his cheeks and wiped his forehead with the back of his hand, leaving a dark smudge on his skin.

Behind him, the still-smoldering coals of what had once been the shed sent spirals of thin blue smoke up into the evening air. The building was leveled, nothing but a pile of blackened rubble with a few blackened timbers left. Surrounding it was a wide swatch of burned grass, a safety perimeter. The nearby trees were all singed and looked like they might die.

"Hope there wasn't nothin' valuable in there," Larry said as he turned and eyed the ruins.

"Not really," Tim replied with a quick shake of the head. "Just some old tools and junk."

"Well, then, I guess we'll be headin' out now," Larry said as he rubbed his hands together. "You might wanna keep an eye on it through the night. Sometimes them coals can stay hot for a goodly time."

"Yeah, I'll do that," Tim said, nodding as he reached out to shake the man's hand. "Thanks for responding to the call so fast."

"Hell, just doin' m' job."

With that, Larry walked slowly down the driveway to the sole remaining fire truck that was parked down by the road. Polly and Tim stood side by side, holding hands as they watched him go. Once Larry backed the truck around and took off down the road, they looked warily at each other.

"So," Polly said.

"Yeah. . . . So?"

A long, uncomfortable silence settled between them as they just stood there, staring at the smoking ruins of the shed. Tim sighed and shook his head. After a moment in which she seemed to be gathering her courage, Polly cleared her throat to draw his attention.

"You probably know what I'm thinking," she said softly.

Anger flashed through Tim as he looked at her, but he was too choked up to yell. Instead, he swallowed noisily and then in a low, restrained voice said, "No, I don't. Why don't you tell me."

Polly gave him a twitching half smile but was unable to look at him for long. Staring down at the ground, she spoke so softly he could hardly hear her.

"I don't just think—I *know* Rob did it."

Saying it out loud seemed to give her confidence. She raised her eyes to look straight at him. Sucking in a breath, she held it and squared her shoulders.

"What the fuck are you talking about?" Tim said, unable to hide the snarl in his voice.

"Your brother deliberately set the shed on fire," Polly said. "That's why he was creeping around out here last night, to set it up."

"Jesus, Polly!" Tim said. He pulled his hand from her and turned away. "Why would he do a thing like that? For Christ's sake!"

Polly grabbed him by the elbow, forcing him to turn and look at her.

"It was a warning," she said in a rasping whisper. "He knows that you know what he did . . . what he *is*, and he's not going to let you forget what would happen to you if you tell *anyone*."

"Anyone? . . . Even you?"

Polly had a fearful look in her eyes as she nodded her head sharply.

"Yeah, even me," she said. "*Especially* me."

Fire or no fire, Polly was determined to pack up and leave. Tim wanted to bring back a few other pieces of furniture, but it was too late to drive into town and rent a U-Haul. Still, they could start getting their personal possessions packed and be ready to go so first thing in the morning, Tim could rent a van and they could load up and leave. They all worked late into the night, packing suitcases and boxes, and stacking them in the kitchen where they would be close to the door.

Sometime after midnight, they all took showers and went to bed, but as exhausted as she was, Polly found that sleep wouldn't come easily. She lay in bed, mulling over everything that had happened to her since they'd arrived in Hilton. While some of it—a lot of it—didn't make sense, she knew now that coming here had been a terrible mistake. She was doing the right thing, making them go back. Even the ostensible reason for their being here—to help Rob because of his broken leg—was obviously moot.

Am I doing the right thing?

—It may already be too late—

Polly was so used to hearing this second voice in her head that she didn't even react. There were times when she was positive that it really was Heather Olsen's voice, that somehow she was communicating with the dead girl. And then there were other times when she was convinced that the second voice really was just a part of her. She worried that she might be schizophrenic or have multiple personalities, like she'd seen on Oprah. Something like that could be causing these two very distinct voices she heard in her head.

What do you mean, too late?

—They're already here. . . . They're gathering outside the white room. . . . Something's disturbed them . . . and they're angry—

Who's here? I thought it was just one person, the bad man, who was scaring you.

—No. . . . There are more . . . a lot more . . . and now they . . . they're angry . . . and they're scaring me. . . . I can hear them trying to get in. . . . I think they all want to hurt me—

Polly had her eyes open and was lying flat on her back, staring up at the ceiling and listening to Tim snore while this conversation was going on. She had a curious feeling of dissociation and could almost imagine that she was here in bed and in the white room with Heather at the same time.

—Can you make them go away?—

What do they want? Can you tell me that?

—I don't know what they want. . . . They're banging on the walls . . . and windows. . . . Can't you hear them? . . . They're mad . . . and some of them are hurt. . . . They're screaming. . . . Listen . . . you can hear them—

Polly raised her head from the pillow and strained to hear, but the only sounds in the bedroom were the steady snoring of her husband and the soft sighing of the breeze through the window screens. Kicking the covers aside, she got out of bed and walked over to the window. She had a curious feeling that she was gliding across the floor, not really walking. Her hands were bone white as she parted the window curtains and looked out at the night.

The yard was as dark as black velvet. The trees on the horizon looked like black lace against the starry backdrop of the night sky. Down in the yard, across the driveway, she could see the pitch-black oval where the fire had been. Eerie, ghostlike wisps of luminous smoke and mist trailed across the grass from the ruins.

Polly watched, her eyes wide open and staring, as she tried to figure out what she was seeing. The moon was down, but there was enough ambient light from the stars to allow her to see . . . *something.* The ground fog or smoke seemed to billow up out of the ground, and every time she caught a glimpse of it from the corner of her eye, she was sure—for just a second—that it assumed a vague human shape.

Yes, I . . . I think I can see them!

A shiver ran up her back and gripped her neck.

—Please don't let them hurt me. . . . Please . . . don't—

Maybe you could talk to them, or at least to one of them. Call out to them and ask them what you can do to help.

—But I'm afraid. . . . And I can't leave here. . . . There are windows, but there isn't a door. . . . I can't get out—

Call to them through the window.

Polly sent out this mental suggestion like a soft prayer, whispered on the night wind. She was still staring down at the ruins of the shed, remembering the face she had seen in the shed window her first day here.

Was that one of them? Was that one of the people outside the white room who's scaring Heather now?

Talk to them, Heather. Ask them why they're angry. Ask them why they want to hurt you.

She concentrated hard on the thought but heard no reply.

The twisted human forms assumed by the smoke and mist dissolved into the night, blown away by the gentle breeze. Far off in the distance, a whippoorwill began its mournful call. The loneliness of the bird's song brought tears to Polly's eyes, and she slumped forward, rested her head on the windowsill, and cried.

Something's gotta give!

Rob's walking cast clumped heavily on the linoleum floor as he paced back and forth in his kitchen. It was almost noon, almost time for his brother to show up for his daily lunch ritual, but today Rob was seething with anger and agitation.

Something's gotta give, and I know what it is!

His hands were slick with sweat as he rubbed them down his neck. He was breathing too fast, hyperventilating. His hands started to tingle with pins and needles, and his vision seemed to get blurry. He felt light-headed, as if he'd had several belts of whiskey when, in truth, he'd only had two. Worst of all, his left leg was hot and itching like a bastard inside the walking cast.

Every time his pacing brought him to the kitchen sink, he leaned over it and looked out the window to the driveway below. Tim's car wasn't there yet, but it would be . . . soon . . . and then . . .

"Something's gotta give," he muttered as he clenched his right hand into a fist and smacked it hard into the palm of his left hand.

"That's what you'll get, you son of a bitch!" he whispered heatedly, and he smacked his fist into his hand several more times, harder and harder each time until his hands went numb. Then he clenched both hands into fists and started banging the sides of his head.

"Jesus . . . *Jesus*," he whimpered through gritted teeth, and then he resumed his pacing.

On the next pass, when he looked out the window, he saw Tim's car pulling into the parking space beside his truck. The tension inside him got even tighter, almost painful. His stomach growled. Acting more on impulse than careful planning, he went to the small pantry and grabbed the broom handle that was leaning against the back wall amid piles of trash and empty beer and whiskey bottles.

He smiled as he gripped the broom low on one end like he was holding a baseball bat. His knuckles went white as he flexed his muscles. The veins in his forearms stood out like twisted blue wires beneath his skin.

He tensed when he heard the tread of Tim's feet on the stairs. Moving swiftly, Rob positioned himself behind the door so he would be out of sight when Tim first opened it. Sucking in a breath of air, he held it and waited when he heard Tim pause outside the door.

Something's gotta give, and this is it! . . . It's show time!

A dry lump formed in his throat when he heard Tim slide the key into the lock and turn it. His eyes were wide and staring as he watched the doorknob turn, and the door started to swing open. Spreading his feet wide, he waited . . . waited until Tim was stepping into the apartment. Then, with a quick step forward and a vicious grunt, he swung the broom handle around in a whistling arc.

It caught Tim at an angle just above the eyebrows with an impact hard enough to snap the broom handle in half. His eyes widened in pain and surprise, then rolled back in his head, unseeing, as his knees buckled. Letting out a watery gasp, he folded up and dropped face first onto the floor.

Rob smiled as he watched his brother hit the linoleum floor and go slack. With his arms spread out beside him, Tim looked like he was melting into the floor or trying to embrace it. His head was cocked to one side, and a thick stream of blood was pouring from his nose and the gash above his eye.

"There you go, you son of a bitch," Rob muttered as he dropped the broken end of the broom handle. Rubbing his hands together, he stepped back and smiled appreciatively.

It took Rob only a few seconds to pull the dead weight of his brother all the way into the apartment. Then it was just a matter of minutes to slap some duct tape across his mouth and, using a length of clothesline, tightly bind his hands and feet. The hardest part was dragging him into the bedroom. After making sure that he was still alive—if only barely—he propped his brother up against the bed.

While he waited for Tim to come to, Rob fished a cigarette from his shirt pocket and lit it. Lowering himself into the easy chair by the door, he smoked in silence while congratulating himself on what he had done so far.

Now he had to figure out what to do next.

The only pisser was the goddamned cast on his foot. It itched like a bastard and made getting around too damned difficult—like last night, when he had gone out to the house and set up the paint brush and turpentine in the old shed to burst into flames.

"Oh, well," he said softly as he watched the cigarette smoke drift from his mouth and disperse against the ceiling. "I guess I have a little time to kill." He chucked when he caught the double meaning of *time* to *kill*.

Yeah, it's time to kill, all right!

After five or ten minutes, Tim started making low, bubbling sounds deep in his throat. The blood had dried in a brick-red streak across his face and neck, and there was a darkening purple lump on his forehead that looked as round as an egg.

Snickering softly, Rob got up out of the chair and limped over to his brother. He could see consciousness returning like dawn, slowly spreading across the morning sky. When Tim's eyes fluttered open, Rob was right there in his face, so close he could smell his own whiskey-tainted breath rebounding back at him.

Tim groaned and rolled his head from side to side, wincing at the pain. Then he grunted with confusion when he tried to move and found that he couldn't. Panic filled his eyes when he blinked and focused on Rob's leering face.

"Hello there, little brother," Rob said, in a bright, chipper tone. "Thanks for dropping by."

• • •

The pain was so bad, Tim found it almost impossible to focus. Splinters of shifting blue light outlined everything he looked at, and there was a persistent, loud ringing in his ears. He had the impression that he was underwater. Everything, even his brother's face close to his, was blurry and distorted.

When he tried to speak, the tape across his mouth pulled his lips back painfully. He tried only once to move his arms and legs, but they were so tightly bound he could already feel the tingling, burning sensation from the restricted blood flow. His heart was racing, and he listened to the rapid, muffled thumping in his ears, feeling each pulse in his neck.

Worse than that, though, was the knife-edged throbbing of his forehead. A spiderweb of pain seemed to be centered just above his left eye. It was especially bad when he blinked. He wished he could touch it to see what it was. A low groan sounded deep in his chest. He tried to remember what had happened, but the last clear thought he had was that he had opened Rob's apartment door and then . . . nothing until he had come to . . . here.

He recognized Rob's bedroom, even though the curtains were drawn, shutting out the daylight.

"Your head hurt?" Rob asked. He sounded genuinely concerned, but his face was too close for Tim to focus clearly on his features, and he thought his brother was smiling.

What's so funny? I'm hurt!

Tim grunted and nodded, but when he tried to form words, the duct tape stuffed them back down. A flood of bad-tasting mucus filled the back of his throat. He panicked, fearing that he might throw up and drown in his own vomit.

"You're probably wondering why you're here like this, huh?" Rob asked.

Again, Tim nodded. His vision was clearing slowly, but

the high-pitched ringing in his head was still strong, almost blocking out what Rob was saying.

"Well, I thought I warned you about what might happen," Rob said.

He drew back, took a cigarette from his pocket, and lit it. The glowing tip of the cigarette danced like a firefly in the darkened room, leaving blue tracers across Tim's vision.

"I *told* you not to tell anyone," Rob said. "Didn't I tell you that?"

He exhaled noisily, blowing a stream of smoke straight into Tim's face. Tim couldn't help but inhale some of it through his nose, and he coughed so hard behind the duct tape that his chest was lanced with pain.

"*Especially* Polly! I *warned* you not to talk to her about it. Didn't I? . . . *Didn't I?*"

Rob's face flushed with anger. His eyes bugged from their sockets, making his face look like a Halloween mask.

"But you see . . . we have a problem, now that she knows about what happened to Cunna . . . especially now that they've found him, so . . . well, you see, I have a few other things, some secrets that I need to protect."

Scooching down with his hands folded in front of him, looking like he was praying, Rob shifted forward. "You want to know what they are?"

Tim could feel his own eyes bulging as he nodded. The movement sent white-hot stabs of pain through his head. He couldn't answer Rob, so he couldn't begin to explain or defend himself. His only hope was that his brother would—somehow—be reasonable.

"I probably shouldn't even be telling you this," Rob continued, "but I guess it's only fair that you know everything."

There was something about Rob's tone of voice that really worried Tim. He sounded distant, detached, almost like he was talking from way far away. Tim knew it wasn't just the bump on his head that caused this. He could see it in

Rob's eyes, too. He was losing it . . . or maybe he had already lost it. He'd snapped.

"You see," Rob said, leaning even closer and lowering his voice as smoke spilled from his nose and mouth. "Cunna was just the first one."

Rob leaned back, took a deep drag of the cigarette, then exhaled noisily.

"After that . . . well, I don't quite know how to put it other than that I realized after I killed Cunna that I kind of liked it. Killing someone, that is. Know what I mean?"

Tim had no idea how to react. He was so stunned that he couldn't. All he could do was shake his head from side to side while letting what his brother had just said sink in. Bound and gagged as he was, he couldn't begin to process or react to what Rob had just admitted, but he had known or at least suspected the truth after digging up what he knew was a human skull in the old garden.

"Yeah," Rob said, chuckling like they had just shared a dirty joke. "Cunna was just the beginning. There've been . . ." He squinted in concentration and looked up at the ceiling for a moment or two. "To tell you the truth, I'm not even sure how many more there have been. A lot, but . . . Hey, you look surprised."

Tim, fearing for his life, knew that he was staring wide-eyed at his brother. He wanted to say something, to talk to him and—if he had to—beg and plead with him for his own life, but the only sound he could make was a low, strangled sound in his throat.

"It was mostly teenage boys or younger. They were fun, but I did in a couple of girls, too." A vacant glow lit Rob's eyes as he focused beyond Tim. "It was fun. I'm serious. Maybe you can't understand that, but I *really* enjoyed doin' it. There's a . . . a *power* you get when you know that a life—a *human* life—is in your hands. Like yours is right now. And I can either let it continue or snuff it out like *that*—"

He snapped his fingers close to Tim's face, making him flinch.

"You should try it sometime. Seriously," Rob said. "When you see the fear in their eyes . . . just like what I'm seeing in your eyes, now. But . . . hey, you don't have to worry, little brother. I ain't gonna hurt you. What did you think, that I'd kill *you*?"

He sniffed with laughter, and a line of snot ran from his nose to his lower lip. He seemed not to notice and didn't wipe it away. Tim was filled with fear as he realized just how unstable his brother was. Straining hard, he pulled on the rope that bound his wrists behind his back, but that seemed only to tighten the knots. If Rob was telling the truth, he was probably very practiced in tying someone up so they couldn't work their way free.

"I gotta tell you the truth, though," Rob said. "I ain't really decided what I'm gonna do with you. You've made this a real conundrum."

As he spoke, a darkness came over Rob's expression, and Tim could see a reptilian coldness in his brother's eyes. He couldn't help but think he was looking at a different person, someone he had never known, a monster that had been lurking behind his brother's eyes all these years.

Now, because of his fear of being found out, the monster was loose.

Rob took a final drag of the cigarette, then crushed it out on the bare wood floor. When he stood up, his knee cracked loudly, and his cast clumped heavily on the floor.

"I hope you understand," he said, "but I've gotta deal with them, first. Course, I can't let Polly live, knowing what she knows. And Brian . . ." He shrugged as though he was absolutely helpless. "He'd be a loose end, and I can't leave any loose ends, now can I? You understand, don't yah? So that just leaves you and me."

He clapped his hands together and rubbed them vigorously, like he was about to enjoy a festive meal.

"I'll decide what I'm gonna do with you after I deal with them. For now, why don't you just try and get comfortable."

He reached behind Tim and jerked the ropes binding him, making sure they were secure. The sudden jolt of pain brought tears to Tim's eyes.

"It might take me a while. You know, it's a real bitch trying to get around with this fuckin' cast on my leg. Things would've gone a lot better if I hadn't broken my goddamned leg."

Tim rolled his head from side to side, all the while making desperate, whimpering noises in his throat. Rob seemed not to notice or, if he noticed, not to care.

"Wait right here," he said, adopting a soft, kindly tone of voice. "I'll try 'n get back as soon as I can."

Just then the telephone rang.

Polly dialed the number to Tim's cell phone for what must have been the tenth time in an hour. Tension and anger wound up inside her as she listened to the steady beep-beep-beep, but Tim didn't answer.

It was late in the afternoon, nearly five o'clock. She had finished with the packing downstairs while Brian was up in his room, disconnecting and putting away his computer. Early that morning, Tim and Polly had driven to Rumford to rent a U-Haul van. They had spent a couple of hours that morning packing up, and were almost done when Tim went into town to have lunch with his brother, as usual. Polly was irritated that he wasn't answering. He should have been back by now or at least called to tell her what was holding him up.

"Damn you," she whispered as she switched off the phone and dropped it onto the table.

For a minute or two, she just sat there jiggling her legs in agitation and staring out the kitchen window. Across the driveway, she could see the wide, burned-out area where the shed had been. A shiver ran up her back when she remembered the wispy, gray figures she had seen out there late last night.

Were they really there, or was I hallucinating again?

Her fear suddenly spiked, and she stood up quickly, knocking the chair over. She practically ran over to the counter and grabbed the phone book. Flipping through it quickly, her hands shaking, she found Rob's phone number and dialed it. On the fourth ring, just as she was expecting his answering machine to kick in, she heard him pick up.

"Hello," he said.

Just the sound of her brother-in-law's voice set Polly's nerves on edge, but she swallowed and took a deep breath before speaking, determined not to let him know how upset she was.

"Hey, Rob. It's Polly."

"Polly. How're you doin'?" Before Polly could reply he went on. "You sound kinda tense. Is something the matter?"

"Ah . . . no. I'm fine. I was just wondering if Tim was still there."

"Still here?"

She heard him inhale sharply.

"No. He ain't been by today. In fact, I was just about to head out your way to see him."

Polly tensed and tried to ignore the cold clutching in her chest.

"He's not home right now," she said. "But he didn't stop by for lunch as usual?"

"What do you mean, 'as usual'? I hardly've seen him all week other than last night."

Polly didn't want to let how flustered she was feeling show, but the cold clenching in her chest grew stronger as her worry grew.

"I . . . uh, do you mean to say he hasn't . . ."

She let her voice trail away, not sure if she dared say what she was thinking.

"Hey look, Polly, I don't know what he's been telling you, okay? But he's stopped by my place maybe three, four times tops since you guys got here. I've hardly even seen him."

He's lying, Polly thought as her anger and worry flared. *That son of a bitch is lying to me!*

"I ain't got a clue where he might've been going," Rob said, "but he ain't been coming here, I can tell you that." He paused again and Polly thought she could almost hear him chuckling softly. "But you know, an old friend of his, Ellie Parker, a girl he used to date in high school, actually, was asking about him just the other day. Maybe he's hooked up with her or something."

There was a brief pause as the words "or something" hung in the air between them.

"Screw you, Rob!" Polly finally said with a snarl. "I know what you're up to. You want me to think my husband's screwing around behind my back. But you know what? It's not going to work. I don't believe you."

Polly started to hang up, but before she did, she heard Rob say, "Hey, I ain't tellin' you anything, all right? All I'm sayin' is that he hasn't been coming by my place every fuckin' day, 'n I have no fuckin' clue what he's been doing instead. And screw you, too!"

The whole time he was talking, Polly kept shaking her head as though that would block out his words and the uneasy feeling they generated. The suspicion that her husband had been seeing someone else had been lurking in the back of her mind for years—ever since Crystal died. Of course, it was natural that the ardor and passion of their marriage—like any marriage, she figured—had cooled over the years. No one can maintain a high level of romance, especially in the face of life's tragedies and problems. But after losing the baby, Polly had spun into such a deep depression that she couldn't help but wonder from time to time if Tim might be seeing someone else for things she couldn't give him.

No! Rob's fucking with your mind! That's the kind of bastard he is!

"Look," she said, struggling to keep her voice steady, "all I want you to do is, if Tim stops by, tell him to come home or at least call me right away, okay? Is that too much to ask?"

"No, not at all," Rob replied, sounding like he was almost hurt by her tone, but Polly was sure that she heard him snicker softly under his breath.

"Thanks," she snapped before cutting the connection with a flick of her thumb.

She was trembling inside as she placed the cell phone back on the kitchen table and shifted her gaze to the window. There were still several hours of daylight left, and she hoped that Tim would get back soon—*right now!*—so they could load up and get on the road.

But where in the hell is he?

Her eyes began to sting, but she told herself not to cry. Nothing had happened. Nothing was wrong. Tim was just delayed for some reason. Maybe he'd run out of gas or bumped into an old friend.

Like Ellie Parker.

She pushed the thought away.

Whatever his reason was for being late, he'd be back soon.

Please.

She wanted to believe that but couldn't. The nagging worries wouldn't go away. They grew stronger with each passing minute. At last, she admitted to herself that she wasn't going to be satisfied until she did something about it. She got up and walked to the foot of the stairs. Cupping her hands to her mouth, she called out to Brian.

"Hey! You awake up there?"

He didn't answer right away, but after another shout he called back to her, "Yeah! What d'you want?"

She heard his bedroom door open, and he stuck his head around the corner to look down the stairs at her.

"For one thing, I want you to take those damned headphones off," Polly said evenly. "I'm tired of having to yell to get your attention."

Brian frowned as he nodded. "Sure . . . okay. Anything else?"

Polly hesitated a moment, then nodded sharply.

"Yes. I'm going to take the van into town to look for your father. He should have been back by now, and I just want to make sure he hasn't broken down or anything. I'll be right back."

"Okay," Brian said.

"You just finish up with your packing, okay? I've got everything else ready to go, and I want to start loading the van as soon as your father and I get back."

Brian nodded again before ducking back around the corner.

Polly hurried back into the kitchen, grabbed her purse and the van key from the counter, and went outside. All the while she kept trying to dismiss her worries, but she couldn't help but feel that something was seriously wrong. As she climbed into the van, slid the key into the ignition, and started it up, she found herself hoping that she would find out that she was mistaken, and that Tim was just fine and had simply forgotten to switch on his cell phone.

That's all it is. . . . Please let it be all that it is.

The first thing Rob had to do was get rid of Tim's car, which was parked in his driveway. If Polly went nuts and called the cops or something, he certainly didn't want Tim's car sitting in his driveway; so instead of driving his truck, he decided to take Tim's car.

Of course, he couldn't very well drive right up to the house in it, either, so he drove over to the construction site on Ridge Road and ditched the car behind a pile of gravel at the far end of the site where no one could see it from the road. Then he took the shortcut through the woods to the house.

He wanted to scout out the area first, just to see what was going on before he decided exactly what he was going to do. He had a few ideas, but he wanted to keep his options open. He liked to improvise as things developed. That was always the best way to do things.

As he made his way through the woods, surrounded by

sunlight and leafy, dappled shadows, Rob couldn't help but remember that autumn day almost thirty years ago when he had broken up the fight between his brother and Cunna Dufresne.

Broke it up? Hell, I saved his fucking life! Cunna would have killed him if I hadn't been there. The problem with Timmy is, he isn't grateful for everything I've done for him!

It was hard going through the woods, especially with the cast on his leg, but Rob made it to the main road and crouched low in the brush while he watched the house across the road.

There was no sign of activity, but his anger sparked when he saw a U-Haul van parked by the side of the house.

"Son of a bitch," he whispered heatedly. "They're moving out and weren't even gonna tell me."

He wished he had known that *before* Tim came by the apartment this afternoon.

That would have changed *everything!*

He was filled with rage, just knowing that Tim had been fucking with him all along.

"You lousy cocksucker!" Rob sputtered as he clenched his fist and pounded it against the tree trunk he was leaning against. He was just about to walk across the road, up to the house, when he saw Polly come around the side of the house and climb into the van. A blue puff of exhaust shot into the air when she started it up and backed around. He could hear the faint rumble of the van's engine and the crunch of its tires on the gravel.

Rob dropped to the ground and, trembling with rage, watched from the brush as Polly drove down the driveway and turned right, heading toward town. Until that moment, he'd been thinking that what he had to do was simply a matter of taking care of business, tying up the loose ends. On the spot, though, he decided that it was going to be a little more than that.

Now he was going to have some fun with them before he killed them.

All of them!

seventeen

As anxious as he was to pack up and go home to Stonepoint, Brian took his time dismantling his computer. First, he wanted to contact all of his friends, especially Croz and Ricky, and let them know that he was heading back to civilization. Then he got caught up in a chat room, and before he knew it, his mother was calling him, telling him to finish packing while she drove to town. He wasn't too keen about being alone in the house, so for once he followed her advice and didn't put his headphones on.

His first task was to throw all of his clothes—clean and dirty—into the suitcases and boxes he'd gotten from his mother. He stripped his bed and folded the blankets and sheets into another box, which he filled up with the few things he had on the desk—the desk his father had waxed so nostalgic about using when he was a kid growing up in this house.

Like it was some kind of big deal!

For a moment, Brian just sat there staring out the window and thinking that this was the same view his father had the whole time he was growing up here. The sun was setting, edging the distant line of trees with a bright orange glow. He watched as the shadows deepened across the weed-choked field that stretched down to the river. Dark, purple clouds looking like fat fingers stretched up from the horizon as though they were pulling the daylight out of the sky.

There wasn't a single other building. Brian couldn't see the river from here, either. Maybe in the winter, when there weren't any leaves on the trees it was visible, but he could just about care. Just thinking about the river made him remember the day he had fallen in and almost drowned. That had been scary enough, but to think that kid Josh had seen it happen and had just stood there watching and not doing a goddamned thing to help him . . .

"Yeah, screw this place," Brian muttered as he set to work disconnecting the cables and hookups to his computer. He was busy at work when he heard a faint creaking sound from downstairs.

"Mom?" he called out, feeling suddenly tense, every nerve on edge.

He was positive he had heard her leave, and he was just as positive that he hadn't heard her drive back into the driveway. It was probably just an old floorboard snapping as the house cooled with the evening, but something made the hairs on the back of his neck stir as he turned slowly and faced the closed bedroom door.

"'S that you, Mom?' he called out, his voice shaking a little.

There was no answer.

The house was so silent it seemed as though he could hear the dust settling in the filtered sunlight. He knew that he had to get back to work putting his computer away. His mom would be really ticked off if she came back and he wasn't ready to go. For the first time since they had moved in, she seemed even more anxious to leave than he was. He sensed that something had happened, but he wasn't sure what.

It doesn't matter, as long as we get the hell out of here!

But he couldn't deny the subtle, creepy feeling he got as he worked, especially when his back was to the door.

When he was a kid, he used to imagine all sorts of monsters lurking in the dark corners of his bedroom, especially under his bed. He knew that was silly, but still, the old fears echoed in his mind.

He jumped and let out a surprised yelp when he heard another, louder snap from downstairs. It certainly sounded as if someone was sneaking around down there. Brian's hands were shaking as he faced the door, quickly trying to decide whether or not he should go downstairs and have a look around.

What's there to be afraid of?

He didn't want to answer that. There was plenty to be afraid of. His first thought was maybe that weird kid Josh was sneaking around downstairs, thinking no one was home. Brian clenched his fists, hoping it *was* Josh. He'd show him what he thought about jerks who don't give a shit if someone's fallen into the river and can't get out.

Moving slowly so the floorboards wouldn't creak, Brian took a few steps toward the door. His senses were sharp and alert, waiting for any indication that there really was someone downstairs, and that this wasn't just his imagination. His fists were clenched so tightly his forearms began to ache, but he moved cautiously toward the bedroom door, coiled and ready to react if he had to.

When he was a few feet from the door, he thought he heard something else: a soft whisper that could have been someone's foot, dragging across the carpet. He ground his teeth together. Realizing that he wasn't breathing deeply enough, he paused and took a deep, calming breath.

There's nothing there. Jesus, you're just overreacting.

But he really didn't believe himself.

On a deep level, he knew that something was wrong.

He jumped when he heard the soft, scuffing sound again. It sounded closer, now, as if someone was on the stairs. Brian swallowed, making a loud gulping sound that hurt his throat. Icy tingles gripped his stomach and chest. He felt a terrible pressure building up in his bladder. He made a soft whimpering sound when an indistinct, gray shadow shifted across the wall opposite his bedroom door.

There is *someone there! In the hall!*

Panic gripped him.

There was nowhere to run. He had nothing he could use as a weapon.

"Hel . . . hello?" he called out, hearing the tight quaver in his voice.

There was no answer except for another soft thump, followed by that dull, dragging sound.

Tears filled Brian's eyes, making it difficult for him to see clearly. That could be a shadow on the wall . . . or it could just be his imagination working overtime.

It was painful to take a deep breath. Tremors ran like little earthquakes through Brian. And then—without any doubt—he saw the shadow, the silhouette of a person, darken as whoever was out there in the hallway moved closer to his room.

Brian wanted to cry out, but his voice was trapped inside his chest. Waves of dizziness crashed over him. He found it almost impossible to stand up. It was with an odd mixture of stark fear and relief when the person out in the hallway stepped into the doorway, and he saw that it was his uncle.

"Oh jeeze," he said, exhaling so quickly it hurt his chest. "I thought you were—"

He didn't finish the sentence because, at that moment, he saw the grim expression on his uncle's face, the cold, hard gleam in his eyes. He also saw that his uncle was holding a length of pipe in his right hand.

"What are you . . . What do you want?" Brian stammered as he took a few steps backward.

His uncle didn't say a word as he moved closer. The cast on his foot made a soft hissing sound as he dragged it across the bare, wooden floor. Brian gave him a twisted smile, but he could see the pure hatred in the man's eyes. He glanced quickly around the room to see if there was anything he could use to defend himself. His panicking brain quickly calculated the chances of getting the window open and jumping outside, but he knew that he wouldn't make it. Besides, he would probably get hurt in the fall, maybe break a leg, and then he wouldn't get away.

"Leave me alone," Brian said, his voice breaking into a pathetic whimper. "Leave me alone . . . please. . . ."

Uncle Rob didn't say a thing. His expression remained fixed, his eyes blank with a cold, reptilian stare. Only one corner of his mouth twitched into what might have been a smile, but there wasn't a trace of humor in it.

Brian kept backing away as Uncle Rob came closer. He saw the man squeeze the iron pipe so hard his knuckles stood out in white, bony ridges. When the back of Brian's knees bumped into the edge of the bed, he sat down hard, bouncing on the bare mattress. When his uncle raised the iron pipe, Brian turned to one side and tried to cover his face with his arms, but the gesture was futile.

He grew dizzy with fear as he watched his uncle raise the iron pipe high above his head and then start to swing it in a downward arc.

Brian never felt the impact. Even before the pipe hit him on the side of the head, he was falling backward into a deep, grasping blackness.

What to do? . . . Oh, what to do?

Rob broke out with a smile as he looked down at the young boy who was sprawled on the bed in front of him. A thick wash of blood ran from the scalp wound just above his right ear and stained the bare blue and white striped mattress. His eyes were closed, and the right eye seemed to be bulging a little more than the other eye against the closed lid.

With his left hand, Rob reached out and gently touched his nephew's upper thigh, giving it a loving, reassuring pat. He was tempted to finish the job right now. Take his knife and cut the boy's throat.

But Rob held himself back.

Why hurry things? Besides, it wouldn't be any fun if the boy was unconscious. He wouldn't be able to see the look of deep terror in the boy's eyes as he realized that he was dying . . . slowly . . . inch by inch.

Where was the fun in just killing him outright?

Rob still wasn't exactly sure what he was going to do next. He had plenty of ideas, but he wanted to wait until Polly got back before he finally decided on a course of action. Until then, he was sure Brian was down for the count, so he shifted the boy's leg up onto the bare mattress and flipped him over so he was facing the wall. Then he propped the boy's head on the pillow so it would look like he was napping to anyone who might glance into the room . . . as long as they didn't look too closely and see the swatch of blood that was drying in his hair.

Satisfied, Rob went back downstairs, moving slowly and cursing his broken leg for making it so hard to get around. He had pretty much decided that he would burn the house down with both Polly and Brian in it. The old shed had just been a trial run. But torching the house seemed like the best idea. If he did anything else—anything like some of the things he had done to those boys and girls he'd killed over the years—it would probably be too easy for the cops to trace it back to him, especially since he still wasn't sure what he was going to do about Tim.

Yeah, good old Timmy . . .

He couldn't very well drag him back out to the house, at least not until after dark, and even then it would be a bitch because of his goddamned broken leg.

So he had to improvise.

But that's what he was good at, improvising. It's what helped him get away with so many murders all these years.

The biggest problem was going to be getting Polly trapped in the house before he torched it. If Brian's body was found lying in bed in the ashes, the authorities would chalk it up to him dying in his sleep, overcome by smoke before he could save himself. But two people dying like that in the same fire would look suspicious.

No, he would have to come up with something else, some other way to trap Polly in the house.

"The cellar!" he said the instant the thought popped into his mind. "That's it."

He walked into the kitchen, unlocked the cellar door, and opened it. Looking down the flight of stairs into the damp gloom, he inhaled sharply, filling his nostrils with the smell of old cement and mold.

Yeah, the cellar was the thing, but how was he going to get her down there?

When he placed his foot on the first step and heard the board creak loudly beneath his weight, the idea he needed hit him.

"Of course," he muttered, smiling with satisfaction to himself.

Dragging his broken leg behind him, he went down the stairs. Over by the furnace, he found a pile of his father's old tools on the dust-covered workbench. The tools were rusted and covered with cobwebs, but he picked up one of the saws and ran his thumb along the row of rusty, dull teeth.

"This'll probably do the trick," he muttered as he walked back to the stairs and set to work, cutting into one of the supports.

The wood was a lot tougher than he'd expected, and it wasn't long before he'd broken a sweat. The rasping sound of the saw blade filled the cellar, and he stopped every few seconds to catch his breath and listen to see if Polly had gotten back to the house yet. It wouldn't pay to be found screwing around down here, but he figured he could bull-shit his way out of it if she found him down here.

Rob was smiling and humming softly to himself as he worked. Sawdust rained down on the floor like artificial snow. After fifteen minutes or so, he had both major supports for the stairs cut almost all the way through. He wanted them just weak enough so when—and if—he got Polly down here, they would give way, but still strong enough so he could get back upstairs without having them collapse on him.

It was a delicate balance that might or might not work. He'd feel like a goddamned idiot if the stairs gave way on him now, and Polly came home and found him down here. He would have to wait and see how it worked, but he wanted to come up with a few other things, too, just to be sure that both Polly and Brian were in the house when he lit it.

Once he was done sawing, he went to the bottom of the stairs and put his foot on the first riser. By wriggling his foot from side to side he made the ancient wood snap and creak loudly. He was pretty sure it was safe enough for him to get back upstairs.

Smiling with satisfaction, he gripped the banister tightly with both hands and started up the stairs, pulling himself hand over hand, and ready to grab on tightly if the stairs gave way beneath him. The wood made terrible, loud squeaking sounds, but the supports held. His face was dripping with sweat once he was back in the kitchen, grateful to have a real solid floor beneath his feet.

"Shit," he muttered when he looked back down into the cellar and realized that he'd left the rusty saw on the floor at the foot of the stairs. He wished he'd thought to put it back on the tool bench so as not to raise any suspicions, but he guessed—he hoped—that Polly wouldn't notice it.

Even if she did, it would probably be too late for her by then, anyway.

"Well, I guess it's time to check on the little whipper-snapper," Rob said with a chuckle. He cast a quick glance out into the driveway to make sure Polly wasn't back yet, then went back upstairs to what had been his and Tim's boyhood bedroom.

Brian was still unconscious and in the same position, rolled onto his side facing the wall. The sun had set, and the dim light in the room made it look all the more like Brian was just taking a nap. Rob was about to go over and arrange him so it looked even more convincing when he heard a vehicle pull into the driveway. The engine cut off with a soft chuffing sound. Then he heard the door open and close, and footsteps on the porch before the screen door opened and slammed shut.

"Brian? You all done packing?"

It was Polly!

Rob tensed as he looked quickly around the room for a place to hide. He grabbed the iron pipe he'd used to knock out Brian, then ducked into the closet when he heard the light tread of Polly's feet on the stairs. Keeping the door open just a crack so he could keep an eye on the unconscious boy, he squeezed the pipe with both hands and waited as she came up the stairs.

"Hey . . . you in here?" she called out.

As he ducked back into the shadows of the closet, every muscle in Rob's body was coiled and ready to spring.

If she goes over to the bed . . . if she finds out he's out cold . . .

It wouldn't be according to his plan, but he knew that he would have to give her a whack, too.

He watched Polly's shadow move across the narrow opening of the closet door as she took a few more steps into the room. Her back was turned to him, and he had to fight the impulse to leap out of the closet and nail her a good one.

No, no. . . . Have a little patience.

Time seemed to stand still as he held his breath and waited to see what she would do next. He knew he could overpower her easily, especially with the element of surprise in his favor, but he wanted to get her down into the cellar. That was the plan, and he was determined to stick with it if at all possible.

Polly took one more step toward the bed, then hesitated. She was so close to him that Rob could hear the soft sound of her breathing. He could sense her indecision. At last, though, she exhaled softly, turned, and walked out of the room. Rob let the muscles in his shoulders and arms slowly relax as he sucked a breath in through his mouth.

He waited—he was good at waiting—as she went back downstairs. He could hear her moving about and by the sounds, he could tell that she was in the kitchen. He heard her pull a chair out from the table and sit down.

Okay, just relax now.

There was no need to hurry. She was alone in the house. Tim was safely bound and gagged at his apartment, and Brian was down for the count.

It's just you and me, Polly.

He tightened his grip on the iron pipe and smiled wickedly as he eased the closet door open.

Just you and me, and now it's your turn to pay!

At first, Polly was furious that Brian was actu-ally *sleeping* when she got home, but she lightened up a little when she saw that all his stuff was packed and ready to go. Her bigger worry was that she still hadn't seen any sign of Tim or heard from him. He still didn't pick up on his cell phone. She'd driven up and down Main Street, even swung by Rob's apartment, but she hadn't seen him or his car anywhere.

So where the hell is he?

As her frustration built, she considered knocking on Rob's door and talking to him face-to-face. She had never liked or trusted him, and she wanted him to tell her to her face that he hadn't seen Tim all day. She was positive that she could tell by his eyes whether or not he was lying.

But she hadn't done that.

She didn't think she could stomach even seeing Rob, knowing what she knew about him.

She opened up the cell phone and dialed Tim's number for the dozenth time. It rang at the other end, but she didn't expect him to answer.

He didn't, so after a few more rings, she folded the phone shut and leaned back in her chair with a disgusted sigh.

—There's someone here—

The voice spoke inside her head as clearly as if someone was standing right beside her, whispering into her ear.

What do you mean? Someone where?

Polly focused her mind, tuning all of her senses.

She looked around the kitchen, now dark with early-evening shadows. Tilting her head back, she sniffed the air, but all she smelled was the dusty, closed air of the house.

—He's here with me . . . in the white room—

Who is? What are you talking about, Heather?

Coiling tension wound through Polly as she looked around the kitchen. She wanted to go turn the overhead light on, but she didn't dare to move. She didn't want to break this fragile moment of contact. There had been an edge of desperation in Heather's voice that unnerved her.

There's someone in the white room with you?

Narrowing her eyes with concentration, she sniffed the air again.

This time, she caught a faint whiff of—*What? Flowers . . . roses . . .*

Her heart skipped a beat the instant she recognized the scent.

But it wasn't the smell of fresh roses. The aroma was strong, and beneath it she caught a powerful tinge of decay and rot. She swallowed hard, feeling a thick lump in her throat that wouldn't go down. When she took another breath, the smell was even stronger.

Polly looked around the kitchen, positive now that she could see or smell or hear that someone else had been here.

Oh my God! Someone was in the house while I was gone!

—He says his name is Josh . . . Josh Billings. . . . He's here with me now—

Josh! That was the name of the boy Brian mentioned a while ago. Is he the one? Is he the person who's been threatening us?

—*No, no. . . . I don't think so. . . . He's lost, too. . . . He says he isn't scared . . . but I can see in his eyes that he is. . . . He's lost and scared . . . just like I am—*

Polly clenched her fists on the table and shifted uneasily in the chair. A cold, tingling feeling went up the back of her neck, like someone was lightly brushing their fingertips against her skin. She squirmed in the chair and whimpered softly as she looked first at the living room doorway and then at the screen door that led onto the porch.

An almost overwhelming urge to get up and run filled her.

—*Get out now . . . while you can!—*

The smell of rotting roses was a sign of danger, a hint that someone else had been in the house . . . someone who wanted to hurt them . . . hurt all of them . . . just like Heather had said!

Is Josh the one we have to look out for?

The feeling of desperation was like poison inside her.

—*No. . . . He's scared . . . and lonely. . . . Down in the cellar . . . you can read about him . . . about what happened—*

Polly's throat made a funny choking sound when she spun around and looked at the cellar door. The key was in the keyhole, and the door was firmly shut, but she felt a presence lurking behind the door that sprinkled goose bumps all across her arms and legs.

—*But be careful. . . . Something's not right—*

What do you mean, not right?

—I . . . I'm not sure. . . . Josh won't talk to me now. . . . He's too scared. . . . He said there's a man who wants to hurt him some more . . . that he's nearby . . . and wants to hurt him—

Every muscle and nerve in Polly's body felt stressed to the snapping point as she rose slowly from the chair and walked over to the cellar door. Her hand was shaking uncontrollably as she reached out and grasped the key.

She turned it slowly.

The latch clicked, sounding as loud as a gunshot in her ears. She turned the doorknob and opened the door.

You told me that I'd be safe down here.

—There's safety down there . . . and escape . . . but also danger—

Polly grew dizzy as she inhaled the cold, moist air of the cellar that blew into her face. The wet cement smell mingled with something else—*Roses . . . the smell of rotting roses*—that made her stomach churn.

Her vision was vibrating like the air was filled with electricity. She felt as though she were moving in a dream. Everything was moving in sludgy slow motion. Even her shadow shifting across the wooden steps seemed to make a low, rasping sound—*like someone sawing*—that set her teeth on edge.

Her hand gripped the banister as she started down the stairs, feeling the cool air of the cellar embrace her like water. She shivered uncontrollably and wiped her hand across her sweat-slick face. With each step, the cellar stairs creaked and groaned loudly. She could only breathe tiny sips of the damp, cold air because it was so heavy with the cloying stench of rotting flowers.

The stairs snapped and shifted beneath her weight, but Polly never loosened her grip on the banister until she reached the cold, hard floor. Her eyes had trouble adjusting to the dim light of the cellar, but her gaze shifted over to a stack of newspapers, yellowing with age, beside the brick base of the chimney.

Were those even there before?

She didn't remember seeing them, but they must have been there all along. She could see a thin coating of dust on the top sheet.

Is this what you mean?

There was no answer from Heather.

As Polly walked over to the pile, she realized that she was breathing too fast. When she knelt down, the cold of the cellar floor spiked her knees. She grew dizzy as she brushed the dust off the top sheet.

"Search for Missing Boy Continues," read the top headline.

Polly clutched the newspaper so tightly it made a loud, crinkling sound, like fire. She quickly scanned the article, not believing what she was reading.

" 'The search continued Wednesday for Josh Billings, a local thirteen-year-old, who has been missing since last Saturday' . . . Oh my God!"

She swallowed noisily and wiped her hand across her face, then continued reading out loud.

" 'He was reportedly last seen walking into the woods shortly before sunset. His parents reported him missing when he didn't show up to help with the evening chores. Police and local volunteers have been searching the neighboring woods and dragging the river in case he drowned. At this point, the police do not suspect foul play.' "

Oh, my God! He did it! Rob did this, didn't he?

Polly licked her upper lip, tasting the salty sweat.

"First there was that boy, Cunna Dufresne, . . . then there was Josh Billings."

—That's him! . . . That's Josh—

Heather's voice sounded faint, as though she were speaking from a great distance. A wave of panic ran through Polly when she realized that she was all alone down here . . . totally isolated. The shadows deepened, pressing in on her.

When she looked over at the flight of stairs that led up to the kitchen, her vision seemed to telescope outward, making everything look impossibly far away. She had the disorienting sensation that she was drifting underwater and looking up at the unreachable sky.

—There are more of them. . . . There are others. . . . They're all outside the white room. . . . They're hurt . . . and they're scared . . . and they're angry—

That's who I've been seeing, isn't it? He's been killing children, and I've been seeing them around the house!

She didn't need an answer from Heather or anyone else. She was certain, now, that was what was happening.

With Heather's help, she had somehow tuned into what was going on, and she was able to sense and feel . . . and sometimes see the spirits of the children Rob had killed!

They're everywhere, aren't they? They're in the house and in the woods and fields. In the barn and the old shed that burned down! They're everywhere!

Polly stiffened when she heard someone moving about upstairs.

Thump . . . skritch . . .

"No," she whispered as she quietly replaced the newspaper on top of the pile. When she stood up, her knees cracked loudly, sending a jolt of pain up her thigh.

Thump . . . skritch . . .

Her heart was pounding so hard in her throat it almost choked off her air as she looked up the stairs. A shadow shifted within the evening shadows at the top of the stairs. Then, like a slowly developing photograph, a dark figure resolved in the doorway. Standing with his feet firmly planted on either side, the man placed a hand on either side of the doorjamb and leaned forward. At first Polly thought she was imagining it when she heard the soft, sniffing sound of laughter.

"This is too fuckin' good," a voice laced with menace said. "I couldn't have planned it better if I'd tried, and Lord knows I tried."

With the light behind him, Polly couldn't see his face, but she knew exactly who it was. Fear and rage in equal measure filled her. His body blocked the top of the stairs, and she knew that he was never going to let her upstairs.

"Do you see this?" Rob shouted.

Polly could see that he was holding up a paintbrush.

"Unfortunately, you didn't learn your lesson when the shed burned down. This is another paintbrush you accidentally left covered with turpentine and wrapped in cloth. What a shame. It started another fire. I wish there was something I could do to help you, but you see, I got here too late. The fire was already burning out of control by the time I got here and could call the fire department."

With that, Rob slammed the cellar door shut.

"You bastard!" she shouted, but even as her voice died away, she heard the faint click as he turned the key in the lock.

Polly knew that it was already too late, but she started up the stairs anyway, taking the steps two at a time. When she was halfway to the door, she realized that something was wrong. The stairs swayed and creaked sickeningly. Then she heard a loud snap, and the stairs dropped, throwing her off balance.

Her hand shot out and grabbed the railing, but the sound of cracking wood continued as the stair supports gave way and the nails holding it up pulled out. The top of the stairs suddenly pitched downward. Polly clung to the banister to keep from falling as the stairs fell out from under her and hit the floor with a loud crash. For a moment, her legs hung free, swinging back and forth, but then she lost her grip and dropped down.

She hit hard, yelping as her left foot twisted underneath her, but she rolled off the collapsed stairway and quickly stood up, brushing herself off.

"Hey! You all right down there?"

Rob's voice was muffled through the closed door.

"I thought I heard something. You're okay, aren't you?"

Polly started to answer, then stopped herself.

Why give him the satisfaction?

—I told you. . . . There's protection down here—

Heather's voice was clearer now, and it was laced with a frantic desperation.

What do you mean?

—Behind the furnace . . . look behind the furnace—

Without even pausing to consider it, Polly ran to the other side of the chimney. The light was dim there, but she got down on her hands and knees and started feeling around the floor near the base of the furnace. Her fingers brushed away cobwebs and dirt, and she felt small things skitter away from her, but she kept searching.

"Oh my God."

Her throat choked off when her hand closed around the handle of a small pistol. Trembling, she brought the gun up close to her face and inspected it in the darkness. She didn't know a thing about guns beyond aim and pull the trigger, but maybe it was enough.

"I hope you didn't hurt yourself down there," Rob shouted through the door.

Her pulse was throbbing hard in her neck as she walked to the foot of the collapsed stairs and looked up at the closed door. She could hear a loud splashing sound, and it didn't take long to realize that Rob was dumping something flammable around the cellar door. Within seconds, the thick, resinous smell of turpentine filled her nostrils.

"You bastard," she whispered heatedly as she hefted the revolver and then raised it with both hands. Her arms wavered as she aimed up the stairwell, where she knew he was standing just behind the door.

"Hey! Did you hear something?" Rob called out, his voice tinged with near maniacal glee.

Polly listened a moment, then heard a faint scratching sound—*like something scratching behind the walls*—which was immediately followed by a low, rushing *whoosh.*

She knew that he had lit a match and set the door on fire. Without even thinking, Polly squinted and pulled the trigger.

The explosion hurt her ears, and the gun kicked back hard in her hands, but she corrected her aim and pulled three more times in rapid succession. The sudden sound filled the cellar like thunder claps, and Polly watched as the bullets ripped through the door, splintering the wood and leaving four gaping, jagged holes. Through the holes, she could see bright, flickering flames.

She realized that she was crying as she squeezed the trigger once more, but the hammer fell onto an empty cylinder. She fell to her knees, gagging, as a hot rush of vomit shot out of her mouth.

"Fuck you!" she cried out, but there was no reply from upstairs.

Did I get him, or was he already out of the house?

She had no time to think.

The flames quickly consumed the wooden door. A line of fire swept up both sides of the door. Thick, gray smoke billowed through the gap at the top of the door and quickly filled the stairwell. Within seconds, the top of the stairwell was filled with smoke. Polly knew that she couldn't make it out the door even if she could get up the stairs.

There has to be another way out!

She looked frantically around the cellar, lit now by the flickering light of flames. The fire was spreading quickly upstairs. It wouldn't be long before the kitchen floor burned and caved in on her. She was trapped and tried not to imagine the inferno the cellar would become soon. She knew that both she and Brian would be dead long before anyone noticed the flames and called the fire department.

Seething with rage, she threw the revolver at the closed door, watching helplessly as it bounced back and fell to the cellar floor, clattering on the fallen stairs.

"You won't get away with this, you bastard!" she shouted, clenching her fists and shaking them in frustration.

The cellar filled with the sound of crackling flames as the fire spread, consuming the old house. A cold draft was blowing across Polly's back as the fire sucked the air from the cellar, using the stairwell like a chimney to feed the flames.

I'll suffocate long before the flames get me, Polly thought, but that didn't make her feel any better.

Waves of despair washed over her as she stood there, knowing she was about to die. Tears filled her eyes, blurring her vision as the fire roared above her. The heat in the cellar was almost intolerable, and she could barely catch her breath.

Then, so faintly that she could barely hear it, a voice whispered to her.

—The white room . . . you'll be safe in the white room—

Polly's head jerked around as she looked at the small room where the old preserves were stored. Her vision was hazy and out of focus, shattering into shards of gauzy light that shifted and blended into each other. She knew she had to be imagining it when she saw a small, translucent figure in the doorway to the room.

"No . . ."

Polly involuntarily took a step forward when the figure—a little girl—raised her hand and beckoned to her.

Above her, the fire was raging and crackling. Even with her distorted vision, Polly could see tongues of flames licking between the floorboards upstairs. A burning dryness gripped her throat and singed her lungs with every breath. Her voice broke when she tried to speak.

"Heather . . ."

The figure of the girl was outlined with shimmering white light that cast long, wavering shadows across the cellar floor. She was smiling, but there was grim determination in her wide, unblinking eyes as she waved Polly on.

—Come with me. . . . You'll be safe . . . with me . . . in the white room—

But I don't want to die!

Tim could feel the blood running down his wrists and into his hands as he worked the rope back and forth, trying to loosen the bonds. Snot ran from his nose as he breathed hard and tried not to think how desperately he wanted to open his mouth and swallow a huge gulp of air.

Through the closed curtain, he could see that the sun had set. The shadows in the room were pitch black. He had tried thumping his feet on the floor to draw the attention of the people who lived downstairs, but they were either out or else ignoring the sounds coming from upstairs.

Jesus! Help me!

He grunted in desperation as he strained to free his hands.

He had to get free.

He was going to save Polly and Brian from his brother, he told himself, all the while trying to ignore the numbing certainty that he was already too late.

He had been bound and gagged here for too long.

There was no way Rob hadn't already killed them both and was on his way back here to finish the job.

But I have to try!

He gave his wrists another savage twist, and the burning friction peeled his skin back. He strained so hard the muscles and tendons in his neck and back cramped painfully. Jackknifing his body back and forth, he writhed about on the floor, stopping only when he hit his head against the metal bed frame. The sudden impact felt like a spike being driven into his brain and made him see stars. A trickle of warm blood ran down his scalp behind his ear.

Dazed with pain, Tim inched his body like a worm until his hands were as far underneath the bed as he could get them. Feeling blindly, he reached up until he caught the edge of the bed frame. It was made of cast iron, and the unfinished edge had a rough ridge that sliced open his finger when he brushed against it.

A rush of relief ran through Tim as he strained to raise his hands and press the ropes binding his wrists against the frame. Grunting and gritting his teeth, he started sawing it back and forth, putting as much backward pressure on it as he could.

He worked until the pain in his shoulders was too much to bear, then rested a few seconds and started again. He had no idea how much—if any—progress he was making, but it was his only hope. The strain ripped at his shoulders and cramped his neck and back muscles. His elbow kept knocking against the floor, shooting bolts of pain up his arm, but he didn't let up. He was determined to keep doing this until he was either free or else passed out from exhaustion and loss of blood. Snorting from the effort, he filled his mind with the desperate need to save his family even though he dreaded that he was already too late.

He was so lost in pain and the effort of freeing himself that he hardly noticed at first when the strands of the rope began to part. After another few passes, the rope separated and the tight, tingling pressure on his arms and shoulders was relieved. Taking only a moment to catch his breath and focus his energy, Tim strained to pull the ropes apart. By twisting his hands back and forth, he eventually freed himself. A second later, he ripped the duct tape from his mouth and quickly untied the ropes that bound his feet.

A wave of dizziness swept over him. He staggered and almost went down again when he leaped to his feet and staggered to the bedroom door. It took immense effort to maintain his balance, but he made it into the kitchen and grabbed the handset of the wall phone. His fingers were shaking uncontrollably as he dialed 911.

"This is an emergency!" he barked into the phone. "My wife and son are in danger! Send a police cruiser out to the house right now!"

"Could you please calm down for just a moment, sir," the woman at the other end of the line said.

"It's number twenty-six Ridge Road! The Harris place on Ridge Road. Have you got that? Send the police out there immediately!"

Without waiting for a response, Tim slammed the phone down and ran out the door. He wasn't surprised to see that his car was gone, but Rob's truck was still parked in the driveway. He fished the spare key out of the ashtray, where Rob kept it, and cranked the ignition. The truck's tires chirped loudly and left long, black streaks on the pavement as he planted the gas pedal to the floor and sped down the street and out of town.

He had to fight back tears and hope that he wasn't already too late, but the cold, sinking feeling in the pit of his stomach told him that he wasn't going to make it in time.

I have to try!

eighteen

Polly could barely think, much less react, as she listened to the roar of flames above her as the fire quickly spread. Staring straight ahead at the ghostly figure, she blinked her eyes and shook her head, expecting the vision to go away, but Heather was still there, staring at her and waving her on.

In the eerie, flickering light of the cellar, the girl's face was bone white. Her blank stare gave Polly the unnerving feeling that she was looking at her own reflection in a mirror, but the girl's hand continued to move in a slow, waving motion. Feeling like she was moving in a dream, Polly started toward her.

—I told you . . . you're safe down here . . . in the white room—

No matter how hard she tried, Polly couldn't look away from the girl. She could still hear and feel the fire as it spread all around her upstairs. It wouldn't be long before the kitchen floor caved in on her and she was crushed by burning timbers, but she felt strangely isolated from everything, almost as though she were in a protective bubble.

Polly hesitated for a moment. With a fearful moan, she glanced up when the floorboards above her suddenly snapped loudly. A shower of sparks and burning embers sprinkled down from between the cracks in the wood. Above, the flames glowed as bright and hot as the sun. The floorboards snapped again and cracked.

I'm going to die, I know that!

She was surprised that she didn't feel as much panic as she expected she would, but a sad feeling of resignation and acceptance filled her, creating a curious calm in her mind.

—No . . . you're not going to die . . . not if you come with me—

Heather's gaze was steady, her eyes glowing with tenderness, but beneath that there was an infinite sadness that wrung Polly's heart. The girl continued to wave Polly onward, and almost against her will, Polly moved toward the small room, resigned that she was destined to die in that little white room.

I can't go in there.

She tried not to remember the jars of horrible, rotting stuff that she had mistaken for entrails and bloody organs. Nausea churned sourly in her stomach, and in spite of the heat prickling her skin, she felt an icy rush of apprehension across her neck.

—Yes you can. . . . You'll be safe in there. . . . That's the only way out—

In her heart, Polly knew that the only way out now was to die. Her only escape was through the door at the top of the destroyed staircase, which had now caught fire from falling embers.

—Please . . . come . . . with me—

In a swift, flowing motion, Heather swept into the small room and disappeared. Fearing as much for Heather as for herself, Polly called out to Heather and followed.
Wait!

—You have to hurry—

Sucking in a breath like she was about to dive into a lake, Polly entered the small room. Noticing again that the walls were painted a dingy white filled her with heart-sinking fear.
This is where I'm going to die! All along, it was just a premonition of where I was going to die!

—Here . . . over here. . . . See?—

A loud explosion behind her made Polly jump and wheel around. She watched in fascinated horror as part of the floor caved in. A swirling shower of sparks and bil-lowing gray smoke filled the cellar as burning planks and timbers smashed onto the floor.

—You . . . have to . . . hurry—

Heather's voice was faint, now, but still distinct above the terrible roar of the conflagration. For just an instant, Polly caught a glimpse of the little girl's face floating up near the ceiling behind the shelves that lined the wall. The fire was flickering madly behind her, creating a disorient-ing strobe light effect, but Polly could see into the darkest recesses, and she saw something that was too much to hope for.
Is that a boarded-up window?
Another portion of the kitchen floor caved in. The blis-tering heat intensified, singeing Polly's back. She heard a sizzling sound close to her ears and knew that her hair had been scorched. The sickly smell of burning hair filled her

nostrils, but it was tinged with the smell of something else: *Roses . . . fresh roses . . .*

Smoke filled the white room, choking her, but she set to work with a furious desperation. Grabbing the front edge of the shelves, she yanked it back with all of her strength. The old nails holding the shelves in place resisted for a moment, but then—very slowly—they began to yield. The room was filled with the loud groaning sound of wood and ancient nails separating. Jars tipped over and rolled onto the floor where they broke with sickening, wet explosions. Polly winced as the gooey mess of their contents splashed against her legs, but she didn't stop.

"Come *on,* you *bastard*!" she wailed as jolts of adrenaline coursed through her body. "Come on! Come on! *Come on*!"

The row of shelves teetered for a moment. Then, with an ear-splitting crash, they fell forward until they came to rest against the opposite wall. More jars of preserves fell and broke. Polly couldn't help but look down at the rotting contents that were leaking onto the floor and tried to convince herself they were nothing but old preserves that Tim's mother had put up so many years ago. They weren't—they couldn't be—the black, rotting horrors she imagined them to be.

Scrambling around the side of the shelf, Polly wedged herself between the shelves and the wall and reached up to the boarded-over window. The planks were held in place with only a few rusty nails, and they gave way easily when she pried her fingers under the bottom edge and yanked back hard. Her heart was racing, throbbing hard in her throat and wrists, but she couldn't help but smile when she caught a glimpse of the night sky through the dirt-crusted glass.

There were no locks or hinges on the window. It was a simple wood and glass frame set into the stone wall of the cellar. The sills were spongy with rot, but the window didn't yield when Polly pushed against it and then tried to pull it inward.

The heat in the cellar was unbearably intense. Polly could feel it, clawing like an animal at her back. The stench of burning hair sickened her. When she realized that the window wasn't going to open for her, she picked up a piece of wood that had been covering it and smashed it. Shards of glass flew everywhere and rained down on her, slicing her hands and face, but she hardly noticed as she worked quickly to clear the remaining fragments out of the frame.

Behind her, she heard a terribly loud groaning sound as a wall somewhere in the house collapsed. The whole house shook with the impact. The air being sucked in through the open window fed the flames with a roaring rush that blew cold night air into her face. Polly paused for a moment and inhaled deeply, enjoying the cool freshness and knowing that this might be the last breath of fresh air she ever experienced.

The window was high off the floor and narrow. She wasn't sure she could fit through it, but she knew that if she didn't try, she would die.

I can do it!

—You can do it—

Grasping the window edge, she scrambled up with one foot propped against the wall, the other pushing off the fallen shelves. Splinters of wood and small pieces of glass dug into her hands, but she boosted herself up, propelling her body through the gap. Her hips got hung up for a moment, but she clawed at the grass outside and pulled herself clear. She got through just as something—she guessed it was the old oil tank—exploded, sending a ball of flame rushing like a fiery cannonball through the cellar. A wall of intense heat slammed into her as it shot out the narrow gap of the window, but she staggered and crawled across the grass until she collapsed face first on the other side of the gravel driveway.

From off in the distance, she heard the rising and falling

wail of approaching sirens. When she finally managed to gain the strength to get up and move farther away from the blaze, she looked back, stunned by the inferno the house had become.

Oh my God! Brian's still in there!

Shielding her face from the intense heat that painfully prickled her face, she stared at the roaring blaze as the fire swept through the rest of the house, quickly consuming room after room. She was numbed and couldn't begin to register what was going on as the fire trucks screamed to a halt in front of the house. The firefighters quickly unspooled their hoses and turned the water on, but Polly knew it was too late to save anything.

"Polly . . . Polly!"

The voice calling to her was faint and seemed to be calling from so far away it was hardly worth the effort of acknowledging it. Numbed and exhausted and bleeding from numerous cuts and abrasions, Polly turned almost zombielike to see her husband running toward her. When he caught her, he crushed her against him with both arms. Her body was as stiff as a board as she leaned against him.

"Brian," she whispered in a croaking voice.

A stab of pain shot through her, riveting her whole body when she looked back at the burning house. She could feel Tim's arm around her, but it seemed like an almost insignificant attempt at comforting her as she tried to absorb the thought that her son—her only surviving child!—was still inside the house.

"He was in the house?" Tim asked, incredulous.

Polly could hear the near hysteria in his voice and wondered why she felt so calm inside. She felt absolutely detached. It was almost as though she were dead, and her soul was hovering above the disaster, watching everything with a remarkable calm.

"He was . . . in his room," she managed to say. "I don't know if he got out or not."

Her gaze was fixed on the flames as they spewed up the exterior of the house and crackled up into the night sky. On the first floor, burning timbers collapsed inward, sending up huge, spiraling showers of sparks. But as she stared into the flames, Polly saw something else. There was something moving in the house!

"Look!" she cried, pointing toward the back of the burning building.

A silhouette etched black against the flames was struggling toward them. Its arms were held out as though to embrace them as it staggered and lurched forward.

"Sweet Jesus," Tim muttered beside her, holding her close.

Polly watched as the figure—unmistakably a person—tried to break through the wall of flames in front of it but was engulfed by them instead.

That can't be Brian!

She knew that much. With a terrible, deep horror, she saw that the figure was limping as though one leg was in a cast.

"It's Rob," Polly said simply, surprised at the lack of panic or sympathy in her voice. An upswelling of satisfaction—*Yes! Satisfaction!*—filled her as she watched Rob stop and then fall into a burning heap on what was left of the kitchen floor. He rolled over slowly, flames outlining his arm as he reached out to them. Polly saw his mouth open as he tried to scream, but the flames had burned his vocal cords, and he didn't make a sound. His fingers hooked into claws that raked at the insubstantial flames, but then his body shuddered and stopped moving.

As she watched, her vision blurred with tears, Polly saw something else—other shapes, moving within the blaze. A corner of her mind told her that it was nothing more than an illusion, but she saw first one, then a few more, then even more until there were at least a dozen small, wavering figures resolving out of the flames and gathering around Rob. Distorted faces appeared and then disappeared into the fire, dissolving into curling wisps of smoke and sparks. And faintly—so faintly she suspected that it might all be inside her head—Polly heard a long, drawn-out, agonized wailing sound of many voices that rose and fell in time with the surging flames that now looked like hands that were ripping apart what was left of Rob Harris.

"Burn . . . *Burn*, you *bastard*," Polly whispered harshly as she pressed her face against her husband's chest.

She couldn't help but smile as the fire and smoke roared into the night sky, taking everything that had been her husband's brother with it, even his soul.

Numbed by her loss and totally exhausted, Polly collapsed onto the grass and just sat there, her body and emotions too wrung out for her even to cry. Waves of vertigo swept over her and almost pulled her under, but she just sat there, watching numbly as the firefighters sprayed jets of water into the blaze. Thick, curling billows of steam hissed like a thousand snakes as they spiraled up, blocking out the stars overhead.

"I'm afraid we ain't gonna save it. It's gonna be a total loss."

Still feeling dazed, Polly turned and looked up. In the flickering glare of firelight, she saw Larry Dunbar standing close beside her and Tim. She nodded numbly, forcing herself not to cry as she took a slow, deep breath of the cool night air and absorbed what he had said.

"It's tough, losin' everything like that," Larry said almost casually, "but at least everyone made it out alive."

Polly made a faint gagging sound in the back of her throat as she looked at him more intensely.

"What—?" she said, but that was all before her throat closed off.

"Your son. Brian," Larry said as he hooked his thumb over his shoulder in the direction of the fire engines down by the road. "He was out on the roof around back when we got here. He'd climbed out once he saw that he couldn't get down the stairs. We was tryin' to get the ladder up to get him, but he panicked 'n jumped. Twisted his ankle. Might've even broken it, 'n he's got a helluva bump on the side of his head, but he's gonna be all right."

Polly tried to say something but couldn't catch a deep

enough breath. Collapsing against her husband's chest, she sobbed and gasped as relief flooded through her, almost sweeping her away.

Thank you. Oh thank you! she thought fervently, not even knowing to whom she was directing her gratitude; but she couldn't help but feel as though someone—somewhere—had been protecting her family all along.

"One person didn't make it out of the house, though," Tim said solemnly as he pointed at the back of the house. "My brother was in there, too. He—"

His voice caught, but only for a moment.

"He didn't make it out."

Larry's expression froze as he regarded them both. His eyes gleamed brightly in the glow of the fire, and Polly saw tears forming in his eyes.

"Shit. *Rob* was in there?" Larry wiped his eyes with the back of his hand and shook his head respectfully. "I—I'm terribly sorry."

But Polly couldn't help but smile as she squeezed herself tightly against her husband and looked past him at the burning remains of the house.

You may be—She shuddered at the memory of the burning figures she had seen pounce on him and rip him apart as the flames consumed him—*but I sure as hell am not. . . .*

Polly refused any medical attention, but they rode in the ambulance to the Hilton Community Hospital with Brian for X rays on his ankle. His left leg was broken, the doctors informed them, but it was only a hairline fracture, and he could probably get by with a walking cast. Because of the lump on the side of his head, they wanted to keep him overnight for observation. They also wanted to give Polly and Tim a quick checkup because of the cuts and bruises they had, but they insisted that they were fine and left after getting the cuts cleaned and bandaged.

It was still dark when they returned to the house, which was now little more than a pile of smoldering rubble. The house had caved in on itself, leaving only the blackened pillar of the chimney standing amid the charred timbers. The firefighters were still spraying water into the flames, but mostly just to keep the fire from spreading to the barn and surrounding fields.

Around dawn, just as the sky was turning pale blue in the east, Fred Hilliard, one of the town police officers, walked over to them carrying a couple of foam cups of coffee. His expression was set and grim.

"Awful sorry about your loss," Fred said, flickering his eyes in the direction of the house as he nodded. He handed them each a cup of coffee.

Polly and Tim both looked at him but said nothing.

"You have any idea how the fire started?" Fred asked. "I know this might not be a good time to talk 'n all, but if you can think of anything that might have—"

"He set it."

Polly's voice sounded strangled and raw from all the smoke she'd inhaled.

"Beg pardon?" Fred said, taking a step closer and leaning down as though to hear her better. "I'm not quite sure I heard you correctly."

The coffee cup was warm in her hand so she put it down on the ground. She cast a furtive glance at her husband, their eyes meeting with an intensity that surprised her. Ever so slightly, he nodded for her to continue.

"Rob Harris, Tim's brother," Polly said. "He set the house on fire. He was trying to kill us—our whole family—because of what we knew."

She paused to catch her breath, finding it hard to take more than shallow sips of air.

"Knew what?" Fred asked, frowning with concern as he squatted beside her, his hands clasped in front of him.

Again, Tim and Polly exchanged glances. This time Tim spoke.

"Those bones they found out by the construction site on Ridge Road . . . They belong to a kid we used to know named Cunna Dufresne."

Fred's eyebrows shot up and he leaned back in genuine surprise.

"You're shitting me," Fred said. "I remember when I was a kid there was a big thing about him disappearing. How do you—?"

"My brother killed him," Tim said. He took a deep breath that made his whole body shudder, but Polly took his hand and squeezed it tightly to give him reassurance.

"He confessed it to me yesterday," Tim went on, "and he knew that my wife knew as well, so he tried to kill us all. I'll come down to the police station later today and tell you the whole story."

"Yeah, I'd like to hear all about it," Fred said, nodding.

"But there's more," Polly said in a broken voice. "A lot more. He killed a lot of other kids, too. Josh Billings, for one."

"That kid who disappeared in the woods years ago?" Fred asked, incredulous.

Polly nodded. "Him and several more. And I can prove it."

Both Tim and the policeman looked at her questioningly as she heaved herself to her feet and turned her back to the destroyed house. Without another word, she walked over to the barn, returning a few seconds later with a shovel in hand.

"Come with me," she said, waving them on as she led them over to the scorched area where the old shed had once stood. Gritting her teeth, she set the blade of the shovel on the blackened soil and stepped down hard. The first few shovelsful turned over nothing but loose, rocky soil; but then she flipped over a scoop of fresh earth. Grasping out loud, she stood back.

"Take a look," she commanded, pointing at the long, narrow, dull white object she had uncovered. Fred knelt down and brushed the dirt away, revealing a long bone that ended with five jointed fingers. A few rotting shreds of flesh still clung to the bone.

"You keep digging here, and you'll find the remains of at least one of Rob's victims, maybe more," Polly said.

Tim was standing close beside her. When he touched her lightly on the shoulder, she squealed and jumped.

"How . . . how the hell did you know?" he asked.

Polly swallowed hard, but it wasn't enough to make the thick, rotten taste in her throat go away. She sniffed and, for just an instant, caught the powerful scent of roses—*fresh roses.*

She smiled to herself in spite of the numbing chill that was dancing up and down her back like invisible fingers.

"I saw him," she said, her voice almost breaking. Tears filled her eyes, and when she blinked, they ran in warm tracks down her cheeks. She looked directly at Tim. "The first day we were here. I saw him in the window of the shed."

"Jesus," Tim whispered, shaking his head in amazement.

"Well I'll be damned," Fred said as he stood up and brushed the knees of his pants clean. Putting his hands on his hips, he scanned the area. "We're going to have to mark this whole area off as a crime scene and have a look around."

"I'm sure you'll find a lot more," Tim said. "Yesterday, Rob confessed to having committed several murders. I wouldn't be surprised if you find the bodies of his victims buried all around on this property."

Fred looked dumbfounded. Pressing his fist against his mouth, he stared intently at the ground, lost in thought.

"I . . . I don't know what to say," he finally muttered. Then he shook his head, snapping back to attention, and looked at Tim and Polly. "I'm going to have to ask you to stick around town for a few days. At least until we can get things cleared up and start an investigation."

"No problem," Tim said with a sharp nod. When he glanced at Polly, she felt a tremendous rush of love and affection for him.

"We can get a room at a motel in town," Tim said. Turning to Polly, he added, "We'll have to buy some new clothes, though. We lost everything in the fire."

Feeling numb with shock and exhaustion, Polly nodded but said nothing. Her mind was filled with other things. She couldn't stop thinking about all the things that, now, seemed so obviously connected: the lone figure lurking under the apple tree, the voices she heard whispering late at night, the strange scents she had smelled. The house, the whole yard was haunted, but she wanted to believe that, now that Rob was dead, the spirits of his victims would finally find peace and rest.

Please . . . please be at rest.

Tears were streaming down her face and neck as she tilted her head back and looked up at the steadily brightening sky. Pale white clouds touched with lavender billowed up over the distant line of trees as the hissing steam drifted away to nothing, melting into the brightening blue of the sky. She still felt strangely isolated from the world, even when Tim placed his hand gently on her shoulder.

—Yes. . . . Please be at rest—

The words filled her mind as she closed her eyes and listened to the soft whisper of Heather's voice and the rush of blood in her ears.

• • •

—Are you sure?—

Polly took a deep, calming breath and held it as she stared up at the blank square of the ceiling. She was aware of the soft, steady sounds of her husband and son breathing as they slept. A quiet, detached contentment filled her.

Yes, I am. You showed me how to get out of the white room. You saved my life, and now it's time for you to leave.

—But I'm still afraid. . . . They're not outside anymore. . . . I can't see or hear them . . . but I . . . I'm still afraid—

You don't have to be. Nothing can hurt you. Nothing! Do you understand? It's only being afraid that can hurt you.

—But what if they're still out there? . . . What if they're just waiting for me . . . waiting to hurt me?—

They won't. They can't hurt you.
Polly sent out the thought like a fervent prayer.
If there's anyone outside the white room now, they're there because they love you. They want to help you move on.
Utter silence filled the room and Polly's mind. The darkness swelled softly around her, like a close-fitting glove. She felt no fear. The darkness was warm and comforting . . . safe and secure.
You helped me, Heather, and now I want to help you, but you have to be brave. You know you can do it.
There was no reply.
The silence was like a vacuum, both inside and outside.
Feeling curiously light-headed, Polly widened her eyes and stared deeply into the darkness, willing all of her internal strength to Heather.
You can do it. I know you can. I have faith in you.
The light-headed feeling intensified, and a soft, fluttering sound, like wings, sounded in the darkness around her.
They're here to help you. People who have known and loved you have been waiting for you all this time. They're here now, and they'll stay with you until later, when your mother and father and others who love you can join you.
The fluttering sound grew incrementally louder, and as it did, a deep, warm upswelling of love and loss filled Polly. Although Heather didn't say anything more, Polly could feel that she was leaving. She imagined seeing a bright, glowing white light grow steadily brighter as it opened up to receive the little girl.
You'll be safe, Heather . . . forever . . .

With a sudden rushing intake of air, Polly bolted upright in the bed.

A terrible feeling of emptiness, of sadness and loss filled her as she looked around. As her vision adjusted to the darkness, she could see some of the fuzzy details of the motel room where they were staying. Through the closed curtain, she caught a trace of daylight. Then, like a hot hammer, a terrible muscle spasm gripped her stomach.

"Oh, no—" she whispered as she tossed the bedcovers aside and stood up.

Sweat broke out like dew across her forehead and neck. Her body was trembling, and she was afraid that her legs wouldn't support her as she lunged toward the bathroom.

Her hand brushed across the wall switch, and the light and fan came on, stinging her eyes and filling her ears with a loud, rattling sound.

Her stomach compressed again, so painfully she had to shut her eyes. She imagined there was a fist inside her that was clenching and unclenching as sour acid bubbled up into her throat and mouth. She snorted and pursed her lips, but there was no way she could get rid of it.

"No . . . please," she whimpered as she leaned forward and gripped the sides of the toilet bowl like a steering wheel.

A third time, her stomach tightened. Then she opened her mouth and made a loud groaning grunt as a flood of vomit shot with a splash into the toilet. Her vision blurred and hot pressure filled her head as she continued to retch time and time again. At some point she became aware that Tim had gotten out of bed and was standing behind her, his hand resting lightly on her shoulder. She turned and looked at him, trying to speak, but threw up again instead until she finished with a low, drawn-out moan as she slumped forward, hugging the toilet.

"Jesus, do you think it's something you ate?" Tim asked.

Polly's face was flushed as she shook her head. Still staring down into the toilet bowl, she watched the strings of foul-tasting vomit that hung from her lips. She snorted, and some of it stung her nasal passage. The smell was thick and rank but then—crazily—she thought that it also reminded her a bit of the scent of flowers—*fresh roses.* . . .

She waited for a few seconds until she was sure that she was finished. Then she smiled and sat back on her heels, wiping her chin with the back of her hand. Tim grabbed a washcloth from the rack by the sink and after running cold water over it began to wipe her forehead and cheeks.

"Feeling better now?" he asked.

Polly couldn't contain the wide smile that was building up inside her. In an instant, it lit up her face.

"Yeah . . . I'm feeling really good," she said.

Even the bad-tasting vomit wasn't so bad because of what she suddenly knew with absolute certainty.

Tim raised one eyebrow as he looked at her, confused. Before either of them said anything more, he took one of the motel water glasses, slipped it out of its plastic wrapping, filled it with cold water, and handed it to her.

Polly was smiling widely as she sipped the water and swallowed. It felt good, cool and refreshing in her throat. When she placed the glass on the top of the toilet tank, she looked at Tim and started to laugh.

"What? What's so funny?" he asked, looking genuinely mystified.

Polly tried to tell him, but her laughter gripped her so hard that she couldn't catch her breath for a moment. Finally, though, she turned and took Tim's hand in hers.

"Remember that morning in the kitchen?" she asked, feeling the mischievous gleam in her eye. "I'm pregnant."

"Wha—? Really?" Tim asked.

He looked like he had no idea how to react or what to think.

"Hey, you guys okay in there?" Brian called out.

"We're fine . . . just fine," Polly replied as she looked at Tim and nodded sharply. "I'm positive," she said. She loosened her shoulders and smiled to herself, filled with an incredible feeling of peace and contentment.

"I also already know that it's a girl."

"Oh? And how do you know that?" Tim asked with a twisted smile. He still looked like he wasn't quite sure if she was putting him on or not.

"Oh, I know, all right. Without a doubt," Polly said as she pressed her hand against her lower abdomen and started rubbing it lightly. "And do you want to know something else?"

Tim didn't say a word as he looked at her, waiting for her to continue.

"I've already picked out a name."

"Really."

Polly felt so full of joy she thought she would burst as she nodded her head slowly up and down.

"Uh-huh. I'm going to name her Heather."

Give sorrow words. The grief that does not speak
Whispers the o'erfraught heart and bids it break.

—*Macbeth*, IV, iii, 209–210.